Vinod Patel works as a Clinical Professor at the George Eliot Hospital NHS Trust in Nuneaton and Warwick Medical School at The University of Warwick. He worked in providing frontline emergency care and delivering the local vaccination programme during the COVID-19 pandemic. He is passionate about good clinical care for his patients, whilst his hobbies include a re-wilding project, planting trees, and eclectic reading, particularly literature. This will be his first and only novel.

Dedicated to Rashmi Shukla, my family, friends, fauna, flora, and fungi

Vinod Patel

GURU PI

THE MAN WHO READ HIS OWN HEIGHT IN BOOKS IN A YEAR

AUSTIN MACAULEY PUBLISHERS™

LONDON ★ CAMBRIDGE ★ NEW YORK ★ SHARJAH

A CIP catalogue record for this title is available from the British Library.

ISBN 9781035846917 (Paperback)
ISBN 9781035846924 (Hardback)
ISBN 9781035846948 (ePub e-book)
ISBN 9781035846931 (Audiobook)

www.austinmacauley.com

First Published 2024
Austin Macauley Publishers Ltd®
1 Canada Square
Canary Wharf
London
E14 5AA

I acknowledge all my friends and family, some events in your life you will recognise in this book, and I am extremely grateful for you being a part of my life.

I am very deeply indebted to my band of personal proof-readers—Nishi Jani, Rashmi Shukla, Bhavna Patel, Jo Wilson, and Asok Venkataraman. This group also advised on some scientific, literary, and philosophical ideas. Shekhar Venkataraman helped with some of the mathematics. Rajiv Nair recommended many on the reading list. Patrick Henry advised on some of the military ideas.

I would like to acknowledge Rheann Saravanan for the proof-reading and advising on the initial draft. Your suggestions were creative and enhanced the narrative. The team at Austin Macauley have been incredibly professional and patient with me. I am so very grateful for your professionalism.

The numerous quotes used form the backbone of this novel, and I am deeply honoured to have been able to include these jewels in the writing. I thank the authors of all the quotes.

Thank you very much too, dear reader, I appreciate you more than you will ever know. Especially, if you do that one extra little act of kindness.

Ultimately, thanks to you – Rashmi, sorry I left you every week at least for several hours over a year to spend an intense day of writing, and thanks for looking after me during my Covid-19 illness.

Ideally, a thesis submitted for the Degree of *D Litt et Phil* or similar,
to a well-known famous University, a less-known University,
or a should be better-known University.

Submitted on Sunday 16th June 2024
Bloomsday and Fathers' Day
Née 16th June 2022

Provisional Candidate Number ≈ 3.141592653589

GURU PI

The Man Who Read His Own Height in Books in a Year

Every life is a novel for those who are curious enough to look into it.

Anne Berest
French Writer and Actor.
Quoted on *Literary Hub*, found in *The Week*

Chapter 1
An Introduction to Pi

"A character? Well, it's an original, a queer chap," I said, and infected by
childish laughter, I burst out laughing.
"It's a kind of freak. Listen, do you know what a dreamer is?"

White Nights. Fyodor Dostoyevsky (1821–1881). Russian Novelist.

It all happened in the time of Covid-19. The French have such a lyrical, dulcet term for the pandemic that riots through the world of humans and the occasional pet that we care about. Positively reducing emissions by 9.4 percent—but also killing too many sentient *Homo sapiens sapiens.*

In the last 12 months, there have been 2,000,000 deaths, which is more than malaria and HIV put together (there are lots of numbers in this story; I do apologise for that). Tuberculosis, we do not appear to care about. Covid-19, we do care about; but do you agree *Covid dix-neuf* sounds better?

It was all going to be quite simple. Swami Krishnamurthydas—the Maha Pandit of the start-up temple Ek Bhumi Ardhnariishvari temple in Sundervagvela—was to cross various waters to come to England and launch the Vedic Foundation of Planet Earth's edition of the *Bhagavad Gita.*

Such a splendid edition; it was a delight that could only be described as a rectangular Fabergé egg. Which is probably not the most apt description for the many strictly vegetarian public in Sundervagvela.

This was—is—a bibliophile's, linguaphile's, art-lover's dream of a tome. The sacred scripture that 1.1 billion of our humanity would swear on and state that they will say the truth—and nothing but the truth—in the event of a misdemeanour (if caught).

A book of the 18 chapters of the *Bhagavad Gita* in Sanskrit, English and French. A translation, transliteration, with each Sanskrit word dictionaried to help manage your body, mind, and soul. Whatever that means. But a worthy guide to just learning about the yearning.

Accompanied by a programme that allows you to build your own personal version as you learn the Sanskrit to the English or the Sanskrit to the French or indeed the French to the English, and vice versa. You can learn the other two if you know one.

A bit like the body, mind, and soul—but probably not. And the accompanying panels of painting or coloured in drawings of the dialogue in gouache, giclee, pastels, oil, the words in traditional Devanagari and of course, a serif font—for easy reading apparently.

Swami Krishnamurthydas did not get permission to cross the *mahasagar* that is the great ocean and seas of the Indian, then the Red and then the Mediterranean Sea and then a quick hop, skip and jump across the English Channel; now again, an official geographical barrier to demonstrate that Brexit was now both legal and closely aligned to the natural geology of it all as well.

The *Shankaracharya* of the higher maths or 'Bishopries' simply barred him on pain of excommunication from the cadre of senior Swamis legible for succession to one of North, South, West, or East seats of Hinduism. Swami Krishnamurthydas had felt very happy that the quartet of Pope-like souls saw the potential in him.

He felt a little like the cardinals must do when invited to the burning of the ballots and witnessing the emanation of smoke from those little chimneys in Vatican City. And he had won. All Swami Krishnamurthydas had to do, mainly, was to present the book at the prestigious (they thought) literary festival in Belton. #Biggest South Asian Community outside of India (it isn't). Durban, South Africa is.

So, what were the other preternatural tasks of Swami Krishnamurthydas? To present the book at several other literary festivals—not the biggies Edinburgh, Hay-on-Wye, Cambridge, Oxford or even Uppingham or Cheltenham. But Belton would be the biggest, then others including Peckleton, Market Bosworth and Nuneaton.

Not exactly the F1 circuits or the Grand Slams or the Big Golfs. Nuneaton, though, was connected to the Elliott Library at the Mater Misericordia School in Sundervagvela. But Nuneaton was of Eliot. A George. A woman. Apparently, once the best-selling female author on planet Earth apart from the scribe of Uncle

Tom's Cabin, Harriett Beecher Stowe. And both firm favourites of the contemporaneous Queen Victoria.

Sorry for the knight's move. Although there is more chess later, I think. And so, Pi went. He was given this sacred task as a punishment. This person was Guru Pi—with a very small g if you were to ask any of his fellow colleagues and friends and possibly family. In fact, Guru was a term of endearment that his young students had used in school, and it had stuck.

Why is he called Pi at all? Nothing to do with Piscator Patel, in what appears to be one of Barack Obama's favourite best sellers—*Life of Pi*. Yann Martel. From Canada. What a country! Second biggest in the world, with just lovely people. Apparently decaffeinated Americans—is that good or bad?

A Premier with bhangra dancing credentials. Is that good or bad? Maybe it is good that Merkel, Boris, Macron, Biden, Modi and Xi conduct themselves more escargot-like *vis-à-vis* a flailing octopus.

Recalling Xi we can segue back to Pi. Sorry for the interlude. Pi, as you know, is 3.14159265358979323846. Or less approximately, 22 divided by 7, or even less so, 3.2. In 1897, the Indiana Pi Bill never did become law due to the intervention of a certain Professor Wald of Purdue University. Otherwise, the burger may well have been a different shape.

Guru Pi was so-called because he had worked out that he was not a Chaturvedi, Trivedi, Divedi or Ved. Of the 4 castes, he was top notch Brahmin and not Kshatriya, Vaisya or Sudra. This all originated from the universal god Brahman, self-generated, and then vivisected into functional castes. Internal promotion was possible and demotion, more rarely so.

You see, the Chaturvedi were the most scholarly of them all. They were the knowers and teachers of all the 4 *Vedas—Rig-veda*, *Yajur-veda*, *Sama-veda* and the *Atharva-veda*. In silver position were the three Ved Trivedi, and then the two book Divedis, then the Ved. Then the rest of human folk.

As a young teacher, BrahmaVishnuShivakumar (Pi as he was known then, this exact strange spelling, Trimurthy for short) was asked by a delegation of scholars from the Nordic Countries what he knew about his forefathers. He stated that he could narrow the field as to who his father was to just one person. There was no need for four nominations in his case.

He then proceeded to do a 17-minute lecture with a flip chart on the various Brahmins and non-Brahmins in his family tree going back 4 generations; as is essential to know, as a minimum, in Hindu lore. Taking into account the

Chaturvedi, Trivedi, Divedi, Ved and the non-Brahmin (there was even an English woman, Jewish at that) the average number of *Vedas* that Trimurthy was descended from was 3.14—even more accurate than that almost legislated 3.2 in the quashed Indiana Bill in that early US history.

There was another reason why it was decided that Guru Pi had to go. He had continued to embarrass the Mahant (or Dean-like college principal), teachers and visitors. Guru Pi had risen the standard of his classes such that the school could no longer apply and be successful in procuring the Ambedkar Funds for Equalising Society Initiative (AFESI).

Results in Maths and English, adjusted downwards, were only a little worse than the private school in Panchgini that the hectic, mercurial Farrokh Bulsara had attended. The state bureau strategically managed to adjust this downwards by including students that were not actually taking the examinations, because of an outbreak of dysentery.

Giving a fail grade to these students resulted in a much better comparison with the local private schools. A cringing apology by the Mahant was also required after a discussion group on Vedic Number Theory by Guru Pi. The visitors this was presented to were the *crème de la crème* from the Rosling Institute outside Oslo, Norway. And their esteemed Nordic colleagues.

Their statistical and factual display skills were well known and had been reiterated in many books and TED talks. All the erudite scholars were doing well on Google Scholar. They had opened the ptotic eyes of those that still thought humans were becoming more murderous, unhealthier, and stupider. Things were actually a little better, alas a little hotter.

Guru Pi had laughed, certainly not in the character of the evil and deprecatory manner of Ravana in the *Ramayana*, after finding that precisely zero of his Nordic class of 23 had gotten correct the question of how many millions of hours we live for. Guru Pi had asked for the answer in the case of an 83-year-old. This being the average life expectancy of a European female. Guru Pi had offered the options of:

A: 1 million
B: 2 million
C: 4 million
D: 8 million
E: 16 million
F: 32 million

To be answered in the time it took Guru Pi to recite the *Gayatri Mantra* in Sanskrit. 19 seconds.

Mainly the Norwegians, and a few other, specifically European community folk had deliberated this carefully but quickly opted, in the majority, for C or D. They knew that Guri Pi had cleverly not given them a middle answer to fall into by default. But they had all got the answer wrong and had been laughed at and felt slighted.

Maybe Pi had laughed a little too heartily at Hans, Eriki, Hexi, Ishi, Kunk, Marzx, Sui and the others. Pi then went on to elaborate the correct answer and announced that they would all probably only ever see a thousand full moons in a lifetime. Also, not helpful.

Hence, the funds to the college were in abeyance. Guru Pi had to go. He could not be sacked; the college was on his mother Lakshmi's ancestral lands. The European delegation had only wanted a visit to India to share virtues, venture capital and extol the college from back home. They were absolutely genuine philanthropists.

A day to the waterfalls and feasting (with the inclusion of the locally distilled Amrut) eventually smoothed things over. A solution that would assuage feelings would be the sending of Pi to a non-European country such as England, and he would no longer be an academic lead on the board of the college for the next visitation of some of these academics.

His mother, Lakshmi had been anguished at the matter of Pi leaving. To her, he was still a boy. She had never dreamt of not seeing her children almost daily. Lakshmi had learnt at an early age that her name was symbolic, the same as the Goddess Lakshmi of wealth. It was also a little-known fact that the *vahan* (or vehicle) of this particular deity was the owl. Therefore—wealth and scholarship. What more could she ask for in the two souls that she had been so blessed with to release into humanity and the world. Well, despite having no wealth, Pi scored 100% in her reckoning and so did Ishverlal, despite no scholarship to speak of but he was a *zamindar* and factory owner. The ancestral lands had been leased; with dated postage stamp upon dated postage stamp on the title deeds as it was leased again and again, uplifted by irrigation and inflation, population and economics.

Some parts had been sold off to the Gandhinagar Building Complex (vegetarian) for considerable lucre. But all the excess profit had been invested in the local school and college, and some small health facilities. The latter both Allopathic and Ayurvedic.

The first cases of a very infectious disease had been hidden for a few days and then announced in the spirit of discovery rather than candour. A New Year's Day gift. Inviting in a happy and prosperous 2020. Wuhan City, Hubei Province, cases 27, serious cases 7, recovering 2, deaths nil. So far.

A few days later, it was clear that this disease was extremely virulent and potentially related to the wet market streets of the Hunan area of the bustling metropolis.

Chapter 2
A Passage to England

My favourite thing about being a teacher is that you meet these children who know so little about the world. When you teach them with books, they come to know things, you help give them a future.

Naluca Mwitelela. Rosa Mystica Community School, Zambia.
Book Aid International Supporter Letter.

Leaving India, it was a farewell like all others. There is always the apprehension of never seeing the same person again, exactly. Heraclitus said something similar ages ago. Going away to a life experience that could be bedevilled or bewitched. Maybe to abandon new ideas for old or vice versa. His brother and mother were particularly saddened. Pi wept. Pi laughed.

A puja was performed under the canopy of the grand, but sterile, quadrangle of mango trees. Apparently shortly to be chopped down to a triangle as the village Jyotish had pronounced that they had brought evil and the last lot of cholera and plague to the village. And many more evils, such as the rats and other stuff.

The whole village had turned up and his brother, Ishverlal, had lacrimated copiously, stood at the back of the crowd of about 150. At five foot five and three-quarters, he had easily been able to see everything. The hoven, burning sandalwood (sustainably supplied), smelt ethereal, with just a small smog to be endured before breakfast with the classic tea that was *Punjkichai*. The recipe was secret.

Ishverlal made small talk with his friend, Babu.

"Has the recipe changed? This tea is tasting odd *hanneh*?"

"*Nahi yaar*—I told you last year. The spices are a little hot in the March blend. The quantities are the same, but the taste is different. What is shocking is the taste of the cinnamon. It is so much less spicy; I think that is due to us no longer having the natural bowel action manure of the *Jungli* monkeys on the trees. And why is that?"

"The *banyan chowk* was cleared for an IT complex."

Secret recipe? Well, the five ingredients were not, just the precise composition of the amalgam. It had *taj* (cinnamon), *muri* (pepper), *lovan* (clove), *jaifer* (nutmeg) and *javitri* (mace). It was the quantities and the fact that the tea was not the meagre tea destined for most tea bags, but the tips of the tips.

Pornk was also served, a spiced millet dish, which would keep one nourished for at least a 20-kilometre walk or 4 hours; which ever came first. The dish certainly catered to the vegetarian, vegan, lactose intolerant and coeliac. A mean feat.

There was a brunch with pickle and some guava and *chikoo* fruits followed by prayers and a reading of the *Bhagavad Gita*. And then the Bharatanatyam and Kathak dancers from the Ardhnariishvari Temple. The sign language too complex to understand unless a cognoscenti of the millennia old traditional dances, but mesmerising and tantalising to the untrained eye, nonetheless.

Bharatanatyam, had a somewhat modest origin, that performed by the Cosmic Lord to dance and drum the universe into being. The dances, started off with the *Pataka hasta* first. These elaborate moves were to request permission and then forgiveness from Bhumi Mata (Goddess of the Earth) for dancing upon her.

This was followed by *Anjali hasta*, to offer salutations to the gods, elders and teachers and indeed, the punters for a paid performance. The namaste hands, sequentially, above the head for the former, then front of the face, and at chest height for the latter.

The dance itself, the cogwheeling, robotic limbs segued into smooth svelte glides, told the story of Radha-Krishna—a favourite of the temple for so many reasons. Krishna; the dark one with the ethereal eyes and the less dark Radha as consort—merging into one single body at the end. The narrative was through the eyes, eyebrows, mouth, nose, hands, fingers, feet and even ear movements that Ishverlal certainly could not see from the back.

The colours and grace would vanish in a flash if evil came on in their darker garb and lighter skins. An angry haphazardness of movement would ensue with Krishna slaying all in the end. The music was all offline and powered only by humans—by the dholaks, tanburs, sitar and bells.

And the food, I forgot to say, was served in tableware that our Greta herself would be immensely proud of. The plates were hexagonal, or the occasional octagon of banana leaf. Utensils were your own cleansed hands. Drink was *chas* (not quite lassi) drunk from freshly made clay beakers.

All to be chucked into the hard core and soft-core recycling areas. In front of the sacrificial fire, now aglow with rough logs blazing was the murti. Looking through the rising warm air from the *havan* created a mirage, with the murti of Radha-Krishna appearing to dance oblivious of the crowd and dancers.

The flowers strewn about, the vermillion and the mandalas added a sense of endless passage into the long gone past; whence the ceremony must first have taken place.

Guru Pi was garlanded. Marigolds would have been in season. The saffron, red, yellow and green perfection with a single white chrysanthemum. As Mark Tully would point out in many of his books and essays—the senses were all assaulted. It was all authentic, nothing too ersatz as in the ubiquitous Ganesha now often made in China.

Guru Pi was garlanded by the oldest person in the village first. The 107-year-old Motiben. Many of the younger relations claimed that she had aged 2 years every year for the last 11 years, adding 3 years on per year when she turned 92. The reasons for this were not clear. Nevertheless, she was the oldest, no doubt about that, with a photo in the *Nava Zamana* newspaper with Mahatma Gandhi and Nehru. From 1939.

And then garlanded by the youngest able human in the form of Gopalakrishnaradhanarayanan. The need had not risen to shorten his name as yet. He was not the youngest at 293 days old, but the youngest who could manage to walk, not vomit, and successfully put a garland around Guru Pi.

Then, all the children from the school put a *chandlo* on him by putting *kumkum* vermillion paste with a few grains of rice onto his forehead. And then the rest of his local clan—all 163 of them in total. There was mass and smaller group photography adjacent to the murti of Rama, Sita and Lakshman leaving for their exile in the forest.

Rama's feet were wept on by Bharat—the brother who had very reluctantly been made monarch during exile. The *Ramayana* is a very long story about their 14 years in exile—that and a whole lot more. This was a little too much, considering Guru Pi was only going for 40 days.

Packing was very easy. The last item to be packed was the *hawejyu*—the spice box. England had diagnosed two patients with coronavirus on 29th January of that year. Valentine's Day saw the first death in Europe, just over the channel, in France.

Had it crept into England from there? Despite Brexit? The virus had by then been finger-printed, its genetic sequence known but its intended message not yet apparent in its embryonic stage, as it became a global body living in millions.

Chapter 3
A Household in Suburbia

Friendship is the hardest thing in the world to explain. It's not something you learn in school. But if you haven't learnt the meaning of friendship, you haven't learnt anything.

Muhammad Ali (1942–2016). Boxer and Social Activist.

And why was Guru Pi even being collected by the Beck household?

It's a long story. Beck Senior was a parasitologist in London. Once the ongoing success of the Victorian sewage system had rendered him almost redundant, he was almost grateful that the British Raj existed in India, as it provided him with the objective of ridding the nation of certain forms of non-human parasites.

Excel, he did in this field; he knew his case of hydatidosis from his leishmaniosis and indeed, from his cryptosporidiosis, toxoplasmosis and the mundane but deadly malarias. There were only four main ones at the time. Now, we have five. An extra one from macaques, until they become extinct.

His son Anton, the deputy CEO of the Beck household, had by then finished his own medical training, almost. During this, he had spent 8 weeks, plus another 6 weeks of holiday, abroad as part of the so-called elective study period. To be honest, most students returned with or on return, constructed a report of often dubious quality to then be allowed to pass their finals and then hey presto; a doctor is delivered to the world.

Anton had submitted a particularly readable report. It was short. With many pictures. Really, it was more like a scrapbook. One should mention that the elective had been at the Beck Institute of Parasitology at Sundervagvela.

If 3 rooms and a microscope and 3 sinks and a consulting room could, and then did, muster the support of the International Standardisation Organisation for

25

such a bold claim as to be called an institute. Then an institute it was. Anton's supervisor had been Pi's father. The latter at the time was the local Public Health Officer for a relatively small district of 5.4 million souls.

Beck Senior had promised future exchanges to England as and when the desire arose, and hence, Guru Pi was to be welcomed into the bosom of this family. Another stitch in this intertwining was the sojourn of Anton's daughter to India. This, then feisty human was well into all things gender-defiant from a young age and had forced her Barbie doll into the cabin of a Tonka tractor, later painting Barbie to a fake tan then to a positively southeast Asiatic version.

She had spent her elective, during her polymath Master's degree course, in Sundervagvela, interviewing adherents and others living in the locality of the Ardhnariishvari Temple. One of her dreams was to have created and successfully marketed an Ardhnariishvari doll for children, locally and globally. This failed.

The temple was probably unique. It is difficult to be precise. This is a country with a lot of temples. The esteemed Hindu councils state that there are 1500 large complex temples (some with their large but no swimming allowed lidos), 15,000 large temples, 50,000 smaller temples and around 5 million local shrines.

This is a lot, and then in a somewhat Mandelbrot fractal idea, the largest ones thread their way through the others into personal individualised worship places in a home or out of the home (next to a tree or large rock or ideally both).

Why be interested in Ardhnariishvari and not the other 3 main or 108 major deities? It is to do with the half female-half male formulation that Anju had found so fascinating. Her research had been well received and carried a mighty citation index of 53—which is apparently high for such a paper—and could lead to a precipitous 3-year lectureship then tenure. Possibly. If sufficient disposable income landed on the department.

In this Beck household, there was also the CEO, of course. Please don't ever call her Mrs Beck. Ruth was the matriarch, stage one. Grandchildren are needed to be an accredited matriarch of a higher league. She worked in an academy, teaching English in the main, and cricket.

The other offspring. That would be Kirk. In childhood, he was told that the name probably originated from the old German *kirche* or church. He aspired to become a suburban vicar. He was certainly apprehensive to have a heathen living under one's roof.

As it stood, the family lived in the most heathen that is non-Christian, city in Europe. That is official. One of the 'godless' cities. Leicester was like a clock, with increasing heathens starting at noon and now at 7.48 pm on the pie charts. Kirk was frankly surprised that there was not a temple for the Asatrú Pagans as this ancient faith to nature and Norse symbolism was growing so rapidly, in Iceland at least.

Kirk was to pick up Guru Pi. The latter had arrived at Birmingham Airport from Kyiv, via Frankfurt, for some reason. He walked quite nonchalantly, looking at the photos he had taken of the splendid airports and the *Mir Vam* posters at Kyiv. He was nicely relaxed having enjoyed a beer (clean with only 4 ingredients) in Frankfurt.

Kirk found him quite easily as Guru Pi was the very last person to emerge from the outflowing of the flight from Frankfurt. Guru Pi had texted Kirk and informed him that he would be wearing an *ahimsa-silk reshmi bundi* jacket. Easily said.

A quick search and a saved picture had led Kirk to conclude that it was akin to a Nehru collar gilet. Guru Pi had also texted details on his distribution of facial hair (including ears), height, weight, and skin colour. The latter was grade 4 to 5 on the Fitzpatrick Pigmentary Phenotype Scale.

"Great to see you," Kirk enthusiastically and slightly disingenuously remarked. Hugs had been advised against and moreover were not part of Kirk's emotional lexicon.

"How was the journey? Did they feed you well? Did you get pissed!"

Guru Pi processed the volley of words for precisely 9 seconds.

"It is lovely to see you and walk in another country. You asked me about the journey. I thought I would be rather uncomfortable. Abdul Aziz, my friend, is always moaning about the lack of space on an aeroplane but for me, it was fine. I wonder whether is to do with the increased body mass index of my friend—or his arthritis."

"I am not too tall for my height, as you can see. I was fed very well. Today, it is an *Ekadashi* fast, *Shukla Paksha* in the lunar cycle, so I only have fluids and fruits. I was fed good and a lot. I accidentally had some wine. But it was good, and had a bit more, and a beer, but I have no regrets. I went to the toilet many times—thanks for asking. The queue was quite long at times though."

Well, that was certainly comprehensive, thought Kirk. The journey back home was uneventful. Apart from Guru Pi asking questions about everything. Kirk was taciturn, but still amiable. All of Guru Pi's conversation was punctuated by that 9-second processing break. Then, the pistol fired for at least a minute or two of slow conversation. He would be a lip-readers' dream.

Guru Pi asked Kirk, "Which football team do you support?"

"Leicester City, of course. I was born in Leicester. They've been an amazing team recently. We won the league a few years ago at odds of 5000 to one. Can you imagine? A 100 quid bet would have won you half a million quid!"

Guru Pi replied, "I support Manchester United. Because my father was a big George Best fan."

Guru Pi asked Kirk, "What religion do you support?"

Sorry to interrupt, but I have had difficulties, recently, processing conversation. I need to compartmentalise. I think, I will adopt a style that Guru Pi would be very content with; that of Krishna to Arjun or indeed all the characters in Shakespeare to each other, or to themselves. Let's not forget Hamlet. So, we return.

Kirk: I do not support a religion, Guru Pi.

His own answer changed something in Kirk, with permanence. Here, Guru Pi's processing interval was less than 9 seconds. The necessity for urgent apologies often had that effect. But not much else.

Pi: So sorry; I did not mean to pry. And it is perfectly acceptable if you are an atheist or even a pagan.

Kirk: I am a Christian.

Pi: Why? But you said that you did not support a religion? But religions are for everyone—they are just lots of interesting ethical stories.

Kirk: A great acronym thus emerges. Nearly.

Pi: You mean?

This conversation was proving a little difficult for Kirk. Kirk's discussion ensued in the direction that religions were not for supporting, but rather adhering to. Guru Pi countered this with the fact that if all religions lead to the same or similar destinations, then why so many creeds?

Maybe, you just support a religion that suits you because of the accident of life, birth and death. Kirk deeply felt that there was a lot more to it than that, especially as he had been baptised into the one true religion. And all could be baptised.

Kirk: No; what you do not understand is that as an atheist, you can have redemption by accepting Christ. You are then not an atheist. And can have all the rewards of heaven, Guru Pi.

Guru Pi: But what would happen if you converted to another big or even small religion?

Kirk: I am not sure, Guru Pi.

Pi: Why not sure?

The repeated whys of Guru Pi only served to make Kirk more irritable. The Guru was dropped. The conversation had to end, as Kirk started to brake.

Kirk: And how is Spikey in India?

Pi: Spikey?

Kirk: Spikey the virus? The pandemic. Chat later, Pi.

Kirk was much relieved as they arrived home and parked. Nevertheless, the two were firmly ensconced in each other's life, for their forever.

In suburbia, the classic 2000 square foot or so of the solid UK household was bannered for Pi's arrival. Welcome to Chez Nous, Guru Pi! —it proclaimed. The most excited was Anju as she had met Guru Pi in India whilst she was compiling data for her dissertation.

She fondly recalled the many conversations they had had on all matters of mutual interest, with some monologues in order to release the valve of self-expression. The latter, a mark of true friendship and comradeship. I think the two are different—I'm just not exactly sure how.

Guru Pi was initially so fascinated, by the vibrant sulphur yellow of the forsythias that he did not notice the humans. Another major distraction were the blue tits. A bird that he had never seen the exquisite form of in India. Anju, Ruth and Anton had all been alerted to the arrival of Kirk and Guru Pi by the signature tune of the cracked exhaust of the Triumph Spitfire—an inheritance passed down from the 1960s.

As a vintage car, there was little road tax, no need for an MOT, and could pollute as much as it liked. Kirk often remarked to his friends these privileges also appeared to apply to the aging silver-surfers. In fact, so many of its parts had been replaced that there was a philosophical conundrum—was it the same car? It was certainly in the final stages of the Shakespearean seven ages of it all.

Anju: Hey man, it's magic to see you again after all these years!

Pi: I am so pleased to see you again. You look as much of a Wonder Woman as ever. And to meet your mother is a gift of provenance, I am sure. Meeting your father too, I suspect, will be equally enlightening for me. For me, seeing your father—a person recommended by my friend and mentor at

Sundervagvela—is a promise fulfilled. I am really looking forward to discussing all things Indian and otherwise. After all, the life expectancy in India has gone up by 12 years in 25 years whilst in your country by 6. More stuff too.

Kirk noted that Pi's English improved if he was less nervous. Pi felt joyful; within half an hour of mundane talk about bathrooms and toilets and the need for the extra pull down, then up and down times two on the cistern to flush stuff away into the sewers of suburbia, all was settled, and Pi was firmly installed into the Beck household at Field Lake Meadows, in the top floor attic room. But what a view. And the great spotted woodpecker appeared on the peanuts. Indubitably male, brightly red-capped as it was.

It was late but Anju was really keen to catch up with Pi. Anju was Anjou on the birth certificate. For that was the intended destination of Anton and his friends' cycling holiday when it later changed to an engagement. Cycling had also happened, just with a fiancée nouveau.

The Anjou grapes to the vin de goutte. The rude health of it all. The bonhomie of the natives, no doubt relatives of Ingelgar the founding warrior via his son Fulk the Red. Redness was everywhere. Ruth had had great sympathy for Margaret of Anjou, our first great English Queen, who was only to be banished and faced an early death back home.

Ruth had also just finished a Master's degree at Queens' College, Cambridge. With a thesis on the despoliation of the character of Margaret of Anjou. For Shakespeare had described her not in the ilk of *women are soft, mild, pitiful, and flexible* but as *thou stern, obdurate, flinty, rough, remorseless*. That was the conception of her despoliation. I'll make a wise phrase to despoil Shakespeare, I thought, but nothing comes to mind. But Ruth had provided the perfect rejoinder and created Anjou, Anju for short.

Pi and Anju had established their old platonic intimacy. But Anju was disappointed and on the point of lacrimation. Her final thesis had not been well received and even failed to make the cut for an open presentation at her university, despite there being an excess of slots in which to present. Apparently, there was a lack of congruency with current thinking in gender politics and future trends.

She was not sure what that meant for she felt she was all things human rights and feminist to boot. Whatever she meant in her thesis was an issue to her tutors. So, they sat in silence for a good quarter of an hour. Because of the tutors' lack of freedom of thought.

Pi consoled Anju.

Pi: Worry not. It is just too difficult for the non-visitor to the Ardhnariishvari Temple to see its relevance for life here. You must live it with all six senses. It is too difficult to see above the high walls of metaphor. People are divided into those who can use the idea of Ardhnariishvari in their lives and those who cannot. They see the binary. You do not. You see the human.

Anju: Yes, the formless one. The one that should be afforded human rights. Whoever they are. This is the division between the people of the book, the Abrahamic religions and the all-pervading oneness of the polytheism of the Ardhnariishvari devotees.

Pi: To call it a division is too absolute, Anju. They understand too. Do not worry. All is one or two.

But she was worried. Anju felt that not presenting her thesis might mean that a publication was unlikely. Her ideas and thoughts did not rise above the block, according to her tutor. The paper would not be published. And then her CV would be less impressive. And then she would be faced with a less than adequate job.

And then she would be severed from all that she had loved to learn and teach and research in order to improve the lives of herself and others. Maybe the university was not a real university, not one where all views could be aired, discussed, and respected; only those eschewed by the well-endowed oligarchy of restricted viewpoints.

Her earlier conversation with Anton had resulted in a less than useful discussion. Anton concluded to her that that was how the world was run. And that was that. He told Anju that every one of the 123 singers and musicians in the Belton Symphony Ensemble, for example, were aspiring greats but reined in—thankfully, he had smirked.

Reined in by only ever playing written down expressions of joy or sorrow of a composer many, many scores of years ago. Very few of the ensemble were ever lost to the freedom of jazz.

Anju felt that there was a certain drabness to it all. The full extent of the world's smorgasbord of ideas would, if food, dwindle down to a few plates of basic meals. Circumventing the unknown and the previously disliked.

Just before sleep, Anju found herself in a state of anxiety but bereft of alcohol and drugs and any other pharmacological alteration of her brain chemistry. The usually empathetic Ruth did not help much either. Anju hadn't even had a chance to air her grievances to Ruth today. Apparently, it was a significant day in the life of the garden.

To Ruth, it was clear that the utopia of Monty Don did exist, in hot composting and the later harvesting of tomatoes, potatoes, and beans. With herbs and flowers, insects, and lazy dogs. Why allow anything from the humdrum of everyday life to float into this world? The garden illuminated all and very conveniently could be switched off at twilight. When the stars and the planets could take over.

There was, however, a bit of useful advice provided by Ruth. Anju agreed that she needed a mission statement of life. Maybe one, two or three statements but at least one based on the garden. Why? Because not everyone from the disenfranchised and meticulously miseducated could become a Premiership footballer on £4 million a year (just an average, a wage-cap is not intended). Or play the national or international lottery and win a cool hundred million.

At least one in 14 million will win a million in the national one. In their own lifetime, unlikely. What can add to the lot of the life of the citizen whether homeless, working, sad or not, rich or poor, old or young, *mens sana in corpore sano* or not? A garden. To Ruth, it was all about the garden.

Pi woke early on the morning of 14th March. The alarm had been set for 10 minutes to 2am. So that he could set a countdown clock and pause it at exactly at 59 minutes past 1am and ideally 26.5 seconds past that particular minute. Last year, he had managed to pause the clock at exactly 59 minutes, 27 seconds and just over half of the next second.

This year, he had managed even better. He had paused the clock on March 14th, at 1.59 am and 26 seconds and 55 hundredths of the next second. Pi thought this was a pretty accurate reflection of the 3.14159265359 that was pi. His favourite number. After, he recited the *Gayatri Mantra*, did the *Aarti* in his mind and read a chapter of the *Bhagavad Gita*.

Ultimately about spiritual salvation but in a war setting, the Gita set Pi's mind wandering to the horrors of the global wars at present. The Afghanistan War, the Rohingya Massacres, the Yemeni Crisis, the Russian Special Wars in Ukraine, the Tigray Offensives, Indo-Pak stupidities, Kurdish wars, East-Indian Conflicts, the ever-present Palestinian-Israeli Wars, Sudan and many other unknown to him.

He felt the horror of an individual fatality or injury that was a life lost or changed. The history of the universe changed, in that event. Just how was this permissible? It was just academic to work through the why of it when killing and maiming each other should be altogether banished from the human psyche. And of other sentient life-forms too. Ideally. But with time.

Pi was troubled. There were no guaranteed solutions. Humans were stupid. Pi lost sleep but by counting the dead he drifted off to sleep a few hours later. Only to be woken rather early at 6.09am by the tawny owl.

Anton was becoming more troubled. Let's not forget Covid-19. But please! There was no need to worry in the UK! We are well prepared. The virus is mild. We can take it on the chin if need be. We can develop herd immunity. We can go to the England versus Wales rugby. And shake the whole team by the hand, with a hug for the captain.

Then what was the logic in ever even considering cancelling Cruft's, the biggest dog show on planet Earth. What had the dogs done wrong for the jamboree to be cancelled? Especially bearing in mind the shorter lifespan of a dog; really that would reduce their possibilities of becoming a champion.

In any category—gundog, pastoral, hound, terrier, toy, utility, and working. And the top dog; the wiry-haired dachshund. Sorry; I almost forgot the 251,684 at the Cheltenham Festival. And the other 500,000 on that weekend of sport. But the virus had been informed to spread only by coughing in the majority. Hopefully, not by shouting *Ingerland, Ingerland, Ingerland* at the football, rugby, and cricket.

Anton needed catharsis, and although one never to keep a diary, he decided to make notes on the pandemic that was affecting him every day at work. The notes would be strictly for private consumption only. That was early March. The first march of SARS COV-2. The ash blades hung like upside down bats at repose. Soon to be banished with life anew.

Instalment One: March

So, my first Sit-Rep. For my eyes only. At the moment. Honestly, the virus does look spikey.

Post Crufts, the six nations and Cheltenham, the UK government had had an epiphany. Maybe this was not to be taken on the chin. Maybe we should at least stay at home from 23rd March. The economic, political, scientific, social, and political again, planets were all in the correct alignment and two weeks after the Worm Moon—the Supermoon. An ideal time for the coming advice that had to be adhered to unless it applied to you specifically; not if you were well connected.

We apparently had 12,637 cases and just the odd deaths. No way near the debacle that was China with its 2000 plus deaths (and all the rest, the press were arguing).

I need to tell you that the naming of the moons was a contribution to world moonology from the Algonquins from the borderless land that was New England to Lake Superior, betwixt the US of A and Canada.

The career of the personal trainer was launched with millions working out at home. We had no excuses to abandon or to not start exercise. It was good. It was what you certainly did more of when under home arrest anyhow. Kirk, to prepare for the inevitable, made his own toilet paper from a combination of various paid-for and free newspapers. Not a huge success, to be honest.

The households adjacent to the Becks were busy auditioning their Creuset saucepans (a tad heavy many found) and wooden spoons to din the streets at 8pm to celebrate the non-suicidal missions, usually, of the NHS workers fighting the virus. Some NHS workers were ungrateful for the celebration as they had just fallen asleep to wake again at 6am for their next shift. But generally, it was well received. From a microbiological perspective, clap for carers would be better than Spikey. At least the clap was curable with penicillin. NHS doctors and nurses die.

By the end of the month, both the PM and the King-to-be test positive. We all worry in varying degrees. But the government declares COVID-19 no longer to be a 'high consequence infectious disease'. We can therefore relax. But the month ends with parliament shutting and an exhortation to *Stay at home. Protect the NHS. Save lives.* 10,000 in hospital with COVID-19. And 1789 dead, their liberty, equality, fraternity lost forever.

Chapter 4
A Visit to the Garden

Certe, adveniente die judicii, non quæretur a nobis legimus, sed quid fecimus;
nec quam bene diximus, sed quam religiose viximus
At the Day of Judgement, we shall not be asked what we have read, but what
we have done; not how eloquently we have spoken,
but how sacredly we have lived

The Imitation of Christ. Thomas à Kempis (1380–1471).
German-Dutch Catholic Monk.

In Sundervagvela, Guru Pi would always wake to a pure human voice intonating a yearning for the Almighty from the balconied peaks of the mosque's towers. This sound had always reminded Guru Pi of a marine navigator looking for dry land in the crow's nest of a ship. In England, it was the church bells at 5.19 am, for some reason.

Really? Thought Guru Pi. He did know that the precision of the many times for prayers, opening shops, naming a child was based on the exact phases of the moon, solar cycle and the juxtaposition of the planets to the larger stars in the major constellations. But he had had no idea that such a system existed in England.

In reality, Bernadette the belling lead had fallen off her motorised scooter and was somewhat late in carrying out her campanological duties on the 3rd Sunday of each month. This was still allowed in lockdown. Or so the edict from the Bishop had declared.

Guru Pi's rather animated conversations at breakfast centred on the division of the 8-part newspaper. Guru Pi estimated that at probably 100,000 words, the paper was longer than most novels. The production of the newspaper was a monumental feat to achieve every week, and indeed it had been carried out the previous 10,192 times.

Breakfast was not Pi's usual at-home staple of *idli dosa*. Guru Pi had also worked out that Ruth would eat no pork, Anton no tomatoes, Kirk no mushrooms and Anju no meat, eggs or dairy. It was one of the family's vegan days. Guru Pi was vegetarian, usually, therefore easy to accommodate. A morning meeting of the Beck plus one household would inevitably consist of a discussion of the justification of one's diet.

Fermented foods were in vogue and Vogue at this time. To be fair, none of the five were so food-obsessed that breakfast, at least, was seen as anything other than a refuelling for the day's journey ahead. Clearly, the beautiful accoutrements of the Peruvian Highland coffee, the Human Race Tea and exotic fruits with the just added tad of the extra CO_2 emission from the Moroccan blueberries, Chinese lychees and the Polish raspberries. In a global village, we share all. If you can afford it. The farmers abroad were grateful for the work.

The paraphernalia of breakfast continued in the form of heather honey and the re-colonisation of the colon with fermented coconut yoghurt, after its initial decolonisation with all things' kale and spirulina.

The origin of the tea was interesting. Apparently, it had been created after a discussion that took place in the early days of the Ruth-Anton relationship. With a smirk, and to the groans and embarrassment of Kirk and Anju, Anton informed Guru Pi that he was not sure whether it was during the chemistry, physics or the biology phase of what to become a 36-year marriage to date.

Anton recalled a conversation with an anthropology lecturer at the Institute of Parasitology and how Dr Venkat Venkat—for that was his name—had reformulated and renamed the human race in terms of migration and physiognomic features and what in those days was crude genetics based on blood types, diet intolerances and the like.

Anton, a keen collector of the National Geographic, had an avid interest in humans generally. The magazines issues were all arranged in their spinal yellow splendour on various shelves across the home. A migrant community of these well-travelled issues was present in every room. The odd decade here, a year there, a season there, maybe a month or so in the potting shed. What he had gleaned from the photos in the main resonated with Dr Venkat Venkat's ideas.

Dr Venkat Venkat—Anton had always liked the quip that Boutros Boutros Ghali had been so called because his parents had liked the name so much, that they named him twice—had come to only four conclusions from his vast reading and academic studies. The categories were the *Africois, Caucois, Vedois and the Chinois.*

These had never caught on as his papers had not reached the attention of the Harvard International Seminars of the Origin of the Human Race, and therefore had not really been read or cited much. It made perfect sense though, did it not? We are all African. Some of us left and went to South India, via the Andamans or overland to South India and went on to become the original Australians all those 60,000 years ago.

Some of us went from Africa through to the windy plains in and around Mongolia and self-effacingly emerged as the *Chinois*. The latter would eventually migrate through the currently Russian and Japanese lands through to Alaska (incidentally, a really good contract for the Americans buying it off the Russians for 1 cent an acre!).

Guru Pi was fascinated by the conversation and felt an internal warming as never before when he had the tea—black. It was indeed the first time he had had tea without milk—in fact, he had rarely ever had it without the spices detailed previously.

The paucity of milk at breakfast was easy to understand after Anju's careful and guarded explanation that maybe humans did not really have to breast-feed and have the milk of any mammal once fully grown.

The warming tea was a blend of the *Africois* Kenyan tea, the *Caucois* Darjeeling, the *Vedois* Nilgiri and the Hangzhou-Suzhou *Chinois* green tea. To be honest, Darjeeling was more *Chinois* than *Caucois*, but the idea was extant and drunk in the Beck household with the blend a staple of Christmas gifting. Usually in home-made origami boxes.

An agenda was being created for Guru Pi through various breakfasts over the next few days. On a day that Sir X (Sir Mark Xavier—more formally) was expected to visit, Ruth and Pi tried to plan a few events that they could attend together or just simply where to go, who to see, to get the best out of what little Belton had to offer. It was plenty for Pi though. There would be a new world for him here, of that he was certain.

Sir X would often pop in to see the Becks, usually around breakfast time after he had finished his jog around the lakes. Sir X had exchanged almost half a dozen sentences with Pi in the last dozen days. He did not talk much unless the topic of conversation was closely related to the running of the country, or a whisky-fuelled conversation with his best friend, Anton. For him, the world was right wing, or the wrong wing.

Ruth: You know, Pi, I am a trustee of the Community Radio and TV Network that is now funded by the BBC and some entities related to Netflix, ITV and even Channel 4. We have a few adverts too but they can only be local businesses or entities. We have been successful in not needing other sources of income or management ideas. My friend Carmen has started a programme. Adapted from a stolen idea. Somewhat.

By now, everyone knew that a 9-second lull was needed to encourage Pi to reply.

Pi: What is it?

Ruth: The format is an interview with an interesting person. And I'm not being rude, but you have an authenticity that is interesting and real. I mean that is what authenticity means. You're like a Crocodile Dundee for us in mild suburbia. Except we have no crocodiles. The programme is strangely called Tea and Toast with a Dost. That is tea with a friend. But you know that, Pi. You could do a yoga segment?

Interferingly but amiably, Anton interjected.

Anton: Tea and Toast with a Dost. What a title! That is exactly what happens when there's an excess of democracy and everyone's ideas count! We do not ask a surgeon to be advised by a committee on what emergency operations may potentially be needed for acute abdominal pain—why are so many things nowadays committee driven?

Ruth: Thank you, Anton—objection overruled. Look, Mark will be at the door. The format is a relaxed conversation with the presenter, Carmen Dean. Her brother runs the Rasta Fasta Nasta café; I must take you there. The BBC edicts of informing, educating, and entertaining all are covered within it and therefore, its *raison d'être*.

Pi: This is actually very similar to a format I have often seen in India where people are interviewed over a cup of chai and a few freshly fried samosas. The interviewees are warned with respect to the stipulated questions. Always within the purview of the person concerned. Books are central to the programme.

They are warned so they can find a short book on the internet and read up on what they are to be questioned about. One of my ex-students also offers a service of providing an audio or written 30 minutes, one hour, or a two-hour guide on any book, for anyone, for Rs 1000 to 2000 only.

Ruth: I think this will be a little more complex and you will be asked to talk about several things. You will need to present to Carmen and the audience a rather tightly formatted curriculum vitae of one's cultural interests and influences.

Ruth usefully spent the next 9 seconds looking at the yellow hammer on the bird table. A canary with a longer tail. *Who needed mindfulness training when Pi was around?* Thought Ruth.

Pi: What is exactly is stipulated? I am liking the challenge of this already.

Anton interjected again.

Anton: I have a challenge for you too!

Ruth sharply, amiably, and irritably cut him off.

Ruth: Anton, sure. Go let Mark in! And let me finish, so I can go and sit down to *Gardeners' World* and—

Anton: Yep you need to find out what Monty the Dictator wants you to do today, whether your garden is 10 square metres or 10 acres! Whilst his lazy dog looks on!

Anton exited at this stage—quite wisely but quite out of character for a man of reduced emotional intelligence such as he was. Sir X was waiting for him.

Ruth: Basically, there will be a general introduction and then Carmen will launch into where you were born and why? That's her favourite question. Bits on the family, its business, character and what your early life was like. Though there is the hidden assumption that really the peak of your life to date is appearing on her programme. Oprah is her president of the planet—and why not!

You will be asked to choose your favourite and most inspiring piece of art, poem, film, novel, hero (in fact or fiction), song, piece of wordless music, and a few other things in general that lighten your life and have influenced it. Carmen keeps it fluid and sometimes forgets the format.

It is not as easy as it sounds though. You will also be asked to spin a wheel, which will randomly decide on either home or away. Dice will decide how many choices you have in each category. What do you think? Then a mirror programme will be done that often has a greater audience then the first show.

Pi: Complex it is. Home and away, what does that mean?

Ruth: Home means that the item under discussion has to come from the culture of Britannia, whilst away essentially means from outside Britannia; in your case, Indic. This method has resulted in a synthesis of ideas and cultures from across the world. A veritable cross hybridisation that any horticulturist would be insanely proud of. But as I said, on the day, Carmen will change the rules as she sees fit.

Had Anton not left earlier, he would have gone on a tirade now at how this was an excuse for the barbarisation and indeed the bastardisation of cultures. Ruth had found it difficult to understand Anton at times. But she had an appointment with Monty.

The latter, the steady man in the lives of so many ungloved, dirty-nailed gardeners across the UK and the BBC's global reach. This was the Maradona of them all, the Pelé of Gardening. The triumvirate in Ruth's life was obvious. There was of course Anton, Anju and Kirk in the heart of it all.

The calming waters and the flow to equilibrium and balance were provided for her by Monty, the David of the Attenboroughs, and all things Greta Thunbergesque. She also had a new charity to talk of, to her Circle of Hope at the Nunnery tea-rooms. It was all so middle-class, I know; but they did some good, it must be said.

Anton and Sir X had written in despair and outrage to their local MP when they had learnt through their chums at the Gate that there were 166,000 charities in the UK with an annual turnover over of £48 billion. And paying little to no tax. That felt, almost irredeemably mean to Ruth, but recently £500,000 had disappeared from the official books of a national football charity with local reach into Belton.

Anton and Sir X had called for a rating for each charity to be included each time it advertised, especially on all their webpages. Like a sort of hygiene certification that restaurants displayed; when by standards or the grace of God, rodents had been absent when health inspectors had visited.

Anton had also proposed an unhealthiness score for each main food item on restaurant menus. As usual, most of his ideas would be rejected. Even though he had a hotline to the local MP, who was Sir X's nephew.

Kirk would be pleased with Ruth's choice of a recent new charity. Kirk was a member of the underground *homo saplings* club. Tree Aid was the charity. A futures investment project; as they say the best time to plant a tree was 20 years ago, and the second-best time is today. One particular appeal was for the regeneration and rewilding of the Metemba forest—I'm not exactly clear on where that is—definitely in Africa though.

The idea was to plant Frankincense trees. Drought-resistant whilst also adding to soil fertility. Named recipients of the bounty would be selling the Frankincense resin produced to make a living. That was incredible to Ruth. The gift that was given to Jesus Christ himself at birth; together with gold (never depreciates, the Earth has stopped making it for now) and myrrh (dubious value at present).

And as the Great Wall of China, but not the lesser wall of Hadrian, is visible from space, the idea was to create the Great Green Wall of Africa. This would also be visible from space. It would start from the little countries jostling at the lower part of the ball that is the hip joint of Africa—Senegal, Gambia, Guinea Bissau, Guinea (minus the Bissau), Sierra Leone, Liberia, Cote D'Ivoire, Burkina Faso, Ghana, Togo, Benin, to the larger Nigeria, Cameroon, Central African Republic, South Sudan, Ethiopia and the Indian coastal destinations of Somalia, Djibouti and Eritrea.

Although some of us marched out of Africa 60,000 years ago, this Green Revolution could unite us all. More lungs were needed for Mother Earth. The UK government was to match, in funding, the money raised for this. And so, everyone wins.

Back to Anton with Sir X and Pi, slowly sipping coffee.

Pi: You have so, so many books.

Anton: Yes. When Anju said goodbye to me as I left for work yesterday, she told me you said that all the books in the house would take 25 years to read. That is impossible! That is my challenge for you—explain yourself! Prove yourself! Without any of this guess and bless and thinking something just because someone else espoused it! That is a crap philosophy—I say it, so it is and therefore it must be respected. I am a man of science and that is *namby-pamby* thinking. Let's chat further on this in the evening.

There was not much time for discussion that day. The household all left to their respective toils of the day. In the case of Pi, not an awful lot was planned. Anton went off to the hospital. On the latter's return home, Pi launched straight back into their conversation.

Pi: And Namby-Pamby was a great poet, I believe?

Anton: No actually; particularly rubbish as it stands. It is not a compliment. Ambrose Philips was dire.

Pi: Thank you. Thank you.

Anton: What for?

Pi: For telling me his current popularity or share price. Appears low *hanneh*. Though I will have to look at his works again. He is certainly immortalised in word. In India, we were taught some of his work in school. His family is originally from Leicestershire, I think? I really like his Winter Piece—it made me think very much of the dampness and coldness you must bravely endure in England.

From frozen climes, and endless tracts of snow.
From streams which Northern winds forbid to flow.

Anton paused and countered.

Anton: You detract from telling me about the books.

Pi: So sorry. Ok, here it goes, exactly and precisely. You have 4 or so big bookcases. A veritable library indeed. In fact, the library of my college is much less extant. In the study, there is a big bookcase that is 7 shelves high, and 2 metres across—maybe a little less. That is 14 metres. And a small bookcase that is 4 shelves high and only one and a half metres across.

I have also seen many smaller migrant communities of books outside the rooms; both on the elephant and on your Hanuman, who holds a pile of books and not the Sanjivani Mountain of tradition. That is clever indeed! Did I tell you, we still read the story your father wrote on his studies in Sundervagvela. To every single class 14 over the last 53 years, they say. There is a lot of homework set on it too.

Anton: You detract again. Which conversation are we having? I, being traditional, can only ever follow one strand of thought. Although, later, about my father's story please, Pi. That sounds very interesting.

Pi: So sorry. In the attic room, next to where I slept, Anju showed me the family library. I was very impressed with your qualifications. Although I am not entirely sure what a Fellow of the Higher Education Academy does. And are there any women allowed to bear such august titles? In this room, there are horseshoe shelves. With a total length of 7 metres and 5 books high. Which is 35 metres.

I think the nomad bookcases are approximately 2 metres and 5 books high. There are some shelves with fewer books as you have the paraphernalia of your life interspersed. I like the rugby ball. So, the total is equivalent to 50 metres approximately—more or less. I think the error interval is a maximum of 5%. The latter with 95% certainty. And so, we have it. You read 2 metres of books a year and Bob is your uncle.

Anton gently corrected.

Anton: It is—Bob's your uncle.
Pi: No; it is a saying we use in India a lot.

Sir X joined them from across the room, tumbler with a peg of whisky, or was it whiskey, in hand. The rest of the day would be dry. Usually.

Sir X: Anton, we can reconnoitre and move on, Pi. You couldn't read 2 metres of books in a year—that is impossible. You could not even read your own modest height in books in a year. Never mind 2 metres.

Pi: I can and will if you challenge me. I will keep in touch with you when I go back to India.

Ruth: Life is so much more than reading, Pi.

Anton: She'll start banging on about the garden now!

After dinner, Sir X came back to discuss and set out the rules for the challenge. He insisted that no dross was to be included. Essentially, he stated that the books would need to be highfalutin, erudite books, rather than dross or mundane. In this regard, there was a duel of a sort, Guru Pi had Ruth and Anju as seconds whilst Anton was a reluctant second for his great friend, Sir X. It was agreed that a 50:50 split was acceptable.

Anju had countered the dross statement with a plea to Anton that had she not been brought up to observe the Gandhian principles of not wanting *my house to be walled in on all sides and my windows to be stuffed* but wanting *the cultures of all lands to be blown about my house as freely as possible* but refusing *to be blown off my feet by any.*

Anton was delighted after his initial perturbation; his daughter had imbibed his earlier ideas and inherited his DNA. He might have lost his. Sir X tempered down his choice of potential books that could be included. A little.

The rules were agreed. At least 10 books had to come from the top 100 BBC books of all time. No children's books within the tower (although Anton had secretly enjoyed Harry Potter and the Philosopher's Stone, and all the other Harry Potters except for the last).

There could only be a maximum of 10% of the total books that could be graphic novels (Kirk had loads—some more graphic than others). Each book had to be by a different author. Some books, Pi would be randomly asked questions about, to verify that the book in question had actually been read. There would be an update every month after Pi's return to India.

Ruth said that this idea would be an international book club, if nothing else. In the meantime, a 31centimetre space was allocated in the hiatus between the two bookcases in the library. This was currently occupied by a grubby-looking but very cheerful Shrek and an equally grubby-looking ET. Guru Pi would plant the books horizontally, once read.

Kirk promised to design and install mini-shelves to stabilise the tower, if needed. A tower of books would arise, whether a modest block of flats or a skyscraper, one would see. The arboreal idea was a *hygge* one, *gemütlich* even. How a book would be planted and grow upwards to be part of a columnar tree of books. Seeds of books strewn into a mind to add to its chaos and order.

He would take photographs every month or so and post them to the Beck household. And to others some in India, USA, UK, Germany, France and the one each in all of Africa and China. And maybe to the Russo-Ukrainian translator he had struck up a friendship with at the airport in Kyiv. Pi was still curious as to what *Mir Vam* meant as it was plastered on so many of the posters and displays at the airport.

Another challenge was posed to Guru Pi the next morning at breakfast when he foolishly started talking to the family without internal rehearsal. He elaborated on his idea that, generally, people had difficulty understanding numbers. This was a non-intended mental victory lap on the million hours incident in Sundervagvela.

In the chat over breakfast, comments on politics, funny stuff and then serious stuff and then sports and then the weather, Guru Pi extolled on the origin, possibly, of the word Google. Apparently, Google was via Googol. A number invented by a doubtless doting mathematician uncle whose precocious nephew had asked him what 10 to the power 100 was and then helped. Thus, the word Googol had been coined.

Anton: This is an impossibly large number and cannot be at all conceived by the human mind. I do not think we can even conceptualise a billion.

Guru Pi: No; it is all possible. It is just a matter of thinking and metaphorising. In the *Ramayana*, there are such large numbers—of trillions and more—that I have already discussed with my year 14 class only. The army of Sri Rama was truly huge. Sorry, I forgot to tell you. Googol is also a village on the banks of the Krishna River in Karnataka. This is where the singing stones are. Reasonably close to my birth-place.

Anton: Thanks for the quick geography lesson. Googol cannot be conceived or imagined. The number of atoms in the observable universe is only 10 to the something of the order of 30. So, can 10 to the power of 100 be imagined? Can you even imagine a million?

Guru Pi: I think I can do that for you and for everyone in the family if need be. I can also get you to imagine a Googol. I think I can show you a million easily. Million is just one square metre. Then divided into millimetre squares. It would easily fit next to the television in the sitting room. Anton, what you cannot think of clearly, you can imagine. So, we can imagine a googol. I will need time though.

Anton: You are impossible. You can read a pile of books that is your height in a year and imagine Googol. Then also prepare for your appearance on Carmen's TV show. You are only here for 40 days! Go for it. It will be fun! Especially the progress reports.

The additional preternatural tasks and labours of Guri Pi were piling up. Although the labours of Hercules were far more difficult, those of Pi were not easy either.

Instalment Two and Three: April and May

Good news, the veritable Minister for Health writes off our hospital's debt. Many thanks, we had quite a bit more than our fair share of the £13.4 billion. Clap again for the healthcare workers. I will also be trained to deliver care in the tent hospitals named after our Florence Nightingale. Several of her avatars are planned across the country.

This temporary hospital in Sunderland, for the cases predicted, is opened by footballers and cricketers and entertainers. Hope we do not need it. It would be worse than the war field hospitals, if it all goes the way predicted.

A five-year-old child dies from COVID-19. The next day, our Queen, delivers her fifth broadcast to the nation and Commonwealth. There may be 'more still to endure' as the previously doubting PM moves to Intensive Care at St Thomas' Hospital across the Thames from his offices.

Captain Tom Moore gets a Blue Peter Gold Badge—the ultimate accolade— and the pressure is on the monarch to knight him. By the end of the month, he reaches number one in the UK chart singles. But we do, often, walk alone in our campaign against COVID-19.

We surpass 10,000 hospital deaths on a sombre day in April. We have not counted the 7,500 dead in the care homes. By the end of the month, all are counted, 26,097 dead. (Pi informed me that this number can be a multiplicand of two prime numbers.) At least vaccine trials have started.

We eased our lockdown. There was no need to just stay at home anymore. But we had to stay alert and be prepared to karate chop the virus out of our lives if need be. Entertainment not so much; not the pubs, churches, cafés, bowling alleys, mosques, bars, temples, restaurants, gyms, cinemas, and synagogues but the garden centres, sport courts and recycling centres. All these centres had their own demigods.

Our senior advising statesman visited Barnard Castle to test whether he was well enough to drive, as he had been having some problems with his eyesight, and to case the joint as a future vaccine production site.

The great idea of test and trace is announced. Within weeks to be world-beating. Just a little delayed thereon with teething problems. The carrot of the pint in the pub awaits if we are all on good behaviour; otherwise, the detentions continue.

We can move on from *'stay at home, protect the NHS, save lives'* to the party line of *'stay alert, control the virus, save lives'*.

To go into work or not to go into work? That is the question. We are all confused, not us though. Hospital work, not possible from home. Where would Ruth agree to house the patients? Ruth will be happy though. Garden centres can re-open. The money tree may have been discovered.

Hundreds of billions are committed to help us all. We have 8.4 million people on furlough and paid. We are tired of clapping for the NHS and carers and will stop doing so after the tenth such banging of saucepans and associated activities.

We know for sure that some ethnicities, obesity, diabetes, kidney disease, dementia, chronic breathing conditions can all mean an earlier death. But we have a drug in Remdesivir, to speed up recovery times and give us that bed back in ITU. We have had 52,222 deaths by the end of May.

Chapter 5
Daily Hadiths and the School Visit

Be fearless. Swim against the tide.

Ellie Simmonds. Paralympic champion. Beijing 2008,
London 2012, Rio de Janeiro 2016.

Changing attitudes is a marathon not a sprint

Jonnie Peacock. Paralympic champion. London 2012, Rio de Janeiro 2016.

The school was inspirational. This was clear from the tree-planting and shrubs and signs to the vegetable garden and Bee Alley. The Ellie Simmonds Elementary School. Doubtless as in India, Pi thought it would have been named after some benevolent benefactor who had lived in times before independence and before a certain cohort, thought it had all gone to the dogs.

In India, it would the Ambedkar High School, Ambedkar Primary, Ambedkar Technical College. All after the architect of the Indian constitution, the lower caste man that he was who aspired for equality but in disdain, changed his religion to Buddhism to stand tall with all of humanity. But no.

The short CV and the photo with the school children revealed that she was a gold medal Paralympian, an inspiration to all the children at the school. The other gender was represented across the foyer by a certain Jonnie Peacock. With a medal or two as well.

Guru Pi was introduced to the head teacher, Miss Virginia Spode, no less.

Virginia: Thank you so much for coming to lead the assembly here at the Ellie Simmonds Elementary School. It is an honour and a privilege to have you here with us today.

Precisely 9 seconds later.

Pi: Why? You do not know me. So, the honour is mine. Thank you greatly.

Secretly, Miss Spode was absolutely delighted for hers would be the first school to have ticked all the boxes with respect to the outcomes, forcefully mandated and negatively marked if not achieved. Pi's assembly being a talk on a religion not rooted in the Abrahamic book would impress the inspectors and the school governors. She was not quite certain which of the 108 main gods would be covered. Just why so many of them, she wondered.

Virginia: Let's rush a bit. Assembly has never started late in the 11 years that I have been here.

Pi: Then why not today. Indian style!

Virginia Spode looked distinctly unimpressed with this quip. Pi was told not to ask any of the children their names. And to only refer to the children in very impersonal terms. And no touching. Anywhere.

Pi: Thank you very much, Miss Spode. Thank you all. I am so happy to be here. I will start telling you all about Hinduism. A person who practices Hinduism is called a Hindu. Why? Because the ideas originate in the main from the area in India around the Indus River.

In Hinduism, we do have many gods. Why? Let me use an example to explain. Imagine any person and what they mean to you. What is your mother or father to you? But then consider—what are they to other people?

There was a tumult as scores of the 141 young souls competed for his attention. "Choose me! Pick me! Pick me please!" were the shouts and screams.

Pi: Please stand up and shout out your answer but only when someone has sat down after giving one.

Though strictly no one should be answering, Pi realised later. Several answers emerged.

"My dad is called the Milkman."

"My Papa is called Farmer Fred."

"My mother is also called Sis."

"Mine too."

"I don't have a mother."

The latter had to be casually ignored by Pi, but the child was collected by a teaching assistant and after a brief chat, the child announced, "My mother is an angel in heaven."

Pi: Great, great answers. So, your mother or father can be looked at in a different way by others. So, there is an idea of God that is different to different people. But what matters is what it means to you. Only you can see the world from your own eyes, hear from your own ears and smell it and feel it and even taste. You are totally unique! There is only one of you. As Margaret Mead said, you are totally unique. Just like everyone else!

Pi was not sure he was explaining anything at all. Maybe the pupils of Ellie Elementary were not quite ready for his other thoughts from the cultural anthropologist and writer on sexual taboos.

Pi: The ideas often come from the stories of these Indic people. Indic includes everyone that is influenced in the main by Hindu thoughts and stories, but later to include everyone. A set of ideas on how to be good to each other happens and that is that. A lot like this.

Pi held up a picture of a lotus.

Pi: What is happening here? What is this?

Spode Junior stood up: It's a lotus.

Pi: Where has it come from?

Spode Junior: The mud.

The following 9-second pause was worrying for Spode Junior as he rarely got things wrong.

Pi: Great answer. The purpose of this is to show you that Hinduism takes all the goodness of its surroundings, creating a beautiful flower.

Pi was not confident that this was working. The teachers and their assistants looked perplexed and seemed like they were looking forward to their breaks. For some, both the caffeine and nicotine levels were becoming dangerously low.

Pi: But to get to the point. All religions believe in the Golden Rule. Behave to one another as you want that person to behave towards you or those that you really care about. And be in awe of everything around you. Look for wonder and amazement.

Hearing this, at least the humanists in the audience who had previously sat rather hackled up, started to clap a little. And the children joined in with much greater vigour. They had not yet reached the despondency and ennui of the teenage years, and still found amazement in these things. The lone Quaker quaked quietly and shook a little.

Pi: And now for the activities. I will hand two or three cards out to each class. Think about what you can see and what the idea is that you think, it is trying to tell you. There will generally be an animal, some plants and something telling you what the job of the Goddess or God is. Teachers, please help the children but I want answers only from them.

Cards that had been posted to him from his classmate who had immigrated to the outskirts of Sydney to work as a doctor, in the less salubrious migrant and indigenous communities, were handed out. *The answers were rather excellent,* thought Pi.

"This one is labelled Hanuman. We can see an ape. He looks very brave. He has a weapon that looks like a broom but with a metal football on the end. I am sure that he would have hit lots of bad people with it."

Pi: Excellent, but Hanuman has a tail, so it is a monkey and not an ape such as a chimpanzee or gorilla or orangutan. The hitting instrument is called a *gada* or mace in English. Yes, Hanuman did hit lots of bad people with it!

"This one must be a teacher. She has books and a guitar, and is sat on a lotus. There are swans and a peacock in the background. She is called Sara— Saraswati."

Teacher (interrupting): Swan, more than one swan is still a swan!

Pi: Brilliant! In the main. One human hurt or loved, is all of us humans hurt or loved.

One child had not had the temerity to stand up and stentoriously present an answer. But she had her hand up intently and was looking at the card with great intensity.

"I can see a spider!"

She was heckled a little. Frissons of doubt looped around the room. Pi was astonished that he had ever missed seeing a spider in any of the cards. Never mind in the 18 he had selected specifically for this assembly.

Virginia: Do not worry that is Maarsi. She often has strange ideas. We are a little time-poor again.

Pi appeared not to hear anything at all.

Pi: You can see a spider?

Pi looked at the picture and there were no spiders to be found among the plants shown or the sylvan backdrop.

Pi: Where can you see the spider?

Maarsi: This God has 8 arms. She must be a Spider God. There are also many eyes and Miss Spode taught us that spiders have many eyes.

Pi looked at the card. It was the universal form of godhead that Arjun had witnessed on the battlefield at Kurukshetra and indeed was beautifully illustrated in the *Bhagavad Gita* that he would or should be launching at the book fairs and the Carmen Show.

The wondrous form of Arjun with his friend and mentor Krishna, expressing the universality of Hinduism. This was the awesome spectacle that Oppenheimer had referenced at the explosion of the first atomic bomb. The whole pantheon was there adjoined into a single form. Granted, there certainly were 8 arms. And many heads, each with two eyes.

Every God was represented in it; Lakshmi, Ganesh, Kali, Shiva, Brahma, Rama, Saraswati, Hanuman. This image, the *Vishwaswarup*, always brought a chill to Pi. There was Ardhnariishvari at the centrepiece of this depiction and then male Gods to the left and Goddesses to the right. The whole greater spectrum of the humanised deities could be seen.

Pi saw all of creation in the eyes of that little child Maarsi, who had been seen the spider, probably for the first time in human history. And he wept. One tear only.

Activity two was a riotous attempt at the 12 steps of the *Surya Namaskar*— Sun Salutation Yoga sequence. It exercised all the limbs of the children and the teachers lost control of them for a short period of time. This was in the main because Pi had added an additional step that involved jumping into the air as if releasing an arrow from a bow.

Miss Spode had gone back to her office to do an email or two, but the noise prompted Miss Spode to anger and walk into the throng and declare the assembly over as the children were jumping up and down and waving frantically.

Miss Spode: You really should behave in front of a guest speaker. You are all so very naughty. Even you, Justin!

Spode Junior: We are doing exactly what Guru Pi wanted us to do. He did a demo!

Pi had hastily revised the Surya Namaskar Yoga sequence from a YouTube video and it could not be called his greatest success. He had also twisted his back in the process. The assembly thus came to an abrupt end.

Miss Spode: Let me thank you again, Guru Pi. To conclude, a final question from us all.

This assembly also counted towards continuous professional and personal development for the staff and was a lot cheaper, being free.

Miss Spode: If I can be so bold, can I ask how Hinduism is different from other religions?

Pi: It is exactly the same. But a little different. But it always centres its advice around the sanctity of life and how each of us interacts with our complex ecosystems. That is why there are so many animals, plants and landscapes in all the images of the deities that I showed you.

The teachers all looked rather perplexed. There was confusion all round; but conversation soon moved over to tea with the handing out of the samosas, kachoris and dhoklas that Pi had brought with him. The biscuit box was spared on this particular tea break. A tour of the site soon followed and later, after another tea break—this time with real tea and biscuits.

He also planted an oak tree, a conker tree, and an apple tree with a few of the children. Pi and the children chatted incessantly. Pi even mentioned his challenge of undertaking to read his own height in books in a year. He then went to talk to the senior class, which Virginia Spode hoped, would be more of a controlled success than the assembly.

Pi: Dear seniors of the school and this English class. I would like to read you a story that we often read at my school in India. In fact, at least 17 short papers were presented on it to the University College for the Srinivas Panditji endowment of Rs 1001! It was written many years ago by the father-in-law of Ruth Beck. She is a governor of this school. No less.

Having given this background, Pi launched into the decades old story. The embellishing notes of the author of the story having seen his first tiger in the wild were recalled by Pi but not mentioned. Only an occasional glance, at the stored document on his phone, was needed.

A Visit by Felix Beck

We had just paid a visit to sedate and relieve the pains of a patient in the throes of death due to cancer of the prostate when on the way to the motorbike, it started to rain. At first just a trickle, then with the force of an average waterfall, within seconds, the mud road of the village became a quagmire of mud and rainwater. This phenomenon is called a monsoon shower.

The doctor, who was well experienced in the capriciousness of nature, explained that the rains would cease soon and that riding a motorbike to the surgery was very feasible. After a ride (that was far more frightening than the average Blackpool Big Dipper), we neared the now familiar road leading to the surgery.

On nearing, the doctor did a spectacular brake, landing us both in a muddy pool from which any budding microbiologist could easily culture the entire intestinal flora of cow and buffalo.

I recovered, unscathed but the doctor suffered a burn on his calf about the size of a hand due to the exhaust of the bike. This meant that the doctor was unable to do visits, so gave this responsibility to his rather reluctant medical student and PhD candidate. I, therefore, became the Locum General Practitioner for the area; albeit under the closest scrutiny possible of the actual doctor.

I did not have to wait long upon reaching the surgery, for a field worker came in and rather nonchalantly informed us that his wife and two children were very sick and probably dying.

My linguistic disabilities in the local dialect were totally exposed as I endeavoured to discover what exactly was wrong, eventually gleaning that his two children had a fever and his wife, diarrhoea and vomiting. Upon reporting this to the doctor, I received the useful suggestion that it might be worth making a visit.

The doctor (with barely hidden glee) parted with his emergency bag and told me to go—on my departing the surgery, I picked up the Indian 'British National Formulary'. The fieldworker guided me to the outskirts of Sundervagvela; past the well, the temple and the post-office until we reached what appeared to me to be an uncrossable field.

It was muddy, recently ploughed, and full of prickly weeds—I was horrified to discover that it was actually part of the shortcut the fieldworker had in mind for me.

On our walk through the field, we were greeted by an army of warty, slimy frogs who made it their Sunday afternoons entertainment to irritate me by jumping on me. According to the fieldworker, the frogs were piqued as we had disturbed some sort of gathering that they traditionally held straight after a monsoon shower.

It was then that the monsoon phenomenon occurred again, all around me. The more astute daisies had already closed their petals and the frog attack had petered off after the first drop of rain sent most of them scuttling to their holes. I retrospectively reflected that I probably should have thought to bring an umbrella.

For the first time, I felt I really understood the meaning of the venerable old cliché 'soaked to the bone'. Another shortcut—or should I say ordeal—in store for me was the crossing of a stream. I took the pointless precaution of rolling up my trousers; but the crossing still resulted in stones in my shoes and insects in my roll-ups.

We had also disturbed some buffalos bathing. A few minutes later, I had the dubious benefit of experiencing the day-to-day of a paddy field worker as they loomed up at us as we passed them—several times.

Seeing the patients' house, for want of a better word, was a welcome relief after this ordeal. My three patients were laid out on the porch in three different beds, ready for the administration of elixirs that would reinvigorate them.

One child was shivering and cold whilst the other was hot and sweating— peculiar, I thought. I examined the chest, abdomen and anything else I could lay my hand on; there was nothing in the way of clinical signs and history-taking that should have been disastrous. I provisionally diagnosed malaria.

To be of little help, it could be Asian 'flu, a respiratory infection, a urinary tract infection or some sort of tropical disease, of which I'd probably never even heard. The worst part of everything was my potentially Oscar-winning performance of a fully competent doctor in total command of the situation at hand. This was in front of the anxious father and the 20-odd people who had begun to gather around.

I asked for the sick woman to be moved inside the house and so she was put onto a bed adjacent to a benevolent-cow and a quite-the-opposite buffalo. She was very sick—almost comatose, her skin clammy and doughy. At least with her, I could make an attempt to treat the dehydration. A cursory stethoscopic examination revealed nothing of note.

I put up a drip (a litre of normal saline) with some difficulty, mainly due to the catheter being strange. Hoping and praying that that would somewhat improve the woman's situation, I went back to the children. A diagnostic dilemma, an infection—bacterial, malarial or viral? Or maybe a life-threatening surgical condition.

It was whilst water was being heated for the sterilisation of a glass syringe that I began to recall a myth I had recently been told.

King Rama (of Hare Krishna Hare Rama fame) was distressed. His brother had been poisoned. The Ayurvedic physicians had pontificated on the illness and unanimously declared that all would be lost unless a rare herb called Sanjivani, located on the faraway Himalayan Mountain of Dronagiri Parvat, could be made available to administer to Lakshmana. Remember, this was the faithful brother who had left the royal palaces to spend 14 years in forest exile with him.

Hanuman—the lifelong friend and devotee of King Rama—volunteered for the mission. With all the attributes of Superman, Hanuman flew off. On reaching Dronagiri Parvat, he realised he had forgotten the exact description of the herb and there were hundreds of plants, medicinal and otherwise on the mountain. So, he did the obvious thing; bringing the entire mountain back with him and saving the life of his Lord's brother.

Using the same sound logic, I decided to inject both the children with chloroquine and tetracycline. It was with trembling hands that I drew nearer to the first child, holding the syringe—I could not remember for the life of me whether it was the top lateral quadrant of the child's backside that I was supposed to avoid or inject. An injection into the sciatic nerve could result in nerve damage and long-term weakness of the leg—potentially permanent.

This was indeed a most embarrassing moment. I mumbled a prayer under my breath and injected the child in the deltoid of the arm. I also administered oral penicillin; with the formulary I had hastily picked up on my departure proving invaluable.

The next day, the fieldworker came to see me again. My heart started to go into overdrive. Had my actions resulted in disaster? My heart was thundering in my chest and into my neck.

He placed in front of me a basketful of freshly picked mangoes. Kaleidoscopic in colour and multi-shaped. My desktop thus adorned, he joyfully announced that his wife and children were much better. I quietly reaffirmed my belief in the grace of God.

The story and Pi's careful articulation were well received with many follow-up questions.

"What was the motorbike? Was it a Triumph? My dad works for Triumph! It's not that far from here, Guru Pi."

"Yes, you should go to the museum!"

"What was the illness in the end?"

"What would you have done if you had killed them?"

"What kind of mangoes were they?"

Time was running out for his session and therefore, Pi plied them with rather vague answers and left. On the way home, he reflected on the events of day so far. He had had fun.

Pi had no straightforward answers to many of the questions but did recall it was a Triumph T100S Tiger Sports. The mangoes were not named, and Pi was curious. At least 101 types, he knew existed from his multiple visits to the All-India Mango Festival at Sundervagvela. He could personally name about 20, no more. His own personal favourites, in no particular order were; *totapuri, kesar, alphonso, rajapuri, langra, badami, neelam, banganapalli,* and *chausa.*

He also wondered why there was only one type of banana in the Belton supermarkets. He also wondered whether the creation and initial manifestation of the Hindu god of medicine, Dhanvantari, had a drip bag! Certainly, coconut water with a pinch of salt had been regularly used for cholera in his health centre.

He wondered about the plight of the coronavirus victims and noted that a lot had changed for the better. Hopefully, improvement would be even faster soon, given time. There was a lot going on as usual.

Pi Staying On

The book challenge could go until May to April or so. Pi was to stay on as a postgraduate student. His colleagues back at the Sundervagvela College would be delighted. He would be absent for a whole year in total. Pi had found out that he had been successful in his application to get the additional 90% funding needed to extend the Gateway Grant.

The latter had helped to bring him over to the Becks in the first place. The usual report would be needed on his observation of the teaching and all things great in Great Britain, for the purpose of inculcation in the course back in Sundervagvela. Especially in relation to health literacy.

In Pi's opinion, his students were better at English and miles ahead in maths. Though this was through rote learning, of course. Nevertheless, this was a reasonable ask and a laudable pursuit; but one that Pi hoped had not detracted too much funding from the Gateway initiatives on malaria and women's health.

For the Gates' millions had to date undoubtedly benefitted inhabitants of parts of the mosquito-infested world and left hundreds of women and babies alive after child birth. Pi vowed to save part of his stipend to donate back to these causes.

The Beck household was absolutely delighted. Kirk told everyone it was going to be a free postgraduate course in Pi Studies. For celebration, Pi went for a solitary walk. Close to the posh bits, or rather the posher bits of Belton (for none were exactly Kensington or even Chigwell), Pi noted a distinct feeling of being rather lost and impersonalised.

In the i-Barista, a brand seen many a time elsewhere by Pi already, he was greeted haphazardly by no less than 4 people who all asked for his order and duly 3 coffees appeared. A fourth was cancelled. Consternation ensued as the manager in the darker t-shirt explained that Pi had communicated his order 4 times and that therefore meant he had ordered 4 coffees.

Pi paid for them all and went to the back of the queue to distribute his excess caffeine. He had spent more than the weekly earnings of a field labourer and was not happy about it. When he got hungry later, he went to Annies. Where the apostrophe was not needed as it was the description of the fact that two Annies worked there.

There was always an Annie present. Their conversations were not all understood by Pi—the "how are you, duck?" especially and the "here you are, son," when given the toasted sandwich ordered. Both Annies were a tad younger than Guru Pi.

He contemplated why a bottle of water from a spring cost £1.85. For only 400ml at that. Presumably for that, there was a man with a few hundred empty plastic bottles risking life and limb, to climb up the scree of a precarious cliff edge, to the tarn, collecting water and bringing it back down. That justified the cost of it all, maybe? Had there been the occasional fatal accident that required compensation, and belated insurance?

Pi had envisaged the West as thinking of plastic as the alloy of the devil. Appearing as it did, as evil everywhere, in land, sea and air. But even the Greenpeace T-shirted locals appeared to be drinking water from plastic bottles. Pi had recently read that bottled water contains thousands of plastic micro-particles per lite. That could not be good? Maybe the tap water was dangerous as it was in Sundervagvela? Often with *Vibrio cholerae, Escherichia coli,* and various *Salmonella* lurking within? Never mind the hepatitis viruses. And maybe sometimes, a mixture of several of the bugs.

Certainly, the water was selling well; especially as it was needed to accompany the masala samosas on offer with a fiery chutney. But then, milk was £1.09 for a 4-pint bottle and only 48 pence a litre. Or only 19 pence for the 400 millilitres that the bottle of water had. That was after growing a cow, separating it from its calf, feeding it, milking it, housing it, and eventually selling it on.

Maybe, money had a different function in Belton. More a token exchange based on frivolity rather than an exchange of the real cost of hard work. Pi was perplexed and planned a chat with Anju, Kirk and Ruth. Probably not Anton as he seemed a little too busy for mundane discussions right now. Especially, now that the Wuhan virus had made its way across the continents and firmly established itself in his hospital wards and the mortuary.

The virus, carried by the usual infirm and the unexpected usually healthy people. There was indeed a virus burning bright; ravaging bodies and playing mind games with the staff.

Instalment Four: June

We got tired of thanking the NHS and felt that that could now be abandoned as focus resumed on the Kardashians; who would may have felt for the last few weeks that they had been globally, accidentally, unfriended. Also, the mood was that muffled drums and stopped clocks would be more appropriate now as Spikey accelerated through the population, in adjacent households, in the streets, through the parishes, the city, the country, the continent, and the world of humankind.

In Belton and its environs came the first extraordinary local lockdown. Fair enough, we had 10% of all the new cases in the country at one stage.

If you dare return to the UK, then thou shalt quarantine for 14 days. You should be grateful—the definition of a quarantine was really 40 days. And with this here, we marked the reaching of the Guardian estimated death roll-call of 50,032 deaths. At this stage, Reuters had only counted a mere 49,646.

Watering plants is banned by hosepipe but crickets' tests are planned. Can the pitches be watered? I must find out. Mark will know. Mark will also be happy that protests have been curtailed due to the conflict of interest with lockdown rules. How so convenient. Could think about a move to Scotland or Northern Ireland, no new deaths due to Spikey.

Pangloss lives on! Apparently, it was always that we *'took the right decision at the right time'*.

The virus is an odd one, and an old politic prevails. Black, Asians, and some other ethnicities are twice as likely to die. Is deprivation an ethnicity in this regard? Need to discuss with Huriya. The trooping of the colours cancelled. The Welsh Guard conduct a responsible, socially-distanced ceremony instead. So safely-distanced; we all celebrate the birthday of our longest-serving monarch.

I am happy. A cheap steroid saves lives. Some of the patients came from our hospital in the mathematically perfect, ethnically odd but sound, clinical trial. Five thousand lives may now be saved. One step forward, and maybe a little backwards too as we, in our tens of thousands, decide to go the beaches. In the league of nation of worst performers. We do well. We are not last, at least. As we are just above Spain, for now. But less than a thousand new cases per day. A veritable nadir with 958 cases on 22nd June.

We can, with safety in place, open the bars and restaurant on 4th July! Why should the Independence Declaration of USA not be celebrated (incidentally, also Ruth's birthday)?

Chapter 6
The Wanderings of Pi

A teacher affects eternity; he can never tell where his influence stops.

Henry Brooks Adams (1838–1918). American Historian

With the first tweeting of the thrush in the morning, Anton had blasted off in his Triumph Spitfire to give it an axial regrind. The only people who could and would complete this further caressing of his beloved (for less than £1000) would be Yarran's Speedy Motors.

He saw the quartet of the immigrant community of the Zimbabwean, Afghani, Romanian and for some reason, a Peruvian on their tea break, with their usual 4 sugars each and a democratic allocation of digestives. The 27 biscuits— reduced from their pre-Brexit amount of 34—were allocated as 6, 6, 7 and 8, reflecting the best solution between a desire for weight loss whilst also feeding the furnace that was their busy bodies.

Anton was waiting for the Australian boss to arrive back from his desi breakfast at Rasta Fasta Nasta Café. For Yarran Ray Jandamarra, Ray for short, loved his masala omelette (skinny) with a *roomali* roti, some seasonal vegetables and fruits of course accompanied by a masala chai. *Thé genuine* with all the spices admixed to a secret recipe.

Ray's wife Shirl had tried at least a three score and ten recipes, but the alchemy of the masala remained a secret. All the admixtures had been gratefully received by 3 mechanics and the talented help. The remains were often discarded to the shop's cactus collection as possibly the most expensive plant food in the world (for Shirl bought her spices at select middle-class supermarkets).

The cacti seemed to thrive on any combination of spice mix. But I digress. The quartet had many questions for Anton regarding the virus, which appeared to be growing closer to them by the day.

For their benefit, Anton provided a mini-lecture on the risk factors for dying from the new peril. All these were present in his audience, often more than once. The male, the older, the diabetic, the minority ethnic, the shrivelled kidneys, and the bigger. Active and a little overweight is fine and protective if diabetic. The mechanics felt so despondent at the conclusion of the chat that they felt that they needed more tea and another packet of digestives.

Anton told this very small band of disciples that his email had stated in black and white, bold font sans serif that all that was needed to get the UK pandemic under control was clear. He had sent this to his colleagues early on in the epidemic.

Just solved Covid-19—self-isolation should be followed by everyone for 14 days.

And was he heeded? No. As his axial rod was being ground and reset, Anton went across the road to the Co-op Taberna—a shop essentially. This was an Aladdin's den of all things viable and green and killed nicely. The new owner was a picture of health and attracted many new customers. The ill health of the previous was no advert to a shop that specialised in marketing a life with all things good alimentary-wise and to wash with and clean with.

Anton recalled those days again and again where he felt things had gone so wrong. The words of our leaders, a week after Anton's email, were to allow the virus to fester, tire itself out and leave, resulting in us all gaining natural immunity in the process.

There had been a staunch and immovable resolve that we could and would take it on the chin. Take it all in one go and allow the disease to move through the population, without taking as many Draconian measures as possible. This was Etonesque, Daedalus and Icarus, Scientist and Politician, in a doubled-winged *folie à deux*. All rolled into a single paradigm.

A ruthless response. Anton was mesmerised with horror by some of the briefings and felt that often it was tantalisingly close to doing exactly the opposite of what science prescribed. The sat-nav was on—as advised by science—but the drivers did not heed it as they knew the way to the man in the high castle.

At the Beck household, Pi was at this moment being rudely woken by the irritatingly pleasant *hoo-hooing* of an owl—possibly the tawny one he had seen just a few days ago. He was mentally churning through parts of a film he had seen with Kirk at the Culture Club—essentially an annexe to the City-Zen Café.

Not a film he would normally watch; certainly not at the Metro Talkies in Sundervagvela that was for sure. Maybe he should read the book. If it was at least 20millimetres and no more than 150 pages. But maybe it wasn't worth reading, the film being so good. Then again, several pandits at the showing had reiterated the same words, so it must be the truth.

That the film was never as good as the book. Pi thought that the film of the recently read *The Unbearable Lightness of Being* was much as Kundera would have intended, but there was no evidence to support this. Until he read the book. Then he concluded that both had to be certified as monumental. Pi had also thought the film of Ishiguro's *Never Let Me Go* was pure art and one of the most sublime films he had ever seen.

The book was one of the best he had ever read as well, thought Pi. He was not sure what the second most was, but understood it without words, but would not tell me. He did not appear to have the right words to express himself; some colours of the palette appeared to be missing. He had been gobsmacked.

He was reminded of how his life's edifice had been completed, shaken and simultaneously destroyed by the death of his love, Priyali. Some things in life just had to be worshipped with reverence. Nevertheless, *The Unbearable Lightness of Being* by Milan Kundera and the Ishiguro had been added to the foundations of a tower. Its final height remained yet unclear, but Mao Tse Tung would be proud. The March of a Thousand Miles had started with a few small steps.

The Jo'burg slums evoked by the words of Athol Fugard's *Tsotsi* haunted Pi all through the early morning. The owl somehow highlighted this, as did the grey and red streaked clouds that heralded rain on the horizon—or so Ruth had warned him. Ruth had also told Pi that there was to be screening of *Tsotsi,* the South African film, at City-Zen Café.

The film ended and the evening session ended with a 5-minute lecture by Edgar Rayner, an amateur know-it-all, according to Sir X. Today, whilst prepping for the talk, Edgar had said to himself that he wanted to be ironic and laconic. A style that suited him best, being as he was a man with several hundred unread but beautifully arranged books, stored in the best tulip wood shelves money could buy.

Edgar's appearance appeared to be a hybrid of Karl Marx and Frederick Engels, and he looked as though his politics were probably similar and equally arcane. Edgar had espoused at length that we know the obvious but do so little. The relevance to the film appeared to be immaterial.

Edgar: We learn not from history. Despite Cato, the Younger living in 46 BCE had attributed to him:

publice egestas, privatum opulentia
public poverty, private wealth.

And Tacitus, a little later similarly cries, many amid great affluence are utterly miserable.

And then what I consider an important yet an altogether forgotten event, the Peterloo Massacre of Innocents. The poor versus the rich again.

Pointing to Pi.
Edgar: Equivalent to your Jallianwala Bagh Massacre.
And even recently, well relatively recently, Martin Luther King (Junior) said:

When you see the vast majority of your twenty million brothers smouldering in an airtight cage of poverty in the midst of an affluent society, then you will understand why we find it difficult to wait.

Edgar's closing comments had been a set of quotes from Pi's hero, the Indian Superman (who even Einstein espoused as such) Gandhi.

Edgar: *Journalist: What do you think of Modern Civilisation? Gandhi has replied! You what he said? "I think that would be a very good idea!"*

The solution in Edgar's opinion was to act to mitigate the seven deadly sins of Gandhian origin.

Edgar: Here are some words that President Carter used at a funeral or two.
The things that will destroy us are:

Politics without principles
Pleasure without conscience
Wealth without work
Knowledge without character
Business without morality
Science without humanity
Worship without sacrifice

Gandhi's cornerstone principle of everyone having enough for their needs but not greed got a look-in. The final dart had been to argue that the one and only thing that Jesus had got wrong was stating that poverty we must have with us always. Edgar stated categorically that he had had issues with Jesus's feet being washed with expensive unction, especially if massaged with the hair of an unmaiden. Some quotes had been judiciously shortened to avoid offence and stricture.

Tsotsi appeared to be about the obstruent affluent society of Galbraith adjacent to the effluent and influent and eloquent and unguent and incongruent. It made no sense. The world was big enough for everyone. Pi thought that he would ideally like to sell this on as the title of a James Bond film. The films were one of his weaknesses that had eaten up a significant 100 hours or so of his life at 4 hours per film (toing and froing included) and the 24 so far.

Attendance for Edgar's talk was high as the pub was having its happy hour. Listening was not compulsory, but Pi was impressed with Edgar's passion and enthusiasm for public lecturing in the most daunting of places.

The day ended with a meal. Vegan this time, due to the Becks' and Pi's proclamation of the necessity of their 21 meals being allotted as 7 vegan, 7 vegetarian and 7 other. The meal came from Lady Guji's kitchen. She also supplied fundamentalist vegan meals.

She had not taken well to breast-feeding in early motherhood; having mastitis and then mastalgia and then more mastitis. A ban on milk was declared in her household and sold cashew and other milks at the same price as milk and had it certified by a friendly dietitian that it has the same nutritional content as milk. A bit of added calcium and a few other minerals and some vitamin further certified even more homology with milk.

Observing the Becks and Pi interact from afar, they appeared to work seamlessly as if there was an invisible conductor playing the Beck household symphony. The essential glue was undoubtedly Ruth. If only this skill of hers was one that could be taught. It was very unlikely that she would be reduced in the foreseeable future into a book called *The Seven Habits of the Highly Regarded (but not very rich)*.

Pi would only leave the bosom of the family to walk to the annexe via external stairs. He needed time to himself to wonder at the moon, always enjoying its inherent yin-yang, or the fish jumping into the water, or the hare.

Wondering why it was that he would only ever see one face of the moon. Then to the stars. Especially the constellation of Orion. And especially his belt.

The three sisters or three kings. Alnitak, Alnilam, and Mintaka. And also, the seventh brightest star he would ever see, Rigel. And the massive Betelgeuse. Its red ochre colour always recalled for him the chewed and spat betel tobacco that superfluously littered so many places in his hometown.

Pi at the Wall

Once on his wanders, Pi expanded his radius to the ruins, which sat a bit further out from Belton. The Jewry Wall. This was, to the disdain of the locally named university, a historical link to the start of more democratic government and the ignoble purging of Jews to the outer walls of the city.

To be defenceless and at the mercy of marauding bands of thieves, weather, and all things inclement or outright deadly. Pi pondered on the reason that almost 20% of all Nobel Prizes out of the still less than 1000 ever awarded were to Jews. This was a fact to celebrate! But why? Could it be a product of their central matriarchy—but Pi had that in abundance even in his part of India.

Men were often just side players in the main edicts and decisions of families. Was it education? And its centrality of purpose; for the sake of knowledge itself and not just for earning a living? And did that happen because money was saved and invested into assets, not cigarettes or champagne or cars or Costa del Sol visits? That could be the case.

Many people in the world today were of Jewish origin but would not consider themselves of the faith itself. Pi was pleased that Elie Wiesel had been so honoured with the Nobel Prize for Literature. He had simply adored *Night,* a personal letter from a friend imprisoned in Auschwitz who had witnessed the deliberate extermination of groups of disparate people scapegoated by the civilised, and ignored by the even more civilised for many years.

Also, the forgotten Roma Community, Special Olympians, Para-Olympians, and those not free to love however they chose. Pi further submerged himself into the sheer horrors of it all, etching them further on his brain as he read the *Tattooist of Auschwitz.*

He continued with *If this be Man* by Primo Levi. These books tightened his heart as he devoured them, losing many hours of sleep in the process. And so, another tribiblio was added. Purely on humanity's shame. Especially, as it doth continue now.

The "D'Artagnan", to the trio, was read in the time it would take to watch two episodes of a popular TV soap. It was the tale of the searing aborted unrequited friendship in *Reunion* by Fred Uhlman. The four, a grand total of 91 millimetres.

Pi Bird Watches

Pi wondered whether his village had such beautiful birds as he had seen in the manicured wilderness at the Beck household, where distinct and precise 1.2 by 2.4 metre areas were left to nature. Where the disappointment was, to head gardener Ruth at least, was why no hedgehogs had appeared as yet in the hedgehog dwelling that she had acquired.

Anton had helpfully pointed out that average property prices, according to the Office for National Statistics, were £1692 per square meter in Belton. And that the hedgehog housing, marketed as the Hodmedod Yurt, was approaching that value for sure. This was expensive real property, *trop cher!*

As he had exclaimed, Pi pointed out after a quick calculation that the hedgehog house would only be 28% of the cost of a human dwelling. That made it alright to everyone, with the exception of Anton. The yurt was just awaiting a hedgehog. Ideally, not just a sole soul, but a family. With them then all reproducing to save the species, as Ruth intended.

Pi recalled that earlier in the week, at the City-Zen Café, he had practically been ordered to get to know his birds and general flora a whole lot better. The conversation group were not really bothered about or impressed by the Sanskrit and Vedic Scripture, and the 211 Bollywood songs that Pi knew off by heart and could sing after a glance at his notebook and a double Pi pause. He could even whistle some.

He looked out at bird feeding station one (Anju's). Here, there was always clean water, with re-fillings every 2 or 3 days. Kirk's was more erratic, therefore attracting many a larger bird when full. And mammals. Which were mostly unwelcome. The squirrel (grey, but red would be better), rats and the occasional mouse. Pi hummed and then sang the classic Bollywood song of old. One of the wandering traveller singing about his shoes being Japanese, his trousers English, his red hat Russian, but his heart always Hindustani. And about his destiny being an unknown entity to him, but maybe known to the One above.

And why was he singing this song? Because he had seen a wandering member of the avian family *Picidae*. One he had seen in Sundervagvela. When Pi had learnt of the family name, he had been intrigued. He would have chosen it as his *vahan*, his vehicle if he ever was to be afforded godlike status. Picidae were not found in parts of the world that had been first isolated from the majority of the world—that is to say they were not from Australia, New Guinea, Madagascar, New Zealand and the Poles, of course.

Pi had also spotted the *Dendrocopos major*. The greater spotted woodpecker. With its red hat. He was also happy that Anju had left such a plentiful supply of peanuts in the bird feeding station such that other inhabitants of the local ecology such as insects, young birds and eggs did not have to be consumed.

In the afternoon, Pi would see the females of the species, capless but with larger redder underpants it would seem. Maybe they were babysitting, so never left the nestlings alone. They certainly did not require a social worker.

He admired the other visitors too. Especially, the *Erithacus rubecula*. *Erithakos*, just simply a bird in Greek. The other word meant red. The robin. Simple. But all wondrous to Pi. He thought about going to the Temperance Bar, apparently only one of a handful left in Europe.

An Episode from the Temperance Bar

At the Temperance Bar, he saw Akbar go the toilet—*sandaz*—as they would have referred to in Sundervagvela, Pi cast his mind back to the retro-evolution there. One day, he would need to ask his family why latrines were called *sandaz* units.

Back home, Pi had been confidently assured by his family that Hindus and Muslims were never a perfect mix, but there had been a vibrant cross-fertilising of friendships, shared art, especially with the shared festivals of Eid, Eid-ul-fitr, Diwali, Holi and many others.

This expanded to include those of the original Christians—St Thomas, who had partied with Jesus Christ, no less, with this influence having been further consolidated by the mercantile and friendly and then the colonising and less friendly British. Along with the refuge-seeking Parsees and the re-introduced Buddhists, in the form of Dalai-Lama. A favourite question of Pi's to foreigners had been what passport nationality was the Dalai-Lama? He was of course Indian.

The same as Pi. In fact, it was a widely spread rumour that Nelson Rolihlahla Mandela had been offered Indian citizenship whilst in prison for that experiential 27-year stint in three 'residences', all more desirable than the previous.

Pi recalled that he had helped Kirk make salad dressing the night before and recalled Kirk's nonchalant admixing of ingredients for his invented dressing; the Egyptian dukka, some pepper, some pink pepper (not a pepper), salt (of the Himalayan pink kind), sumac, smoked paprika, and cinnamon—the oldest spice of all. Having been thus coarsely ground, it had been added to 10mls of the finest light Palestinian olive oil and the equivalent volume of Modena balsamic.

Then it was all shaken up, Kirk gyrating his pelvis like Elvis of Memphis in the process. The emulsion that resulted added spice and a warmth and breathed life into a rather mundane salad of carrots, assorted leaves, tomatoes, onion, and cucumber. Dandelion and nasturtium leaves and flowers of the latter added the final panache.

Yet, Pi thought, in the emulsion that had been India, at its best, there were forces afoot that had rendered a settling to differences rather than a constant admixing to the commonality of a life fulfilled and enjoyed. This made Pi sad.

His more joyful thought, on seeing Akbar return, was his recollection of the Bollywood mega-hit *Amar, Akbar, Anthony*. Why? Simply because it was a crazy, daft, roller-coaster of incongruous events and ideas. But it was one of his very favourite Bollywood film hits.

The film had been a desperate plea to the idea that all religions can live together—there were so many bits to the film that any film critic (whilst not the Kermode who was eclectic in his taste and totally unpredictable) would have deemed cringe worthy of the highest calibre. The fact that these three boys had been separated from their mother and raised as Hindu, Muslim and Christian respectively was the least of it all.

Pi had remarked on the superbly advanced blood transfusion sciences pictured to his friends at the time. The critically injured mother was in intensive care. And who better to give her sustenance through their blood but the complete trio of Amar, Akbar and Anthony. The three brothers had coincidentally volunteered at the same time to donate blood.

Thus, the triple simultaneous blood transfusion was born, and a scene reminiscent of Frida Kahlo ensued when the mother had three streams of blood flowing into a single cannula, *eodem tempore* from all three of her sons! His friends had surmised that many such innovations do happen in India first but that the Western world always got credit upon its rediscovery, in due course.

In a universe of infinite possibilities—Bollywood—such things can happen of course, a lot more frequently, and a lot earlier. Just a few multiverses thus spared.

Guru Pi got out his notebook from the centre right pocket on his green Nehru gilet. He had decided to plan his sojourn across the literary landscape. Dechunking the task would make it much easier. The caste system, or the Varnas might help?

The *Varna* system, the caste system, was a construct definitely needed for a functional society, in Pi's opinion. Its mythological origin was a vivisection, of sorts, of the universal deity itself. It consisted of the *Sudra* to the ankles, the thighs were the *Vaisya*, the *Kshatriya* to the shoulders and the peak of the *corpus universalis*, the head, the *Brahmin*.

This was all a bit casteist and didn't sit well with Anju or most of the clientèle of City-Zen Café, but was not intended in a bad way. It just meant that we are all important. Which the scriptures do make clear. But maybe this wasn't a good example. A better example was that of the Karate, Kung Fu, Jiu-Jitsu, Taekwondo and Kendo belts. The martial belts.

Quick research at the library had revealed to Pi too much information to be remembered. Copious notes were needed. Scrap paper had been surprisingly difficult to acquire, and trust was not forthcoming as he asked to borrow a pen. The librarian, wonderfully accented in Brummie, said that it was against library policy Section 3.5.8 to give out stationary to 'clients'.

Pi was happy and willing to pay for a pen, as a client. His allowance was in good surplus. But this was not allowed either, explained the librarian. She had not been particularly enamoured with Pi from the very moment he had come into, what the locals, called the Pork Pie Library. Pi had circumambulated around the inner wall and then marched across the diameter of the reading hall.

Freya: Pray, what are you doing?

Pi: So sorry, but I was quietly calculating Pi with my steps. It is very accurate! Many thanks! Very exciting!

But then looking at Guru Pi's benign Buddha-esque smile, her heart had melted like the proverbial chocolate tea pot. Writing paper was retrieved from the blank pieces of paper and others with a logo alone, from the confidential waste. It would have been a great training exercise for would-be spies to work out the importance of the confidential waste that had to be locked with heavy Gorilla-branded handcuff grade plastic ties to be ferreted away in a dirty diesel van and shredded at reasonable public expense.

Then incinerated to generate that little bit more CO_2 for us all. But she, the Brummie-accented, was a tattooed Goth-like creature and it was unlikely that anyone would be brave enough to ask her opinion. Certainly, not before completing her media study degree through the university of not actually going to university.

Freya was a carer and Zoom and Microsoft Teams had been a godsend for her. Pi's writing kit was completed by Freya donating to him her own flashy 4 colour pen from her tartan sporran bag.

Some research later, Pi had the necessary facts. There were 6 main belts; the white, orange, blue, yellow, green, brown and then the coveted black belt. The belt was called an Obi. Guru Pi wondered whether Obi-Wan Kenobi was thus named as a Master Jedi. The 'bathrobe' worn for these martial arts was called a 'dogi'.

In the Shinkyokushin system, white appeared to be the sign of a complete novice. The orange signalled a knowledge of the basic moves and an ability to fold the dogi properly. *These basic moves were unlikely to threaten even a librarian,* thought Guru Pi. With blue, there had to be evidence of strength of balance, co-ordination and even flexibility.

Along with some control of the mind. And *kumite*. Which was friendly sparring with strikes, attacks and defences. A blue belt marked better progress with the mind and body too. And yellow conveyed harmony! Green marked advanced techniques and brown a less friendly *kumite* with (potentially) deadly blows.

To obtain a black belt, there was an exam that needed to be passed; a viva and demonstration of it all. Of the body and mind in harmony. Of course, one cannot be truly original, *plus ça change, plus c'est la même chose,* and all that, but Guru Pi wondered how then did the belts relate to the snooker balls. They were certainly in the wrong order. But black was the highest accolade in both.

Guru Pi decided to go for the belts, and for the more erudite and intellectually refined, he would invoke the chakras. The chakras would serve his purpose perfectly too, adding a spiritual dimension for those that required it. The *muladhara, svadhishthana, manipura, anahata, visuddha, ajna* and the *sahasrara* were thus recruited. The root, sacral, solar plexus, heart, throat, third eye and the crown.

There was apparently a red belt for the 'exemplary' masters of Judo, Karate and Jiu-Jitsu. Was there a *kenobi* belt? There wasn't much on that in the library search engines. Although Guru Pi's legs were short and subsequently his height not the tallest, the task in hand would have to be broken down in manageable chunks. This was discussed with Anju.

Guru Pi: I have an idea about how to de-chunk the idea of reading my height in books and making it towards the stipulated endpoint of a year. I think the chakras will help to manage this. There are seven of them, whilst there are also six main karate belts and a final black one.

And the red one that I certainly would not even mention in the context of my silly little challenge. That's the highest that Kyokushan karate would ever award. A sort of Nobel Prize of the karate world.

Anju: What do you mean?

Guru Pi: Well, so to my knee would be the *muladhara* root chakra—so the white belt. The *svadhishthana*, the sacral would be the orange one. That is the knee to the sacrum. Then there would be *manipura*, the blue belt, which would be equivalent to the solar plexus.

Anahata, the yellow which would equate to the heart. *Visuddha*, the green, to the throat. Almost there now! Anju, to the third eye would be the brown belt. The *sahasrara*, when reached, is the crown of the head and the black belt.

Anju: That was a lot to take in; please do write that down for my benefit. Do you think you're actually going to wear them?

Guru Pi: I've made notes, I'll show you them. If need be, I am prepared to wear them. I've already got a plan, I will get Darzi Ali back in India to make them. He has a shop that I named for him, called Kanga Roo. Roo means cotton, by the way, in one of my languages.

The confidential wastepaper notes were shared. Occasionally, Guru Pi was referred to as "Guru Pi" at the Beck household. He insisted that he preferred to be called Pi only.

Anton Visits Beck Senior—First Lockdown

And Anton was off to visit his father, his dad, Papa. You know, one of the few people that you have generally known all your life. Until they die. The home he was in could have been designed by a wise community of Spock-like individuals catering for the fourth stage of the Hindu life or the *sans teeth, sans taste, sans everything* of Shakespeare's scripted life for us all. The misery of Covid-19 had granted many the release of death, albeit unwillingly so. The living continued sans taste, sans olfaction, and sans energy.

The south-facing yew tree grabbed his attention. He knew all the facts. This yew tree was celebrant of and co-contemporaneous with the arrival of Augustine in 597 AD and the start of Christianity. Although the errant recurrent thought, surely one or Romans would have been Christian 500 years earlier?

It was not clear but the yew no doubt attracted funding, awe and pervaded the air with peace and tranquillity. One had to forget that its poisonous matte red aril berries were deadly to casual eater but also refined, deadly to some cancers. Good for humans and the well-insured occasional canine or feline.

Anton, albeit with a bit of a heavy heart, greeted his father, the longest living resident of the home of St Augustine's, a cricket pitch away from the home itself. Anton was proud, despite being a microbiologist, that he had been able to procure the statin, ace-inhibitor, aspirin and many unpronounceable heart failure protection drugs for his father, admittedly after many a battle.

One interest, recalled Anton, had its origin in another general poison, this time from the root bark of the much less long-lived humble apple tree. As a matter of principle, Anton would always follow the clinical advice of Dr Huriya Alkuhs, a passionate supporter of the primary prevention of life-threatening events such as heart attacks, strokes, cancers, diabetes, or even death itself. Huriya had recently been decorated by the Queen for services to the hearts and brains of Belton and its environs. That is the rest of the world.

Anton's was dressed in his usual Sunday attire of a blue shirt and the maroon, blue, and green stripes of the parachute regiment. Astride the winged horse Pegasus was Bellerophon. The other insignia declared within it *Utrinque Paratus*—ready for anything. Alas, probably not in the case of both of them.

Talk was small but touched their mutable souls directly and immediately. Connections were created as Anton exposed his father's feet for his nails to be cut, his feet washed and massaged with a little oil of wintergreen. Drug-eluting stents, bypass surgeries and kidney transplants were all thankfully fully available, however, foot care was a little more difficult in the health system. Everyone called Felix Beck, Beck Senior at the home. His careful, sharply clipped elocution was always a joy to listen to.

Anton: So, Papa, let's do the beaches again.

Beck Senior: I feel sharp today, you know and think I'll remember them. So, the beaches are Gold, Silver, Utah. Yep?

Anton: And two more, Dad?

Beck Senior: Need a clue.

Anton: Your favourite play. Though certainly not mine! About the troubles in Ireland. Something about the Peacock.

Beck Senior: Paycock not that is Juno! Juno beach. That's all of them bar one.

Anton: Separated from Utah by the interspersed state of Colorado is Nebraska—the capital of which is?

Beck Senior: Omaha.

Anton: Yep—all 100% correct today.

Anton was becoming increasingly concerned that clues were far more often needed than even just before Covid-19 had started. The nails were cut. The feet washed and massaged. Anton had been to a talk on the left and right sides of the brain and the red, blue, green and yellow bits. He certainly at this moment was feeling like this, an integrated whole. Connecting to his father through touch, DNA and the strangely asymmetrical yet not unpleasant smell from one foot but not the other.

The right was that of a camembert, brie or even akin to the Welsh Caws Cenarth. The left, a little rancid. But the end result was a perfumed set of feet adorned with the gentle smell of wintergreen. He had also noted that there was no evidence of the various fungi that had laid waste to his own toenails—that was a good test of his medical knowledge for him indeed.

He scored himself full marks as he internally enunciated the causes of tinea unguium or onychomycosis as *Trichophyton rubrum, Epidermophyton floccosum* and *Trichophyton interdigitale,* to himself. He felt he knew his disease-causing fungi. Especially, the ones that tried to decompose humans whilst still alive.

Beck Senior: You know son, we nearly forgot Omaha. Pujji would have been shocked.

For Anton the RAF Squadron Leader Mahinder Singh Pujji DFC, was the uncle he had never known. Pujji had been a good friend of his father's brother. This uncle he did know and had landed in France as part of Operation Overlord. Anton's promise to his father was based on the latter's promise to Pujji's brother to visit the statue of Pujji in Gravesend every year and lay a commemoration poppy or two. This story, strangely, Beck Senior never forgot.

Anton did not press his father for further snippets of information about the Normandy landings, as he knew that he would only have recalled these on waking in the morning. Anton lamented not being able to join his father at breakfast when he was usually at his sharpest. Anyhow, Anton could relax a little now. He would join Pi at the Temperance Bar.

Temperance Bar

In the Temperance Bar, Anton introduced Pi to an array of drinks as had never been imagined before. If these were the drinking choices for a pint or two, then life would be at such a higher standard in the fishing villages of Sundervagvela. There, the males, in Pi's opinion, seemed to drink too much with the excuse being that drink was needed to rest their muscles at the end of a hard day.

Hayward's 15 was a beer a little too strong for him, rotting the brain and muscles, never mind the liver. The long hop-induced dequenchment of thirst with its many consequences. The most infamous of all was the *Pyassa Schorr*—the infamous 'get rid of your thirst'. It appeared to cost 20% of the average daily wages. The local bar proprietors were all very contented with this cut.

The Temperance Bar had the 3 standards of the natural, orange and lime, and the fruits of the forest—indeed implied was all of them called as it was *tutti fruiti di bosco*. Then, you could choose your hop cordial, mashed in sprouted barley or wheat in certain months.

Of the hops, today, Crystal was an option or the favourite Kent Goldings. And then comes the vehicle of the drink; a slightly salted soda water or some sharp sparkling Welsh water (for the bartender was a handsome Cullen with the standard 2 letter Ls in the family surname).

The business brains of the bar were Brianna and her partner, the intelligent Quinn. He was greeted in the most non-proto-Indo-European of all languages. And I must add that the happy hour was three drinks for a Lady Godiva. Not bad for a fiver. Yet another act of benevolence from the wife of the tax-hiking Earl Leofric, Earl of Mercia. Her 1000-year legacy lived on.

Cullen: *Bora da*!

Pi: For sure!

And paused. It seemed to him to be a neutral greeting of sorts.

Pi: My name being Pi and yours?

Cullen: Cullen, and good day to you, young man, what would you like today? We only serve non-alcoholic beers. We make our own!

Pi: And what would you recommend?

For he was thirsty.

Pi settled down to a pint—he wondered why that measurement was used at all. In India, it was all 500ml or the horse, which was a big bottle. He had enjoyed the occasional beers with his peers, appreciating it even more with his non-peers, however (for its ice-breaking capacities). He found the drink most refreshing and *turu*, he said to himself as he quaffed the first 100ml sip.

He liked the clean, astringent hopiness of it and the tiny popping sensation of the bubbles. But he had no idea what he was actually drinking and avowed that he would return with Anju and Kirk.

Pi had been told by Kirk to wait for Peta Oblonski. Apparently, a living Ardhnariishvari if there ever was one. According to Kirk. Peta strolled in, dandy walker style with a stick out in front. Pi recognised Peta immediately from the description he had been given of a dungaree-clad human in a red t-shirt with strategically placed holes that revealed a plethora of tightly wrought tattoos; a smorgasbord of beliefs, wishes and commemorations. There was even a *Mir Vam. He too wanted world peace,* thought Pi.

Peta: Hi, I'm Peta. As in Pet-her and not Pete—ere, as in the stuff you should not be using my dear gardener!

Pi (a little confused): Hello, my name is Pi. So lovely to meet you! I can get you a drink; my allowance is underspent again.

Within minutes of another beer arriving, the phrase *yaki da* was repeatedly called out and explained by Peta. Peta sketched out a brief curriculum vitae. He had qualified as an engineer at the Pushkin School of Art. Once enrolled at college on merit (or a hefty subscription) the student could construct a course for themselves that was individualised and across a minimum number of disciplines that spanned across the arts via the humanities to the hard sciences of physics, chemistry and through to mathematics.

The polymath, thus endorsed with a degree, was free to work in so many different walks of life. Peta had chosen Sculpture, Modern Art, the giants of Russian literature, Human Rights, Political Change, Earth Science, Engineering,

Theoretical Astrophysics and Vedic Mathematics. Pi felt deeply envious of such a course.

Pi explained to Peta his need to think of a way of portraying a million, a billion and a Googol. Pi also admitted his other intent and extra agenda of using such a depiction to allow children and adults a vision of the number of hours in a human life. Was that a possibility?

Peta: Portraying a million is easy and can definitely be done using my million table that I created and sold as a student in Odessa. It was simply a sheet of quality graph paper that had on it an exact one metre square. This was subdivided into 25-centimetre squares—in total 16. Each of these was subdivided into 5-centimetre squares and then into 1-centimetre squares and finally each centimetre square was divided into 10 millimetres by 10 millimetres. Equating to exactly a million 1millimetre squares per sheet. The colours of the sub-divisions also made it look aesthetic indeed. Many people bought it, and then the owner of the graphic could watercolour it themselves. Timelines and whatever. Why are you interested?

Pi did not want to repeat the story of what had pushed him to the UK in the first place. He changed the subject. He was moved that Peta had had the same vision of depicting a million though but did not share it with him.

Pi: I'm sure you're aware that we live for considerably less than a million hours, Peta?

Peta: No mate, it's millions and millions. I forgot to mention earlier, the paper for the million picture was hand-made—rush and grass paper.

With this, he whipped out his smartphone. The phone was always smart, Pi recalled in his previous discussion of the subject.

Pi: Peta, please consider that the average UK lifespan for a UK woman is 83.

Peta nodded. But did not entirely agree with its possible relevance as he was Russo-Ukrainian.

Peta: See here; it is 7,270,800 hours with a bit more for the leap years, I guess! So, just over 7 million then. Still not as much as I thought.

Pi: Your calculation is good but technically incorrect. No, Peta—I'm so sorry to have to say this—you appear to have added an extra zero at the end.

Peta rechecked.

Peta: What the hell! So, every hour I waste is more than a millionth of my life? In fact, one and a third millionth of my waking life! Sorry, but with all due respect, maybe now that I have found out how short my life is, I should just be leaving now. God knows I haven't even been out of Europe—yet. Oh my God, it may never be possible now because of coronavirus. I don't want to die before I have seen Japan, India, Peru, Madagascar or Chile! But anyway, tell me your idea.

Pi: I am glad that a million has been depicted and the chart that you mentioned could be used to project things onto or even to draw and paint onto. My idea is to depict a million but in 3D! Which I'd like to be able to project milestones of life such as birthdays, the length of childhood and the like. I saw a beautiful little key chain dongle that was a cube of plastic with etching inside. We could do that—and have a cubic meter with laser-cut lines inside to divide it up into 1-centimetre cubes? Then into millimetre cubes to potentially depict a billion?

Peta: You wouldn't even need a million though, will you mate? Less would do; Perspex isn't cheap?

Pi: I agree; it could be expensive. But a million would look nice! And the fact that it is much less than the million unless you live for 114 years and 28 days! Some do. I believe mainly in Japan. Our normal life, if of 83 is only that of around 1000 full moons.

Pi recalled that that particular fact had also annoyed that Sundervagvela Nordic delegation.

Peta: What would the size of the smallest cube be?

Pi: 90 times 90 times 90; that is 729,000? That seems near enough—that would be a cube within the cube with a good border of 5 centimetre all round. Let's do it! I will cost it and see. I might even be able to get a grant for it.

Both were excited. By the time they were into the husky dregs of their second pints, they had covered the lighting of the cube, what they could depict in a human lifespan and generally how they could use it for other purposes like historical timelines.

If they had, sharply engineered, laser-cubes of one millimetre dimension, then a cubic meter could depict a billion. Eight of these would do to portray the entire human race on planet Earth! Just fourteen would be needed to depict the age of the universe. This excited them both enormously.

Peta also left Pi with a recommendation to read Pushkin's *Eugene Onegin*; on the level of any Bollywood story. They had both already agreed that *Sholay* was one of the best-ever movies and that a billion Indians were probably not wrong in thinking this. Pushkin would also tick so many diversity boxes—he was foreign, probably gay, probably dark-skinned and Russian. He could maybe read a Gogol after the Tolstoy and the Gorky. Or even a Turgenev and definitely a Solzhenitsyn, if not a Pasternak. *Which of these would the Beck library hold within its folds*? thought Pi.

Pi stayed on for an hour or so, distributing gifts of small snacks of dates with cashews and almonds and glasses of water to passing folk outside the Temperance who were coming up to iftar on the way to the mosque. Ramadan was almost halfway through, and there was to be a magnificent full moon that night. Each passer-by was greeted with a Ramadan Mubarak.

The evening's convening with Anton and Kirk was essentially a progress report. The triad showed off what they had learnt to each other but as the conversation got deeper, they agreed mutually that there were such major blind spots in all their thoughts and values and behaviours. But luckily, there was no perfect answer for those, and no guilt required for progressing on the journey that is one's life.

Pi to Work

And then the news came. Guru Pi could not to go back to India just yet, even for a few weeks to see his family. Quarantine rules were such that once back in India, he would not be allowed to fly back. There had also been an outbreak of cholera, coronavirus and the odd case of bubonic plague in his locality.

Ruth secured him a bank teaching post and got his visa extended to cover paid work. There was a national shortage of mathematics teachers. Also of psychologists, pharmacists, doctors, radiographers, occupational therapists, nurses, speech and language therapists, teachers of science, physics, Gaelic, social workers, paramedics, nursing assistants, chemical engineers, physical scientists such as geophysicists, geologists, engineers—civil or mechanical or electronic or design or process or elsewhere not classified, IT folk, vets, actuaries, architects, artists, dancers, choreographers and welders.

Really? I hear you say. Despite the UK's 164 universities. We still have to steal personnel from other countries, having saved on their education and training. Though we have footballers in excess, thank goodness for that at least.

Now that Pi was certain not to go back until the year was complete, he wondered whether the pujas that been performed were a tad too much for his original shorter stay, so God had decided to run Pi's credit dry by extending it. Whether Pi would enjoy the extended stay or not was not in doubt.

In England, a general lockdown was being threatened for a good few days now. And indeed, the weekend that it commenced, the population was isolated indoors in the main. Unless you had to work in London, in which case you could utilise the Tube.

Surely by being encased in a long metal tube, you would be safe from the virus. No masks were needed at present; the taking of it on the chin would be on a maskless chin. The diligent Taiwan and Korea were wearing masks; however this was not based on evidence. Oddly though, Anton thought, there was very little evidence for the use of parachutes.

Yet, they were definitely quite handy at times. His uncle Frederick (a member of 1 Para) had certainly found one useful when jumping out of a Dakota Transport as part of Operation Market Garden in an attempt to liberate Arnhem.

Instalment Five: July

Independence Day, super Saturday. We can now eat out! And help the economy too. Go to the pub. Even cut and colour and wax our ears. But not in Belton and environs. Have the locals been naughty?

Face masks are now mandatory with fines for the non-compliant.

Tom Moore has been knighted. He became a Captain for his time served in India and Burma. But knighted for being our patron saint in these most awful of times. The Spitfire and Hurricane fly overhead. Guard of Honour by the 1st Battalion of the Yorkshire Regiment.

Having seen the Spitfire and Hurricane flown in anger and now peace brought happiness to Sir Tom. Now immortalised in the table of Sir Toms of all time. Sir Tom Jones now slips to a still highly commendable silver position of honour. For now.

There were many clinical trials underway. The plasma, bit more Oxygen, the unpronounceable '*zumabs*' and '*amabs*'. Experiment to save lives or not. None were working. Apart from the steroid.

New cases were then picking up everywhere it would seem. Tens of thousands of job losses. A less prosperous future promised with the service pensions lost. Even the 33-year-old Phantom of the Opera closed due to this wretched pandemic.

We plan an independent enquiry in the COVID-19 pandemic in our country. I would put my friend Devi Sridar in charge. But that will never happen. The truth will hurt too much, I suspect. The Russians may be spying on our vaccine development work. We should let them. We worked together on the Space Station, why not this issue?

And incidentally, the ethnics, had not been naughty when adjusted for their economies at home and the people they say hello to every day at home in their taxis, shops and other duties to society.

We are usefully informed that we are 'not out of the woods' yet. I agree as we have had the highest number of excess deaths in the last 4 months in all of Europe, and the second highest peak of deaths. Thank goodness for Spain.

Vaccines by Christmas, we think, the government buys 190 million doses in advance.

Chapter 7
Visits to the Citizens of City-Zen Café

They have more 'voice' than ever before (a meme or a YouTube or TikTok video can reach millions), but they have a sense of diminished agency in 'real life' (institutions and political and economic systems seem locked, inaccessible to them, and wrong-headed).
They are often optimistic about their own generation but deeply pessimistic about the problems they have inherited: Climate change, police violence, racial and gender injustice, failures of the political system, the fact they have little chance of owning a home or doing better than their parents.

From *Gen Z, Explained: The Art of Living in the Digital Age* 2021.
Roberta Katz, Sarah Ogilvie, Jane Shaw, and Linda Woodward.

At the City-Zen Café

Polly and Jeb knew which side their respective parathas and crumpets were buttered on. They had successfully, in the words of the local economist Tin Phin Hien, segmented their clientèle to optimise income and use of the paltry resources, and not particularly wealthy patronage that the City-Zen Café premises offered them.

The F&F stood for Flora and Fauna. The entire idea was that of Kirk's friend, Erasmus Philips. Named as he was after an invaluable Dutchman who had lit many a torch in Europe's Age of Reason. This idea was that of the cataloguing the local environment in comparison to the segmented whole. The three divisions were water, earth, and air.

The completely democratically autocratic rules meant that you could only ever have membership of one of the triad. Or none at all, of course. Here at City-Zen F&F, the currency was the Zeit Coin. You coined a Zeit, which simply enough was an educational presentation slide that you added to the 'bank' on behalf of the F&F community.

Division one was the one that secured 63% of the afternoon takings at the café on the water, earth, and air day, which was usually a Thursday. This water division, so called as it used a lot of water in the gardens. The scriptural writings were those of *Gardeners' World*—digital and for the higher clerics, the magazine. Its new testament prevailed, the old testament prophets had largely been forgotten, even the major ones such as Thrower, Hamilton and, Titchmarsh. The second coming of Dón had prevailed with his coterie of Carol, Arit, Frances and others.

These were the most welcoming of all to the foreigner plants but were also equally joyous with the humble foxglove (as long as it stayed put and did not invade the Hosta aka plantain lily, although apparently related to the asparagus, originally from China, Japan, Russia and both Korea).

Division two was the one that secured takings in late afternoon and early evening, this was the ragged band of the Earth sisters and brothers. An assortment of the very young and seemingly impossibly mobile older folks. This band were celebrating the fact that they had managed to procure an allotment.

The parcel of land, in rods or poles or perches, which is now exactly 250 square metres had simply not been available to them for the last 8 years. Alas, there had been an untimely Covid-19 death and it was a dead man's legacy of beautiful soil in knee high beds. The tennis court slice of Earth that will be forever their England until passed back to the parish council.

Clearly, no sub-letting was allowed. Not bad for 15 pence a square meter! These coterie of 'grow your own' were also the economic anchor of the local garden centre. Tin had calculated those tomatoes had cost £17.31 a kilo— assuming a minimum wage with no costs for pension, national insurance and holiday.

Potatoes were a mere £11.79 a kilo. Clearly, the earth brigade were not quite ready to compete with the supermarkets. Tin had failed to measure other outputs; President Ruth would contend. And that the approach of the Bhutanese might be better. The folks were happy.

Division three were the regular posses that would descend on meadows and fields and canal bank to photograph and catalogue life in all its forms in the local wild ecology of it all. They were restricted to the parish boundaries as this was a local stock take only. Confluent with the boundaries of the annual litter pick. Now, of necessity, monthly.

The parishes had their own web-sites in several cases. These saw themselves as the natural heirs of the English amateur natural history bods now mightily equipped with instant photo creating equipment allowing 12-million-pixel paint strokes in a moment.

There was consternation that a mere gardener had found a grass snake in their compost bin. And taken a photo worthy of a worthy mention in any photography competition. The *schadenfreude*, jealousy and ire only an Othello would understand. This was beginner's luck. The compost heap had not been turned as instructed. Thus, the hot and tropical had attracted the snake.

Kirk and Co had recently—in lockdown one—launched an underground unit within Division 3. The mission of this unit was to disseminate native British trees throughout the parish. Saplings would be traded, *gratis* usually, or bartered without negotiation, for a swift pint or two. Most were tiny and exchanged in well aerated '*Kireen*' bottles.

This had been invented by Kirk and Cullen over a pint at the Temperance Bar. You got a PET bottle, often 2 or 3 litres, cut it across two-thirds up, slit 2 centimetres perpendicular to the cut top end, and this could be inserted into the bottom end to create a miniature greenhouse. If draining was needed, then you just perforated the bottom with a hot screwdriver.

Usually, a tree would go into a *Kireen* bottle, be exchanged at the café and into the ground within a day or two at most. Several of their members, childless and blessed (mostly), had declared themselves as a member of the Hova community. *Homo obliterans var abor*. The human obliterated, sub-species tree. To hug tree, yes, never to hold a hand against another human.

They were wretchedly staunch in this, despite the unwashedness at times and the apparent poverty and distress. They were *Ents*, they were of *Groot*. They also played a lot of computer games and watched a lot of fantasy films.

The saplings would end up being planted in hedgerows, in parks next to dead trees, the sides of ponds, canals and the River Nun. Essentially, anywhere where these anonymous Banksys could get away without incurring official or local ire. There was even an unofficial map of where the trees had been planted and what they were.

The tallest of these was already over 2 metres high. If bought at Chelsea, this would be £1215 plus VAT. This was from an acorn, picked up in Stellenbosch by Hanse and Edile, then gifted to the Becks on a visit to Belton years ago. Others approaching 2 metres were the silver birches planted before Covid-19 visited. There were plenty of rowan, hornbeams even. No ash was allowed as it was being ravaged by the fungus *Hymenoscyphus fraxineus*, renamed from the cuddlier *Chalara fraxinea*. Anton was a useful source of micro-life information.

Those that did undertake tree-planting as part of this Homo saplings group, would often paint or sticker a green dot on the wheels of whatever description vehicle—cars, cycles, motor bikes, scooters. Even a pram and a wheelbarrow had been seen with the mark of the Homo saplings unit.

To be fair, one of the reasons for the Homo saplings club being driven underground as it was because the words Homo saplings were not allowed and reportable by the internet police. Each such tree planted would appear as a green dot on the introductory page of the Division 3 site.

There had been 191 such trees planted since inception and most of these were in lockdown one—facilitated by the more solitary walks and less curious walkers who were just out striding homeward to their castles and put up the drawbridge as soon as possible, so as to not miss the daily despairing updates from the chosen trinity of the day. Often the PM, ideally the health minister and the always welcome, Professor JVT and his boss.

Today, there was to be a debate for and against the planting of a monkey puzzle tree. Was this native to Britain?

Havier: I am welcome in Belton but not my tree? It is my national tree. It is endangered, it was around when the dinosaurs were. *Aruacaria araucana* has been here since at least 1795 when—

Kirk: Look mate, the oak supports 500 plus flora and fauna. Never mind the fungi! The monkey puzzle is sterile, meaning no nests and blending with the native broad-leaved trees that contribute the most to the taking of CO_2 out of the atmosphere. Each of these trees is an ecosystem that blends in.

Havier: This is xenophobia! The jays and your beloved red squirrels feast on the pine nuts. Why does the Woodland Trust sell them?

Kirk: It is not a pine. And is there not a traditional saying that speaking whilst passing one will bring bad fortune and grow you a monkey's tail? Look, let's vote on it at the annual meeting. But please, do not plant under the aegis of the HS work. We also have 31 trees in *Kireen* bottles to plant out! Who wants one? Again, please do not plant ashes until the existing die and disappear.

The 11 members of the underground unit received two or three saplings each. The silver birch, the oak, the hawthorn, hornbeam, the rowan and the sycamore were gratefully received and would be put in the ground over the weekend to come. Kirk had become particularly partial to the rowan—it reminded him of the awesome fearful beauty of the coronavirus particle.

He also liked those waxwings, redwings and other thrushes that fed on them. He was of the opinion that a meal of berries might just dissuade a song thrush from smashing open a snail on a stone and eating it alive. The songsters appeared to Kirk to have the most inaesthetic of names—the blackbird being *Turdus merula*, the song thrush was *Turdus philomelos* and the redwing *Turdus iliacus*.

The rules in Division 3 were quite simple. You were only allocated one Zeit Coin each week. This was to reduce the Hermione over-performers from discouraging the Harrys and what's his names of the world. The model worked well and in the 15 months since its inception (the May of the year that coronavirus had wreaked havoc), it had catalogued 241 plants and fungi, 173 faunae including 7 different types of slugs.

The retired teacher Professor Marma was the final arbiter of what went on the website. Her rules were strict; and in general, you did not raise your voice with her or argue with her at the risk of a fine or that look. All she wanted was a slide with a picture.

They were all strictly templated with all their Latin names in italics and their etymology explained. There had to be some history included, and ideally, its medical or societal use in times gone by or present.

Pi was astonished to learn that the snowdrop had given humanity a chemical that had been the basis of a drug for dementia, the humble ubiquitous foxglove one for heart failure, the rare French lilac one for diabetes and that the bark of a member of the willow family, a *Salix* was the source of the original aspirin— used by millions on Plant Earth to reduce chances of an untimely death.

Not forgetting the anticancer drugs derived from the periwinkle and yew. And that the latter could live over 3000 years! Certainly, in Sundervagvela no tree could live that long, as the Panchayat (the local parish council, made up of usually the 5 most prominent men of the village) would call in a shaman periodically.

For a fee of Rs 1000, the shaman would walk through the village and pronounce that certain flora had to be destroyed as they were casting a spell on the village; blaming them for everything from the failure of the mango harvest that year to the reduced birth rates of its buffalos and cows. And possibly, the scandal and fertility of the head teacher in his congress with the lab assistant.

The last such incursion had resulted in the condemning of an esplanade of trees that had shaded children to and from school for around 200 metres for all the years since Independence. If the choice was his, Guru Pi would have preserved these for the simple fact that Mahatma Gandhi had remarked on their beauty as saplings just a few years before Independence and had actually planted the first two himself.

They had taken 75 years to grow, and when cut down, a gift of Rs 25,000 was given to each of the Panchayat. The wood had been cleared away to the wood mill. This reminded Pi of Boxer the Shire horse from Animal Farm, who had worked tirelessly for the Animal Revolution only to be sold to the knackers' yard, to be converted into glue and leather, to fill the coffers of the ruling elite, rather than to be pensioned off. A brilliant, prescient book, but alas only 8 millimetres thick.

Prof Marma

Pi was then to meet Prof Marma in the bar. This had been arranged after they had met very briefly at the F&F gathering. The ex-teacher. But really, once a teacher always a teacher. The description of the clientèle in the Temperance Bar would have been of the pink, the black, the olive-skinned and the bronzed.

Olive-skinned was always problematic—are we talking about black olives? Surely not green. For this was a local bar; not one teeming with aliens gathering in for a welcome watering after traversing the galaxies.

Pi noted that every four to five minutes, someone would go up to Prof Marma, chat, and offer to buy her a drink. One such brand accoutred bloke had a briefcase—a sight never seen in these parts. And after a chinwag, he went up to the bar, handing over a note with a flash of Boulton and Watt that was recognised by Anju as a fifty-pound one.

Anju was looking forward to having or even seeing the Turing note that had recently been released in June but had not quite made it to her purse. Prof Marma now had £783.54 credit behind the bar.

Anju filled Pi in with the details. Prue Marmaduke—*probably no longer a follower of the Irish Saint Maedoc*, thought Anju but did not tell Pi this, as many of her compatriots never appeared to be interested in her etymological knowledge. *Was this a wasted interest of hers?* Thought Anju.

Prue had become a professor, a title bestowed on her by the fledglings of Ellie Elementary that she had taken under her wing in evening classes whilst the parents went out for a quick meal or a walk or God forbid, a rare attempt to conceive the next member of their family.

Prue had been the informal social worker and evening tutor of a particular echelon of Belton society for the last 23 years and had been awarded an MBE for her efforts. Bestowed upon her by the Queen, no less.

The United Nation of British children, thus assembled, had run riot through basic Maths and English with a passion that had lit the fuse to their future successes as nurses, builders, computer programmers, police officers galore, and many others. They were all eternally grateful.

An extension had been built onto the library as a tutorial room for the children. The children had metamorphosed Prue into Prof and the Marmaduke easily into Marma—motherly as she was. She was their own Professor Minerva McGonagall. And even a slight look-alike.

Anju and Prof Marma often worked together—often over the ether though— comparing notes, and in reality, both together were often the final arbiters of what went on the City-Zen Café F&F site. Prof Marma had agreed to meet Anju with Pi after she had supervised her class in learning about Pythagoras's theorem, and other bits and bobs about triangles. Including the bit about the deltoid—the site of so many painful injections received and to come—being a triangular muscle.

The Covid-19 vaccine roll-out was being planned. Apparently, the promised vaccine was nearly here now. That much was clear from the fawning press and politicians' self-expressed valedictions. Pi had been very excited to meet Prof Marma. He was sure that she was a local dignitary, and he approached her with hands in prayer and his head slightly bowed.

Pi: Namaste.

Prue offered her right hand, with the left remaining concealed. Anju remarked to herself that one was a Sanskrit implication that the divine and the spark of Brahman is the same in you and me, with the handshake being a gesture of stating that you had no weapon in your dextrous hand—though one could be presumably concealed in the sinister hand not seen.

The usual conversational forage into each other lives followed, and then the more serious business of book choices that was to be the main part of this informal BASALT meeting that Kirk had arranged to advise Pi on his reading.

Sorry, that acronym is rather tortured; Books: A Strategy and Learnèd Tips. Small talk over.

Pi: What am I to read then, Professor?

Prof Marma: I am not a professor but if you insist! Ok. Some books are a great challenge, and may be difficult for you. I am not being patronising at all in saying this; however, my nephew recently informed me that he had passed his law degree. Great news in itself—though he also texted me a photo of him standing next to a pile of books that was about this high.

She indicated a height of 2 feet, maximum.

Prof Marma: Apparently, this including all his books of law and those of leisure as well. Tom loves his books and likes to read a book or two a month at times. But discourage you, we certainly will not. Even if your challenge does seem a lot more like a marathon compared to his half-marathon.

Anju: He can but try!

Pi: I will try and then if I fail, I will try again in India and post you a picture back of my attempt! Even if I only get to the manipura chakra in my abdomen, I will be happy in failing to that extent.

Prof Marma: Whatever. We must face the challenge, especially as I do not want you to lose to Mark. Sir X to you, I suspect. So, what shall we read? You must acquire a thick edition of Fiela's Child. This is the best book I have ever read. I was reminded of it in the light of the recent brutal murder of George Floyd. Day 25 of the month of May 2020, will go down in history with infamy. It's ridiculous to think that in this day and age, people can believe that Black lives do not matter as all lives equally do. What did he do to deserve that? What construed society to make that happen? 25th May in the year of our Lord 2020. In even accepting that the year is two thousand years after the birth of our Lord who told us to be kind to each other. Full-stop end of story, end of all politics, end of religious discourse.

Anju: Just awful.

Pi: I—

Prof Marma: This is a turning point, Pi—Anju, you note what I have said.

For Anju, no speech was needed. She just touched Prue, and on eye contact, shared her shame at the lack of progress on the planet generally, and specifically in the USA since the emancipation of all human folk on New Year's Day in 1863.

Pi was saddened.

Prof Marma: We live and we must learn. I re-read Dalene Matthee's book this week. Never has the calamity of losing a child been expressed in such raw terms. The story being that of a White child foundling bought up by the Black Fiela. For the child to then be re-introduced into the so-called proper Christian life of the White people around him by the Apartheid bureaucracy, an unforgettable epic indeed. It has even been translated into Icelandic and Sinhalese.

Guru Pi: I am so lucky to hear your personal recommendation. I will have to read the English translation. Was the original in Afrikaans?

Prof Marma: Yes. I will remember that book forever. I had a privileged childhood, but the day I finished reading that book was the day my innocent view of the world disappeared. Age 16, I think.

Namaste would be an ideal greeting to adopt in these times of the virus. A mutual thought shared by the trio on parting.

Kirk found the book for Pi. It had been easy to locate on the app that he had developed with one of his best friends, Keke. Find a book locally, easily— FABLE. Not terribly financially rewarding, but it worked every now and then. Pi agreed to meet Keke at the City-Zen Café to collect *Fiela's Child*.

Keke at City-Zen Café

Pi had only met Keke in passing before. On the day of the book collection, it was Keke's significant birthday do and so, a buffet was to be inflicted on his friends and the occasional erstwhile foe. Carmen would also be there, an added bonus to all.

The word inflicted had been used by Kirk. Why? Keke's diet was simple enough. No wheat, no meat, no heat, no teats. It was terribly bland. Anju had chosen the menu which Kirk claimed was a double whammy.

The wheat free, vegetarian, milk-free, non-spicy, no things raw buffet consisted of not a lot, but included variants of hummus, rice-cakes, refried beans, corn chips, spud patties and veggie sausages.

Pi was sat with the nondescript. The less gregarious. The unnoticed. It was almost as if Pi had held his hand aloft and offered for them to crowd around him. The tired, poor, huddled masses yearning to breathe freely. Surrounding their new Colossus. In Pi, they found a gentle spirit who listened, always giving you that 9-second window to continue to converse.

Around Keke and Kirk and Anju and Freya, there was far more competition for a chance to air a word, a thought, a sentence. Pi's little huddle, meanwhile, was mesmerised. They were looking at the fizzy drink in a fluted glass. What was being observed was the short-term perpetual motion of the blueberry sinking to the bottom of the glass bubbleless, acquiring a bubble at the bottom of the flute and floating back up again.

Repeat. Repeat. Repeat. This makeshift lava lamp had ended all conversation between them and had inspired a segue into private thoughts of life and death and karmic return and creation and destruction.

Pi felt somewhat paralysed with joy. Pi was in a world of Pi alone, but eventually explained that he had seen the creator Brahma in the bubbles at the bottom, the preserver Vishnu in the short journey as the berry floated to the top, and then the destruction of the bubbles enacted as per the role of the great destroyer that is Shiva.

The trinity of it all enacted in the café whilst normal life continued around them. Especially the urgent chat on the footie, the rugby and even darts.

A lot of the chat was to do with books. There were useful and less useful bits of advice being freely given. Pi was running a little behind with his reading and was fast coming to the conclusion that realistically most of these highly recommended tomes (that seemed to be the favourites of the literary illuminati) would have to be shortlisted to read and possibly bought to display on one's shelves back in India.

George Eliot, Pi learnt, was a woman who had to be read if one was serious about reading at all. *Middlemarch* was the centre of the literary universe. Indeed, the location of the purported town of Middlemarch was not that far off the literal centre of England. The country that had ruled over most of humanity some time or other. The ruling over of India, China and USA had certainly given England a head start. A forever forwards in any future epoch. But the book was too long and very densely printed. Investing time to read its 316,059 words would be folly for Pi's undertaking. That was probably one for later. Pi, not being the fastest of readers, would need a good 37.5 hours of week-long to give it justice. Also, at 31 millimetres, the book would be a thickness too little for the amount of time it would take, although the magnificent Folio Edition was a hefty 59 millimetres.

Similar rejections had been the tome that started the American Civil War, (if certain historians were to be believed) Uncle Tom's Cabin by the best-selling author of that time, until the great JK Rowling and her compatriots came along.

JK's Harry Potter would be rejected by Sir X. There was little doubt about that. Sir X had made it very clear from the outset of the challenge.

Pi continued to enjoy local Sundervagvela conspiracy theories. If they can be called that. That the Potter boy was Indian! One believes what one wants to, and it was clear on MuggleNet that this hero of heroes was Indian via the mixed heritage of Fleamont, his father. Whilst, his mother Euphemia was Indian.

On the way home, Kirk shared an observation with Pi and Anju. And now that several members of the City-Zen Café had lost their sense of smell, noxious emissions from the distal end of the alimentary were being let loose at an alarming rate by these miscreants. This was asymmetrical warfare at its best. Drone strikes with no human responsibility.

At home, Pi finished reading *Casual Vacancy*. This proved to be one of Pi's favourite reads. It was less traumatic than *Shuggie Bain*, but a great story of the down-trodden, the exploited and the exploiters of a society cracked at the seams with rudderless lost characters and the hyenas that took, took, and took. The action in Pagford revealed an idyll poisoned by the machinations of the schemers.

Stuart would see through it all; and saw that many of us were ashamed of who we are, then try to be someone else. Fail at that. And then despair. The messages of how society treats the messiah and pariah, the labelled mad or the criminal sounded very familiar to Pi. A precept to avoid, that he had read about in the *Bhagavad Gita*. With an invocation to treat the highest sage the same as an eater of dogs, and indeed gold and a stone.

Although some gold in the bank would certainly help anyway. To Pi, every interaction in the community was a casual vacancy of sorts to fill a bit of a life, maybe to enrich and maybe to not. But that always went to count towards time together shared if nothing else.

A cracking read and at 34 millimetres, it was a job well done. Apparently, there was a film too. He vowed, to himself, to watch it. Also recommended for the life Scottish were the Ian Rankin novels. Pi would need to seek one out.

Soviet Tea in the City-Zen Café

Yeke, the café owner, and I, would just listen to Pi and notes would be taken. As to the tea, Pi-style. It had become a quickly established firm favourite in the café. It was certainly not the exact formulation that his village, Sundervagvela, was famous for. Just as only a closed triad knew the formula of Coca Cola, the recipe of Sundervagvela's masala tea was a closely guarded secret. Known to the triumvirate elite of the local *chaiwalla* guild only.

What Pi did, in Kirk's opinion, was to essentially introduce a licence to print money. Or at least a cool Rs 20,000 that he could remit to his school every month. Yeke had agreed to give Pi 25 pence for each beverage dispensed. Irrespective of whether it was a *vente, grande* or *mucho grande.*

They all seemed extortionately priced to Pi, but really, they weighed in at a healthy price being a third lower than the rate charged by the one named after Captain Ahab's Quaker First Mate on the whaling ship Pequod in *Moby Dick.* The café with the logo of the initially bare-breasted, but now a more demure, mermaid.

Plus, or minus barista oat milk, if so desired. Cow's milk, if you were choosing to annoy the vegans. There was, always of course, the almond, hazelnut, coconut, pea, and tiger nut milks.

Pi was not one to keep secrets. Rather, he was incapable.

The City-Zen Café regulars soon teased out of Pi that there were 5 ingredients. They sounded more exotic in Pi's particular Hindi dialect. The main ones were, you remember, *taj* (cinnamon), *muri* (pepper), *lovan* (clove), *jaifer* (nutmeg) and *javitri* (mace) in that Sundervagvela blend.

Local quality and availability dictated that Pi could only resource a more mundane cardamom variety, reasonably good cinnamon, reasonable clove, and excellent Vietnamese black pepper. Everyone started to call it Soviet tea; for the recipe was CCCP. It was a big hit and at festive times such as Diwali, the Eids, Baisaki, and Christmas, sales tripled.

Soviet tea was freshly ground and a veritable powder keg of explosive flavours ready to cleanse the palate of the aftertaste of food. A samosa, muffin, burger, or bagel. All could be cleansed. Edgar quipped that it was enough to spark the mental firing of a barista into the sharp incisive sparring death kill delivery of a barrister of the highest calibre.

Nobody quite understood what he meant. With time, the spices became the best available, the thinnest Sri Lankan cinnamon, the cardamom sourced locally from a select area of Turkey, the cloves from an African Women's Co-op. Not sure where exactly, the packet just narrowed it down to Product of Africa, just the 20% of the Earth's landmass, but about the same part less than the area of the moon.

Pi was always happy to grind spices fresh in the granite mortar, lovingly pestling them by hand. Who knew, this hand grinding might even have some minor but distinctive health benefit. Anton had made it known to all that listened among his family and friends that cinnamon, being related to willow-bark, contained aspirin-like properties.

The Ombudsman and COP 26

Another time, Pi saw Keke walk into the City-Zen Café and go up to the bar to order a drink. The luxury of offering other people drinks wasn't for him. The coke had a sling of rum slipped into it from his Lenin hip flask—although he carried it in a pocket close to his heart for several reasons, presumably for protection from a stray bullet. Though rare in these parts of the world, it did happen every 7 years or so.

Keke glanced across to see Pi and Edgar in deep fraternity but total non-conversation. Edgar thinking about whether COP-26 would achieve anything. Would Greta be annoyed by it? Was he, Edgar, even allowed to have a view? As he would be dead by the time the planet was even more over-cooked. How would the hypocrisies of the giants of diplomacy be exposed this time?

He recalled that COP was an allusion to the first such conference on all things climate in Copenhagen. Like the fairy tales that had come out of Copenhagen since old Hans.

Edgar in his optimistic gloom realised that it would be the Little Mermaid and the Little Matchgirl that would be saddened as the Emperors' and Empresses' new clothes would prove to be inadequate in Anderson's story, but politically adequate against the warming atmosphere present day. Maybe the Snow Queen would never have been written on a warmed-up planet.

Pi was engaged in less esotericism. He was recalling the death of his grandmother from tuberculosis all those years ago. The TB had been latent, but malaria had weakened her and left her ravaged with the incurable disease. Pi was sad.

His mother's mother had only been 59. Granted not the 1000 moons oft promised to those well-behaved, followers of ancestral rituals and those up-to-date with all the temple subscriptions. He was reminded of one of his favourite films.

Another incident in his life that had landed him in trouble almost a decade ago. About the film *OMG!—Oh My God!*—he had posted, on the college

99

newsletter a remark, attracting consternation from many. His simple post, for he knew it verbatim, was:

Superb film! Clearly exposes malpractice in religion. None of the big 3 in India are spared. Each religion does have a benevolent counter-character, as the great spiritual founders would have wanted. Based as they were on compassion and not financial trading as the key mission. The film is not anti-religion—just more pro the things that religion can do and should do to improve the lot of humankind and all of creation.

Please, please can we end the practice of sacrificing life-giving, cow-distressing foods such as milk and ghee as oblations? They end up in the sewage system, which is good for no one, and warm up the planet with diyas that shed no light.

His recollection of the aftermath of this post was not pleasant as near riots had ensued. In modern parlance, he had not consulted the key stakeholders that had to be consulted in a democracy before anything controversial could be voiced, working as he did, albeit through a distorted route, for the government and higher education.

The dairy farmers were particularly disenamoured with Pi. They felt that it was the pinnacle of their endeavours that their milk was the chosen brand for pouring over the *Shiva-Ling* and *Yoni*, carved from a single piece of Himalayan black granite in the most auspicious of the local Shaivite temples.

The milk would be poured over the cosmic dome to cascade down into the grooved surrounds that was the yoni and onto the sand and pebble beach of the jet black *shilajit* mineral. The latter milk-imbued would be collected, with small amounts of milk to be used as a universal medicine by the revered Ayurvedic practitioners of Sundervagvela bazaar.

Shilajit mineral pitch, an amalgam of plant matter, presumably baby coal and minerals. The best was from the Himalayas. Especially the Indian and Tibetan, it would appear. Its myriad properties included improved brain function and hence was effective in combating Alzheimer's, ageing, anaemia, and viruses of all sorts. And chronic fatigue, altitude sickness, liver cancer, heart disease, obesity, and of course, infertility. It probably was of some benefit as it had a lot of iron in it, or so I am told.

Pi had been invited to do a short speech at the Hanuman temple in Belton and was apprehensive about potential bad press if he was to talk about dairy products again. He would need to keep on message and only talk about the

Ardhnariishvari Temple as per his specific remit. Or at least he would try his best. But the speech was a few months away.

Keke: Hi guys! You're looking deep in thought today. The Ombudsman and the perfectly slim Billy Bunter.

For Edgar did, now come to think of it, look like Billy Bunter. A small cap, a black short jacket with a braided border. Paired with tweed trousers and a waistcoat. And very shiny shoes that seemed never to have trodden bare earth. Keke had always been fond of the adventures of Billy Bunter and in different books, the more adventurous Biggles.

Edgar: Thanks for the compliment. The god I worship has been exposed! But Pi is a teacher; not an Ombudsman?

Keke followed his eyes to the Om emblazoned on the badge on his sleeve-less Nehru jacket. Then to the two empty Bud bottles and the one currently still in operation. Pi followed Keke's eyes and smiled.

Keke: Pi is also the very meaning of Ombudsman. A person of utter integrity that you could call on to investigate and can count on to be fair and balanced and totally incorruptible. Unless he behaves otherwise.

Gentle banter between the three of them kept them in a cosy atmosphere until closing time—which was unusually early at 9pm as the owner was off to complete the three peaks challenge over the weekend. On his way to the toilets, Pi saw a mirror image of the sign navigating him, ideally masked, to the toilets.

He was pleased to discover—in a truly massive contribution to humanity—that toilets was an anagram of TS Eliot. But that would be Eliot of the George? As in the authoress of Silas Marner, which he had just finished. How did TS spell his surname? Was it Elliott, Eliott, Elliot or indeed Eliot? He had no reception on his phone neither to check or share this discovery. Pi recalled his very unsuccessful sojourn as a poet in Sundervagvela. But he still had a hidden collection.

Walking home, Pi ruminated on the cosmos; as he always did when he could see the stars. It would help him figure out how to depict a Googol, for sure. But he was in no such mood to today. It was not so much the black dog, but a dark cloud that was creeping up on him.

This had been triggered by the accolade of Keke attributing to him the characteristics of an Ombudsman. Pi felt like a fraud and somewhat disappointed as he vividly recollected his essay to himself—*The Kalma of a Thord.*

Throughout his early years, the edicts of the Thord had carried so much weight that may as well have been etched onto stone pillars that Asoka has strewn across his Mauryan Empire many millennia ago. Across Afghanistan, Nepal, India, Pakistan, and Bangladesh.

In Asokan days, there could have been hundreds; but today only 19 had survived etched with the wisdom of humans generally and of the Buddha specifically. Sadly, to Pi, his edicts appeared to have been made of hard ice; as they had melted away gradually but surely.

He had started off as purely he felt. His idea was not that of poetry but of casting his thoughts directly through his own words, unpolished, into a vat of water to crystallise yet remain unchanged. Hence, this direct combination of thoughts and words. He felt himself the first self-declared Thord; in his own small world at least. Eventually, Pi could no longer resist rereading his rejected collection of Thords.

He got out his phone and went to the pdf of his Book on Thords, and read words written over a decade ago. He would read them in detail later. That night, Pi settled down to read his own notebooks. He wondered whether he was brave enough to discuss his old Thord ideas with Anju or Kirk or Ruth or Anton even. Pi opened his raw cotton and *ahimsa*-silk clothbound notebook. This was volume one of three. His early formative years of his *Brahmacharya*—or student days.

Conceptual Thord

I am amongst other things, a Thord.

Hopefully, no-one challenges the originality of this word.

It was carefully chosen and is an extremely mature concept.

It would be a life-spark if someone would do likewise.

This is obviously asking too much.

I am not the first, probably, but I coined the word on this auspicious day, 26th January, the day of the anniversary of the original Republic Day of India.

I recall the Constitution and its promise of Justice, Liberty, Equality, and Fraternity to all its Citizens. This, I will enact in my life.

The word. Thord. It consists of the primary stem of the word thought.

That is the 'T' and 'H'. The rest contains the letters all but the twist of 'word'. Simply, a Thord is therefore a noun. In event of translation into other languages, I would like it to be feminine. Eg. Die Thord or La Thord. The whole concept if of use to anyone else is wholly dedicated to Sarasvati—the Goddess of Art and Learning—if such a concept exists.

Thord. A noun. Meaning the direct transfer of thought to paper via words. I really must stress and clearly define what I mean by direct transfer. One really must understand because this is the whole perception of the phenomenon.

A poem is an artful articulation of thoughts onto paper. One has thoughts and then this is translated, the latter is an extremely important punch-word, into a poem.

The Thord (now the person who writes thords or indeed just a thord) is at the end of a line that starts from the lyric writer to the Thord via a poet.

The lyric writer is a person who translate a subject into word eg words. She is not necessarily in a creative mood. Talent is needed to be truly good. The poet translates a thought into words that other people will understand. There has to be certainty of this, because if the poet is not appreciated a living cannot be earned.

Some 'poets' eg. Keats, one classical poet, in this sense above—just read To Autumn. It is superb. Each word blends into the next visually, audibly, verbally, thought-wise—plump-fruit oozings, etc.

Other poets such as Blake were more Thordist if not complete Thords.

I want to finish now. But I want to say that a Thord wants to express himself or herself and about the milieu that they are in—nature, society and the broad canvas of the universe itself. In fact, all that is important that can overcome the natural inhibition of having to write it down.

In their own words, a Thord wants to photograph thoughts in which they star and convert them into words. An added bonus would be words that are understood and ideally liked. There has to be complete honesty to distil the individual. Amen.

Pi felt that maybe this was a vindication of the verity of his writings being declared *buckvass*. And that maybe his erstwhile critics had had a point.

What followed next in the notebook, after a few pages of abstract art was a long list of edicts. Even the fact that he had been called an Ombudsman today immediately grated with the first idea. Integrity. What integrity? And then all that had occurred with his first love had erased many more. For the sake of revisiting his naïveté, Pi put himself through all of the 37 self-edicts. In a capitalist world, why have only Ten Commandments when you could have 37?

Some, he recognised as being prescient as lived in a relative backwater, as Anton would refer to Sundervagvela. Others had had to be abandoned shortly after being written down.

A few simple ideas to use.

1. No drinking of alcohol even at home.
2. No smoking.
3. To correlate actions with thoughts as far as possible—few wild imaginings.
4. To forever live, I hope of having an arranged marriage—the belief behind this is that all humans are equal and in the happiness of my family especially.
5. To speak the truth with friends. The family will be spared some details.
6. To eat good foods only, not any artificial foods.
7. To be simple in needs and wants.
8. Study hard both English and Hinduism—the latter to uphold my cultural heritage and find my own self.
9. To spare anger, be understanding as possible.
10. Never to return injury.
11. To take care of the body by exercise, good food, sleep, etc. in the belief that the body has a profound effect on thought—the most important distinguishing faculty of humans.
12. To opt out of competition with everyone as an end to follow my own life.
13. Same in praise but to change if criticised rightly.
14. To be unpassionate of anything and anyone.
15. Spread an understanding of people as a means to a proper interaction with them.
16. Not to pursue any large action selfishly.
17. To be unselfish but not to the extent of falling to a degradation with neglect to all my other points especially smoke + drink + work.
18. Uphold academic work as the most important 'course' of life now.
19. To give up the eating of meat at the end of next term. Why?

    - Meat is flesh-produced by an act of violence.
    - Meat is unhealthy—fat, etc. not simple.
    - Ecologically inefficient as a source of food.

- *To adopt a more humane attitude by not eating meat.*
- *Meat being a favourite source of food (especially red)—my not eating entails a sacrifice, a sacrifice in remembrance of people who don't even have enough food to satisfy hunger.*

20. *Never to waste food—saving food to feed birds or return to the soil—only to be followed when alone. So not to embarrass others by unseemly piety.*
21. *To pray daily at dawn simply and more formally at night. With a chapter of the Bhagavad Gita to be read every day and keep a note of days missed to catch up. And a small passage of the New Testament. And a part of other wisdom, especially the Quran.*
22. *No small snacks—have a good morning, evening and afternoon meal.*
23. *To learn to live with the weather and not let this ever hurt me, eg. rain, sun, wind.*
24. *Carry on writing Thords. As a means to record my journey. To write something in dedication to my future partner and friends. Why leave out the foes even?*
25. *Save all my annas and paise for charity always at school and at home if budget allows. Money to the Orphan Society or other very useful cause.*
26. *Work for the local, then regional, then state, then national and then international literary and charitable societies to spread good education to the deprived. Make others, especially closer friends, more aware of global problems.*
27. *Restrict use of foul language.*
28. *Be active and therefore, not be untidy or dirty.*
29. *Think practically in terms of paying off family debts, house repairs, gardening, etc. To follow a course of action as well as thought and education.*
30. *Not to tie myself with people which might leads to passions, serious angers. To pursue a simple display of love and respect for all human being.*
31. *To be especially responsive to a people in need. When sorrow strikes, illness, etc.*
32. *Uphold to be a disciple of Gandhi, thus having a place, always for humility and modesty.*

33. *To hold all humans equally—each as a product of their environment. Never to think myself better. Or worse. If I am different, if positively so, it is due to my luck in life alone.*

34. *To be an Advaitist—a monist. Integration of, and beyond, simple good and evil. Give advice, but not criticism to all who state my way is better than yours.*

35. *Uphold never to hurt anyone.*

36. *To pray to the Cosmos daily by engaging in a simple sense of awe. To see as many of the 1000 full moons as possible in my life to come. If my life is an average lifespan,*

37. *To develop a consciousness based on all sources of Traditional Wisdom, Perennial Philosophy and the experience and experiments within my life and those around me.*

Here endeth the paper and my points to live my life by. Please adeptly adapt and adopt.

A good hour had passed during which Guru Pi had read and cogitated upon the edicts in silence, in English and then internally monologued in his mother tongue. Even scores of Asoka's edicts had survived. Pi noticed that he had a prime number of edicts. But many of his, he felt, had been skittled away akin to India's wickets at the recent debacle in Australia where they had been skittled out for 36. This was of the deepest embarrassment.

The lowest in their test history. Adelaide. Luckily, Christmas, which shortly followed was not to be celebrated in great style by the team. Media wits had coined the definition of the *delaide*. A *delaide* is the humiliating defeat by a population of 1.38 billion by a country with a population of 25 million (living in a country twice that size though, and the diameter of the Earth's moon). However, the phoenix had risen from the ashes of defeat and the outcome was pleasant for Pi to recall. Despite a century by the magnificently named Labuschagne. The headlines were unkind. RIP had been underlined, and Australia added beneath, in the name of the Man of the Match, Rishabh Pant and lauded everywhere.

A few of the edicts were still standing and unbroken, and set in reasonably firm stone. The acid experience of life had eroded many and dissolved some altogether.

Reading Animal Farm that night, he dreamt that many of his personal edicts had been chalked on a barn wall adjacent to the Orwellian changes such as *four legs good, two legs bad* to *four legs good, two legs better. All animals are equal* to *All animals are equal but some animals are more equal than others. No meat eating except at Eid, Christmas and (weekends). No drinking of alcohol except when you want to. To have an arranged marriage—arranged by myself alone.*

Maybe he, Pi, was a hue man. A rainbow of colours to behold. Not the pure Sattvic blue. But a rainbow through the red of Rajas and dark greys of Tamas as well. A changing with the winds type of person, but hopefully one still sailing towards his original intended destination; albeit off course at times due to his personal whims and also the exigencies of the winds and calamities.

He was certainly not a child of the Mahatma. Pi needed a walk. He was not certain whether anyone would truly ever understand him.

Vindication of Vik

Another time, Pi met Vik. Vik had nestled into the sign-posted Hygge Corner of the northern designation at the café. He was in deep chit-chat with his Uncle Chimay. So many topics had been covered but not in any meaningful detail. His impending hip operation was covered, and the matter of the operation was going to be particularly challenging technically, never mind the complicated anaesthesiological aspect of it.

The latter because of Uncle Chimay's old tuberculosis affecting part of the joint, the diabetes, the heart, the kidneys as well as his hypertension. Apparently, the liver was bearing this strain remarkably well despite the cirrhosis of obesity. Vik would always indulge in a bottle of Chimay when with Uncle.

A parody, he thought, both on Uncle Chimay's religious tee-totalism and the fact that the Christian monks of the Trappist Order of Hainaut, Belgium had radically different ideas on how to achieve Nirvana.

In Vik's opinion, their four beers and their four cheeses were the perfect accompaniment on one's journey to Nirvana. Along with some bread, this was the perfect packed lunch and supper. The beers; the rouge, the bleu, the blanche and the one-fifty.

Pi entered the café with Kirk and Anju. Vik invited them over although Hygge East was empty. The seating style of this section was cushions galore on the floor, meaning this was usually the first to be taken despite it being less conducive to conversation than the classic round table of the north point of the café. As was Pi's habit, a general hello was followed by an enquiry of the elder's health.

Pi: How are you, Uncle Chimay?

Uncle Chimay: *Billcool saru ché*—everything is really rather very good.

The latter was added as he was aware that Kirk and Anju's Gujarati might not be quite up to scratch. Or even Pi's.

Uncle Chimay: Even my bowels are completely in the clear.

Vik: Really, we do not need to know such alimentary details, *Uncleji*!

Uncle Chimay: But he asked me!

Vik: Not directly. And anyway Pi, I must talk to you about your conversation with Edgar earlier. You were waxing lyrical about how Joyce in the Wake of whatever included many mentions of ideas with Sanskritic and Indic origins.

Pi: TS Eliot too! On the way to the toilets, I saw a mirror image of the notice and it spelt TS Eliot backwards almost! His *The Waste Land* had spurred on so many poets in my college, especially, because of the vindication of the Sanskrit language into mainstream poetry the world over. The word *Shantih* in its final lines. Echoed to grant and wish for peace. *Shantih, Shantih, Shantih.*

Vik: What are you blabbing about? It's also a spelling error!

Sensing a heavy discussion, Kirk and Anju sauntered off to the bar.

Pi: Yes, I did have a long chat with Edgar—is that not really interesting? The bits about the *Upani*—

Vik: You are unbelievable! Five thousand years of Indic civilisation and you need it to be vindicated by Joyce and others—really! I suppose that the *Bhagavad Gita* only exists as a backdrop to Oppenheimer seeing a nuclear bomb go off! It was a misquote anyway!

On returning from the bar, Kirk and Anju sensed that Vik was upset with Pi, although the conversation had moved on to things Vik-related—specifically his property businesses. Safe territory, thank goodness.

On the way home, Pi lagged a little behind as the Beck siblings planned an imaginary ski-trip. He wandered, lonely, but soon came across, in the grikes, the clover red, sorrel yellow and purple of the poppy, the eggs and bacon of the bird's foot trefoil and the direction home from the compass plant. He noticed a flash in the sky. A meteor, no doubt. And there was Jupiter, Saturn, Mercury, and Venus. His loneliness was cured. Tomorrow, he would go to the café again.

Kalushi

Pi met Kalushi at the café. Colourfully dressed Kalushi reminded Pi of the wandering Rabari of Rajasthan, Gujarat, and the Sindh desert. They would occasionally send a few of their tribe to sell intricate trinkets and bangles in Sundervagvela bazaar. These would invariably sell out once their prices became affordable. Kalushi, Kal for short, had come over from Ukraine via Germany.

He had been in Germany on a *Willkommenskultur Fachkräftezuwanderungsgesetz.* Everyone that talked to Kal would hear about his command of the German language, particularly these two words. This, the welcoming culture, and the new labour immigration law for skilled workers had allowed him to prosper and then move to Belton.

With Kal's presence, Belton was no longer devoid of a man who knew the ins and outs of everything from solar panels to barista machines to washing machines to cars to roofing to windows and even lawnmowers. Pi was always excited when chatting with Kal as he would discover so many words that adjoined his languages with German and even Ukrainian.

Kal had declared the bunch of allotment folk a coterie of plotters, a band of *demütig mitmachen volk.* Humble folk who got stuck into everything, especially anything local. This certainly made for an interesting life, if not a very diverse and extremely heathen one. The plotters would get stuck into anything and everything local.

The charity drives, the Disasters Emergency Fund projects, the Literary Fair, Safety at the travelling fairs, and especially any festival with an edible slant. The latter would be, not inclusively, Chinese New Year, Eid al-Fitr, Eid al-Adha, Diwali, Holi, Vaisakhi, Hannukah, Vesak-the birth of the Buddha and even Christmas and Easter.

Keke and Xipi

The same day, Pi also struck up a friendship with Xipi, whose thoughts and ideas were gratefully received by Pi. Xipi felt just so out of the world of Keke and especially Carmen, Keke's sister. Xipi's Trinidadian Indianness had installed a set of hybrid views that were rarely reciprocated by friend or foe.

The occasion of Navratri had been his favourite festival in the smorgasbord of festivities that the Caribbean community had offered. And why not as part of a dance whereby two rings of dancers danced with each other—what was there not to like? Each male would dance with each female, and eventually, every pair was possible. The dance had always reminded Xipi of nuclear particles hurling around each other and occasionally pairing, in that big doughnut that was CERN, hidden beneath the mountain betwixt Italy and Switzerland.

The cadence, rhythm and grace alone were hard enough to describe. The women's costumes themselves looked like they hailed from an alien designer shop. All the colours of the rainbow and some the creator appeared to have forgotten to put into the usual colour wheel. The diamond mirrors, the circular mirrors, the iridescent mirrors with jewellery befitting the Queen of Sheba. Not to forget the bells.

To Pi, the feminine was being celebrated here. A force that was always there for him, in the multi-potential that was the mother, the grandmother, the daughter, the sister, the acquaintance, the lover, the wife, the partner, the friend, the foe, the colleague, the niece, and the babies in his life, past, in the present and in the future.

With Navratri incoming, Xipi rehearsed the stories of the Goddesses that were celebrated. The purpose of which, in the main was to recall the details that he would no doubt need to know, as his two children would inevitably ask him. He was doing his part of their homework too. Were parents even allowed to complain that homework was becoming too difficult?

Was there home tuition for parents? An appraisal to ensure that an appropriate standard had been reached by said parent. Were holidays or sick days allowed? And what was a past reflective intense pronoun? Would a plumber or bus-driver or nurse or physiotherapist or retail assistant or gardener or a neurosurgeon ever really need to know or care about these things in the future?

Yet, they did not teach in schools how to make cheese on toast—what the posh called Welsh Rarebit. Or popcorn or pasta sauce or a curry (a basic right of all humans, as he regarded it) or an omelette. With complete coincidence, it was the NorthWalesFire.gov.Wales that ended up giving him a useful initial recap.

Quite why the North Wales Fire and Rescue Service were so enamoured with this festival was a mystery too difficult to solve in his time on Earth. The nine nights of the Navratri festival were dedicated to the worship of Durga, it said, but that he knew that anyway. What he did not know in detail, he was confident that Pi would help him. And did previously.

What Xipi was unclear about was the nine avatars. He liked all things avatar, the Vishnu ones, and the films with the blue beings. He understood more about the colours. A good many things were purple. Including the former artiste and his rain.

Maybe he could design a nine-coloured rainbow a velodrome depiction with 9 colours. Each of the nine Goddesses had their own colour. The *Pratipada* yellow of the spring Carlton daffodil, the *Dwitiya* green of our wild euphorbia leaking milk, the *Tritiya* grey of the pregnant cloud, the *Chaturthi* orange of the Dutch Royal carrot, the *Panchami* white of the bleeding stalk of daffodil. Nearly there.

The *Shashthi* red of the paper cut, the *Saptami* deep blue of the chicory petals, the *Astami* pink of the riotous Himalayan balsam—the escaped migrant. And the *Navmi* purple of the yeasted sloe. Which reminded him, it was nearly time to take his van up to Chalkstone Gorse and gather some sloes to add to gin and sugar to create his Nox—the nectar of Xmas in his house.

So that's why the costumes are so colourful and indeed the professional groups did wear a different main colour each day. The final day being *Dussehra*—the tenth day. The end of the battle of Goddess Durga with the evil of the Demon Mahishasura.

Xipi recalled that *asura* meant demon, so that bit about the demon probably wasn't necessary. And it had to be a woman that killed Mahishasura; as the creator Brahma had given a boon to the aforementioned demon that he could not be killed except by a woman. Macbethian, in its complexity of how exactly one could or not be killed, just a lot earlier. The battle had lasted nine days, hence the nine nights of Navratri. Pi was impressed with the overall knowledge that Xipi had and just had to fill in the details.

In the *Dandiya Rass* dance, if you particularly liked someone, the sticks would be played more forcefully, with added gusto in the steps and swirls. In fact, it was at a Navratri festival that Xipi had met Keke. This had been his quantum fusion moment.

The *Dandiya Rass* dance was Morris dancing on a different level and scale; although he wondered if the origin was in fact in some quiet corner of Caucasia. The bells and sticks were present in both.

The avatars were interesting but might be too much for his little daughter. Especially as many were terrifyingly depicted. There was the daughter of the Himalayan mountains, Ma Durga Shailputri, who rode the bull, Nandi. She is offered ghee to guard against disease and illness.

Anton joined Xipi just as he was having a quick smoke and imagining the nine avatars. Just outside the hall. Both settled down for a quick drink.

Anton: And Goddess Durga, presumably against coronavirus now, one would think. Pi mentioned her recently.

Xipi: I like Ma Durga. The Brahmacharini was the deeply meditative avatar with her sacred dried reddish-hued berries necklace of *rudrakh* and is it the *kamandalu?* She is offered sugar for longevity.

Anton: And presumably the sugar is out of one's home. Therefore, one does not eat it. One does not get diabetes. Longer life. Done.

Xipi thought that Anton must be a little drunk, especially as the usual banal pleasantries had not been exchanged and a camaraderie befitting a shared bottle of wine had already been established within seconds. Next was the 10-armed crescent mooned Chandraghanta riding a tiger; who was offered *kheer* to drive away pain.

Anton: I am not sure what *kheer* is?

Xipi: Rice pudding.

Anton: I'm still not convinced that would help with pain. Morphine helps. Unless you add morphine to your kheer, Xipi?

Xipi: Ma Durga Kushmanda, the egg of energy from which the whole universe was created. Her offering, the rich sweet fried bread that is *Malpua*. Offered for intellect and good decision-making.

Anton: Is this the Big Bang? I must ask around. Raj in the Big Bang Theory would know. If not, Sheldon always would.

Xipi had no idea what Anton was banging on about.

Xipi: Do I carry on? Or should we talk about you instead?

Anton: There's nothing interesting to talk about, mate. Let's just carry on.

Further flips in conversation led to the Goddess Skandamata. The mother of the peacock-associated Karthikeya, the God of War. Who was apparently fond of bananas and then to Katyayani, the sword wielder, the lion rider. Katyayani, so far, the most ferocious of them all. Xipi was disappointed that there were no more quips coming from Anton. Then to Ma Durga Kaalratri, who oddly rode a donkey. Her skin was dark, reportedly for an unexplained reason. Her third eye contained the whole universe. The internal eye was unlimited, to the edge of the universe and beyond. The offering for her was *jaggery*.

Anton: Not exactly a war horse, is it? Not that would have been my choice either. *Jaggery* is dried molasses, I believe.

Xipi: Correct. Apparently, it helps to bring happiness and the removal of obstacles.

Anton: We all need that.

Xipi: Goddess Mahagauri rode a splendid white elephant. Holding a drum and *trishul*, which signified perfection. Sesame seeds were offered to her for safety from natural disasters.

Anton: I think the devastation caused by Covid-19 qualifies—don't you think, Xipi?

Xipi: Yep, although we should have gone to Taiwan or South Korea and copied their strategies. They are almost democratic. Sorry, I got that wrong. Coconuts are offered to Ma Durga Mahagauri. It is the ninth avatar Siddhidatri (who sits on a lotus) who is offered sesame seeds.

Anton: What is the one on the elephant offered?

Xipi: Pi did not say.

That was a fruitful school day, thought Anton. Their following conversation brought them down to earth; with news of the toll of the virus and the migrant crisis and the rapes and shootings and the multiple wars currently ravaging Earth. A set of Durgas was certainly needed. Distracted as he was by the chat with Anton, Xipi did not dwell on his feminine side as he had often done over the many Navratri festivals he had been to since the age of 9.

The feminine energy at the festivities had been and was still palpable. Sometimes, the men would retire to the pub across the road, but the women would not be detracted and would continue with renewed energy.

Pi joined them and settled in with a Hanaa—the coriander-flavoured, hopped and non-alcoholic beer that had been the Temperance Bar's latest creation. It was inspired by the Belgian heritage of Anka, a new hire to the bar.

The morose turn of conversation had led to the obvious conclusion that men had caused all the problems of the world. Even in the Navratri allegory, it was Lord Brahma that had inadvertently caused the principal conflict by granting Mahishasura the boon of not being killed by anyone or anything but a woman.

It was eventually a joint conference of Lord Brahma as the Lord of Creation, Lord Vishnu as the Preserver of Creation and Lord Shiva as the Destroyer of the universe that had created Durga and commissioned her to destroy the evil-minded Mahishasura.

Xipi: Maybe the world will end because of the masculine ability to perennially cock things up. To warm up the world, pollute it, to stockpile resources instead of sharing the bounties of the Earth. It is a disaster.

Anton: And spread disease.

Pi: But there is hope. No? I can see a future where we grow much closer to perfection. The end of the world is predicted, but maybe only for men.

Anton: The virus certainly kills more men than women!

Pi: I hear that there is a process of parthenogenesis in nature. Whereby snakes and other animals, like birds, produce young without the aid of a male.

Anton: So, if we really mess things up, then evolution would occur in the manner that males would altogether disappear?

Pi: We are only halfway to being destroyed totally as the sun implodes or explodes—disappears anyway and we all become—what do you say— smitherings!

Anton: Smithereens.

Xipi: But will that be anytime soon?

Pi: In five billion years, give or take a few hundred million years.

Anton: So, I can sleep soundly tonight at least?

The Collective

On the way home, Pi joined Anju at the bar. They settled into a comfy seat, for the sole purpose of relaxing together with a drink or two and some *bitings* to wash away the bitterness of the hops. These were utterly cherished moments for them both. Today, in the green corner of the café, the WUBANA Collective were holding a meeting.

The Worker's Union of Belton and Nearby Areas. They were a prickly lot in their views. They had become powerful recently by officially joining the non-aligned worker's unions. No longer taken for granted by any of the big parties, each major party now jockeyed to help them.

The WUBANA Collective had successfully implemented fairer working practices in Belton such as overtime payments, improved health and safety and a chance to progress at work through up-skilling, and further general education.

The hot debate today was on how to sanction certain members of their union that appeared to be just a bit above the law to be arrested. Just below the radar of polite society to care. But very much below the human right standards adopted by the union. Koki, Aoife, Elle, John, Richard and Sam and many other agreed that the situation was universal but unacceptable.

The cancer was there, slowly maiming the foundation of their organisation. The WUBANA knew that at closing time tonight, the pubs would slowly become empty; with the beer-battered folks of a certain type moving on to battered fish and chips and battered saveloys, then home to their battered children and partners.

A situation alien to most and powerless to help with. Yet their subscriptions were in. Surely, we can could educate our own members? Graphic details, occasional deaths and injury details were shared. Another unresolved issue which would undoubtedly need to see the light of day again. Pi and Anju felt dismayed and helpless.

Pi and Anju went out into the starry night, both avowed to be able to name a few more stars as the nights became longer. The true glory of the night sky would be exposed on the coldest of nights when its covering blanket of clouds would come off and the naked sky was revealed. Both spotted Venus and Jupiter, the belt of Orion and several other constellations. Satisfied, they went their separate ways to bed.

Anton's Sit-Rep on Spikey

Instalment Six: August

Let's all eat out to help out! 50% of the bill was to be paid by the largesse of the Chancellor, which was initially served without a mask and then presumably, after paying the fine, appeared masked.

Gyms, swimming pools, and leisure centres can now all open too. Time to shed those risky pounds put on during the lockdown and the 64 million enjoying the great British Eat-Out. But was this not spreading infection? Or was it a cheap way to get the younger vaccinated by spreading the virus among themselves? We will never know.

Bad news as the educational gap between the social classes widens. But schools open in earnest to tackle the issue, possibly. Many businesses close. Including many of my favourite sandwich shops.

Portugal in the clear, no quarantine needed. But Austria, Croatia, Trinidad and Tobago are off the exemption list. Scotland, go independent and take Switzerland off the exemption list. But watch this space, things keep changing. Then later, you had to be quarantined coming back from Belgium, Andorra, and the Bahamas. But you can go to Switzerland, Jamaica, and the Czech Republic but not Cuba.

And thrilled were the footie fans who could now go and watch the Brighton Seagulls play the Blue Pensioners Chelsea, the band of 2500 non-Chelsea supporters, who saw a goal at 4 minutes and then nothing much except for a penalty save for the next 86 minutes. But that was more than enough for them, much more than enough. They were already promoted. Women's football is back with Chelsea playing Manchester City.

Incidentally, and uselessly, I now have a collection of 53 different insert labels from face mask boxes from Pakistan, Wales, and the rest from China. But we still do not have to wear the masks in most workplaces. Mine, yes of course. All of Pi's reading festivals have been cancelled though.

Not much usually happens in August. The end of the month sees a total of 53,805 or is it 41,499 dead souls due to COVID-19?

Chapter 8
Covid-19 Strikes

And when they are taken to task for these things, and many other unseemly
things that they do, they think that they have sufficiently discharged all their
grave burdens to reply,
"Do as we say and not as we do,"
as if it were possible for the sheep to be more constant and stouter
against temptation than the shepherds

The Decameron. Giovanni Boccaccio (1313–1375).
Italian Humanist and Writer

And then coronavirus hit Anton and Pi, almost simultaneously. They both complained at breakfast that they felt as if they had run a marathon overnight and had a few bouts with a very energetic Muhammad Ali. Each was then confined to respective single rooms—well ventilated, of course.

Ruth had to be dragged out of Anton's refuge, practically kicking and screaming. But it was the advice of her specialist General Practitioner, Dr Desdock. For Ruth was in possession of those rebellious antibodies that attacked her various organs often instead of any viruses at hand. Her calculated immunity was low, putting her increasingly at risk of the worst of all coronavirus outcomes However, all was quiet on that front, at the moment at least.

Anton felt fully vindicated with respect to complaining about his distress and pain. His female colleague, Dr Fiona Bayeaux, had posted, on Facebook, that her Covid-19 backpain was worse than the labour pains associated with the induced-delivery of her first-born.

Anton recovered as the weather improved, only for the household to be plunged back into sickness with Pi's go at the virus. His initial days were racked by pain, one that seemed close to that of the inquisitorial rack, thought Pi self-pityingly.

His brain felt all mushed and foggy and a panicked Pi started to recant all of the parts of the *Bhagavad Gita* that he had memorised. Was it accurate? None could surmise. Especially, chapter 2 in a morbid morose manner, those verses beloved of all at the Hindu cremation ghats.

It was reasonably clear that Anton must have picked up the bug via his on-call duties at the hospital on the bank holiday. That particularly August day; only 9 days after the day celebrating the tomfoolery of the response to it all. The ups and downs of the graphs on the rates, mortality rates and PPE supplies.

PPE, Personal Protective Equipment was no longer just the business of the smirking teenager thinking about their responsibilities in relation to contraception and preventing the evils of chlamydia, gonorrhoea, syphilis and other sexually-transmitted infections. But now the need to avoid touching teddy bears and banisters and library books but being crammed 150 to a stainless-steel tube hurtling at snail's pace to 60 miles an hour, or if you want 96.561 kilometres per hour, being allowed.

Through all 272 stations serving the 11 lifelines of the metropolis. And one more to open in the jubilee year to come. The line of Elizabeth. Masks were still a quaint, irksome folly of the faraway Southeast Asians. Suffer, as they would in the future, without the demise of their elderly population with all its attendant costs.

That weekend, Anton had done his usual rounds, but it was clear that 87 patients with Covid-19 would be a bridge too far for Dr Hoku Gurung, the imported respiratory specialist from the foothills of the Himalayas. She would have far more difficult decisions to make, however, on who was the illest of them all.

Brutally rational but ultimately based on the best fix equation for the resources available in terms of the intensive care beds (too few), the high dependency beds (plenty) and the staff (brave, terrified, but relatively calm and extremely competent). The new external management consultant had pasted a new slogan onto numerous hospital noticeboards. This month, it was—*non c'è coraggio senza paura*. Yep, no courage without fear. *Not so helpful, and please join us on the wards*—thought Anton.

Anton had dusted down his Sprague Rappaport stethoscope, and agreed to clinically examine and review the cases and report back to Hoku. For Anton could assess, think, plan management, but not actually write out the solution if prescription was required.

Much like most of us in society. In full advised PPE—for there could be no deviation from the cast iron rules of Sister Jo-Jo Wilson—the FFP3, blue gloves and plastic apron were in place.

Pi had calculated that the amount of plastic aprons, at one square meter each with one or two being used per day per NHS employee; in a year, this would be in excess of 600 square kilometres and therefore, be enough to cover the areas of the Isle of Wight ($380km^2$), Jersey ($120km^2$) and Guernsey ($65km^2$). The latter where Pi's hero had lived and worked for so many years.

The issue was (not obvious to Anton, rule follower that he was) that there were flaws in the infection control arrangements. Later inquiries would reveal that in comparison to elsewhere in the world such as Korea, we in the West had given the virus the status of a middle-weight boxer.

Hence, the suspected ability that we could take it on the chin, seeing this agile but less hefty foe. Elsewhere in the world, there had been containment areas. Staff would put PPE on outside the single room patient facilities, see a patient in a well-ventilated room, take their PPE off when going into another area, and then often going out into the fresh open air to wash their hands and having completed this, into work again.

This was a laughable aspiration for Anton. He had heard about this, having seen the film *Contagion* and knowing it was true to life in the faraway southeast. But we in the West preferred, it appeared to Anton, the dictatorship of the virus invading our bodies and killing us rather than comparatively benevolent human dictatorships that allowed *homo sapiens* to live in droves rather than die in them.

The illogic was that Anton went into the single bay of 6. This was six of the same obvious gender, same coronavirus status, for even in these trying times, the plagued and unplagued should not mix.

He saw all the patients. He did his *'SOAP'*. The subjective asking of the patient. Quite why this step was construed as being subjective and not objective was something he had never got a satisfactory answer to; other than to say it worked and patients were not always reliable witnesses to their illness and indeed even pain levels. Usually underplaying distress.

The objective co-location of data that was scientific—that is measurable. The vital blood pressure, oxygen saturations and the clinical examination. Then the assessment, a beautiful, constructed listing of the diagnoses and problems and whether in expert judgment the patient was improving or not. And the plan was a finale edict or a further attempt to sustain life.

Alas, the decision was often not to resuscitate. Although Anton had avoided the automatic call not to resuscitate people, such as the grand old Duke of Edinburgh, as they would be too old, too frail, and downright liabilities on the road.

Anton made mental notes. Later, these would be transcribed into illegible handwritten notes. There were international and national standards on everything medical; including the requirement to throw away thousands of unused but expired vaccines despite scientific evidence that these were still kosher and halal. But it was the printed expiry date alone that mattered.

There were no such standards as these, however, for handwriting legibility. And hence, Anton's clinical notes often attained the highest standards of patient confidentiality, incognito to all but himself. And often not even that.

Within the bay, he had changed his magic plastic apron and gloves in between each patient encounter. However, then came his near fatal error; he took off his mask and the rest of his PPE inside the bay, as instructed and absolutely mandated, washed his hands and exited the bay. It was presumably at this point that he had taken a few breaths of air from the bay, which was filled with the admixed expired air of the ill 6. All of these patients had been clad in a clear plastic helmet, which would then give them high doses of oxygen under pressure; or had a mask tightly stuck onto their faces to achieve the same effect.

Anton recalled their awful shortness of breath, the near drowning of them all. It was a very homogeneous disease, Covid-19. But his patients were incredibly resilient and stoical. When asked how they were, they would reply with Churchillian spirit, that they were doing better. Alas, their vital signs would often indicate otherwise—with the inevitability of death facing at least 1 or 2 of this band of half a dozen. Daily.

The impartial nature of the virus was demonstrated in the diversity of these patients, none of whom would ever have met in real life. This bay of six contained a retired miner, a recently retired Gurkha Major, a teacher, a care worker, a traveller tarmac-man and a Windrushed bus-driver.

Who would then share their final destinies? Which, was often death in a matter of days. And then adjacent to each other in the makeshift mega-fridges that served as impromptu morgues.

Yet, Anton felt that he was highly qualified and wanted to help. He was a doyen of the national drive that had essentially eradicated MRSA, Norovirus and the awful diarrhoeal *Clostridioides difficile*. The latter so-called as it was difficult to grow and resembled a bulged spindle. And now even more difficult to spell than hitherto.

Simple ideas of infection control had eluded them all. For a decade or so. Anton was particularly aggrieved as his hero Ignaz Semmelweis had been ignored again. In Vienna that had happened, in Victorian time, driven to despair he died broken in an asylum for the insane. He had been beaten up too and died from gangrene of the hand.

Louis Pasteur rediscovered the ideas and actually found bacteria and the rest is history. All the way through to even tinier invaders, SARS Cov-2 itself. Now obviously things were better, at least prior to Covid-19. Everyone washed their hands between seeing and examining patients. But oddly, thought Anton, only he ever cleansed his stethoscope between patients.

As a nation, we saw ourselves, unable to follow strict rules but dozily accepting of poor advice. We needed to be told that masks were important. We needed to be dictated to; though this was obstructed as our health pandits were forever tempered by the comings and goings of different politicians.

Hoku had effusively expressed that she was extremely grateful for the help that she had had from Anton. She would later email the clinical director stating the same.

A few days later, Anton came down with fever and a cough. He felt as though he had been forced to run a marathon and a bit more, such were his muscle aches and back spasms. If these were labour pains, then he was forever grateful to Ruth in yet another way.

This made him feel somewhat better. His positive result had come in just the next day after his test and he had been advised to stay at home. Pi was ill a day later. Pi was only unwell for a few days. There was initial delirium which worsened and as it worsened, Pi asked Anju to give him the two tomes of the sumptuous *Game of Thrones* to read.

This was a wise tactic as the books were a commendable 92 millimetres with the slipcover and the well-wrought and eventually well-drafted maps of the lands that would be on the minds of millions more than any other landscape including that of the Earth that they inhabited.

Enthusiastic though Kirk was, the TV series had been banned after the Beck parliament had met and Anju had vehemently denounced its gratuitous violence and orgies. Although the books had been read, none could be too sure that Pi would remember any of the details if asked about these 92 millimetres of reading.

Ruth was now the *de facto* leader of the household. As always, really, if truth be told. Anton was ill, very ill. He had last been struck down, oddly on an alternate day basis, when he had malaria as a student. It was delayed in its diagnosis as he told he had exam nerves. But this was worse.

He recalled that the last time he was off work for illness was rather a long time ago. This had been the day of him receiving his first wage packet as a doctor and then taking to the wine lodge as never before and needed half a day off. He had needed to be carried to bed. With his Covid-19 infection confirmed by antigen immunoassay, he had gone from the good health of a butcher's dog to a valetudinarian in two days.

Ruth: Let's all work together to do the best that we can for Anton and keep him at home. I understand bits of what we need to do. But not everything, so guys, any advice would be great.

Anju, Guru Pi and Kirk agreed to search various sites and other sources of advice and meet. Ruth made Anton's favourite soup of diced potatoes and mushrooms, and a toasted sandwich. Or shandwich, as Anton so often said, hailing as he did from Edinburgh in some of his schooling.

A motley crew of advice thus assembled, and put into place, Anton made an uneventful recovery. Most of the ideas were less immediately acceptable to Anton. Anton talked at the speed of Yoda but with the Queen's English syntax intact. And looked as pained as Marlon Brando talking offering godfatherly advice.

Anton: Pi, where is the evidence for the turmeric and honey steaming— please? What exactly do I do?

Cradling his hand, Ruth quipped that there also no evidence for paracetamol and revisited that the evidence base for parachutes was still lacking. Even the 1st Battalion Parachuters had recently acclaimed this on TV.

Pi: It is from the good doctor friend of your father in Sundervagvela. He has WhatsAppèd me. He has even sent a video. I insist never on anything else but please try. It is working so well in India.

Anton: I give up. What shall I do?

Pi: Nothing. We will do it for you, with you, *hanneh*. Boiling hot water is there. One litre, into a bowl. One teaspoon of the best ground turmeric.

There was an interlude where Kirk told Pi about the redundancy of saying ground turmeric as that is how it comes. Then Pi explained that turmeric could be used in the same way as ginger when fresh and was often used in pickles. Pi went onto to mention other members of the ginger root family such as the more subtle fragrant galangal for noodling as Pi put in. The culinary conversation was brought to an end by the thousand words of disdain expressed by the picture of Anton's eyes.

Pi: *Achsha*. Good, boiling hot water is there. One litre, into a bowl. One teaspoon of the best ground turmeric. Then a full finger stick of honey. Put you head over the bowl. Heavy towel on top and that is it. Sorry but I forgot the salt.

Ruth: And a full finger stick of honey is?

Guru Pi: Well, we dip a finger into a honey pot and stir in. Or nowadays, many people will use a stick like a finger to do the same.

Ruth: I am sure that Winnie the Pooh would be proud of that method of getting honey out of a jar.

Pi questioned the Winnie Pooh mention and Anju said that she would explain later.

Anton: How long for, Pi?

Guru Pi: Well, strictly speaking in my culture is for the *Gayatri Mantra* followed by the *Aarti*. Twice daily please.

Anton: I give up. Ruth, please can you advise me. What is Pi banging on about now?

Anton slipped back into slumber, exhausted, brain fogged as he was.

And thereon hence the Beck household was introduced to the mighty *Gayatri Mantra* and the *Aarti*—the daily hymn or blessing or communal singsong at daily pujas solely, in families, temples or a few hundreds of thousands at a time and occasionally a million on the shores of the Ganges at so many places including Haridwar, Varanasi, Gangotri and on other rivers such as the Hooghly, aka now the Kati-Ganga, in Kolkata. Please note that the 2013 Kumbh Mela Festival, on the Ganges had 120 million people attend over several days.

Pi elaborated that Gangotri was near where the mighty Ganges descended from the heavens its flow modulated through the dreadlocks of Lord Shiva. Ruth recalled that Cyrus, whoever he was, was mentioned as doing something similar in finale of George Eliot's *Middlemarch*. She had forgotten the details. Was it all this communal gathering and singing that later could have had a part to play in the daily dissemination of the Delta variant at the Kumbh Mela? I do not know. But Anton thought it likely.

The Aks and Lakshmi version, with the query mother of one of them, was judged to be the best version of the *Aarti*. The translation was passed as *pukka* by Pi. The *Gayatri Mantra* was spoken by Guru Pi followed by the 5 minutes and 12 seconds of the *Aarti*. So, it was about 6 minutes.

At the end of the 11-day illness. Anju knew all the words of the *Aarti* off by heart. And could be heard singing some of her favourite lines, especially whilst walking in the garden feeding the birds.

Om Jai Jagadish haré — Om, Praise to you, Lord of the Universe

Bhakta Janon ké sankat — Dispeller of all the sorrows of your devotees

Kshan mé duur karé — These You banish far far away in an instant

Kashta mité tan ka — Any suffering of the Body and Mind is removed

Tum ho ek Agochar — You are the Invisible Power

Sabaké Pranapati — Of all breathing life

They all worked together, even more seamlessly than before. They had a collective endeavour to keep Anton as well as possible. When washing up, Anju noticed that Pi was frustrated. One of his washing-up rubber gloves was wet inside having punctured. As often is the case, it was the right-handed one. Anju quickly retrieved a left glove from the many collected under the sink and blew it inside out.

Anju: This will work for now, Pi

Pi: Ingenious! This reduces wastage!

As Pi smiled at her, Anju felt as if she had been handed over the Noble Prize by the King of Sweden for *Advances in Digital and Manual Compartmentalisation Device Reconstruction Engineering in a Crisis using the Inherent Intrinsic Property of a Levo structure to invert into a Dextro structure.*

After the recovery breakfast, Pi, Anju and Kirk remarked on how Ruth had been the force that animated the household to a different conductor and seen Anton through. Ruth would not take any praise though. Through the Scylla of keeping Anton at home and monitoring him and improving him to the Charybdis of needing hospital with all its well-meaning and often successful treatments but also wrought with unintended consequences.

But Anton had sailed through now albeit *sans taste, sans olfaction, sans power*, and lacking that certain sharpness in his thoughts—the brain fog. During his illness, Anton had reviewed all of human existence through reading Tales from Shakespeare by the Lambs. His four big themes, and there does need to be others, were all there.

Love, Sex, Power, and God. Anton re-entered the lives, trials and tribulations of Hamlet, Portia, Shylock, Beatrice, Cordelia, King Lear, Othello, Desdemona, Juliet, Romeo, Nick Bottom, Ophelia, Polonius, Puck and the Macbeths. And his favourite of all, Katherine.

But his would be an untamed shrew played by his favourite actress Josette Simon. The beautifully illustrated edition was highly recommended to Pi. Pi rejoiced it was 51 millimetres thick and read it during the prolonged recovery of his illness.

Anton's Sit-Rep on Spikey

Instalment Seven: September

There is an enthusiastic start to the months with all the schools opening. I have to say I am impressed with the work that Marcus Rashford is doing to combat child food poverty. I feel that I can no longer tell you about the countries on and not on the quarantine list. It is too difficult to follow and keep accurate.

More than six in a meeting and it's all over. This would be against the Law of the Rule of Six. But I hear, source secret, of parties within the governing party. Surely not? Especially as the Home Secretary declares that families stopping to talk to each other in the street or park would definitely be in breach of the Rule of Six Law.

Captain Sir Tom Moore gets busy and inspects soldiers at a graduation ceremony at Harrogate Army College. Dogs are now more expensive too.

And then Spikey starts the second wave itself. An idea, from the Stasi, of informing on the neighbours unsurprisingly does not take off. Net curtains oft were twitched but the misdemeanours of neighbours were not snitched on. Street drinking becomes fashionable, as imbibers of alcohol get disinvited from pubs at 10pm.

We have trouble, at one point over a hundred new deaths a day. Local lockdowns are back.

The world is changing. The rising cases have created a Hokusai Tsunami on the daily graphs that appeared on TV. And the death toll a weekly 2004 Tsunami. The latter of the height of 23 metres, 23,000 Hiroshima-bomb detonation power, and the 230,000 lives lost.

Death rates. *Only the 998,867 deaths and maybe (definitely) tomorrow a million just before October starts. World 33,173,176 cases. UK 439,013 cases. 42,077 deaths. USA 7,122,754 cases. 204,825 deaths. India 5,990,581 cases. 95,542 deaths.* Were all counted everywhere? What about the lonely deaths? The Eleanor Rigbys of the world?

Next year, it will all be over, thank goodness. I think the vaccine is on its way.

Chapter 9
Mainly Anton

If you want a happy ending that depends, of course,
on where you stop your story.

Orson Welles (1915–1985). Director, Actor, Screenwriter and Producer.
Quoted in *The Week* from *The Times* (2022)

Ruth on Anton

Ruth wondered when it was that the silicone rubber expressiveness of Anton's face had changed. In the spring of their relationship, Anton's mind could be read from the lift of his eyes, a squeeze of his eyes, a billow of his nostril, or even a twitch of his philtrum.

He had the most splendid expressions of his Cupid's bow. And that had ensnared her willingly into the rest of his life. It had all been sealed, Cupid bow to Cupid bow, vermillion to vermillion, gently and passionately, one day at college. And then, forever, on the holiday in France. But now his face appeared vulcanised into a much-reduced portfolio of expressions.

Many, a little low in mood. The causes of his consternations were not clear to Ruth. Was it the ongoing and relentless dementia of his father? Or the earlier death of his mother—or current issues at work? Anton had never felt fully at ease in these modern times of progress.

For all good reasons, but something irritated him. What he found especially irksome was that he would never be able to rise to the higher echelons of the world of microbiology. In pursuit of academia (especially the genomic sequence of the bacteria that caused human disease *vis-à-vis* canine and feline disease), he had not completed the stipulated seven years of higher training.

Known as the brainiac of his peers and the only one with a PhD and an Associate Fellowship of the Academy of Sciences, he had the discomforting distinction of being paid a quarter less than his duly qualified medical colleagues. He had some ideas that had been reported a long time ago but not developed. The square Petri dish, to grow microbes in, was one such invention.

He felt perfectly allocated to a position at work where the little people of Lilliput tied him down and hindered his progress. Where the Brobdingnagian giants essentially ignored him or squashed him underfoot. Ironically, Anton was also thinking in parallel with regards to all things Swift.

Should he recommend the travels and travails of Gulliver to Pi? He felt that the swift answer was no. There would be little to overlap between the mind of Pi and the Dean of St Patrick's, Dublin.

Nevertheless, Anton was the rock on which Ruth had built her life. And what was happening now was a melting of the face into just these extra distinctions of expression and especially the less straining smiles when Anton spent any time with Pi. Ruth was even jealous at times. But only ever fleetingly.

Anton had told her of putting a certain Damyenti on a pedestal whilst he was out there in Pi's town. But it was not that at all. It was the fact that Anton saw in Pi, albeit reluctantly, a human stripped of the concerns of promotion, mortgage, tax, education of his children, the leaking conservatory, the failed investments, the deteriorating car and the death of family and close friend. One by one. Some tragically, a quarter of a century too early.

Pi seemed to live in a world inhabited only by all things good. The cares of his world were limited to spending his allowance, reading, chatting with his friends, generally wandering around Belton, digging for his coterie of mates at the allotment, planting the occasional tree, and spending time in the Temperance Bar and the City-Zen Café.

Pi was truly the opposite of a *schadenfreude* being. In fact, he was quite the opposite. The word in English eluded him. And when Pi wanted a higher level of stimulation of the GABA-receptors in his deep brain, he enjoyed the non-temperance drinks at the Gate.

He admired the Teflon personality of Pi that all could rest on him but never stain him. Anymore metaphors like that and he would be emulating his hero Professor JVT even more.

Anton was also rendered irate by the increasing death toll of the UK and the Western world in general. How could the countries that produced 90% of the world's scientists in the field of virology and disease control end up in this fix? It was beyond belief that the smaller so-called tiger economies were doing so well.

He fixated on his theory on why and how he had caught the coronavirus. Infection control advice from on the highest in the land had been followed to the letter and detailed iota. Otherwise, he could be instantly suspended of course. He replayed the mind's film of event that day, over and over again.

Anton has been advised to enter a bay of 6 Covid-19 infected humans, in a full gown, double-gloved, fully masked and visored. Then to see the patients and examine them. He would perform the rarely observed rite of cleaning his stethoscope between patients. He would, however, always wear his often frowned-upon tie. But it was not too much of a catastrophe, as his was always tucked away.

Then after the round of six had been completed, he would discard his gown and his current set of gloves. Take off his mask. And breathe in a few droplets of speech and the breath of patients soaked with the virus no doubt. And then exit through the same door. An email from a colleague in Korea outlined his different precise journey at work. Walking into a bay, through a door, into a hallway. Into the bay of potential contamination. And then out through another door into an outside corridor to decontamination. Then he would disgown and decontaminate and re-enter the hospital.

It was good exercise too. Although most ill patients were nursed in their own individual rooms, and rarely in the barrack style of our nations. Anton was sad that he did not give clinical care for his patients in well-ventilated clinical areas.

Although these nations had rendered the Bali, Javan and Caspian tigers extinct, their sense of all things viral decontamination was still very much intact. Our ill-advised stock approach was happening in all the hospitals of the nation. And in many other nations too. This was what was really stressing Anton. The notion that he was totally powerless and unheeded.

The Visit to Beck Senior

As soon as possible after recovery from Covid-19, Anton went to visit his dear father. Anton knew that his father's layers of thought were being slowly eroded away. The most recent first, by the winds of change, in true geologic form.

The contents of breakfast were not as fast and indeed totally disappeared but not the first day at school, first love, the marriage, the birth of Anton, his siblings, the tragedy of the loss of his wife.

Anton had been referred to as Pujji. That true hero; who was albeit of a dark latte complexion in real life. So, it was not Max this time but Pujji. When quizzed on the beaches, the score was a mere 60% that day with the forgotten Utah and the 23,000 landed US personnel and Omaha, bloodiest of all with 2412 dead.

The British Gold and Sword, and Canadian Juno were all remembered. And to us many, who would give such little, the allied 4414 dead and the equally dead enemy. After tea, normal service was resumed, and Anton was called Max again.

Beck Senior: Max, Max, Max—it's just great to see you! This may be the end you know. They told us at breakfast that there would be no more visits.

Anton: Good morning.

Beck Senior: One of us died, you know. Suddenly. He was only 91. Fit as an old fiddle—ha ha!

Anton: It's the virus—Dad. It's me, Anton.

Beck Senior: What virus? We have always had them; they cannot kill us. Unless we for some reason need to die.

Anton: There is an awful virus going round. It started in China, but its official name is SARS Cov-2. Severe acute respiratory syndrome coronavirus 2. I do not think severe is a good enough moniker—it should be called DARS Cov-2. It is deadly, not severe.

Beck Senior: Could have started anywhere, Max.

Anton: Well, it was China. In the wet markets. Live animals for eating *vis-à-vis* dead ones. *Vis-à-vis* live humans and now dead ones. Enough to drive anyone vegan or so we thought. The market has re-opened.

Beck Senior: Don't worry, we can take it on the chin, and all will be well. That is what the PM said, or so I am told. We have survived many wars, you know. I will be happy, I think. To not see so many people that I do not know. That do not say hello. And many are actively rude.

Anton: I hope you mean the visitors and not the staff.

Beck Senior: My Gloria and Becky are lovely. Sidney is a bit off today. Amali is never here in spirit. Problems back home, I think.

Anton: Can I help?

Beck Senior: Probably not.

The conversation flitted from shore to shore. Landing here and there and to take flight again. Breakfast, lunch, and the evening meal were not recalled. Through the walk, again not recalled and the bitterness of his lost career. Especially his sacking from being a director when the firm got taken over by a huge global behemoth. It was Jonah swallowed by the whale, never to be spat out.

Max was the one person who Anton almost despised with utter admiration. Another person to *schadenfreude* again. The lucidity of prose and historical capture of the epic battles in such devastatingly mundane factual terms but veined through sparkling with humanity was just too much to bear, but utterly brilliant.

Anton recalled Max's Armageddon and now his father's. The cognitive decline would be his final decisive battle and the defeat would herald the *sans everything, sans toute* predicted. The invading army of the *tau* proteins would tangle up his thoughts and aspirations and memories of the past, present, and future into a congealed mess of despair, frustration, anger, and grief. And incontinence. It made for a harrowing combination. His memory was being hacked, with a clearing out of the present first and then an extension of its tentacles into the past to taser it byte by byte. Then, hopefully, would come an unknowing. With the inevitable, death, sedated by nature and aided and abetted by psychotropics. As if the brain needed altering at all.

Seven days later, his father did die. The funeral was a paltry band of 6. That was all that was allowed at the small chapel. The body was not allowed to be seen by the family and friends and carers. Even if in privately-resourced, relatively-adequate, barrier PPE.

The virus could be held at bay by a plastic apron and a mask and eye protection whilst in front of a coughing patient with life in their lungs. But apparently, it was still dangerous lurking in the dead cells of a lifeless pair of lungs, never to breathe again.

Anton on Children

Anton very much hoped he had been a reasonable son. He thought about children a lot in the days following the funeral. Anton had shared his ideas on children many a times with Sir X, Mark to Anton. Mark too found considerable solace in talking to Anton on the same and other subjects. Mark's knighthood had been stripped or rather dissolved away. For one of the standard politicians' crimes.

People had been openly gleeful. But to Anton, he was his best friend, flawed or not. As long he was sincere in his regret and good with his family. Crime and punishment was over, as far as Anton was concerned. Back to children. Anton had found them a gift in the Khalil Gibran trope of arrows to fling well nurtured into the future of humanity as the guardians of the planet and its contents. Hopefully, at least.

Unfortunately, Sir X had not been so lucky and had had rather different children. Despite the extra tuition and the years spent at private school, his boys had been monstrous, and indeed had been in trouble on more accounts than the speeding fine which was the zenith of Mark's usual criminal behaviour.

He felt that the boys could have been modern-day future non-violent Krays for all the disdain they had shown in all matters civic. Sir X was clear. Babies were developing computers that had experience drummed into then by well-meaning parents.

Then only for the kids to start thinking for themselves and go AWOL in relation to all the benevolent intentions that had been expected of them. He was just so angry. His wife had committed suicide on learning that their eldest had been arrested on a heroin peddling charge, but the downward trajectory had started when Hugo had started peddling his home-grown cannabis and the parents had turned a blind eye as to what was happened a far corner of the paddock.

To Anton, consciousness was just the accumulation of experiences—visual, auditory, olfactory, touching, tasting and the internal ruminations of which the final result was a life. Your life. A unique life. Some more unique than others. A computer developed over times. Sometimes it went to sleep. Organised itself. Dreams were the overnight pressure valve of the brain's spare energy.

The brain jogging itself before waking afresh, ready to reboot. Dementia was just the expected downward memory gain from the peak that was Mount You. A few children, he felt, were just juvenile delinquents. And accurately listed in the synonym dictionary as offenders against good humanity, crooks in society, thieving felons and breakers of the law and hearts and minds and souls. He was so utterly grateful that his children were different.

Anton and Sir X shared the malts during this particular conversation. Sir X, the ardent whiskey drinker and Anton, the whisky drinker.

This shared agenda meant that the spirits accompanying their chats were not just respectively Irish and Scottish but now and then stretched to the Indian, the Japanese and even the Welsh Gold.

Anton was sad that the universe had not blessed Sir X with the joy of Kirk and Anju. Especially Anju, as Kirk was Ruth's favourite. Or so it was claimed at their family breakfasts.

Benedict had also contributed to the most recent discussions on the subject. Sir X's brother, Benedict visited Belton only infrequently, nested as he was, alone in a tiny little village in Wales, which had the sole positive attribute of having two well-functioning pubs. He would use time efficiently when in Belton and almost always managed to spend a few hours with Kirk and Anju as he was particularly fond of them.

To them, being an arborist and planter of trees himself, he would espouse the benefits of trees versus children. The former needed no costly upbringing, not too much emotional investment and could always be relied on to never talk back and be ready for a hug anytime.

To him, it was a no brainer. It was also better for the planet. But he loved Kirk and Anju. And sometimes when he saw them, he wished otherwise.

The Juggler

Anton was dropping the serotonin. He recalled an educational video of a mime artist juggling serotonin, dopamine, acetylcholine, oxytocin, and a few other neurotransmitters. When the serotonin was dropped, the artist had become depressed and had mimed so very expressively as to rival Pierrot.

All was resolved when his androgynous partner turned up and gave him a peck. And so, the mime had continued. On dropping the acetylcholine, dementia appeared. The dopamine balls went higher, and mania ensued. There also CART. He had heard about this one only recently.

It was a pleasure centre. He really had to further explore this cocaine—and amphetamine-regulated transcript peptide idea. Eating, drinking and all other rewards were linked in. Some more so than others.

The bag of chemicals that was his brain was suffering from the anxieties of work. His Covid-19 illness was segueing into the vaguely described Long-Covid condition. Coronavirus had knocked him out so much more than the originally prescribed taking it on the chin. Anton had been particularly affected by the image that was currently replaying in the cinema of his mind on a loop.

These sometimes could only be shut down by alcohol or Ruth or sleep. The loop presently on repeat was of Inad, the refugee from Afghanistan that his hospital trust had hired with pomp and ceremony, to many accolades in the local press and regional TV.

To be honest, the trust had had a major shortage of certain staff. Not many locals were interested in giving up a guaranteed income to have to work 35 hours a week and come out better off by only £45. However, he was so very grateful that many of the hospital staff did, indeed, do that.

Anton had gone to the shower rooms. They had the cleanest toilets and were only used by a handful of cyclists. Currently, it was too chilly for cycling and the electric bike revolution had just started but was too expensive, so they could pretty much be relied on to be empty.

Inad was in the corner of a shower, quietly sobbing with her face turned to the corner. She quietened on noticing that Anton had come in and walked into a cubicle, hiding her face.

Anton: Hi Inad!

Anton was not one to know the cleaners in his hospital personally but the huge yellow badge that could be read from 25 metres away was pretty useful. He did however know the names of all the cleaners that worked in his department at the hospital. His favourite interview question came after the interviewee had been lulled into thinking that they had it in the bag.

He would then ask them the name of the cleaner in their current place of work. A candidate had once even seen it fit to answer that the only reason, he did not know it was because the cleaners did not have name badges such as in Anton's hospital.

Anton: Can I ask what the problem is, and I will at least try to help?

Anton was confident that he would be able to solve this issue relatively easily.

Inad: I am fine. Really.

Anton inquired as to whether it was to do with work. Inad hinted that it was in fact work-related and that her family were doing very well now that she had a job. Inad had been so very grateful for any job. She could not now work in her own country of Rumi, as the primary school teacher that she was. Essentially, the genetic abnormality of too many X chromosomes.

Anton: I am the Hospital Lead for infections—is it related to Covid-19?

Inad went on to explain, very slowly and diligently, as if she was on trial, how on her very first week at work she had been allocated to the Intensive Care Unit but that as she would not be less than 2 metres from a patient, a white FFP3 mask was not needed.

A blue one would do instead. She had been upset that Sylvia, another cleaner had been off ill with the virus and had now been admitted to another local hospital very ill with it. And dying.

Anton, feeling completely disingenuous to himself, explained that the white FFP3 mask was not necessary for her and that the blue surgical mask would do. It was official national policy. So, it must be followed as it would be scientifically correct. We are an advanced nation. Anton felt otherwise but could not really express his thoughts to anyone.

Anton knew that he had completely failed to allay and reduce both Inad's tears and fears. He did not believe that current PPE was adequate despite the edicts of Her Majesty's government. There were issues of ventilation, the air exchanges and the still prevailing belief that the surfaces carried infectious doses of the virus and that the airborne theories in relation to the transmission of this virus were not generally accepted.

So much of the government's advice was a mixture of science and politics. The pandemic in the UK was being run via political science rather than scientific politics. Often the worst possible mixture of the two, it appeared, at times. But at the best of times, he felt hopeful for the future as he read the news and emails from his colleagues in Oxford and London that vaccine development had been much faster than anticipated. The Turks and the Germans had really worked well; *zusammen* rather than as *gastarbeiter* and were probably heading for a Nobel Prize.

The world could be one when needed. Anton felt a little optimistic. He usually thought of the world as dying. One factor was the political cancer that was all things Palestine-Israel. This was his personal political obsession. He had borne witness to the amity of the Arabs and Jews when he had stayed at the Kibbutz many decades ago and had felt so optimistic.

But he had been young, and the world was indeed rose-tinted. The geopolitical cancer that had spread from an insignificant (geologically and oil-wise) and yet, a most significant part of the world where the first crops and settled societies of humanity had first arisen.

The cancer that had spread to trains and then to the bus outside Tavistock Square in London—as Mahatma Gandhi had looked on—and claimed 52 lives and several hundred injured. The unresolved problem from the clarion call that was from the demolition of the Twin Towers, with the abrupt ending of 2763 lives and the almost 500 rescuers. And the Kenyan Mall and the Taj Hotel and even to New Zealand.

Anton's Curriculum Vitae

Anton was going through a time of reflection and deep cogitation about his life in the aftermath of his Covid-19 infection. Anton was bemused and somewhat in despair. He had done all the right things in life. The private education gratefully received without drugs, expulsion, or a pregnancy with the local lovely ladies.

The highly governanced and useful work for the labs, despite the outdated and dysfunctional equipment and the paucity of the latest better antibiotics at times. Always with the chronic 'beck-breaking' work as Beck Senior so often alluded to.

His was to serve because the elders in society, the college chiefs, and the occasional chiefess knew what they were doing. But now, he was the older, more experienced, wiser generation, and little progress had been made beyond yearly changing platitudes, with the occasional 3 steps forwards then the sneaky 2 back to save that little bit of money or assuage the durable influential MPs.

There was the early starter programme that quickly got withdrawn. The increase to the retirement age and the royally endowed honour to the civil servant who saw through the changes, who then retired early! Anton was just so irritated, vexed even.

Why was there not even slight positive movement on the year-on-year line of progress that was set out, agreed and adhered to? If not in our best of the flawed forms of government, then where?

Anton started to wonder and wander after his two large glasses of the mid-range, but perfectly adequate, Chateau Neuf Du Pape—*why was that just so-called?* thought Anton. *Was it the ninth of the papal Chateaux in the vineyards of the Catholic Christian God, whilst Protestants languished in the Lambic and Saison beers of northern France and Belgium?*

It was clear to him that a mission statement was needed. He now had Kirk and Pi as his audience, albeit with smaller glasses. Ruth and Anju were bonding elsewhere.

Unbelievably, they were making samosas and talking about its similarity and difference to the Cornish pasty and the kachori. Having discovered and accepted their philosophies of life they did not have to waste time in the manner of the Chateau Neuf du Pape triad invariably would end up doing.

Indeed, Anju and Ruth could have written a paper for the World Journal of Gastronomy. Its working title would be The Homogeneity and Heterogeneity of culinary skills, gastronomic appreciation and nutritional content of a staple: An exploration on the Cornish pastry, samosa and the kachori.

It was clear to the triad that a mission statement for life was needed. Or maybe more than one; or two, or three, or more. As not everyone from the materialistically, educationally and often spiritually disenfranchised, through dint of accident of birth would become Premiership footballers or somehow win the national, Euro or global lottery at the odds of scores of million to one.

Kirk told the group that the kids of Santanu Varan and Keke Swizekle had both enrolled into the city academy in their respective gender groups—and were being paid the median wage of the UK at the age of 17. Along with a part-time scholarship at the sporting lyceum supreme that is Loughborough University.

Kirk: So, they can become doctors and lawyers if they score enough goals!

Anton: Only doctors and lawyers if they are no good at scoring goals, actually.

Anton thoughts were rather random. Surely enlightenment could not be found through working at the supermarkets, other tiring retail work, toils in technology, building and IT? The trials of tribulations of healthcare and education; were they a better path? Or could this be found in building, policing in any form, travel, helping you eat and drink and be merry?

Or in arts, music, novels, and poems? Or in gardening, or nature; forests and shores and seas and rivers and streams and mountains and glaciers. Or maybe it was impossible to find until retirement. And then to mundane reflective activities such as gardening. Pottering in the fashion of India Knight. And doing jigsaw puzzles. And scrapbooking, cataloguing lives lived. Yours. Mine. Theirs.

Anton knew that to Ruth, it was clear that a Monty-inspired utopia existed in faffing around in the garden, plus or minus lazy dog. And that crocosmia, gowri, begonias, the bees, beetles and spiders were the citizens of that place. These were the little lamp-posts that illuminated her every day, lighting up the dark corners of a fashion magazine-described humdrum life. Easily switched off at night without the aid of any substance. The faf. The flora and fauna, and everything else of life.

Later, Pi and Kirk continued with some threads of the conversation.

Pi: Alas, it is just not a problem I have seen in India. The older just appear to get on with it; they have no other choice. They have the solace of prayers and its communality of spirit.

Kirk knew that this idea of Pi's was patently not true. The naïve universe that Pi appeared to have come from was not extant anywhere much outside of Pi-land! The volley of fury that he had gleaned from his friends at the City-Zen Café created an image of India where there was internecine violence of the body, mind, and soul.

The internecine differences wrought by religion, caste, historical, economic and gender differences. Kirk even wondered whether the general populace in Sundervagvela had protected the all-too-well-meaning Pi from the worst of life. He had been protected probably, in a lite version, of how Prince Siddhartha Gautam was protected from all things unsavoury by his father, the King.

The Prince, later to become the Buddha. But only after having experienced and seen all of life's reality around him via the four signs of the old man, sick man, the corpse on its way to the cremation grounds, and the monk in meditation under the canopy of a tree.

Even the second bottle of wine did not resolve anything. Surely, if resolution was possible, then we would all be hermits wrapped up warm in the Lake District, Cairngorms and the Black Mountains? That would not be a great result for the vineyards. Or the stock market.

Or the local pubs and restaurants and cinemas and theatres and churches and mosques and temples and synagogues and parks and even the rubbish tip. And what if we developed acute appendicitis? To work the next day was a daunting reality and Anton declared bed-time.

Petri Dish

To Anton, the Petri dish, that every single person who was involved in anything scientific would have paid at least scant attention to, could be confined to history. Why? Because he had invented the Beck Plate. Petri had had enough time in the books and common lore.

130 years in the microbiological limelight was overly sufficient. The agar enhanced with blood, salts, carbohydrates, amino acids and various indicators. Fleming had discovered that bacteria were killed around some inadvertently introduced fungus, presumably from the gonorrhoeic and syphilitic streets of Paddington where it would prove so useful in the future for clients and workers alike. This had just happened to land on a Petri dish and then, penicillin would be discovered when he was decluttering his workspace.

Anton's middle name Julius was shared with Petri's first name. This had been purposefully intended by Beck Senior. History could therefore see it as a seamless passing on of the microbiological baton, for at least a few more decades. Petri had only written a 300-word paper on his idea.

Anton's presentation on the square dish ran to 3000 words and the paper to a little over that. His Beck Plate was a square dish. The mathematical rationale being that the easier tessellated fit of these was more space efficient and furthermore allowed the bacteria and fungi freer rein to wander. A somewhat further distance to judge the rigour, success and often, failures, of the antibiotics set against them in the dish.

Pi was minorly acknowledged in the paper as he had calculated the percentage space saving and the fact that the bacteria could edge a further 21% into the corner recesses of the square dish.

The potential for antibiotic choice being expanded was there. It had even been calculated that 11% less incubator and fridge space was needed now. These ideas he had published in a peer-review journal, albeit for a small fee.

Anton was in a foul mood. The subject of his ire was Stephen Fletcher, his chief lab technician who had decided to dress down the day before the visitation to his labs, by the CEO of Gagarin Pharmaceuticals. Dieter Templeford was to visit the lab and see the Beck dish in action. He wanted to buy up the patent, produce and improve efficiency in labs everywhere. The initial pilot would be local labs, clinical, teaching, and research. And then the world.

Anton: I do not care whether it is fashionable or not. This is against the code of smart professional attire that we all signed up to. Fashionable means *à la mode*. The mode is the middling idea. Therefore, usually the worst, because most of us still aspire to mediocracy!

The point of discussion was Stephen's socks. They were deemed too short for the visit.

Anton: When you meet a CEO such as Dieter, you wear real socks! He sincerely does not want to see your ankles.

Stephen: But I aspire to a world where we use less material—this is surely a greener solution?

Anton: Then stop eating those disgusting burgers in my lab. Go put some real socks on!

There was little point in talking when Anton was in such a mood. Octavia and Seni had been reprimanded, earlier in the day, for their attire and excess facial piercings. And the tattoos that they could do little about, ever. Neither did they want to, ever.

Anton had rarely engaged in badgering his team, but he felt that it was justified as so much hinged on the visit. This visit was potentially a critical juncture in his life. An invitation to leave behind a significant invention. To see his artifices in all the microbiological incubators and fridges the world over. There would also be saving of plastic and energy resource. He would make some money, possibly.

The actual visit of the potentate of all things laboratory did not please Anton either, for the fully socked team were greeted by a mop-headed brunette in a loose cheese-cloth shirt, corduroy trousers and sockless sandals. Dieter arrived with a small entourage in his Lamborghini Bravo—a very mustard yellow one.

He had come in an inflatable jacket that was see through. Later, Seni pointed out to Anton that the jacket was a prototype worn initially and modelled by no less than Rahim the Sterling and then produced in a batch of only 25 to be sold to the very deservingly wealthy only, at a £2495 plus Vat.

True enough though, the Beck Plate had been well accepted by Dieter, clad as he was. The idea sold for a handsome £75,000. To be shared 50:50 with the taxman and the hospital.

Instalment Eight: October

England divides among the old Anglo-Saxon and Daneland ideas and there is more alertness here and less there, with Manchester particularly upset for reasons outside of football.

Abdullah of the World Food Programme gets the Nobel Prize and weeps. The irony of getting the prize for peace when it was war that caused almost all the hunger in the world. He presciently warned of all things COVID-19 affecting the near future of his work in the war zones, refugee camps and COVID-19-stricken areas across the global village. The latter an idea for sharing markets but not necessarily relieving hunger.

Now, coronavirus deaths are greater than AIDS, though still a little less than TB. For now. The years of life lost still numbered less than poverty, diarrhoea, accidents, suicides and AIDS. *There was yet no vaccine for poverty, diarrhoea, accidents, suicides and AIDS,* thought Mark and I together. But Mark just wanted more growth and wealth and it would trickle down to the masses in due course.

There had been a lot to upset us in recent times. The deaths were mounting, local, national, global. After early promise, the vaccine had been delayed. Bodies were floating dead in the oceans and rivers. In 2020, a simple virus could not be controlled. Never mind everyday human tragedies. The end of this month heralded a total of 63,451 UK deaths on most calculators.

Mark and I also agreed, after much debate, the conclusion to the COVID-19 enquiry that will inevitably happen and cost a tenth of a billion pounds or more. It was written by a certain Russian, many years ago.

Germans are self-confident on the basis of an abstract notion—science, that is, the supposed knowledge of absolute truth.

A Frenchman is self-assured because he regards himself personally, both in mind and body, as irresistibly attractive to both men and women.

An Englishman is self-assured, as being a citizen of the best-organised state in the world, and therefore as an Englishman always knows what he should do and knows that all he does as an Englishman is undoubtedly correct.

An Italian is self-assured because he is excitable and easily forgets himself and other people.

A Russian is self-assured just because he knows that he knows nothing and does not want to know anything, since he does not believe in the possibility of knowing anything fully.

Leo Tolstoy (1828-1910) War and Peace. Book 9: Chapter 10 1812.

Chapter 10
The Strategy of Reading

I believe humans should be plants.

Notes. Yi Sang (1910–1937). Korean Poet.

Pi at Breakfast

November 11th was one of Pi's favourite days. There was sadness to it today, for sure, as it he was missing his brother, Ishverlal's, wedding anniversary. It would have been his wedding anniversary. The family were juxta-positioning at breakfast, each to their tasks, synchronised breakfast making at its best, worthy of a medal.

Pi: The doff bread is just great! Just amazing; especially the Stilton one from Bellvoyer.

Kirk: It's sourdough from Beaver.

Pi: No—I mean this one. It clearly states Sour-Doff from Bellvoyer.

The label, sourdough from Belvoir was duly paraded in front of Kirk by Pi.

Kirk: No really, it is pronounced sourdough from Beaver.

Pi: This is illogical. How can you teach children to read when the rules make no sense?

Ruth then Anju and then Anton all lined up to the Kitschen brand whiteboard.

Ruth: This is tough-tuff, rough-ruff, enough-enuff.

Anju: Bough is bow, cough is koff.

Anton: And this is Luff-boro—spelt Loughborough. Not Low-bo-ruff! Or indeed Loo-bo-roo.

Kirk: So, when I say that Keke is my soul-mate—could I mean fishy sole, footy sole, is he from Seoul, or we both adore soul music, my deep friend, or is he the only one?! And if I say I love you—is it that I love ewe or yew or even you! It adds mystery, you see, Pi. English is thus very creative.

Pi: That is still illogical. But thanks a lot. I think English would have benefitted from having its own scholar. In Sanskrit, we had Panini who sorted out all the grammar and pronunciation, scientifically and logically 2500 years ago or so.

Kirk: Panini is a bread too!

Anton: Yes, but think of all those extra English teachers that are needed! English is also so much easier to type having only 26 letters. If all the accents and larger number of letters are counted, then Sanskrit and Chinese both have several thousand letters. Hence, English takes the title of the *lingua franca*. Ironically, it is not French! A pukka Hindi or Mandarin typewriter would need 120 keys, or so I have been told.

Ruth: Italian, that most expressive of languages, has only 21 letters. There is no J or K or W or X or Y.

Anton: I think the lack of letters explains the hand signals needed when speaking Italian! Even on the phone!

The conversation switched for some reason to the Bitcoin.

Anton: Some countries are thinking of using it as a legal currency. It is the biggest con in history. It is not money that makes the world go round, it is the exchange of goods. I give you this and you give me that.

Ruth: It is not as catchy though is it, Anton. We actually sing 'Money makes the world go round, world go round, world go round'. That is surely better than the exchange of goods makes the world go round, world go round, world go round.

Kirk: Yes, but money itself is a con. The dollar, pound, euro and all the big currencies are exchanged to each other commensurately to the work of an average worker in that society. But not so to the Rupee, Naira or Rands. This means immediately that the work of a Nigerian, Indian, or South African is valued less. The Bitcoin in a future avatar could potentially get round this.

Anton really did not like it when the young were so succinct and could see through the rubbish of prevailing ideas, but he was extremely proud of his son. And daughter.

After breakfast, Pi read but at exactly 11 seconds, past 11 minutes, past 11 in the morning, he took two minutes silence with the Beck household. This was the actually the first time in his life he had undertaken this observance. He was distracted by something that his brother had shared with him many, many years ago.

The fact that 111,111,111 multiplied by 111,111,111 is 12345678987654321. It reminded him that the full potential of one could be that magnificent number. And also, of the ebb and flow of the latter number always reminded him of the spiritual opulence of the universal form of deities depicted in the *Bhagavad Gita*. Then to the exhibition.

Because

There was an exhibition of new writers at the Belton library. Many writers were popping in and out of the pork pie-shaped library all week to sign versions of their written *opera magna*. Pi, with chagrin, recalled his humiliation at the reception of his little book. It had had a print run of only 250, at the price of only Rs 75.

He wanted to hold a collection of hitherto unprinted, uncommunicated works by himself specifically and his favourite stories of Beck Senior. Pi was very pleased that the book still had a place of honour on the Beck bookshelf. Next to Dostoevsky on one side and a Tagore collection on the left. Ironically, the Dostoevsky was The Idiot. Pi wondered whether this was Karma indeed. The expression of the law of singularity and entanglement.

The poems were admittedly dire, bits and tranches and diatribes of the young communalist romantic that he was. This was the official review in the college journal and specifically of the journal *Literature: North, East, West and South*.

At best, the prophetic utterances were mocked, and others were sung to altered rhyme with the worst swear words chucked in. The simple 'Tinned people pollute the air I breathe' was rendered into quatrains on human emissions rather than those diesel and petrol.

The most distressing incident was a video recording that had made the rounds and then had later been re-enacted many times in college. Often whilst Pi was walking down a corridor. A variety of students and the occasional teacher would overtake him and scoot into an empty classroom and start the sketch grouped around the chalkboard, the 'teacher' with a pointing-cane in hand.

Nothing original, of course. That, they were incapable of. But gleaned from the original on the Tube you all use. The oldest or the most teacher-sounding of them all would stand in front of the blackboard or in the innovation suite the whiteboard, back-arched, stern, and head thrown back.

Teacher: Classroom, namaste! Welcome to the English language spelling class.

The teacher would take a gentle bow of reverence to the class of students. Usually less in number than the toes of a camel and equally educated.

Students: Good morning, Sir. Namaste!

The students would then respond with even more reverence. Taking in all the body language of the teacher. Along with an obsequious head bob.

Teacher: Please repeat after me. B.

The teacher would begin writing each letter in turn.

Students: B.

Teacher: E.

Students: E.

Teacher: C.

Students: C.

Teacher: A.

Students: A.

Teacher: U.

Students: U.

Teacher: S.

Students: S.

Teacher: E.

Students: E.

Teacher: *Buckvass*!

Students: *Buckvass*!

Teacher: The book is complete. It is complete *buckvass*—there are no bits missing at all! It is the very dregs of the literary dreck!

And the teacher and students would keel over in a deep-felt cruel laughter. For *Because* was the title of Pi's book. The mispronunciation, *buckvass*, the national word for all things rubbish and useless, total, and utterly so. The professional reviews printed, and now archived forever, were no less cruel.

Although the scholar in Pi made him wonder whether the word *buckvass* had anything to do with buckwheat and *vass*. Was *vass* water and *buckvass* a Proto-Indo-European word for beer? And therefore, *buckvass* was what we verbally regurgitate when we are so drunk? He knew he would never know for certain.

Good Progress

On a brighter note, the recommendation of the librarian at the Belton library was a useful 28 millimetres and to boot as oft discussed in book clubs throughout the world, it had allowed Pi to enter the life of another without the hours and weeks and months needed to establish a friendship with a character so out of the orbit of his experience.

No time travel machine was required either. Pi and Kirk remarked that there were many such people maxed out on their credit cards and bored senseless as their nature ordained brain had been exercised so little beyond the seams of experience via media—some social, via TV, more TV, films, and films galore vis the endless choices that eventually distilled to the one more disappointment so often.

And then the amputation of their lives and careers through being the almost sole carer for the next generation. Another truism also manifested itself. Oft quoted—sex happens in novels and then children in real life. The book was Gustave Flaubert's Madame Bovary.

Madame Bovary's humanity shone through brightly, and Pi lay awake in bed thinking through the dilemmas in her brain and the universality of the tragedy predicted. There was this utter realism that Pi found in this and other novels that defined, for him, a deep but bridgeable division.

Bridgeable with the sort of dangerous rope bridge that Indiana Jones would have had to overcome in the dying minutes of a film. On the one side of the chasm were for him the huge and splendid libraries of myth, legend, and spiritual thinking tomes with their tales of valour, romance, despair, death, and comedy.

But these were the infrastructures of development that were a commonality to a group of people defined by geography, religion or ethnicity or culture. It was the novels that had provided a collection of personal programmes to imbibe or not into his experiences for the future.

Novels were far more personal, but both were needed. A sharing, then a personalisation. A re-programming or more hopefully just a version update. Restricted as he was from reading Tolstoy, at least so in this first year of reading fearlessly, Pi was enamoured by many Tolstoian Quotes.

Especially, as he learnt that Leo had had a deep friendship with Gandhi, the Mahatma, no less. Many could be amalgamated and thus pages appeared in Pi's notebooks:

Everyone thinks of changing the world, but no one thinks of changing themselves.

Wrong does not cease to be wrong because the majority share in it.

If you look for perfection, you will never be content.

If you are not enjoying your work, either change your attitude or change your job.

If you want to be happy, be.

The only thing that we know is nothing and that is the highest flight of human wisdom.

Pi was confident that the above could be rendered into a slow, soulful song by his nightingale-voiced sitar-playing colleague and friend, Mirabai, back in Sundervagvela.

Next, Pi read a Brontë. And not having chosen Emily Brontë's Wuthering Heights or the higher acclaimed Sister Charlotte's Jane Eyre, Anton was offering Pi a way out of being Brontëless in his Life on Earth. That Pi liked books about servants was an added bonus to Anton.

It is true though that Anne Brontë's heroine *Agnes Grey* was a spirited woman who tries to rise above the quagmire of convention, gender-rights and all things Victorian whilst working as a governess. If unmarried, this was the only path to tread.

Untouchable by Mulk Anand took Pi back to the familiar pasture of his everyday life back home that was still happening in India, reworked all over the world in different settings and translated into many languages with many different actors. A world discombobulated for Bakha the cleaner of latrines—the *Bunghee*.

The lifelong imprisonment, granted and adjoined to his life at birth, the one of those proven guilty of the crime of being born an outcaste. A heraldic shield inherited that could feature the sewer pipe and the sweeping brush. Disconcertingly to Pi, the *Bhagavad Gita* offered the reason for Bakha's being doomed to the lowest rung of the caste ladder. It was his Karma. Pure and simple. A result of prior deeds.

Pi cringed. He was embarrassed. Memories flooded back in, and he belatedly winced at the slaps that Bakha had gotten for forgetting to ring a bell to announce his approach on a public road, or accidentally touching a person of a higher caste. Bakha had not gratefully welcomed his God-given pariah status. All from his caste were thus treated.

There was the ignobility of the beautiful Sohini having to wait at the end of a queue determined by caste again when collecting water at the well and then later assaulted in body and soul. But treating everyone equally, featured an awful lot in the *Bhagavad Gita* too.

Maybe the idea of Karma was just an ethical ploy to make everyone behave, thought Pi. Or maybe in the long run it all pans out. Pi recalled one of the heroes of the *Mahabharata*, King Draupad, eventually getting his revenge on the almost unconquerable Drona. A mega-war, all for an insult.

The final book in the trilogy of servant books was Umrigar's *The Space Between Us*. A beautiful and poignant dialogue of the servant, Bhima and her mistress, Serabai. A water and oil that could never really fully mix. To his mind, these three books were a testament to the craft of a real writer.

The books had made him direct a film in his mind's eye at a pace suited to the ruminations of the thoughts and actions of the characters. With actors chosen from his collection of humans met to date in person, play or film even. One clear choice would be Amitabh Bachchan as the untouchable, although he was a little too tall and well nourished. And Mahatma Gandhi had appeared in a cameo shot too in the *Untouchable*. That part could only be played by Krishna Pandit Bhanji, again.

A credible and worthwhile 57 millimetres had been added for the triptych that were the 'servant books', as Anton called them. The three covers made an impressive photo to speed across to update his brother, Ishverlal.

Sir X had given, he said, special dispensation that the odd 'H' volume, in the literature Nobel Laureates series, would count as 3 books. In the scheme of Pi's actual task, this was of course immaterial as it was the height that would be final arbiter of achievement, not the quantity of books.

Pi devoured and felt enriched by Hamsun's *Hunger,* Hesse's *Siddhartha* and Hemingway's *The Old Man and the Sea*. The three H authors in a single volume. Nobel prizes all. This led to the only Nobel Prize for Literature for an Indian, Rabindranath Tagore being re-read by Pi.

Pi could easily have read and often re-read books by this Gurudev. The Nobel Prize had been won for Gitanjali. But there were plays and novels and a collection of paintings and drawings. Anton showed him a copy of Gitanjali with the author designated as Sir Rabindranath Tagore. This book was from 1918.

After the Great Peace, there was the debacle and loss of 379 lives and thousands of lives wrecked on the day of the Jallianwala Bagh Massacre by

General Dyer. Tagore had felt self-compelled to give his knighthood back, 4 years after the King had bestowed it.

Tagore, the founder of Shantiniketan, later Visva-Bharati University in Calcutta (later Kolkata) also had in his immodest outputs, a handy three National Anthems. The Indian and the Bangladeshi and the (heavily influenced by the former) Sri Lankan. All this was a favourite même of Pi's.

Sir X could not believe that Pi was entirely happy sharing the above with him recently. Without blame. He had however felt blamed about this particular massacre. Pi in his simplicity just liked the story, historic though it was.

Pi read Tagore's longest of his twelve novels, *Gora*. Intriguingly, *gora* means white and could be considered an attempt to meld all that is best of the West and the East together. Its discussion ensues on all things under the sun and more—the meaning of life, the meaning of wife, the meaning of friendship, spirituality, and feminist discussion.

Pi thoroughly enjoyed this book. The film of the travails of *Gora* and Sucharita, Lolita and Binoy repeatedly played many a time in the cinema hall of Pi's skull. *Gora*, at 33millimetres was fair progress.

Progress, Conjoint with the School

There was confidence in Pi. His trajectory was upward. Characters had been archived, their drab or colourful lives thriving in Pi's mind. He felt them to be his forever friends. The aspired full height of books seemed within reach. Even at the Ellie Elementary, progress was going well.

It was the sponsored responsibility of the school to undertake a reading height of 143.75centimetre. The latter being the average of the 144-centimetre tall 11-year-old girl and 143.5-centimetre boy.

Anton had been taken on to give advice to the Ellie Elementary and the local library. The local library had shut again because of Covid-19. And was then delayed opening due to cuts in finances. But now it had opened. *Evidence from science had been used oddly,* thought Anton.

It was true that closeness of people would and could lead to infection. But then masks were not advised generally at the beginning. Yes, the virus could survive on paper, but to an infectious dose. Not sure. The books were to go into quarantine for at 72 hours then released for circulation.

Anton had created a complicated spreadsheet to catch and document the first infection from a book and then gave up. He knew it was a talking with, breathing with disease. Not a disease caught by reading, or touch alone. Usually.

Anton, as a governor of the school had blessed and encouraged Pi's reading project for children at the school. His donation of some mini biographies proved to be a big hit at the school. Sir X, in reckless rejoinder he later surmised, had even donated half the value of the books in hard cash.

The Beck household, Pi included of course, had chosen the lot. A veritable smorgasbord of the illuminati was represented. There was the black, brown, white, man, woman, and child, a cosmopolitan tribe of the famous.

Among these were the illustrated books of Rosa Parks, David Attenborough, Captain Tom Moore, Stephen Hawking, Amelia Earhart, Martin Luther King (Junior), Anne Frank, Albert Einstein, Bruce Lee, Ada Lovelace, Kobe Bryant, Steve Jobs, Frida Kahlo, Marie Curie, Coco Chanel, Maya Angelou, Emmeline Pankhurst, David Bowie, Michelle Obama, Mindy Kaling, Ru Paul, Hans Christian Andersen, Kamala Harris, Marilyn Monroe, Rosalind Franklin, Andy Warhol, Ruth Bader Ginsburg, Jane Goodall, Mother Teresa, Agatha Christie, John Lennon, Michael Jordan, Zaha Hadid and Harriet Tubman.

Greta Thunberg and Malala Yousufzai were the most thumbed. Anton bought a copy of Audrey Hepburn for himself as well, and Ella Fitzgerald to distract attention from the ever-vigilant Ruth. Pi had complained. He rarely did. He was affronted by the fact that the BBC Man of the Millenium, Amitabh Bachchan, and on a different note Lata Mangeshkar, the latter having recorded 39,119 songs was not given this particular prize of being the central character in a book in this collection. Maybe the West, were more aware of Inquilab Shrivastava as the son the famous poet Harivansh and Teji, in Allahabad or now Prayagraj?

The local press was covering this idea. Photos of children posing around books made for good press, and sold papers. A classroom of children would immediately launch the sales of an extra 100 papers, at least, for the parents and the often even prouder grandparents, uncles, and aunts.

A flurry of bibliophilic adverts helped grease the wheels of commerce. The height of 143.75 centimetres had been achieved within a term by the schools and therefore there had to be a reset. Each class would take on the challenge of reading the average height of their year within a year or less.

Lots of photo opportunities meant lots of sales, and for the children, lots of reading done. Guru Pi was to give out medals and belts to the children. Ellie Simmonds had, of course, been the first choice. She had promised to come along in the future, saying she wanted to start reading again too.

The sponsorship from immigrant businesses had been generous in this regard. They especially recalled the unaffordability of books in their childhoods, having often floated into business as a route to their *roti, kapada aur makhan—* their food, clothing, and housing.

Sir X had reviewed Pi's early progress and had rejected double inclusions. There were two Umrigar books. He stated that he had clearly stipulated different authors. He also complained that some books were over-illustrated. Sir X pointed out that if they were all the ilk of a Michael Connelly or a David Baldacci then even, he could complete the task in a year. He announced that he was reading *How to avoid a climate disaster* by a certain Mr Gates and told everyone that he had written to this author to suggest that he should write a book on avoiding pandemics.

Another triad of books was rushed through that month. In quick succession, he read *The Vegetarian* by Han Kang, which interested Pi as it was the story of an anguished being who had, unexpectedly to family and friends and against the flow of her society, decided to change her diet as a protest against barriers to her personal freedom, and common human cruelty.

The bonus being that a book from Korea had been read, albeit that of the sister of the northern bit of the country. It was intriguing to Pi that the book had been reviewed as 'bizarre'—it was surmised that changing diets for this reason was difficult and improbable. Nevertheless, it had won the Man Booker International.

And hence, the recommendation by the slowly drifting towards veganism that was Anju. To Pi, it was about an unread book that would now never be forgotten having been etched, indeed pyrographed into his mind. The call was of the taken for granted spouse who throws off her shackles and declares, as crafted on a Wedgwood plate—*Am I not a Man and a Brother?* Then to the re-awakening of her body (detailed), mind and spirit.

Interested in Korea as he now was, temporarily at least, he read *The Book of Masks* by Hwang Sun-won. The author born of the country of the brother in the north but from when the family lived under one roof. Pi learnt of connectivity of the past and present, the young and old, the sacred and banal. This particular tribiblio was completed with the reading of the deeply disturbing, but fascinating novella of falling into a senility—*Diary of an Mad Old Man* by Junichiro Tanizaki. Alas, all three only added 37 millimetres for the tower of books.

He wanted to read more of Han Kang's books, but the stipulation was that only one book per author counted towards the height. She had written her books with great pain—from her repetitive strain injury. Possibly, the last handwritten book. It could be read, of course, but he was behind on his trajectory. By at least around 3 weeks.

To hurry it along, he read *The Spy who came in from the Cold*. This *Le Carré* was so tightly wrought and brilliant that it would put off generations of would-be writers. Quite how he had managed to write it in 5 weeks was well-nigh on unbelievable. And he had had a full-time job.

Anton had discussed this at breakfast and concluded that the author clearly did not have a manager or appraisals to prepare for and must therefore have been free to work, rest and play. Pi imagined himself on Friederich Strasse at Checkpoint Charlie, delivering humans from the warm constricted pre-ordained confines of the East to the cold freedom of opportunity in the West. On both sides however, it always appeared to be raining. The same rain.

Some of the reading was undertaken at the allotment. It was often cold though and damp to boot. Watching the plotters coming in from the world, beyond the plots, where there were bills and debts, loves and deaths, bad news (some good), the continuing and growing menace of Covid-19, the looming of yet another death, yet another funeral. Two plotters had died, John and Peter, both would have had another decade, at least, to enjoy their pastures.

The Le Carré was a reasonable step in the right direction at 37.3 millimetres. Accurately measured courtesy of a cost-efficient supermarket digital caliper. It was a scrumptious Folio Edition. But to further accelerate his book-worming, it would have to be books from the burger van library of Xipi.

Old Man Xipi had a van and on that van, he had an eclectic collection of well-thumbed books. He felt that his customers were so unreasonable. No one would come for long stretches of around 2 hours and then the hordes of the hungry would descend impatiently. And if he had prepared 24 veggie burgers, then the demand would be for 11, and if he had prepped 12 meat burgers, then 24 would be needed.

The wastage fed the homeless at least, that he encountered on the sojourn home. His own diet was largely dependent on what the customers had not bought off him that day. The healthy bit of the meal would be being prepared at home; completed with his input, of course.

In fact, the option of a free salad with a burger was very rarely taken by the clientèle. In fact, the burger van advertised its food as *Junk Plus*. The acronym was that burgers were the Juxtaposition of Unbalanced Nutrients Kind but that the Plus of his salad of leaves, vegetables and seeds made it ideal. Or so he thought. Anton had told Pi that Xipi was technically correct. Salad was often supplied by the plotters, grown with love and devotion, but sold cheaply.

Xipi accelerated Pi's progress with the recommendation of another exciting and even thicker 400-page Michael Connelly, the bit longer and absorbing John Grisham and then the thrilling *Da Vinci Code*. A very useful 93 millimetres that was not to be sneered at.

Pelé

Pelé was a slow read. But Kirk had recommended it (and had underlined his favourite parts in blue) and had borrowed it from Xipi (who had bought the book and had underlined his favourite parts in a furious smudgy red). Pi decided to underline in pencil.

An HB pencil; easy to rub out if the need arose. Pelé was dying. Although Pi argued that Pelé would never die in the human psyche until another football avatar would exhibit such brilliance and win three World Cups. Possibly never, ever.

Another book from Xipi was *Natives—Race and Class in the Ruins of Empire*. It was imminently suitable on both the score of high recommendation, prior underlining to facilitate understanding and dialogue with the previous readers and most important of all, the 28 millimetres height. That was a perfect kaleidoscope of learning.

Pi admitted in discussion that he had been deeply ignorant of the rich tapestry of folk that made up the UK population. The teaching and viewpoint in India (especially through that most important of sources, Bollywood) was that the UK was a White country.

Usually populated by well-meaning people who were in no immediate competition to the love interests of the hero and heroine who would languish in UK for a few years, studying or working. Always to return home. In reality, Kirk knew that these erstwhile British colonial subjects of old would settle as soon as allowed to aspire to generate the next generation of doctors, accountants, pharmacists and business entrepreneurs, especially the very successful ones. A Prime Minister was predicted from this nouveau generation in the media, printed and virtual.

The point of Blackness being an autosomal dominant trait in modern thinking was apparent in the books, but to thank one's lucky stars, no longer legislated and defined. Apparently, in 1910, anyone with 1/16, (Pi calculated 6.25%) or more pure Black blood—would be defined as a coloured or mulatto.

To be White, you had to have pure White blood or no more than 1/16, 6.25%, American Indian blood. The rules relaxed in 1930 and the Virginians removed the mathematical stipulation, replacing it with the apparently more humane definition of there being just the evidence of 'any ascertainable negro blood'. But what had been underlined, circled with an adjacent fish hooked exclamation mark was the word Pelé.

Kirk and Xipi had done some research. It would appear, to them at least, that Edson Arantes do Nascimento (admittedly a mouthful, making it difficult to scold him at school or home) was called Pelé as he was a *pelé*. This was the novel idea that Kirk and Xipi claimed as their own original one.

As a child, Pelé was called Dico by his parents, then Pelé because it sounded like the local hero Bilé—the Vasco da Gama goalie. Kirk and Xipi, after reading the Akala book, felt that they had discovered a hidden gem of a controversial story.

Kirk explained to Pi that *pelé* was just one of 500 possible racial subtypes of Brazilian society. Other racial variations included; *branco, claro, cabo verde, roxo, gazula, roxo decabelo bom*. So that was why he was called Pelé. In an otherwise excellent book, both Kirk and Xipi were perplexed as to why the genius of Akala had missed this point.

Alas, Pi recalled that in India it was the same, and just incredibly more subtle in all other societies in the world. A distinct pecking order would be established very quickly and usually with a degree of harmony but not always. Pi despaired that, very obviously even in Sundervagvela, there was *homo sapiens sapiens var varan, modh, modi, dhobhi, mistry, mochi, khumbar, patels* (various village numbers, various religions, some claiming descent from either Lava or Kusha, the twin sons of Rama and Sita). The Sikhs also claim descent of their Gurus from the sons of Rama and Sita. All complex.

He wondered whether the post nominal *sapiens* applied in this Anthropocene world; whether it had ever applied or if it was just a self-conferred title. As in the

His Excellency, President for Life, Field Marshall Al Hadji Doctor Idi Amin Dada, VC, DSO, MC, Lord of all the Beasts of the Earth, and Fishes of the Seas and Conqueror of the British Empire in Africa in general and Uganda in particular.

Kirk had also picked up the *Good Immigrant* by Nikesh Shukla. In fact, he had purloined this from the Temperance Bar as he had forgotten to sign it out. The bar had a photo of the author with older relatives, parents—mother in a saree, and three co-authors. This was signed by the quartet of authors and had pride of place above the small bookcase.

Pi was riveted by these three books, and they were all finished within a week. He felt that sitting in the Temperance Bar, or the pub, or the café, he would be observing the characters in *Natives* and *The Good Immigrant* flitting in and out of these social stations, as would the potential Pelé or Beckham or Vardy or Bronze or Earps. The latter four, dreaming at this stage, walking past the windows, tired after playing on their way home from the soccer games in the recreation park. Pi wanted to catch up with Anton. Pi felt he had not seen enough of Anton recently. They had grown closer together after they had both gone down with Covid-19. Their plasma antibodies were commendably high and both had started to donate plasma for clinical trials. *Today*, thought Pi, *Anton would undoubtedly be in his study*.

Anton on Bugs

Anton had a big passion, as one must have. As Darwin had his barnacles and later the Origin of Species. Linnaeus in his classification of life itself. And Marie Curie, not forgetting Pierre on all things nuclear. Anton was going to finish his work, unlike the fictitious Casaubon in Ruth's favourite book *Middlemarch*, who had never quite determined or finished the Key to all Mythologies. More later.

Hence, he must continue to take the statins for which he thanked fungi again. Apparently, as Dr Alkuhs had informed him, they would on average give him an extra 4.1 years of life. The 95% confidence interval being 4.2 months to 7.8 years. It was probably worth it. He did not have the muscle pains that Sir X got with statins and was on some other medication.

Anton recalled his buying of the statins through the private sector for his father. Statins were a little too expensive for the NHS at that time. *Rightly so*, thought the slightly right-wing Anton. He could afford the £41.33 per month.

Admittedly, the Chateau Neuf du Pape had disappeared off the domestic wine racks and had been replaced by bogofs at the German supermarkets.

If so desired, then 80% of us could afford these drugs. By saving on our lifestyles. By buying a less salubrious phone or putting up with a few less than the 93 paid-for TV channels, perhaps. Each tablet could provide 43 extra minutes of life. A good quality of life at that. Full-stop, end of story.

The rest could have them for free if authentically unaffordable. Anton was never unkind, not on purpose at least. But now, we could all have them. Thank goodness for generics. Anton's real excitement was that the drugs had originally been extracted from micro-organisms. It was all about the bugs.

Pi walked into the study. Anton, for all his external armadillo crustiness, was always happy to be visited in his den. As long as it was on his own terms and conditions. He had grown fond of Pi. Pi noticed that Anton was making notes on index cards.

Anton: It's all here, Pi. It's all about the bugs! The microbiology. I think we know less about our microbiology than we do about the moon, planets, and stars in the universe. Such nonsense, our so-called learning! There is so much we don't know about the trillion bacteria inside all of us.

Pi: You must write your book, dear Sir. I will certainly make sure that all the students and faculty are recommended it as my personal choice on the yearly roster of recommendations that I am allowed to do as a founding academic of the institute.

Anton: Thanks for the advance sales, Pi. No accolade of Sir, please. But look; here we have In *Jane Eyre*, Helen's tuberculosis. My favourite patient would be—Ippolet. He also had tuberculous in Dostoyevsky's *The Idiot*. My favourite of his tomes. In real life DH Lawrence, Anton Chekhov, Emily Brontë, Frederic Chopin, Robert Louis Stevenson, George Orwell, and Franz Kafka all died from TB. John Keats, of course too. In this Maggie Farrell book—I think Hamnet dies of the plague. As Shakespeare's son probably did. And in Roth's Nemesis, we had the polio-stricken character of Cantor. Who never marries as he implores his fiancée to leave him?

Anton knew that he had to pause for Pi to start talking.

Pi: Exciting extra material for your book. What are the bugs causing such devastation?

Anton: Not a book. A DSc, and then the book. Some books are not for you to read—just yet. They are not thick enough! Get cracking with stuff that will add height and just be easier to read. My old paperbacks are just tough on my old eyes at least. I want you to succeed.

The DSc might just be too difficult an undertaking for me. I want to be a proper historian. A little bit of a Max Hastings or a James Falkner. The bugs in the illnesses I just mentioned are, respectively—*Mycobacterium tuberculosis*, *Yersinia pestis* via the flea *Xenopsylla cheopis* and that via *Rattus rattus*—the rat! The last is the polio virus—*Picornaviridae enterovirus C*. You that polio was called the Heine-Medin Disease originally? Polio just means grey in Greek!

I wanted to be more than the clinical doctor I wanted to be as a kid. I wanted to be a proper doctor.

Pi: What do you mean by a proper doctor? You have a medical degree *hanneh*?

Anton: *Hanneh*? Let me tell you a story.

Anton told Pi of his career trajectory that had sky-rocketed a little too quickly in his early years. He had left clinical training after 3 years, seduced by the limelight of research and higher academia as a researcher, a discoverer of new knowledge.

He had gone on to explore the role of gut bacteria and parasites on nitrogen fixation (where the parasites or a word that he had invented, but never caught on—*symbiososites*?) Anton had simply woken up one morning with the realisation that all human bodies were just the stuff of rain, air, solar energy, and bits and bobs from plants and animals that were also created from the materials of rain, air, solar and some earth elements and micro-organisms.

Essentially, we all need nitrogen to fix via bacteria or plants or both and make protein. Or does the gut do that too? This had created a frisson in his small world, and he had embarked on his research. It did not quite deliver, and he had ended up as a clinical microbiologist, not as a senior clinical doctor.

Despite the many awards and the papers and the initial grants, they dried up when the topic was no longer à la mode. For Anton, the peer-reviewed life did not work. He had learnt from Ruth to be himself and not compare, although it had its benefits. With a smirk and a grin and a smile, Anton told Pi of the oft repeated remarks of Edgar. The impersonation was somewhat less than perfect.

Anton as Edgar: *If I want to look tall, I stand next to the diminutive Peta. If I want to look slimmer, then I stand next to the even more portly Curtis. If I want you not to notice the hairs in my ear, I stand next to Vivek. One day, I want to meet my perfect friend. The three in one!*

Pi never did work out the meaning behind this remark or what Anton had intended to communicate. But he had enjoyed the conversation and time spent together.

Doubts

Later, relaxing and reading, Pi recalled meeting Anton for the walk home. Pi had gone for a solitary walk around the lakes and then picked up Anton from his usual Thursday evening sanctuary that was the Liberal Conservative Labour Club. It broadly appealed to the middle class of all parties. And eclectically drink champagne or bitter ale.

Almost a reflection of parliament, though, yet radically different. This was the King's Court where Sir X had restated Pi's task to Anton on many an occasion. Progress was assessed at every meeting by Sir X with Anton. As deep friends, there was so little to discuss now. They were living parallel lives and knew each other's views on almost everything.

Both read the party leaflets and edicts, both partook of the same rabid tabloids, and both had the whole world of the BBC to assimilate and be blessed by. Both were happy in their lives. Internally at least. Externally usually too. Both had the same view on all things Covid-19.

On the Panglossian calculus that they had created for their lives was the perfect view that they were grateful that they did not have the lives of those poorer or richer. The rich, they felt, were too encumbered by their wealth to be really happy. But a little extra was always welcome.

Sir X: Anton, you say Pi is progressing well but really, I don't see how Pi is managing to read a series of books by different authors to the equivalent of his own height. The rules have to be obeyed! I will check! I, myself, do not read more than one book every two months and I have a First-Class Honours in PPE. May even have been a cabinet minister if not for my illness 14 years ago! I certainly have the level of pomposity and self-adulation required!

Anton: There is something special about Pi. I do not know what it is, but he will deliver if it is humanly possible for him to. You have made this point several times already.

Sir X: But he is not erudite enough to tackle the task. He will not be truly reading. I cannot read many of my classics collection. They look good on the shelves, however! Got Kiera a lovely young professor for a fiancée. It's also great wallpaper for all those Zoom and MT calls that I seem to live in daily. Pi thinks he can imagine Googol too! Simply not possible! I have never heard of that. I am sure it exists on the net, but he wants to come with a depiction *de novo*. An act of discovery unlikely to be done by a man of limited education.

Anton: I really think you underestimate his credentials. These guys are smart. What you call these Johnny Foreigners are ahead of us, the ones are tucked away in the bubbles of Europe and North America, in so many ways.

Sir X: Are you going over to the Dark Side? I think Tolstoy named a book after Pi?

Anton: Really, Mark! Pi is going to tackle a great Russian novel soon. Certainly, when he goes back to India. We will gift him the Folio Edition of *Anna Karenina*. By the way, *The Idiot* is by Fyodor Dostoyevsky, not Leo Tolstoy.

Sir X: You draw from Pi rather than the Black Wells. I remember the motto from my days in Oxford—From the Black Wells draw ye the Muses' draughts. *Sumite Castalios de fontibus.*

Anton: You've lost me, Mark. Another whiskey? Or whisky?

Sir X: You are losing your Latin, Anton. What do you want to drink? Considering you mentioned your trip to the Croagh Patrick earlier, it can be whiskey with the E of Eire. I will have the 12-year-old please. Are there really 365 islands there?

Anton: I didn't count them, Mark! Do you have any recommendations for Pi?

Sir: How about Finnegan's Wake to slow him down? Even Joyce's wife could not read it!

Anton: That I would not wish on my worst enemy!

Pi was informed of Sir X's choice over the day's chit-chat on the walk home from the club. Pi was riveted by the idea that a book could be unreadable. Apparently, it was the most famous book never read. Pi had the idea of reading a few pages. But unreadable it was.

Even *Ulysses* by Joyce had been deemed too difficult to read by Pi himself. But he had diligently listened to all 22 episodes of the unabridged CD version (if allowed, this would have been a very fruitful 7.1 centimetres!). The bulk of the narrative related to Leopold; but the erotic bits at the end were a definite reason not to include the book in his quest.

There was the brother and sister-in-law to report to. The couple would almost certainly Google a synopsis. Both would be upset for sure. This narrative was certainly Pi's literary peak of this genre, albeit in audio-form.

Back to *Finnegan's Wake*. Pi eventually mastered the meaning of the title. But on further dips into the book, he discovered that there was an intriguing amount of Sanskrit to glean from almost every 10 pages. But it seemed to make no real sense.

Sandhyas, Sandhyas, Sandhyas was even there. Then *Arans Duhkha*. And *Agni araflammed* and *Mithra monished and Shiva slew as mayamutras the obluvial waters of our noarchic memory withdrew. Every talk has his stay, vidnis Shavarsanjivana, and all-a-drea perhapsing under lucksloo at last are through. Vah! Suvarn Sur! Scatter brand to the reneweller of the sky, thou who agnitest! DH!* There was a lot more, especially near the end. The *'Vayuns', Tasyam kuru salilakriyam! Pfaf! Svadesia salve!*

This he understood—something about one's own country, pleases you or is a salve? He was not too sure. Perhaps this could be about Gandhi's swadeshi movement of using only or mainly products locally produced? But he was not entirely sure on this interpretation either.

There was an interesting podcast that claimed that the word quark had been 'borrowed' from *Finnegan's Wake*. This Pi found utterly profound; that an odd book had given a voice and a name to the most elemental of the bricks of existence. The soul within the mind within the body. Made of particles and waves, within it all and without it all.

What did the rest even mean? It was not for him. Maybe he could do a PhD on the Sanskritic material. Possible title? What about *Finnegan's Wake by James Joyce: Profound thoughts, joy, or nonsense?* At the university of somewhere cheap. He could see himself writing a 50,000-word impenetrable and grammatically correct thesis on the subject. But the illustrations in the very expensive edition of the book were something else.

A world of the highly imaginative opened to him through the 12 plates of vividly coloured etching. Especially the *frontis*. Pi had lost 3 days on his reading journey, he had become joyfully lost, but none the wiser. *Finnegan's Wake* then, a contribution to quantum mechanics but alas, not to Pi's tower of books.

Back to the David Baldacci; that would add a useful 33 millimetres. Pi was looking forward to Ruth's biscuit club the next day.

Ruth's Biscuit Club and Madeleines

For the next meeting, Ruth, knowing that Pi was tackling the graphic novel of *Swann's Way* by Proust, made some madeleines. The book itself was deemed too long. Ruth recalled writing an essay on madeleines for her gastronomy course. And how the author of the Man in the Iron Mask had claimed their invention for Madeleine Paulmier, cook to the Perrotin family, when preparing a feast for the exiled king of Poland—Stanislas Leczszynski.

Further details had been forgotten by her. However, she also remembered there was that bit about the pilgrims who were on their way to the burial site of St James in Santiago di Compostela in Spain via the Camino, wearing scallop shells around their necks.

This being the symbol of St James, the Gospel writer. Shells had been used as the original mould for the cakes. But now plentiful supplies of *Pecten maximus*, the large comb mollusc, were no longer available. Here, the miracle of silicon was put to use in creating the moulds.

Early mornings, Pi was often to be found rereading his scriptures in the conservatory. Ruth found Pi, reading one *Upanishad*, sipping tea. Ruth had some cards to write out. She never forgot to send a card for the birthdays, anniversaries, and festivals of her closest friends and family.

As long had been customary, she inserted a bespoke or somewhat unusual teabag into each of the various cards she sent out. Her tentacles and synapses of happiness to friends and family and those bereaved of any ilk. A *joyeaux anniversaire* there, an *alles gute zum geburtstag* further afield, a wondrous sounding *tanti auguri buon compleanno*, and all the more mundane sounding, but equally heartfelt English ones.

Pi's second drink was changed to coffee by Ruth, this being the traditional drink that accompanied the madeleines. He was offered madeleines, which he greatly enjoyed. The usual group of Ruth's biscuit club were ensconced in the library. Away from the humdrum, especially related to children, of their daily lives. Ruth left Pi to join them.

Ruth: Here's a lovely quote. Madalista, a twelve-year-old from Malawi. *"We felt very happy when we first saw the books. There was no library in the school before. We only had textbooks and no story books. We are now able to read many interesting stories."*

Book Aid International was, of course, accepted. In fact, there was very little that Ruth could not persuade the biscuit club to do to help her causes. It was difficult to argue with the fact that 1,007,449 books had been successfully despatched to 24 countries. All new books, that is. Pi informed the biscuit club that another 10 books would have made a prime number. There was discussion and discontent around the fact that the various charity walks and runs remained cancelled during these times of Covid-19.

At the afternoon tea, the madeleines were very well received by the rest of the Beck household. The potential full *hyggeness* of parsley, sage, rosemary and thyme was missing. But these madeleines were made using the latter two herbs. This beverage ceremony was presumably being paralleled across the channel at the 4pm French equivalent, *Le Goûter*, albeit usually with coffee.

But was it tea or coffee that Proust would have dipped his madeleine in? It rapidly became Pi's favourite dessert. Or as Pi usually said, desert. Pi could not understand the redundancy of having two words for the lemon drizzle cake, banoffee pie, apple crumble, chocolate cake, and the Gobi, Thar, Sahara, Arabian, Namib, Sonoran, Takamakan and the Atacama. Were his usual sweet favourites *rasmallai, jalabis* and *barfis* legitimate desserts?

Pi was happy to have been recommended a graphic novel. He had lost a lot of time on *The Idiot*. Pi had decided to read it after all. Anton and the possibly priesthood leaning Kirk had agreed there was no better example of the Christian creed in action. Dostoyevsky's good and beautiful man.

Anton felt that the other cheek had been offered a little too much by Prince Myshkin. The author, in his real life, was a man battered in mind by the mock execution, and body by epilepsy and the soul yet to emerge flourishing. In the book, there was the beauty and life of Natasya Filippovna torn betwixt the compassion and love of Myshkin and the obsession and passion of Rogozhin. If all truly read Dostoyevsky, then none would bother writing in this genre. For none could write with as much heartfelt pathos as he.

Ironically, it was time that had prevented Pi from further reading Proust's *À la recherche du temps perdu*. He did, however, avow to read it in the future. It was rather long. Long at seven volumes and a mere 1,267,069 words. Pi gleefully told everyone that this did also not weigh in at a prime number. Though it was only 2 words off.

Two less words were needed or 34 more. The 34 words of a translation of the *Gayatri Mantra* from the *Rig-Veda* would have fixed it. Pi found it interesting that Proust had more to tell us than the Bible at only 788,280 words, but less than the *Mahabharata* at 1,800,000. Of which the *Bhagavad Gita* could be construed a fractal, as it also had 18 chapters.

For the future though, Pi was inspired by hefty, light books of fiction. Especially, those in the ilk of James Patterson and Rosie Goodwin.

Instalment Nine: November

Let the second lockdown begin. Maybe it was then *Eat Out, to Infect others*. We haven't quite figured that out yet. We will later, I am sure.

Ironically, although we are dying earlier due to COVID-19, our engagements into death—the mortgage—are extended. If we are alive, we can pay it off over a longer period of time. Controversies galore including the Reform Party declaration that more lives have been lost due to the lockdown than it hopes to save.

We all die but at present, one in eight, maybe one in five, of us are dying from COVID-19. Is freedom of expression for the Reform Party a good thing?

There are further animals to blame. So, we ban the Danes. They appear to be infected with a mutant strain picked up via their, particularly unfriendly, mink population. But mouthwash may kill the virus. No details of how to use it etc. are given out by the University of Cardiff though.

Two vaccines, the BioNTech and the Pfizer one, both appear to offer 90% protection from developing the full-blown COVID-19 disease. It is even more effective in those 65 or over, at 94%. The present of a vaccination by Christmas is on the Santa list of all the gentry and sundry.

Town and countryside. Rugby leaguers and unionists. Tall or short. We have bought 7 million doses from 7 vaccine suppliers. Three of them definitely have an effective product, we think. Just awaiting delivery now.

The three wise men suggest that there may be a 5-day ease of lockdown to collect Santa's presents and visit family, if one so desires. There is even the idea of extended bubbles over the 7 days of Christmas.

There came an early present from the blood transfusion people for Pi and me. A bronze medal indeed. For a bag of plasma counts as 5 blood donations. Belton is in Tier 3, a lot more restricted than London and Liverpool in Tier 2. Cornwall, Scilly Isles, and the Isle of Wight are the best places to be. They are in Tier 1.

An accolade of sorts. We stand slightly stooped with USA, Brazil, India, and Mexico. We are that band of citizens as we become the one of the first five countries in the world to admit to 50,000 deaths from COVID-19. On my most reliable website, 77,113 UK dead are declared at the end of the month.

Chapter 11
The Plotters

*And your Lord inspired the bee: "Make your home in the mountains, and on
the trees and the trellises that they erect. Then eat from every kind of fruit and
follow meekly the ways of your Lord."*
*There issues from its belly a juice of diverse hues, in which there is a cure for
the people. There is indeed a sign in that for a people who reflect.*

The Quran. Al-Nahl. 16th Sura. Revelation to Prophet Muhammad
(*Sallallahu Alaihi Wasallam*, Peace and Blessings of Allah be upon Him),
570–632 CE.

*Upon this handful of soil, our survival depends. Husband it and it will grow
our food, our fuel, our shelter, and surround us with beauty. Abuse it and the
soil will collapse and die, taking humanity with it.*

Atharva-Veda. Sanskrit Scripture, c. 1200 BCE.

Wildflowers

Pi wandered a lot in those days. Alone usually but always thinking. About
everything under the sun. What had been a source of consternation was that he
had not paid much attention to the wildflowers that surrounded his home in
Sundervagvela. He felt that he had previously been going about life unaware of
the splendours of the ubiquitous wildflowers. Never to be called weeds.

Those plotters could get extremely annoyed if you called any plant a weed.
They would point out that humans had wrecked the planet in 250 years, whilst
wildflowers had beautified it from at least a 100 million years ago. The same
idea for the insects.

171

Now in autumn, he missed the abundance of wildflowers that he had seen earlier on in the year. But his brain had catalogued many, especially through the activities at the City-Zen Café with his friends.

Heaven was indeed present to behold in a wildflower. Or so thought William Blake and his past, present, and future acolytes. These inhabitants of Mother Earth have long outlived us, having appeared as blooms from the Cretaceous.

The evolutionary plot was to convert the photons of sunlight via quantum mechanics to sugar and create a flower and seduce the insect to visit or else times to eat it altogether. Whilst we slowly plodded onto the scene about 6 million years ago. If the life of the Earth was but a day.

Flowers were late too at 40 minutes to midnight. But we did our hobbling first at 3 minutes to midnight. And started writing a fifth of a second before midnight. A long legacy indeed and probably so close to destroying a lot more of evolution in the next hundredths of a second.

May, June and July were the best months, or so Pi thought. But there was never a day when a wildflower could not be found. So, he had liked March, April, August, September, October and November quite a bit too. These wandering hermits of no fixed abode could be spotted anywhere.

Some, like the foxgloves, in the most unlikely of places. Blown away from their origins and dispersed on the wind. For there had been many particularly boisterous winds that year. Covid-19 had started with Atiyah, then Brendan, Ciara, Dennis, Jorge, Ellen and Francis.

The rest of the allocated names thankfully remained unused. Gerda, Hugh, Iris, Jan, Kitty, Liam, Maura, Noah, Olivia, Piet, Poisin, Samir, Tara, Vince and Willow would need to await a time in the hopefully very far future.

Many of the wildflowers remained unnamed to Pi, even though he had access to Anton's father's sumptuous collection of books on the subject, many Victorian. The ones he knew, he knew well. Their etymology too. Pi was not one to shrink from sharing his acquired knowledge and had made cards for the plotters on common wildflowers in his environs.

He had also created a slide set that he would love to replicate as an App—if a few hundred pounds were forthcoming from any direction. For each flower, there would be a Budding Press picture, kindly purchased at mates' rate, then a photo and a description and what Pi inappropriately called 'juicy facts'.

Edgar, and even Sir X were particularly enamoured by the project. They told all that listened that Latin had been second nature to them in the dim and distant past of their erudite education. And that Latin was a founding bedrock of Western civilisation.

Pi was not accredited with its mini resurrection. Especially as Pi kept on claiming that Latin, Greek and Sanskrit were all closely related from that most ancient of written forms—the Proto-Indo-European Language. *Another Pie*, thought Pi.

Pi enjoyed his journey through the field of bindweed, hitching a ride towards light on an unsuspecting and benevolent sloe, navigating upward via tendrils. The black sloe thorns protecting the bindweed from harm. The leaves heart-shaped and the trumpets of flowers declaring their continuing presence here after a 100 million years. Still thriving, mocking us.

In folklore, it was the perennial morning glory. Even the Brothers Grimm had a little tale to tell. That Mary, mother of Jesus, used the flower to drink wine with to strengthen her to help push the wheel of a cart stuck in mud. The negativity of weed in its name offset by its real moniker, *Convolvulus arvenesis*. Alluding to rolling up and wrapping round and living in open fields.

A consequence of Pi's bout with Covid-19 had been his anosmia. He had enjoyed being introduced to the smell of chamomile tea and even to a plant in June. Which was apparently unusual. Or so said the plotters. To his chagrin, despite with the abundancy of chamomile this August, he still could not smell a thing.

For others, the scent was enhanced by the drying and maturation of the flowers in the slow sun of August. The plotters claimed that the scent was released when they walked on the chamomile, dense as it was, in the paths around the allotment. For Pi, only the visuals were there; but he saw this as glory enough. We bow down to you, *Chamaemelum nobile*.

The earth-apple of nobility, as the Romans named it, for such is its scent. Even Beatrix Potter, via Mrs Rabbit, sent the mischievous Peter Rabbit gently anaesthetised to the land of Morpheus aided and abetted by chamomile tea— after he had engorged himself on a few too many of Mr McGregor's cabbages. Not for reading by Pi though, for Sir X had stipulated that no children's books were allowed.

Pi was ashamed that he had learnt to recognise so many more flowers in his short stay in Belton than he had living in Sundervagvela. He had prepared cards on the daisy (the standard and ox-eye), garlic mustard, meadowsweet, the water plantain, wood anemone, the orchid hellebore, the wild garlic, wild strawberry too, the carnivorous Lords and Ladies, cross-leaved heather, foxgloves a plenty, herb Robert, red and white campions, red thrift, pheasant's eye, the ubiquitous poppy reminding us of the blood of others a life wasted in war, the scarlet pimpernel hidden in crevices, the bluebells that existed for a limited time only, the bleed stopping bugle beloved of carpenters of old, the exquisite columbine.

The cornflower was an even bigger favourite, the devil's bit scabious was there, the gentle harebells, the towering teasels and the hogweeds, the up-coursing tufted vetch, the cough treatments plants of cowslip, the dandelion for ersatz coffee, the St John's wort for depression, the lesser celandine for joy and its cousin the several buttercups, the silver weed (a tea plant if you like).

The irises, daffodils, yellow rattle and snake's head fritillary. Although an invader, he also enjoyed the Indian Balsam along the canal banks. Just nearly forgot, did you know that the daisy is so-called as it closes at night and opens in the day—the *day's eye*?

There were many that he still did not recognise. As to the mushrooms, abundant now, they mainly remained nameless, but their architecture was vividly remembered. Pi was especially intrigued by the mushrooms King Alfred's Scones, Wood Ear, Wood Bluewit, Shaggy Ink Cap, Dead Man's Fingers and Toes, Candlewick, Fly Agaric, and Turkey Tails.

Actually, these were the only ones he could identify. Pi had been somewhat envious of Anju who had recently found a gigantic mushroom called Chicken of the Woods. He would search for it in vain for many wistful hours.

Pi had learnt a lot about earth itself. The plotters had vowed to stop digging a lot. In previous years, they had gone along to Tools 4 U from Us and hired a diesel digger for the weekend. Everyone had chipped in a quid or two and all the plots were dug by them or for them by a willing workman. But they had bought into the current evidenced trend to not dig too much.

They saw the earthworms as a deity of all things horticultural. Pi was suspicious of this, considering worms remained unclaimed by even the multitudinous panoply of the Hindu deity. But maybe a trick had been missed because of the inherent bias towards vertebrates. Pi recalled that Vik had been supported of snails in this regard. He was keen to point out that his Mother tongue had called the snail *gokalagaya*—the wandering cow, as opposed to the more vulgar *nakha*—nail of the Sanskritic.

Our common worm is called *Lumbricus terristris*, the Linnaeusian 'earth-worm', an oddly unimaginative name for much an important link in our food chain. But the German, *gemeiner regenwurm* had a hint of sourness in the common bit and the romance of their appearance after rain. Even the Danish *Stor Regnorm* had a mark of Norse godliness about them.

Although the actual truth was that rain could drown them, especially during a thunder-plump, and that is why they had to surface to breathe. This much like, but then again completely differently from the whales, dolphins, and porpoises (pray what is the difference betwixt these three?).

The plotters no longer wanted to destroy the delicately engineered tunnels and highways that the earthworms had built underground. The tiny casted piles of the purest fertilised growing soil were collecting on the surface of the soil, creating viable passages for roots to grow into with their fungal companions.

The air pockets that prevented the freezing of the soil when Jack Frost visited. After a warm rain, the, as yet, unclaimed by Chanel, geosmin earthy perfume. Organic, betruffled and alien.

The Plotters had decided to absolutely minimise digging. Because how would we humans feel if the London Underground was destroyed on a yearly basis?

Pi — Stray Thoughts

Pi dabbled in stray thoughts at the café. This was unusual for him as life previously had been a lot busier and more regimented. He had been entranced by the idea of a tattoo of the testosterone molecule on a nomad in the filmed book *Nomadland* by Jessica Bruder. The latter he had enjoyed reading a lot.

He had found the world of the bit-time workers totally fascinating. He had sketched out the design of the female hormone and then the male testosterone on a piece of packaging of a six-pack of beer bottles—quite why one of the listed ingredients was glucose syrup, he could not quite fathom. Pi thought that this was certainly not in obeyance of the German Purity Law of *Reinheitsgebot* from 1516 put into place by the grand old Duke of Bavaria, Wilhelm the Fourth. *Is that why only 4 ingredients were allowed?* Simply water, barley, malt and hops.

The admixture of the female and male hormones, was of the hydrogen-carbons of pentagon, hexagons and the twigs going off to the two oxygen each. The difference between a female and all that dictated a male was just the one extra carbon and four hydrogens for the latter.

Pi created a rainbow in which the oestrogen and the testosterone overlapped at the shared pentagon in green. The other colours were arranged sequentially, going from the right to the left of the rainbow colours. Within a day, the rights of the design had been bought by Xipi's partner and had been installed, tattooed, on the forearms of several (and the backside of one). Pi felt that he was raking it in at the large commission of a pound per tattoo. Which were, untaxed, put into a pot for the homeless at the bar.

The summit meeting with Anju, Pi and Kirk started off a little patronising as Kirk gave a synopsis of the three best books he had just completed. All on rewilding—plus or minus the odd wolf in the case of Knepp. At the outset, he stated that the three were a step removed from being suitable for Pi for his labours. He categorised them as being too dull. Certainly, they were long.

Kirk: *Walden* by Thoreau is a transcendentalist's dream to escape into the woods. About how he builds a log cabin in a wood and lives there for a year, sneaking back into town every now and again for supplies, the occasional meal and alcohol. *Feral: rewilding the land, the sea and human life*, is a phenomenal collection of ideas on rewilding and re-introducing wolves, lynx, bison and even the sabre-toothed tiger, ideally. Monbiot's always a little crazy; according to Dad anyway. Lastly, the realistic Knepp Project authored by—can you believe it? By a Tree. A certain Isabella Tree! The book is called *Wilding*. An interesting title considering it is about rewilding.

Great quotes, thought Pi flicking through the book, *one from an ancient* Veda.

Another suitable PhD topic, Anju thought, *but let's see where the funding comes from.* Even in scholarships, he who calls the piper calls the tune.

By now, Anju and Kirk would always respond to his lifting of his chin, knowing they needed to give Pi his 9-second pause.

Pi: Have you been taught about the four stages of a human life?

Clearly not, thought Kirk, *yet another omission from the theology college curriculum.* Anju's eyes widened slightly in interest. Maybe it was time for an *Einklarung,* as was bandied around so much at the City-Zen Café by Leken, the real Saxon. Kirk wondered how Pi would now segue back into book-talk.

Pi: In Hinduism, there are four stages of life. The four ashrams or the places that you live your life which are as follows: Firstly, *Brahmacharya*—the stage of the student. Where knowledge is fixed and the tools for a fulfilled future are gathered. Then that of the householder—*Grihastha*. The family, the household, the upper echelons of work. Then the one that made me think of Walden.

The stage of *Vanaprastha*—forest dwelling. To be one with all of creation. And then *Sannyasa*—a renunciation—in order to die fulfilled. There are merely four stages; I know that Shakespeare describes seven.

Both Anju and Kirk wished there was a PowerPoint slide or two to run along Pi's still relatively strong accent.

Kirk: Makes sense. I would ideally like to skip the householder stage.

Anju: What and not gift another Kirk to the world! Surely that's a great blow to humanity! I shall be staying in one stage for a very long time, your gods willing, Pi.

The Wildflowers and Clouds

At the City-Zen Café, the slides were coming in thick and thin. There was a lot more time as the days were shorter and therefore, more time indoors. Thick on Mondays and Tuesdays with the weekend work coming in, in direct contradistinction to the low death rates from the virus on Mondays and Tuesdays. One wondered if they had stopped counting the dead or certifying them at weekends? Or did they not die at weekends?

The democratic, but self-elected, senator in charge had come out with some rules. There were to be no more than 2 new additions to the virtual scrapbook per week per person. And that included wildflowers, trees, and fauna. There could also not be more than two submissions, per person per month, in each separate category.

The digital image added to the scrapbook had to be an original taken by the submitter. These were just the rules I understood. These rules had led to the early corruptive practices of befriending a fellow member in order to legitimise one's submission.

There was Tiberius who had wanted an additional category of clouds. He was most assertive in his asking and if adopted declared that he could see himself financing a re-hash of the website à la local zoological society fashion. The leader would have no such thing. Especially as he was the semi-capitalist (for he did not make much money) proprietor of the Well-Read Well-Red bookshop. His personal philosophy was one concordant with his heritage and all the maxims of Confucius. Especially *"The beginning of wisdom is the ability to call things by their right names"*. And clouds mattered, particularly to Tiberius.

The sign for his shop was a tome of a red book with a Hammer and Sickle underlined by a quill. (PS-if you ever fancy finding it, it's 5 shops around the corner from the equally red Bolshie and Banana—the vegetable and fruit store). The leader did allow a description of the cloud to be specifically included when there was one to be seen in the photos of the flowers.

This led to the underground dissemination that if a decent picture of a cloud was included (that Tiberius wanted included) then he would gladly buy you a bottle of the cheaper of the two champagnes at the Gate. He was always glad to taste the stars that Dom Perignon had declared were present on discovering champagne way back in 1697. Thus, the low-level cotton balls of stratus, nimbostratus, cumulonimbus, cumulus and the stratocumulus appeared often in the backgrounds of these photos. Occasionally, the mid-level altostratus and altocumulus could be spotted. Less often included were the Himalayan heighted cirrostratus, cirrocumulus, and the wispy cirrus.

The digital address of each image was confirmed by Idris. The whizz-kid of all things digital. The photos had to be within the bailiwick of Belton. And at that, parish boundary only. The borders were digital and more absolute than the Trumpian invisible wall between him and Mexico.

The flowers tumbled in.

The snowdrop—beloved of the demented. A drug galantamine from its biochemistry. And later, the other bulbs would appear; the Lenten lily aka daffodil. Not forgetting the wild garlic, so often picked, and put into sandwiches to inspire the bland cheese to becoming edible.

The grape hyacinths and the most beautiful native of all; the snake's head fritillary. The reference to the check pattern was added by Anju. Each card had to have a natural light photo, often champagne-happy. The flower and its leaf had to be included.

A short description was then produced, fronted by the flower's Latin name, its etymology and common names. Uses, if not pragmatic, could be 'beautification of the universe'—*Botu*. Additional ideas were permitted, in these most brief but Anthropocene of times. A list follows. This was the animation of the wildflower. This society of Blake indeed saw their heaven in a wildflower.

- The Foxglove: *Digitalis purpurea*, the withering potion from the Birmingham Witch. Having no property rights in those times, her name is unknown. Its use was for heart failure, especially for those with the random but stepped bolero of atrial flutter and fibrillation.

- The Snowdrop: The Eid, the breaking of the fast for many an insect that had to hibernate over winter. The first release of the bulb to distil in the pistil to a drop of nectar.
- The Yew: An identity hewn over thousands of years. From the start of Christianity, the triad of Yews hold watch over the gravestones of the last 300 years in Belton and elsewhere over Neolithic burial sites. From a tad over 5000 years ago. Now used to treat cancer, still in these most modern of times.
- The Dog Rose: *Canina rosa*. The petals could be eaten as jam as in the Kashmiri *Gulkand*. The rosehip for the vitamin that only we, *Homo sapiens* and guinea pigs appear to lack, particularly.
- The Dandelion: Good enough for Fabergé to craft and to tell the time if you really needed it (plus or minus 3 hours). You could eat the leaves and roast the root, thereby saving on coffees and filling less the coffers of the coffee shops.

I could do more, but I am afraid I will bore you even more. There appeared, within months, the rarer sightings of the Milk Thistle with the allegorical milk of the Virgin Mary on the leaves, and the extravagant Cuckoo Pint with its riches of rowan-like berries.

The mushrooms had proven controversial, so had been given a sub-category. This was headed by Pedro Fernandez, whose interest in all things mycological had been sparked in infancy when informed of the tale behind King Alfred's Scones. Thereafter appeared the mesmerically beautiful *Amanita muscaria*, the regents of the kingdom of fungi.

Class: *Agaricomycetes*. Order *Agaricales*. Family *Amanitaceae*. Rare, now, with poison guaranteed. The common earthball was included. And later, the alien collared earthstar had come in. The fragile inkcap, the spikey common puffball. The trees appear to listen to us all through the jelly ear—the *Auricularia auricula-judae*. The stinkhorn, shaggy parasol and the wax taper fungi were all there. And the impossible design of the common bird's nest fungus. Not to forget the yellow brain.

The lichens joined. The red, the orange, black and white. Often to be found in a harmony of adjacent mapped countries or intermixing. The barnacle, bearded, and others were all there. A superpower treaty between the fungus and bacteria or algae.

A treaty thus signed in DNA or RNA that would live on until the decay of the sun in 5 billion years' time. Pi informed me that the lichen was an essential ingredient of the very best biryanis. The *patthar ke phool, kalpaasi* can be 10% of the very choicest *garam masala. Patthar ke phool*—the aptly named flower of the stone. The best from the pure air of the Himalayan foothills. But Pi was going through a morose patch.

Black Dog-Priyali

That latter half of that particular day at the City-Zen Café had not gone well for Pi. Then the night neither. The Churchillian black dog was chasing Pi through the night. He lay restless, his mind a vortex of mercury. Usually, his sleep was a still reflective lake. The dog was chasing him, trying to take a chunk out of him and floor him.

He was missing Priyali. He did not think this lightly as Pi fully appreciated there was no belonging to each other in anything but two robust trees standing apart growing but in not each other's shadows as elaborated by the prophet Gibran.

The lacrimation of the rain was pelting the leaded windows as he sank into the despair of memory, recalling the last days of Priyali. To Pi, she was Priya.

He recalled his mind's film of how Priya had stepped out to cross Mrudvali Road, skipping to the bus stop. He had seen her both in his mind's eye and the reality of the photons received into his retina as she turned around and waved to him, as he brushed his teeth standing on their balcony.

He watched her hourglass figure move in her tightly wrapped saree. Priya, as was customary for her, lifted up her saree just above her ankles to avoid the puddles that were gathering with heavy warm drops of the growing rain. She put her foot on a crisp packet.

The packet had caterpillar-tracked beneath her champal and she had slipped, falling forwards into the road. A few seconds later, a motorcycle had ploughed into her and ran over her chest. The ubiquitous, perpetual non-recycled litter of the lazy citizens of the world had killed her almost completely then, and then killed her forever, a few hours later.

Pi had been but married a mere 11 months and Priya was already with child. The marriage had been the simplest of ceremonies; they had garlanded each other

180

with marigolds and proceeded to do the *saat phera*. To translate that for the ease of you, dear reader, that was the name of the ritual of the seven circumambulations around the sacred fire of the Goddess Agni.

The colours and aesthetics were in place, the witnesses were in the wings— Ishverlal and sister-in-law. Lord Ganesh obviously made up the rest of the small wedding party, ever-present to thwart any obstacles to the wedding. Though there were no objections. Certainly, Pi's brother was utterly delighted that Pi was settling down with such a cool, calm, and collected epitome of a human in the form of Priyali.

Even though she hailed from a different community, that was entirely *Veda*-less, with just the one, very busy, God listening to 7 billion prayers a day. Around the clock, through all time-zones.

The fire delivered their prayers and intonations to the gods above in order for them to deify, sanctify and certify the marriage. Pi recalled it all in vivid technicolour. His weddings vows were brought to the front of his mind. Inscribed into his mind in Sanskrit.

Phera First: The first to, with the Deities as guides, to live with honour and respect, let us walk together, work together, to get nourishment for our bodies.

Phera Second: Then, with the Deities as guides, let us walk together, to be joyous in an enjoyed life. To grow together in strength and overcome our weaknesses. Let us walk together.

Phera Third: Then, with the Deities as guides, let us walk together, to share joys and pains together, and create prosperity that benefits all.

Phera Four: The fourth to, with the Deities as guides, let us walk together, to live, respecting and helping our elders and family. For we are part of them, and them of us.

Phera Fifth: The fifth to, with the Deities as guides, let us walk together, affirm to observe acts of charity, and a family if desired. And to agree to provide any children with love, education, care and to value the lives of others.

Phera Sixth: The sixth to, with the Deities as guides, let us walk together, to work towards improving health and looking after our bodies, to have a long and fruitful life together. In good physical, mental and spiritual health.

Phera Seven: The final step, with the Deities as guides, let us walk together, to be friends as wife and husband. A commitment to live a life of love, friendship and fulfilment.

The final step, of the *saat phera*, fully sanctified the marriage. It did not matter whether it was witnessed by the priest and a couple of witnesses, or the crowds of relatives bussed in from all corners of India and the global diaspora of relatives and friends that attended the jaw-droppingly expensive 'society' weddings.

Pi recalled how he had insisted on having Priyali lead on several steps as well. Traditionally, it would be one or even nil! Usually, the last circumambulation was granted to the female of the species. After duly socially and legally sanctioning the marriage, the household had become vegetarian and alcohol-free. In preparation for a life enjoined.

Pi was gut-wrenched in despair as the image of Priyali on a ventilator, frothing at the mouth, was carved into his memory. She remained unconscious, but with epileptic fits. Later to die from collapsed lungs and an infection.

The song that he recalled most was *ek pyar ka nagma hai*—from the film *Shor*, sung by Lata Mangeshkar and Mukesh. The former was in her nineties now and had had a 75-year career in recording songs. The latter, his all-time favourite male artist. Pi knew that both of these would never die in human history.

These were unknown to the Beck household, such that the sentiments could not be shared. The song, a homage to the destroyed Priyali roughly translated as being something about this love being the melody of his life.

His book *Because* had been an output for Pi, and some others, to remember Priyali, forever in print, but it had been savagely mauled by critics. He recalled his mind and soul, driven by Priyali's death, had constantly echoed '*scatter my ashes quickly, I wish to live with Priyali again*'! He had felt an utter loss.

The *Because* collection of poems had been a testament for his love for her, which would endure then, now, and always to come. But in the barrage of tweeting and disliking on social media, it had sunk like a lead weight. Why is it called 'social' media at all?

The term lulls you into a sense that it is a positive thing only. Pi felt that his heartfelt book had been a part of him, transplanted into the community and then very violently rejected. But he had not been the only one thus treated in Sundervagvela.

Art Group

Those that can create art create art. Those that cannot, critique. Pi recalled how critics had caused the disbanding of the PALS Group at college. This Pals

Art and Literary Society had consisted of the acronymic Pi, Arjan, Leena and Shazana.

The Hindu, the Sikh, the Christian and the Muslim had all been equally shot down in their artistic ambitions. Sunken with Pi's *Because* book was Shazana's sculpted mesh of crazy strips of polished metal in the hues of silver, gold and bronze that strained out of a cage.

Her creation *Infinity escaping from a cage* had attracted the meagre sum of Rs 250 in scrap metal value. It had taken her several months and at least 200 hours to cut, weld, polish and bend and give form to the idea that had swirled around in her mercurial brain; she was in the possession of one of those minds that saw all that was indefinable in the world and wanted to mould and fashion these ideas into solidity.

The effervescent symphony of non-traditional instruments that Arjan had created oddly worked well. The quartet of typewriters would never again be heard in the magnum opus that is human music. The clickety-clacks of the Belton-made, *qwertyuiop et al* would be silenced forever. The multi-coloured keys of the Imperial-brand typewriterpiano—as he called it—were already demented to the extent that words could not now be forced out of them onto paper.

The clickety-clack symphony was a second childhood. The transition from old visual, to the words, to the recreation of 50 multi-coloured keys, and then to odd music that had been ceased forever by the critics.

Beethoven, if alive, could probably legitimately sue Arjan, as the melody he had created recalled Ludwig van Beethoven's Pastoral Symphony in so many ways. But it was also true that Arjan had not even heard it and only knew a little of the manic genius beyond the detritus of his life, his infamously congenital syphilitic hearing loss and poverty.

Leena, a painter of abstract depictions that were easier to decipher than Picasso, Braque or Chagall, simply sold her canvases for children to re-use at a local school. After painting all over them in a fashionable off-white shade. Pi felt that the group had been a little permanently broken. Their wings had been clipped; despite the fact they had never flown.

Also clipped were the artistic ambitions of the score plus pals of PALS. All had reverted to social chit-chat and banality of sharing pictures of dishes prepared, fashion worn in herd behaviour and the general *schadenfreude* comments. The social media mantra, the ill of others is the joy of me. Is this really the pinnacle of humans, so far?

Arjan still drove a taxi. Leena was still a nurse. Shazana was still in retail sales. But none dared take up their art again. Pi was looking forward to the next day but knew that he would be exhausted and would need a nap. He was going to Ellie Elementary to judge the art competition. He wanted to see their outputs but really did not want to judge. How can art be judged? Even if it only holds meaning for the artist that is art. If it has meaning for others, then that is a bonus.

At the school there was an incredible outpouring of art. To see the children shyly giggling was unforgettable for Pi. It made him proud; he felt that he was walking on sunshine. These children all had a superpower and had declared their ownership of it within their creations.

Today, they had put to one side all the toxic under-aspiration that would thwart them in the future. Today, they said to themselves, lose yourself, head to a future paradise, as an astronaut.

A lot of their art was based on the rainbow, praising the NHS and care home workers for their efforts during this particular plague of ours. There were several early Pollocks, it would appear. Fauvism and Cubism had also been re-invented and de Kooning had been given some close competition.

The winner was a small Zen Garden, Fibonaccian at 34 centimetres by 55 centimetres. It was populated by fresh flowers—a buttercup, a daisy, a cosmos, and Pi's favourite—a marigold. There were also stones, the colour of zinc patina. Fossils recalling a belemnite swimming in the Jurassic and Cretaceous 100 million years ago, more or less. Also, present were the ammonite and devil's toenail.

The former fossil, Pi was rivetted by. He recalled the *Shaligram* in his local temple in Sundervagvela. This was an ostrich egg-sized black stone with an ammonite fossil, and part of daily worship as the earliest avatar of Vishnu. Pi wondered—*Did the Shaligram auger an anticipation of human consciousness from over 200 million years ago?*

Other items in the Zen Garden included a flint that recalled early arrowheads. Several perfectly cubed crystals of pyrite added wonder, as did the miniature cones of the alder. The winner was 4 years old! Everyone got a prize though; art was not to be undervalued at this particular school. On the way home from the school, Pi had arranged to see Rodavan at the allotments.

Rodavan of Belton

On the way to the allotments, Pi was enchanted by the caterpillar he had seen crossing his path. On its way to a certain death, as the dog walkers behind him would catch up to it before it had made its way into the hedge. It was likely that the yellow hairy caterpillar was heading for the *mille feuille* yarrow. He would do so if he was a caterpillar.

He gently coaxed the caterpillar onto a leaf and placed it into the base of the copper and green beech hedge. Later, he worked out that it would not turn into a colourful butterfly but instead the rather drab, but beautifully sculpted, pale tussock moth.

Rodavan was also known as Bob. His origins had been pretty much lost; all that was known was that he was the grandson of the first Rodavan who had died in the needless massacre that was war, always unilaterally justified and bilaterally regretted. The war with big sponsors backing each side. So much for civilisation.

Rodavan was Slavic; his name came from the element '*rad*' meaning happy, and '*van*' from the root of many words that meant soul. Rodavan was indeed true to his name. As an apiarist, he was also known as the Beekeeper of Belton. And therefore, Bob. He preferred to be called that rather than the accidental Radavan, a name so very besmirched.

Although it was obvious to all that he was not a man of many words, Rodavan had a deep interest in Pi's undertakings and had recommended several books. Kirk approximated that Rodavan had spent more time talking to Pi than all the allotmenteers put together that year.

Rodavan had offered up *The Unbearable Lightness of Being* by Kundera, *The Life of Ivan Ilyich* by Tolstoy and Solzhenitsyn's *A Day in the Life of Ivan Denisovich*. Pi had thoroughly enjoyed the latter two; he had already read the first. These were new vista to explore, another TV channel, another set of programmes.

Rodavan just adored his Eastern European DNA. It was quirky and fresh. And he was open to learning a lot from everyone who had better personal and national balance sheets. He always enjoyed his conversations and silent walks with Pi.

At the allotment, there was all of humanity, distilled to the special tincture of those earth connected. They were another tribe planting seed, sending the tiniest of plants to nursery, and then to prick out and send onto larger troughs and then to Mother Earth itself for the final growth spurt, fruition and then to unselfishly die for the next generation after gifting a meal or two. Pi thought this was the cycle that the Vedic scholars had defined and stratified for the human. It was so much clearer with plants.

The allotments took on a life that would not have been obvious to passing pedestrians. Separated as they were by a narrow hedge, the incurious public hardly ever ventured to wonder what was going on during their especially raucous Thursday afternoons.

The allotment plots made up a drone's eye view of an arcade of sheds, in front of which were still the classically Anglo-Saxon defined pieces of land at 10 poles square. Approximately, 250 square metres. Pi told me that an Anglo-Saxon pole would then have to be 1.58 metres. At 5 foot 2 inches, this could be the size of the average erstwhile Anglo-Saxon.

This double tennis court of land was the country of the Belton Allotment Society leaseholders. If it had to be twinned with a country, it would be Bhutan, measuring outcomes in human happiness and blessèd produce. The last fight at the allotments had been 7 years ago. Over a football game. Or was it cricket? Or rugby?

That was the last time the First Aid kit had been opened at the Mont Gnomery. It was so called because of the Band of Gnomes that appeared to be climbing the 3-metre-high rockery that was laid in the exact centre of the focal 7 by 7 plots. There were at least 61 garden gnomes at last count, hidden in and amongst the saxifrage, gentian, trailing bellflowers, thyme, aubretia and house-leeks.

It was beyond understanding as to why the latter was called that. Also called hens and chicks—succulents that thrive in our land. Seven of these gnomes were definitely intent on looking for Snow White. It was also no modest achievement that the rockery had been nominated in the Garden Gnome of the Year competition—at the European level.

The competition from the Germans and the French had been especially strong this Covid-19 year. Mont Gnomery actually had its own live webcam. This webcam attracted scores of watchers; namely 13,611 over the last weekend. The plotters would, on a rota system, move the gnomes twice a day, at sunrise and sunset. Thus, were created stories of the gnomes on Mont Gnomery. This was easy.

Most of the gnomes were at leisure, but many appeared to be gainfully employed as teachers, anglers, at a desk with a microscope or telescope, driving a taxi, helping children across a zebra crossing. Those humans less enamoured by gnomes felt that the Mont Gnomery was an allusion to the most famous Monty of their screens. But a salve in these times of Covid-19.

The less desirable plots were behind Mont Gnomery. The latter served as a den for the allotment owners. Although they saw themselves more as custodians of the land. Some particularly well enriched folks did not like the idea that at the age of 63, they had to rent leasehold land from the society.

They even stated that they would be happy to pay a hundred times more than the required £199 a year to own the plot themselves. But really. A life lease seemed like a good enough offer. Rodavan, as a builder, knew the planning regulations inside out and so, built a communal public house.

It had a stove pipe, a cedar tiled roof and bold loggy planks. At 10 square centimetres less than the 30 square metres allowed and less than 3 metres height (a special bonus for having a pent roof). It was completely legit.

This was home indeed away from home for the Belton Allotment Society brigade; a place separate from the humdrum everyday society where they could engross themselves in all things carrot, leeks, potatoes, onion, garlic, bean, chilli, aubergine, parsley, coriander, fenugreek and courgette. It was particularly, when walking into this public house with a tattarrattat, that Pi felt positively demalayalamed, losing his own heritage to merge with all the folk there.

There were soft drinks, harder ones and always some spare communal fruit and veg to share. There was always, of course, teas and coffee. Dandelion roots were roasted, and genuine *ersatz* coffee made. Or as Saxon Smith asked, which came first? The dandelion coffee or the acorn tea or the coffee arabica or tea Chinois. Clearly, it was the former. So, who was *ersatz* now!

Although bananas and mangoes were always desperately missed, there were strawberries, raspberries, apples and pears in abundance. And sloes for those that fancied making their own gin. Also, impressive and worth an honourable mention were Rodavan's effect to harvest rain water—Rain$_2$O—as he dubbed it.

Collected in glass, shaken up to add oxygen and shared with all. He was also working on the glass bottle shed—almost completed now. The project had started 4 years ago and was progressing consistent with international building standards, with respect to its rate of progress towards completion.

Pi, Kirk and occasionally Anju would often go to the allotment together. They had to be ushered in as guests by existing allotmenteers. However, they were always welcomed warmly. They often brought small snacks as a token of their gratitude, ranging from flapjacks to samosas to pastries or biscuits.

Kirk and Anju had registered for an allotment and were confident that their time would come soon, as the waiting list was only 41 long and people were sadly dying at the rate of 2 or 3 a year. Many of these had left the plot unattended for 12 months and were therefore 'released' from the strict regulations, returning to normal life unencumbered by 250 square metres of land to look after.

The arrival of Rodavan in his Defender created an effervescence. It was akin to the one that Pi had observed at the Pakistan-India border betwixt Amritsar and Lahore, at the point of the National Highway 5 from India meeting National Highway 5 from Pakistan, at the Wagah border post.

The aggression of the nuclear armed powers in the pomp and ceremony of the changing of the guards was evident. Yet, they would also settle down together in food and celebration of Eid or Diwali or Dussehra or Christmas. Later in the Mont Gnomery hut, Kirk dug up the video of it on the internet. Some would consider this the supreme tourist attraction in that part of the world.

Rodavan's Defender would drive down the side road of the allotments to the beehives at the bottom of the plots. This was Bee Alley, his pride and joy. He was the caretaker of 17 beehives. Some were double-deckered, some were standard boxes whilst others were constructed of woven willow and thatch as was traditional—looking much like Marge Simpson's hairdo. Though obviously not in blue, of course.

As he parked, he would roll his windows down and he would turn on his music. The first song would always be Fanfare for the Common Man. Copland's tribute to all of those who fought in the Second World War. Quite why this was chosen no one dared ask.

At the end of these 3 minutes, Rodavan would emerge from the car. Clad now as proud as one of his compatriot pioneering cosmonaut comrades, Yuri Alekseyevich Gagarin and Valentina Tereshkova. Looking the part too, being covered neck to toes in his bee suit. Astronaut white, carrying his helmet under his right arm.

The smoking gun of the bellows in his left hand. The music at this point would have changed to the Blue Danube, the Johann Strauss composition from his favourite film. Then the short, but spacey, odyssey to the Bee Alley having been completed, further music would follow. This would be calm and serene, with the occasional inclusion of, Buddhist or Gregorian, monks chanting.

Rodavan was now to visit his millions of subjects. Rodavan, the Emperor of Bees. As it was late autumn, he would give them some feed today as late pollen yield had been depressed by the rains. He appreciated that the honey-producing bees, incidentally all female, worked extremely hard.

They produced around a tablespoon of honey per bee. Rodavan informed the allotmenteers that 683 bees would fly around 32,500 miles, gathering 5.93 pounds of pollen from 1,185,000 flowers to make one 9.5-ounce jar of honey. The metric alludes me just now. The beehive work would be completed and Rodavan would then return to his car, get into civvies and go to the Mont Gnomery hut and chill with his friends. In the event of the death of a queen, he would play Saint-Saëns' Carnival of the Animals—number thirteen. Le Cygne, the Swan.

All who were present at the allotment would stop what they were doing and come outside, standing in the elements whether rain or sunshine, wind or calm. Until the music finished. The dead queen would then be buried, in a matchbox, 2 hands deep into Mont Gnomery. And gently watered.

And later at the Gate, where Pi informed Rodavan that the same number of humans had died due to Covid-19 in the UK, as the number of bees in one of his beehives. With the global deaths exceeding the number of bees in all of his beehives put together. Rodavan acknowledged this but was more worried about the bee parasitic mite that had been found by other local apiarists—the *Varroa destructor* mite—oddly wider in width at 1.6millimetres, than its length at 1.1 millimetres.

Pi and Radovan later discussed books. This was especially centred on the academic controversy of the title of a little Tolstoy book, named the *Life of rather than the Death of Ivan Ilyich.* Then again, there was not much of a life described. Pi was looking forward to seeing Elle and Evinive the following day.

Evinive and Elle

One of Pi's favourite couples that he often encountered in the City-Zen Café or the Temperance Bar were Evinive and Elle. These two had found each other 4 years ago on the match-making sites that made the middle-aged lives of so many people a little more exciting and less redundant at times. Evinive had advertised for a like-minded partner and jokingly added that she would ideally prefer another palindrome.

Elle had responded, much enamoured by what she saw, though this erupted into something else, within seconds, when she actually saw her. They had fallen in love. By which we mean—no, let's leave it at that. They exemplified the *wabi-sabi* view of life. Theirs was perfectly imperfect.

Today was particularly exciting for Pi. He was going to do one of his tours for Evinive and Elle. This idea of Pi's had been advertised at the café and at the various local pubs. It was priced at £5 each, the proceeds of which would be donated to their charity of the month; this month it was Water Aid.

Pi had also recreated, with Anju, the *nimbu pani* masala. They quipped that this was lemonade for Water Aid. The £733 raised so far would lead to 6 wells and a water bowser. For parched humans, somewhere.

Evinive was to push Elle along the cindered path created within the plots. The money for this had been donated by the Chamber of Heart Specialists that was led by several that had been recently honoured by the Queen for their endeavours. On either side of this path were lines of marigolds.

The theory was that they kept the flies at bay; or did they? Opinion was divided. Marigolds held a special place in Pi's heart, as a garland back in Sundervagvela would often be the centrepiece of a Hindu festival or rite of passage such as births or weddings or funerals.

The design of the path was incredibly intricate—when seen from the bird's eye vision of a drone. A path was sketched around the plots, outlining a heart and its chambers, its ears and its two little bellies, outlining curls of electrical pathways. Each and every plot was thus served.

The weather-dependent promise was to go around the plots and have a discussion with a 'guide'. Pi even had a small badge for his designation in this regard. The guide would carry a pack of cards of the 'stuff' that would or could be seen on the walk.

I have used the word 'stuff' here because a collective noun for birds, bugs, trees, wildflowers, human heritages and clouds does not readily come to mind. On the walk, Pi would give out a card with a picture of the item or a flag of the heritage. And a few basic facts. You would keep a pack of the 'stuff' that you encountered. Other cards could be bought, of course. Most of the things in life can be bought. But not all.

Pi felt joyous on meeting Evinive and Elle. There just seemed to be so much to embrace in the world today. He wished happiness for all the people he knew. And for all those that he did not.

Cards were handed over for the ladybirds—there were three different ones of them canoodling, smooching, petting at the Bug Mahal. It was not certain exactly which species they were even with the magnifying glass duly proffered by Pi. The robin was spotted and then the murder of corvids—in this time of Covid-19.

The raven, the carrion crow and the rook. And later, a magpie—or was that a corvid with a glamorous paint job? The oak, the ash, the beech, the birch, the lime, and the hawthorn were all there. And even a survivor of a pandemic of old, the elm. The clouds were a little more difficult to delineate. But that was a cirrus for sure, and those looked like the cumulus, the stratus, and the cumulonimbus—just a little bit further off.

The weeds, sorry wildflowers, were resplendent. The daisies, buttercups, dandelions, hogweed, the early yarrow and the scarlet pimpernel. And its close relatives, the speedwell and the forget-me-not. More bugs followed; a vivid green cricket was seen on the path and then its larger cousin, the Usain Bolting grasshopper.

The damsels showed off next to the bulrushes on the pond. Taunting us. You mighty humans can try to recreate me if you dare. Thousands of swarming midges, though harmless to us all. A carp jumped upwards to make a mouthful of the midges. Three worms at least had been identified.

The blood red ones all over the compost dump, the fat juicy standard ones and the thinner threads of a white one. Pi was struggling with the names of the worms. There were 4 types of spiders and two types of ants followed.

The flags and facts about Ethiopia, Sudan, Baltic States, Poland in Unity with Romania and Ukraine, Turkey in partnership with the Greek Cypriots, the Indians and the Pakistani and Bangladesh, West Indies had been encountered on this most United Nation of places.

The target of 52 was easily achieved on the walk, and they concluded by walking back to the Temperance Bar. Back they went to the Welshman. Bore da, Mae'n Dydd Gwener indeed. Today, it was the announcement of the winners of the sunflower and other flora competition. And PS. The patron saint of crows, and possibly, therefore, all corvids, is St Kevin.

Pagan Harvest

The triad of Pi, Kirk and Anju's sunflowers reached well over 6 metres. But in the Belton Sunflower Competition, it was the red Russian giant sunflower from the little girl that lived down the lane that won. Anton fared better on the potatoes. His Blue Danubes (which were actually purple) took the silver ribbon.

Whilst Ruth's wildflowers topped this new category, Anju won on the wild mushrooms. Though controversy surrounded these wins, as disagreement as to whether the competition should be allowed at all reigned. Picking wildflowers and mushrooms was apparently illegal. But it was allowed.

This was explained carefully in a 3-minute lecture at the Temperance Bar by none other than QC Jane Henton. The latter was Edgar's new incumbent as guest lecturer and took on the topic *pro bono*. After a brief introduction, a summation was given.

Jane: Wildflowers can be picked for personal and non-commercial use, provided that the whole plant is not uprooted. What is forbidden is the harvesting of anything from a National Nature Reserve, a site of Special Scientific Interest or a National Trust site.

Though bluebells and daffodils cannot be picked, as it is likely that you could be saddled with a £5000 fine. Always allowed is foraging from hedges; this was granted to all commoners before the Magna Carta. To sum it up:

A person who picks mushrooms growing wild on any land, does (although not in possession of the land) not steal what is picked, unless it is done for reward, for sale or other commercial purposes. But do not trespass and follow local regulations.

The sale of the produce took place, after what some would consider a pagan harvest festival. The variety of the produce was in itself visually exciting. The carrots were not orange, the onions not just a boring cricket ball size, the melons and gourds were every colour of the rainbow (except blue).

There were alien-looking fractal cauliflowers and otherworldly-looking mammoth pot leeks. The Nadine and the Winston potatoes. The Alderman pepper and the redskin pepper. The Cheltenham green top beetroot and its cousins, presumably, the Boltardy, Red Ace and the Pablo.

The Lobjoit lettuces and the gladiator parsnips along with the Hative de Niort shallots. The beans were there in all their glory too, the Longpods, the Prince, the Enorma and the Liberty.

But the supermarkets had reduced these tribes of vegetable to well-behaved hot-house slaves alone. Today, what particularly delighted the ornithologists in attendance was the presence of the sparrow hawk at the post, adjacent to feeding tables, in the Temperance Bar beer garden. This had never been witnessed.

This zebra-feathered bird of prey looked on in a bored manner whilst the punters imbibed and chatted and imbibed more. And took many, many photos and videos. After almost half an hour, to everyone's discontentment, it flew off. Only to return with the head of a field mouse, very dead, with its 30-centimetre entrails dangling.

Honey

Another time at the allotments, Pi visited some plotters as they were concluding their first drink as the sun set for the planet and activities, horticulturist, and apiarist. One of the other apiarists, Dini, had an important announcement.

In attendance were most of the plotters and many of the main corvids were feasting or otherwise engaged around a dead squirrel. The raven, rook, carrion crow, jackdaw and the magpie. Rodavan was there too, but very quiet and totally attentive. Pi had made it very clear to Dini that he wanted a detailed explanation of everything as he knew so little about bees.

Dini: The results from the analysis of the honey are in, from the National Honey Monitoring Scheme no less. The SK map reference was a prime number of 8 digits. Pi said that boded well. Quite why that is so, I do not know. Technically, its Brix level is 81%—a decent sugar content.

Its Baume Scale specific gravity of 43 is also commendable. The disclaimer was that honey, being hygroscopic, could have attracted water. This would render the results a little inaccurate.

Rodavan: What is the water content?

Dini: Wait, wait—it is a long report. It appears to be 17%, which is ideal. We, as registered apiarists, aim for less than 17.8%. Above this and yeast will grow, eventually spoiling the honey. Less than this, appreciably, and the honey will crystallise.

Rodavan: And the flowers?

Dini: Please wait, Rodavan; the crops first. Areas of crops included in descending order, from around 33% to 1%: wild grasses, winter wheat, potatoes, oilseed rape, maize, spring wheat, winter barley, field beans and spring barley.

There was a lot of others from the crops we grow, or let grow, here on the allotment.

A growing impatience was sensed from the crowd, but Dini continued with the report.

Dini: Please hang on. We have new pollen members here. Please do look at my t-shirt. Local design. Locally printed. Hopefully, not with underpaid labour. But one never knows. This is the structure of the pollen. Tiny. 7 per millimetres to a 100 per millimetres. I did the direct microscopy with my mates. If you want to know, these are my melissopalynology chums!

We detected all the top ten broadleaf trees locally. The oaks, ash, silver birch, lime, beech, hawthorn, sloe, conker, sweet chestnut, hornbeam and loads of willow, poplar, and aspens.

All looked intently at the t-shirt. Some more intently than others. Mostly educationally, one would hope. There was wonder and bewilderment in the eyes of most and even a tear from Rodavan. The beauty of the alien shapes—many of the exine spikes of pollen—reminded people of the coronavirus particle.

But this was a different alien planet with different sets of aliens. A better world. To think that the tiny germ cell in a pollen—only 35 microns across—that is 30 or so to a millimetre—could result in an oak weighing 50 tonnes and living 1000 years—in some cases at least.

Dini: This analysis from the National Honey Monitoring Scheme looks for DNA fragments in honey and found evidence of the following: *Rubus fruticosus, Fragaria vesca, Trifolium pratense, Tripleurospermum maritimum, Rubus sylvaticus, Myristica fragrans, Trifolium repens. Persicaria lapathifolia, Filipendula ulmaria, Persicaria maculosa.*

Once Dini had perceived enough gratifying looks of appreciation, a translation was forthcoming. Cards were handed around respectively for the following, in order as above. Blackberry bramble, wild strawberry, red clover, sea mayweed, another bramble, nutmeg, white clover, pale persicaria, meadowsweet and redshank.

The nutmeg was a surprise. No one had seen this plant. But the bees had found it! Or was it a mistake? It was never all idyllic though.

Plotters' Disarray

Pi was not always to bear witness to it, but it was not always idyllic with the plotters. At times, it was very far from it; for local jealousies and feuds and general shenanigans were always boiling under the skin of it all. The plotters were in a tad bit of a disarray. Their famous *hygge* was in abeyance. Even though one of the signs inviting you into the allotment area and its surrounding stated *"Friluftsliv this way'*.

It was due to the impending Annual Horticultural Show. The Valleyshires region, née Canuteshires region, and the Maganshires, née Alfredshires, were both vying for the attention of Belton's Horticultural Society, mainly based at the allotments. Over the years, there had been a complex waxing and waning of friendships and loyalties.

The hostilities had reached a peak several years ago when fake news abounded in relation to the honey of Valleyshire being contaminated with neo-nicotinoids via the mid-season pumping of sugars into beehives to increase the yield of honey. It had poisoned hundreds of bee colonies.

The Valleyshires had struck back against the Maganshires and had stopped the sharing of the charcoal soil improvers that the latter had become so dependent on. The national rules were quite clear. Any local level society could only enter one regional event. Only then could the winning entries compete on the all-encompassing national stage, for the grandest prizes and the most coveted trophies and ribbons.

The tack and clutter to gather dust and then be sent on to charity shops by the inheritors. This was never to be resolved considering how firmly entrenched each individual plotter was in their own views. Yet, they had all managed to co-operate for the local fête and it had all gone so well.

£3984.52 had been raised for the Afghanis, the Syrians, the Yemeni, the Rohingya Muslims, the South Sudanese and increasingly so, the Ukrainians from the east of their country. The Venezuelans had failed to make the list.

Pi had difficulty understanding the issues, and felt very uncomfortable when asked to join sides.

Wissismistic Society

Other feuds happened too. It was quite a rowdy meeting, considering the purpose of it was a discussion on joint operations and ventures. The Homo Saplings Society and the Wissismistic Society had difficulty in agreeing on anything at all. The latter society was the brainchild of Edgar who fully appreciated that wars were the lifeblood of interesting yet inhumane history.

Otherwise, history would be frankly rather boring, he thought. But war is so stupid. As was the name of the society. It mainly existed to visit sites of rather infamous battles.

The war is so stupid, society agreed that the various *bogoff* offers with respect to the Wi-Fi, the treasurer functions and printing and the like would result in mutual cost-savings to further the benevolent works of each. Despite their bonhomie being lubricated by 4 pints of the non-Zeer beers, Edgar summed it all up with a frown and exercised look.

Edgar: I am sorry, but this is proving a lot more difficult to resolve than the *Deutsche Wiedervereinigung*. This, the joining together again of the two Germanies after 45 years was a damn sight easier! That happy anniversary was only recently celebrated—3rd October, in fact. I use this example as both these societies were the creation of my brother and myself. Which you know, I am sure. Rayner having died, appears to have left his society to a band of young delinquents! Ironic really, as Ragnar means judgment warrior. Rayner appears to have let himself down on this occasion!

Kirk: But you are just too focused on the functions; you refuse to tell me how the union would help us. Apart from reducing costs by a few hundred pounds each way.

Edgar: It is always about the money!

Kirk: Thanks for leaving out the word stupid when describing me! But for once, we have so many new members—who seem to want to join both societies. And did you ever see religions merge? Strength is in being apart and maintaining our unique identities!

Edgar: Not merging is folly indeed. We will plant less trees and visit less memorials of the dead. If that is what you want.

Kirk: Our independence is important—so I am sorry, but my answer is no to the merger. It's my round!

So, the societies, despite sharing many mutual members, stood apart as before. Homo Saplings, loosely associated as they were with the plotters, remained unattached officially with the Wissismistic Society. Pi regretted learning about this undercurrent of non-harmonious living.

There was a realpolitik to be assuaged and conquered before any meaningful change could be affected. Pi sensed that Edgar wanted to feel closer to his sibling, who had died a long while ago now. In those days, there were no drugs that could control the HIV virus that would ravage the lives of hundreds of millions and had 36 million deaths to its name in the last 40 years.

Edgar recalled the heady days of the 1980s and 1990s when he had pyrographed many of the wooden boards with quotes that hung from the trellises and the eaves of the huts on the allotments. When he had worked seamlessly with his brother in almost everything.

The sign *Langsam aber sicher*—the slow but sure—he remembered well. The one in the allotment barter shop was *Wandel durch Handel*—change through trade. Several dotted around were on recycling matters. The local recycling had dramatically increased from 43% to 96%, the council had attributed this to the living example of the plotters and the leaflets in the shop at the allotments.

The most carefully constructed plaque that the Wissismistic Society had put up, was professionally etched onto slate and chalked in. This was hung in the Temperance Bar. It read:

"I would only make one stipulation," continued the Prince. "Alphonse Karr put it very well before the war with Prussia. 'You think war unavoidable? Very well! He who preaches war, off with him in a special legion to the assault, to the attack, in front of everybody else!' "

Anna Karenina, Leo Tolstoy, Part 8, Chapter 16.

Instalment Ten: December

The second lockdown ends and we become the first country to approve both the main vaccines. Our rapid approval is disapproved by our Big Brother across the pond. Why the seminal approval in UK? We are working so much quicker due to the wonder of Brexit, apparently.

We must be cautious, however, and not get *'carried away with over-optimism'* warns our PM, so much wiser now as having hosted the virus. I think there is over-optimism as one of the daily triad claim that hospitalisations and death will be cut by 99%. No research facts have ever stated this much predicted joy.

One aspect of the business of the supermarkets completely eludes me. Why did five of our biggest supermarkets agree to pay back £1.7 billion of rates relief? What benevolence. I remain cynical. Or is the world changing? Sincere thanks though. Especially as there was panic buying of eggs, rice, pasta, soap, and toilet rolls, again.

The 8th of December is a truly glorious day. World Vaccination Day versus the SARS Cov-2 virus and to make COVID-19 of historical interest only, we hope. I should tell you that this was just down the road from our hospital. The very first time on planet Earth in a clinical setting, rather than trials. A Patel doctor in charge there, Pi had proudly informed me.

Margaret Keenan, age four-score and ten, is vaccinated and will have a place in history, forever. Clad in her blue penguin t-shirt, with its falling snow, close in shape to the falling viral particles of SARS Cov-2. The second so honoured, is William 'Bill' Shakespeare of Warwickshire. A tad younger but still four-score and one. Probably, no relation of the Shakespeare, but no genetic studies to confirm or refute.

Over the next 8 days, the pizza boxes of vaccines have been delivered and served to 137,897. I would have vaccinated more, as I almost always got that extra dose out of the vial intact and accurate.

A big worry, and we had some local cases, there is an aggressive variant, VUI or Alpha that has cleverly changed its spike protein to slip under the radar of our immune system even more efficiently. Then there's a South African strain too.

Christmas Eve, we enjoyed our loud doorstep bell-ringing to announce to all the lonely people that they are not alone. Or have we just informed them that there are other lonely people too? On Christmas day, the Queen tells them that they 'are not alone' too.

Christmas is changed for children everywhere. Santa and his elves are on furlough too, I suspect. But three households can meet in many areas of the country. But no Christmas bubbles, if you are in Tier 4.

On 29th December, Margaret Keenan, returns to have her second dose of the COVID-19 vaccine and thus become the first person to complete the stipulated recommended.

There was one incident that I will never forget, I think (although there is a bad family history that I must heed). Ruth phoned me at work. I was in full personal protective equipment. On this occasion the full works due to the new strain. I was clad in double gloves (taped), FFP3 mask, coverall gown, goggles, face-shield, head cover, and overshoes. I briefed my entourage of adoring educationally-hungry students about the clinical cases and, as I was about to enter the bay of patients, my phone rang. The phone was on the nursing station, it was Ruth calling. She never phones me at work unless there is a compelling urgent reason. I had to take off a substantial part of the full personal protective equipment. Ruth first words were 'Where's the mop kept, Anton?'

The year ends with 44 million people in Tier 4. New Year's Eve is cancelled. I assume just the celebrations. 180,000 retail jobs lost in the year and a total of 94,077 dead from COVID-19.

Chapter 12
Musings and Chit Chats

"What would you understand?" Seria Mau asked it.
"By the idea, 'Evidence of myself'?"
"Not much," the fetch said. "Is that why you did this? To leave evidence of
yourself? Over here, we wonder why you kill your own kind so ruthlessly."
Seria Mau had been asked this before.
"They're not my kind," she said. "They are human."
She greeted this argument with the silence it deserved

Dated 2400 AD in *Light* by M John Harrison.

Anju's Taze

Pi thought that he would like to sit in on one of Professor Pritchard's creative writing classes. Anju was allowed, indeed encouraged to bring a guest student (to sit quietly and strictly in the back row only, a little apart from the enrolled students). Pi was confident that he would learn a lot.

Professor Pritchard was intensely proud of his skills and his Indian links. It was his ancestor that had had mastered the 200 metres race and won two silver medals, hurdles and running. Albeit in Victorian times, in 1900. Paris at that. This ancestor had not been chosen to run for Great Britain but the International Olympic Committee had certified that he could compete for India.

So, well over 50% of the Indian Athletic Medals, ever, had been won by his ancestor. Pi was grateful for the gold medal that Neeraj Chopra had won for throwing his javelin far greater than the diameter of his beloved cricket pitch at Chennai, the mighty MA Chidambaram. And the throw was almost 90 metres.

Today's exercise was Professor Pritchard's Taze exercise. Last week's Haikus had gone down well. One was beautifully poetically palindromic. But the professor's claim, in this instance, was that he had invented the Taze. A sentence where each word starts with the letters of the alphabet.

In order—A to Z. No one was quite sure as the verity of this claim. He carefully explained it to his class of 17, split into 4 groups. The class were given 30 minutes to compose this. The favourite Taze of each group was then selected.

Professor Pritchard made Pi an impromptu classroom assistant. The frisson in the class was palpable, especially as Pi wandered around with volume two of the 3743 paged Shorter Oxford Dictionary. There were actually many X words that would be handy to the groups.

This letter needed a designer t-shirt thought the class. In our daily lives, the Xs were missing and could well become extinct if we were not careful. Where were Xanadu, Xanthelasmata, Xenial, Xenon, Xenopus, Xeres, Xerophagy, Xeroderma, Xhosa, Xiphisternum, Xylan? Sure, X-rays and Xylophones were there. But not the Xylorimba. Z was in a similar predicament. But not the zebra, of course.

Van Gogh could reasonably be accused by his critics of Xanthism, thought Pi. There was probably too much yellow in his paintings, as a recent critic had announced to the world. But, maybe, they were perfectly imperfect anyway.

Anton later concluded that Xmas probably should be extinct. X was now replaced, at the time of the holiday, by shopping, drinking, over-eating, bargain hunting, garish decorations, dubious office parties, killing of many trees. In fact, anything but a celebration of the birth of Christ.

Anju's was chosen and appeared to have some meaning but that took a good 6 minutes and 27 seconds to be revealed. As the words had to be coaxed out of another group by charade.

It was: A boxed-in clever dervish effortlessly flows gathering Hegel's intentions, joyful Kantian letters, Marxian nuances, Oppenheimer's platitudes, Quine's rationalism, Sophocles' tales, Umberto's views, whilst X-raying your Zen.

Professor Pritchard later gave the mark as ABCDE: *Anjou Beck Completely Dreadful Effort.* It was easy to start, and made sense, then there was repetition, and a nonsense ending that made no sense. *C'est la vie.* C minus, the grade on the never to be changed University Assessment System version 1.7.

The Latin

Another time Pi had sat in with another class, Anju had composed a poem. She thought the poem compostable too! There was a lot of recycling. The breakdown and learning of it could contribute to other learning.

ad astra per aspera —To the stars through difficulties

alis volat propriis —He flies by his own wings

dum spiro spero —Whilst I breathe. I hope

mirabile dictu —Wonderful to say

omnia iam fient quae posse negabam—Everything which I used to say could not happen, will happen now

exigo a me non ut optimus par sim sed ut malis melior—I require myself not to be equal to the best, but to be better than the worse.

This was the idea; but it was not well received by Elton Flaherty—the Master Emeritus of poetry at the college. The Call to Latin had been written in 41 seconds of thought, courtesy of a smartphone app. Such super efficiency Anju had never thought possible.

The initial mark was a hefty 17 out of 20 but once the confessional Twitter feeds had reached Dr Flaherty, it was downgraded to a mere borderline pass at 8 marks (out of 20). The amended report from the master was:

aut insanity homo, aut versus facit—The fellow is either mad or is composing verses

poeta nascitur, non fit—The poet is born, not made

trahimir omnes laudis studio—We are led on by our eagerness for praise

This was a bind. Merits and distinction would now forever be out of reach, with this accusation of possible plagiarism. Anju recalled that her potential to be a prefect, as a teenager, had been taken away from her with her third detention in a month. Apparently, in school regulations, it is a criminal offence to share paracetamol with a fellow student. Even for the pain of the unwelcomed monthly. Anyway, Anju was somewhat comforted. She would be meeting Pi later that day at the Rasta Fasta Nasta, so that would be fun. She also felt destined for other things.

Pi had sat down with great earnestness and had finished the book that he had brought with him from India. He wanted to discuss it with Anju and give it to her as a present (after the final reckoning of the tower of books by Sir X). The book was relatively unknown in England. Umrigar's *Secrets Between Us* was a captivating read for Pi and it was a creditable 36 millimetres thick.

It was one of the servant books that Pi had completed. The emotional relationship of the women caught by accidents of birth in disparate castes was poignantly cast into words. The pathos and atmosphere were captured so accurately that Guru Pi yearned for another of her books.

Next, he tackled a recommendation of Ruth's. Abraham Verghese's *Cutting for Stone*. Guru Pi was overwhelmed by the selflessness of the medical team in Ethiopia dealing with the desperate plights of women damaged by childbirth. Although a novel, there was an uncomfortable amount of contemporary truth in it.

It also made a decent contribution to his goal at 38 millimetres, but it had taken him a whole 14 days to read. He was way off schedule. Kirk had informed Pi that the reading schedule was at least 6 books under. He had informed Pi that this was a triple double bogey. Pi needed help. A summit meeting would need to be scheduled with Kirk and Anju.

Perturbations of Anton and Pi

Anton and Pi had discussed their worries about the number of unsubstantiated claims that were dictating the lives and spending of millions around the word.

Anton: Look at this—unbelievable! Apparently, you wear this piece of plastic as an insole and you walk off those pounds of extra flesh! Flesh, that you would have spent good money on to add to your body in the first place.

Pi: What is the scientific basis of it all?

Anton: Not to be pessimistic but the only pounds you're losing is the ones from the wallet—real or virtual. Apparently, wearing something that looks like the thing you urinate on in posh restaurants makes you lose weight. Dr Ritz—who is definitely very rich having sold 100,000 of the things—claims that you can lose 2 pounds from day 1, 19 pounds in only 30 days and stay slim forever.

I am sure that he is currently developing a version that can be neatly tucked into your pants!

Kirk smirked and Pi did not.

Pi: And the costings?

Anton: No, to answer your first question. The scientific basis is that the little plastic irritant bits of the insole act on parts of the feet that are directly related to the organs that are responsible for keeping you fat! Maybe there is an instruction in small print to not eat at all or to use the insole to jog around the UK!

Kirk picked up the advert and read out a testimonial from a customer.

Kirk: Look at this! *"I ate as normal and continued to drink alcohol but hey presto; the weight dropped! I had not exercised more or less. My body was just miraculously drained of excess fat."*

Anton: And the costings, Pi? 30 quid or all three of us could each have a pair for 70 quid! Not that we need them. But Pi, you must be a bit thinner than the rest of us. I am informed by Huriya.

His microbiological mind was irked even more with the second advertisement. He admitted to himself that he completely did not understand the how and why of it all. This was a patch that, if placed on your body would supply your gut with good bacteria—the *Bacteroidetes*. And less of the *Firmicutes* that made you fat.

Anton was speechless. He recalled the awful stench of foot ulcers infected with *Bacteroidetes* and felt that he did not want those in his gut. The patch also somehow provided the recipient with more prebiotics—a special type of fibre.

Beautifully svelte slim people who looked as though they had won an Olympic Gold or a BAFTA or an Oscar were advertising it. *Some*, thought Anton, *looked as if they had won all three judging by the size of their smiles.*

The discussion between the three took on a very serious tone as they talked about the various promises humans made to each other based on very little science, lots of faith and usually no evidence at all. Usually, lubricated by the exchange of hard cash or power, or both.

Anton launched into a speech (that Kirk had heard at least once a season) about the duping of humanity in the Iraqi Wars where dustbin bombs had been found but no mustard gas invented by the Brits and used in war by their belligerents.

Ironically invented by the man who had also created a process for making the most ubiquitous and cost-efficient of all fertilisers—the ammoniacal ones.

Then there was the debacle of various land divisions the world over; the Balkans, the Palestine issue, the Kashmir border wars and many others.

The contentious subject of heaven dependent on which culture or religion you had been born into was only lightly discussed for fear of offending anyone—either those present or in virtual stance in the community in Belton.

Kirk's conclusion, as always, was that the only item of world output that could solve all these issues was strict adherence to the 1948 declaration of Human Rights. Anton had not vouchsafed this completely, but generally agreed. Sir X had spent a lot of time trying to persuade Anton that Human Rights, from the UN, were too restrictive if the economy was to be developed at a pace.

Anton agreed as much as any father could to a son. That is never completely. There was no particular edict in the Human Right Declaration that he did not agree with in his psyche. But the main issue was the not invented here components and the fact that the ruling party was doing a revision with less strictures.

This was even though the late Nelson Mandela and Desmond Tutu had led a movement to get a billion human souls to re-pledge themselves to the Universal Declaration of Human Rights. Anton, and indeed Kirk, and even Ruth and Anju it was understood were less enthused by its support of by their erstwhile heroine Aung San Suu Kyi. But the latter had been given the benefit of the doubt, as a person caught between the devil and the deep blue sea.

Kirk simply could not understand why his father no less, and his knighted friends at the golf club had led a petition to have the UK parliament less dependent on referring all things legislature to the United Nations Declaration of Human Rights.

It was not just Brexit that was craved but an exit from the global human societies generally. Kirk imagined spaceship UK exiting Earth by launching itself into space away from it all and towards a new horizon in a different galaxy. But then, Kirk's avowed PhD subject was always contemplated as being '*A modelling of the objective beneficial effects of the UN Declaration on Human Rights and its related nine core treaties on human society*'.

These had only addressed marginal subjects—believed Anton and his compatriots—on refugees, racism, equality, dignity, apartheid, women, torture, children, and migrants. There were other considerations that would need to be included. Such as, Sir X suggested, the right of a company of people to profit from their endeavours independent of the concerns of some of the above.

Pi contributed very little except:

Pi: Hansa Jivraj Mehta changed the line all men are created equal. That is what Eleanor Roosevelt had suggested. Hansa, incidentally meaning swan, changed it to all human beings are created equal. My father knew her even though she was a Gujarati. Her translation of the *Balakanda*, *Aranyakanda* and *Sundarakanda* parts of the *Ramayana* are so very readable in English.

Kirk teased Pi about knowing all the most important people in the world somehow.

Pi went to bed and reflected on the great myths and scriptures of India. The *Ramayana* and that it had given him the most wonderful stories and a stance on all subjects that really mattered, or did they? The opening of the *Bhagavad Gita* had started as a narrative with Arjun in despair and the description of his mouth parched, limbs weakening and quivering, and piloerection.

All due to fright and anguish. Then, there was scripture, interspersed with dialogue. It was like a novel in many ways. But the myths were not an invitation to enter into the life of another; rather an exhortation to be read and learnt from, rather than just enjoyed as a programme of insertion into one's psyche.

These programmes had to be accepted entirely without discussion or argument to prepare the soul for what came after. Unless you wanted to change the religion entirely. Or a bit only and have your own sect. Nevertheless, they remain his ultimate refuge albeit tempered by his own life experiences.

Pi read for a bit. He had completely fallen in literacy love with Josef K in Franz Kafka's *The Trial*. Surely this was not fiction, but themed on the world's bureaucracy. Especially his, back home. A knight's move to Anton. But the book was a slow read and would have to be read interspersed with other books.

Anton at the Golf Club

As for Anton's friend Sir X; he was no longer in the inner circle of knights. He lost the great honour of being a Knight of the Garter, a while back. He still had the medal from the monarch proudly displayed in his library at home. He had made the mistake of being involved in a dubious tax haven that had been discovered to be illegal in its dealings, but only after a 4-year investigation.

Unfortunately for him, it had just crossed the very fine line from tax avoidance to tax evasion. Did I mention that Sir X was a shortening of Sir Mark

Xavier? I think I have. He had taken on the nickname Sir X as people had difficultly pronouncing his name.

Sir X: I am still not sure that Pi can read all the books possible for him to read his own height in books in a year. I have been stuck reading *A Spy who came in from the Cold* for the last 6 weeks.

Anton: No. He is perfectly clever and well-read in his own way. I just think that many books may be difficult. But a challenge is a challenge. Pi will try his best for sure.

Sir X: Well, I keep telling you that I tried reading the classic novels at university and failed and even now, I cannot get myself to read them. How can Pi? Many are unreadable even to an Englishman educated at a proper school.

Anton had heard these sorts of remarks from Mark a little too often. He chose to ignore Mark's ignoble thoughts. A friend is a friend. Anton's inherent conservatism was of a different alloy to Sir X's, it was obvious. The undermining of the different to him and his thoughts was so often implied in such a lot that Sir X ever uttered.

Anton: I am sure that he will do OK. I just cannot recall a time when my kids were so happy. They love Pi. Ruth loves everyone, of course.

Sir X: Obviously, I do know the classic books. Many have been made into accurate films. I do admit that that saves time from reading them. Which is the polar opposite with a certain genre of films. Reading comics, for example, would be a damn sight shorter and less of an inconvenience than the 3 hours loud white noise of a film. But don't tell Kirk that; otherwise, my share price with him will sink even further. Let's see what happens with Pi. There is also the ethnic programme that he will be doing.

Anton: Yes. Ruth has got Pi to do *Carmen's Cultural Journey: Home and Away*. Which should be fun for him. I need to brush up on my Indian culture and recall some of what I loved years ago when I visited Pi's village in my undergraduate days—well, you know all about that, Mark. You know how much I absolutely loved it all.

Looking around the bar, Anton noticed a void. There was something in the home comforts of the golf club that was lacking. There was not the hustle and bustle of bars elsewhere. The food was particularly bland and usually based, needlessly it seemed to him, on the carnivorous side of things. It was like being anaesthetised from the reality of life.

He imagined the fun and vibrancy that Kirk, Anju and Pi were participating in at the City-Zen Café. No doubt Ruth would drop in for a quick drink with the trio after the weekly shop. And why did women still lack a presence at the golf club? Despite them having been allowed in since 1992. Anton knew for certain that the City-Zen Café would be anathema to Sir X.

Anton wanted to pop into Lady Guji's on the way home. He wanted to see if he could buy a *murti* or small statue of Sitala-Devi. Pi had told him all about Sitala-Devi. This was the Goddess for smallpox. Previous generations had prayed to her to mitigate the disastrous effects of this virus.

Both to prevent the condition happening altogether in their locality, but also to prevent death from it. The local temple had held regular *Bajan* and *Aarti* sessions dedicated to the Goddess and given her a remit to act against Covid-19 now that smallpox had been eliminated and HIV mostly controlled.

The mini sermons now allowed as lockdown had eased covered a lot of ground, including the idea that inoculation was carried out in China and India at least 1000 years prior to Jenner and his ideas. And that, intriguingly, the British Raj had tried in vain in 1804 to ban the tribal practice of using cowpox to vaccinate against smallpox in Bengal.

But we forget Lady Mary Wortley Montagu observing the beautiful non-poxed skin of Turkish women in the communal baths. She surmised that this was due to the traditional vaccinations that the community undertook. Back home she had inoculated her 3-year-old daughter, greatly perturbing polite society. This worked, in 1721, and this was a tad before Jenner's scientific endeavours in 1796.

Pi had also told Anton that he learnt from the Brahmin Pandit in Sundervagvela that Sitala-Devi had been assigned other responsibilities and that her portfolio encompassed several diseases, all infectious; tuberculosis, leprosy, chikungunya, meningitis, encephalitis, dengue fever, HIV and even (to pre-empt Covid-19 it would appear) SARS and MERS. But Covid-19 would be the current and near future biggest challenge for the Goddess of the smallest things.

Anton texted his son and arranged to meet him on his way home.

War Chat

Pi, Kirk, Edgar and Keke were having a chinwag over a few drinks. Starting at the Gate and then moving onto the Temperance Bar. Anton joined them and instead of having his spirits lifted, they were dampened. Another inconvenient trope revisited. All were saddened by the present rampant disgrace of war and violence across the world.

The legalised killing of another. Sanctioned through the legal attack route or the legal defence route. Yet, death was still death. Maiming was still maiming. And rubble was still rubble. Tears were tears. They agreed that usually, there was a complex algebra. Once again recalling Arundhati's Algebra of Infinite Justice.

Often, you had to be clear in your support of one side. As if it made any difference at all. One warring disaster of a nation's stupid idea versus another's. Often, both were equally stupid. But one had to choose. *Pro patria mori* again. Maybe not so much dying for one's country but agreeing its direction and waving a banner in support.

The algebra was inevitably based on a calculus of oil, arms, imports, exports, the overlap of religions, hubris, and then back to oil and other fossil fuels. And always history. There was often fighting between one's prize-fighters in the course of war, our little theatres of war where our weapons were tested and refined and supplied to the ragged armies.

To protect the big boys if the worst should happen. Their number one priority was, of course, to protect themselves. But let's supply weapons and let everyone else slug it out. We the ultimate seconders of the duel supplying lethality. Until *digga*—all hell breaks loose.

The idea of war had to be fossilised forever, agreed the quintet. And to home they went.

Pi would continue to worry about war that night. He recalled Edgar's chat about nationalism causing wars and the acceptable rationale being patriotism. Edgar had been crystal clear in his definitions of the two and how mixing them up was dangerous, often being a popular pretext for conflict.

Pi recalled his words almost verbatim. Patriotism is a positive force that celebrates past positive progress in the culture, history, and development of a country of identified people, hopefully always endorsing the rights of all humankind.

Hence, Edgar had stated, "*I support England in cricket—miserable as they are at present! And Pi, you support India, with Bangladesh and Pakistan in reserve. Look at the Italian rugby supporters, they will lose almost 50 matches on the trot against the top teams, but their fans feel that they will win the next one. One day they will!*"

He had also added.

"*But nationalism is believing that your country or nation is superior to others and has a legitimate right to subjugate, maim and kill others in achieving the non-human rights agenda of your country. That is war—whether declared or not.*"

Pi had a lot to digest.

Instalment Eleven: January

The New Year starts with, often futile, attempts to break up illegal parties celebrating the new epoch of vaccination against COVID-19. Christmas and the even the smaller gatherings may have been a disaster as 57,725 cases are reported on only the second day of the new year. An estimated 30% of the NHS bed capacity, that is 26,626 patients, have COVID-19. I know this to be true in our hospital.

Lockdown, an encore.

But the light at the end of the tunnel is visible as vaccination drives plough a way forward. The oldest and infirm are the first to be vaccinated. An estimated Titanic load of deaths will now be avoided every month. A hundred thousand volunteer to help. GP surgeries to prioritise vaccination over all other routine care.

Armed forces will also help with the delivery of vaccines. The vaccine was beginning to reach the 'less important' people in society. Such as the staff on the Intensive Care Units in the smaller hospitals. Also, the two unpronounceable drugs, tocilizumab and sarilumab, have evidence that they can cut death by a quarter in certain select groups of patients. But the cheap steroid, Dexamethasone, is even better in some patients. I note that some of the research was done in our hospital.

Our death roll exceeds the yearly death toll in the Second World War and more than a quarter of the total as the landmark of 100,000 dead is surpassed. One day, there are 1161 deaths in the land of Sir Tom Moore, who tests positive himself. And tomorrow, there will be 164 more deaths than that. I think that was our peak daily death per day recorded. Or was it a bit later at 1820 deaths recorded?

Ironically, the release of the James Bond film—*No Time To Die*—is delayed. Presumably, the audience needs to be alive, even if sleeping.

A really virulent Brazilian strain emerges. We must wear masks to shop. If we do not, then the shops do not have to let us in. There is an odd 'Can you look them in the eyes'? campaign showing lots of coal-face healthcare professionals, to dissuade the public from leaving their homes.

Another campaign to urge people to stay at home, shows families at home but with men loafing on sofas and the woman home-schooling their children, and doing domestic chores.

Clap for Heroes takes over from Clap for Carers. I am officially a hero! At last. The extraordinary hero that is Sir Tom Moore is admitted to hospital with COVID-19. I think we have lost control. For we lived in an age where we all know Mr Bean, but not Mr Alan Bean; the fourth man to walk on the moon and a professional artist.

And as on the moon, there seems to be a lack of oxygen in many parts of our planet. For us humans, that is. And a little too much carbon dioxide is noted.

The most fortunate CEO of Gasworld explains that it is all to do with logistics and nothing much else. The air we breathe has enough oxygen. Just not concentrated enough. Affected are all the corners of the world. Egypt, Nigeria and India get honourable mentions. Replete as they are with spare humans.

We passed 100,000 COVID-19 deaths a long time ago this month. Officially, we have had 129,420 deaths.

Chapter 13
Random Ideas of Pi

Ten masts at each make not the altitude
Which thou hast perpendicularly fell.
Thy life's a miracle. Speak yet again.

King Lear. William Shakespeare (1564-1616). Playwright and Poet.

Pie Conversation

The Beck household had, for once, all showered and lumbered down to breakfast with Pi already in the conservatory having just finished his *Surya Puja*. They had all showered using the tarn technique. Kirk had made the, yet to be published, observation that it was laboriously dull to have to keep squeezing out a glob of soap every time you moved onto a different part of the body.

So, his idea, under trial in the Beck household, was to put a large blob of said shower gel on the hair and keep using small parts of it to clean the body.

The bottle of wine from last night was studied. There was the Latin: *Labor omnia vincit improbus*—work conquers all. The dizzy heights of *omnia vincit amor* to even *mors vincit omnia*. The Beck Tarn was devised to solve the problem. Pi wanted clarification from Kirk. And got it in some detail early in the morning though it was.

Kirk: You basically put a large dollop of the chosen cleansing fluid—priced according to your pocket and gullibility—onto your hair. Then to approximate the rule of nines as a rule of 10s. Thanks Dad, for helping with this bit. One mini-dollop to the front—20% there, 20% on the back, 20% to a leg each, even minier 10% dollop to the arms, 10% to the speedo trunk areas, all done and the head to finish, if not done already. This shaved off a bit of time and saved on water too!

The whole family agreed somewhat with the idea. Although it would be difficult with the depilated or the tonsured among us. In the rather random conversation, Kirk shared the fact that Keke's father was to have dialysis because of 'sugar diabetes'. The Becks thanked their lucky stars for their functioning kidneys, liver, spleen, heart, brain and all things else inside.

The conversation that day had been a tribute to Pi and PIE, whilst eating pie for breakfast. It had started off with a wink between Kirk and Anju, and one or two between Ruth and Anton.

Anju: We should have a conversation using at least one word per input originating from Proto-Indo-European.

Kirk: The tarn shampoo technique works—I shaved a good minute and a half off my shower.

Anju: Today, I will wear my bangles and my cashmere jumper but not my Jodhpurs. A dungaree will be most appropriate for the trip to the godown. I think I can harvest some potatoes.

Anton: I will wear my cummerbund tonight at the hospital as I will be presenting the NHS Hospital awards this year. If you enter, then you get an award. Seems fair! I am sure that the bandana-ed Derek will win something for his cushy number in setting up the vaccination drive. A pandit he is not, but very politically astute. He certainly knows which side his naan is buttered on. I hope it's Wacras to get the top gong!

Pi: Tonight, I will cook a dal curry and a smoked haddock kedgeree.

Kirk: I will drink a bit until I'm doolally. I will make a punch for the gymkhana thugs later.

Anton: Please don't loot my best liquor, chor!

Ruth: I will see you on the veranda. I will be in my alternate avatar doing yoga and ignoring you all!

Pi in non-sequitur, but the urge was there:

Pi: My family were so worried about me coming to Blighty.

Kirk: You dropped the ball! Checkmate!

Pi: Afraid be not. That sentence of yours counts as a ball not dropped, which is probably from the PIE bol meaning stone in fruit and later, all things sport-wise. Checkmate is, of course, also PIE. Blighty comes from vilayet—which means abroad or foreign.

Breakfast conversations were often hard work. Especially if there were no scandals in the news.

The Prince Dies

The Prince dies. Five million of the Duke's Awards given out. And now the full-stop on those. Dame Kelly was thus inspired towards her brace of Gold Medals and the one Bronze via the life work of the almost Centurian Prince. His gaucherie will always be exposed and displayed for all see again on WhatsApp and Twitter. A ratio of his say 50 maladroit occurrences—actually that is not the right word as that means badly right—so I mean gaffes—to the 5 million of his awardees is 30 seconds to the seconds in a day that is a ratio of 2880 to 1. Particularly upset were the Yakel and Yaohnanen tribes on Tanna Island in Vanuata. Honestly, so. The Prince had been deified as the pale son of the Great Ancient Spirit.

For them, he was the avatar predicted, that of a human representing all that was good in their culture and the idea of promoting peace in the world—the *Kastom*. There was also something about him leaving and returning with a very powerful woman. Which he did do. These devotees held a mourning ceremony.

Anton was shocked. Truly shocked. About the rumours of the party via Sir X. Anton was also oddly sad about the death of the Prince. He had never been a monarchist, but he had heard from the best economists via Sir X that the monarchy as an institutional and tourist attraction had increased our scoring on the Global Prestige Index by about 15%. It could not be a total disaster that the 18.7 million square kilometres of the Earth still had our monarch on its coinage and monetary notes.

It then became printed news that on the day before the funeral of the Prince of Endeavour, there had been a party at the abode of the First Lord of the Treasury. Really. Preceding quips were rampant. A COBRA that is Cabinet Office Briefing Room A, meeting with a difference.

Days before the funeral, they had organised some real fun for themselves. With Cobra beers, the papers had suggested, whilst all the rest of us were barred from visiting the lonely, seeing our dying for the last time, and burying or cremating our dead.

On his walk, Pi was encountering doubts again in his mind about some of the issues in his scriptures. He had heard of several Christian missionaries that had had doubts about their scriptures too. Especially, when their potential wife-to-be had refused to convert from Islam or Hinduism to wed the Christian.

Doubts in Hinduism were rare as it was such a broad church; though it was a non-Abrahamic religion, all of Christianity was somehow somewhere encompassed within it. That there was a supreme entity or even just an idea of something greater, Pi had no doubt. The latter especially, as there was no stipulation to have to believe in anything concrete at all.

There had to be a force—even if it was just the Big Bang, which had created us as its aftermath. Were we all, flora and fauna, all mere accidental side-effects of randomness? The thing of it all then had its *lila* or play and there was consciousness. Whatever that means. Consciousness being the sum total of all that we express internally and externally.

Maybe a super-computer that could recall events, ideas and perceptions to guide us towards a solution, absolutely necessary, given our current spate of global crises. Would that be consciousness? We exist, so we each step into this river and we make things happen so the history of the universe changes, forever, that creates the future. Janus indeed or the triumvirate of Brahma, Vishnu, Shiv-Mahesh. It was all muddled thinking.

Another issue was Karma. How could the blame for a disability be attributed to a callous calculus that coldly considers positives and negatives and then assigns you to be in the existence of a slug or tortoise or, a lower caste or higher caste or, a super power or a handicap?

Pi was adamant that this could not be true. We are a sum total of what we do individually, as a family—core or extended, community, population, country, continent or globally as a whole. This was certainly what he had concluded from that great little book of Greta's—*No One is too small to make a difference.*

The children's one, Pi had also read—*Skolstrejk för Klimatet*. But that could not count, Sir X must be obeyed. And the human rights for all ideas in that other greatest little book by Chimamanda Ngozi Adichie called *We Should all be Feminists*, extolling us all to be (mildly decaffeinated at least) feministas.

Then another difficulty arose. There were three books imminently readable and interesting to Pi. And indeed, could prove to be a future necessity after he had got over Priyali. Kirk had recommended the *Kama Sutra*, a rare edition with many lithographed pictures stamped as needing to be censored from the Indian public under the British Raj.

Clearly, they wanted the population to go forth and multiply using only the rather restricted menu of the missionaries. The Khajuraho temples would have been in the blind spot of that particular British Raj department. The other was the *Perfumed Garden*, a bit of an unknown entity, which could account for the under population of the old Asia Minor.

The final one of the discarded triad was the medieval scientific sexology manual that was the *Koka-shastra*. Pi had not been persuaded to even think of reading the Joy of Sex—he felt that the pictures were too filled of bearded individuals. There was also little in the way of skills such as flower-arranging, perfumes, and bedroom design as in the others.

The reason for this reluctance was not the potential lack of approbation from the Beck family but the definite disapproving mien of his brother and sister-in-law. He had promised and had delivered regular updates to them. The mysteries and various machinations of how his homeland had created over a billion souls in just half a century would sadly not be part of the book tower.

Though it was quite likely that the books had originally been picked up by Beck Senior to while away those later hours during his spell in India. Anton was similarly in deep thought on various issues.

Anton at the City-Zen Café

Anton was having difficulties with the news again. Ruth knew that it would take a few days for him to get over this particular but everyday occurrence of spates of bad news items. There had been several news items that had irked Anton. In relation to his favourite topic at the moment, it was the fact that all policies coronavirus were driven by *political science* rather than *scientific politics*.

He kept discussing the issue with himself, for he had no audience. Sir X especially, and his work mates, thought themselves far too busy to even think about things that they could not change. What was it exactly that stopped us from simply going into lockdown a little earlier, rather than waiting until the horse was bolting and then making attempts to pull it back in by the tail?

It was our inherent superiority complex. Or disease, as Anton preferred to refer to it as. On the two or three occasions that Anton had met Edgar, they had fully agreed on most things political and historical, but they had not quite clicked so as to be close friends. They had arranged to meet at Edgar's 'lecture hall', the City-Zen Café back-room snooker suite.

Anton: Why did we not emulate the stricter well-run democracies that had taken precautions to chop off several heads of the monstrous Hydra that was coronavirus? We appeared to be offering it a shave and haircut.

Edgar: And a head massage at that!

Anton: Taiwan, Finland, Singapore and Norway are all doing relatively well and we have the top ten deaths per million in this country. We are globally second when it comes to the death toll! Honestly, at the beginning in March, I would have settled for 1000 deaths a month and everyone laughed. And now, we are clocking 1000 deaths a day. In the UK! In the advanced UK. I am just embarrassed. Did we really think that the virus would afford us special privileges and behave more respectfully in the UK?

Edgar: We were thoroughly prepared, we were told. It was only old people that were dying, some said. Also dying were the frail and the those with learning issues and the diabetic and the immigrant. But thankfully not the overweight, unless very much so. Good news for me at last!

Anton: The same profile that totalitarians usually want to kill. It appears to be a fascist virus!

Edgar: Not to be too Panglossian, but things could have been worse.

Anton: But so many deaths could have been averted.

Edgar: *C'est la vie.* Where else would you want to live?

Anton: That's the ace you always play. Here, of course. This is my home. But I believe in home improvements too!

Anton and Edgar always offered each other solutions to all the major ills of the world. There was nothing that Anton could not fix with an email or two as long it was decisively enacted. The solutions were based on the philosophy of how football was tamed from occasional deaths on the field to a series of rules and amendments with the referee as the underpaid less important arbiter of all, as fair as possible but human too.

Occasionally to be shot; but that was especially in South America. Another favourite metaphor of his was the separation of the craniophagal twins. Anton knew a little about the 19 operations that had taken place so far globally. Another one was being planned at Beersheba hospital. These were twins joined at the head rather than elsewhere, which could also happen in Siamese twins.

The siblings could often never see the other directly. But shared a destiny. The only way forward, ironically, is separation. Edgar always had difficulty understanding this idea fully but gave it credit via the sage nods he offered Anton every 10 seconds or so.

Discussion also ensued on Batman and Robin. They wanted to explore how the Batmen—the vendors of bat meat in that dreaded market had been robbing lives every day since December 2019 and would continue to do so for years to come. This idea was dropped for fear of offence and ridicule. Although Edgar did use it briefly in a lecture piece. But today, Edgar was not the main speaker. They would need to get a move on and get to the Temperance Bar soon.

Raw Tea

The invited speaker at the Temperance Bar was a very far-off relative of Scott of the Antarctic. As we all are. The talk, the usual 10 minutes only was extended today. Usually, it was a maximum of 10 slides otherwise the chair, Edgar would go ballistic and red, and sweat. Interesting enough, today's talk was on the Life and Times of the River Thames.

Pi, Kirk and Anju were there to hear the talk and enjoy the seasonal raw teas from local herbs. Only snippets of the talk were picked up by most of the small audience. There was too much going on in their own individual worlds to pay much more than scant but polite attention.

Speaker: And did you know that the River Thames had been declared '*biologically dead*' in 1957? But was now home to over 115 species of fish including three kinds of sharks. The tope, spur dog and starry smooth hound.

The flights of the raw teas were another pragmatic approach to learning about local wild flowers and creating a loss of absolutism about the notion of the caffeine drink. The flight of drinks was often exactly phenotyped to the customer as long as they had signed up to paying a tiny fortune for it.

To be fair, many of the teas were disastrous in taste and most tasted of grass. For the base was often the very different architecturally goose grass, nettles, dandelions, pea shoots and the ubiquitous nettles. Except for the rare Roman Nettle, which was originally bought to us by our colonialists. The Urtica pilulifera was used for purposes of self-scourging, to inflict skin injury—to keep warm. Hardy bunch, those Romans!

The dead nettles were actually minty in taste, more colourful too with the red, white and pink flowers. But they were not true nettles. Once rose hips were added or the crab apples, then the zinginess was imbued. But always, it was cheaper and more interesting than the barista staples.

And no objective criteria for good or bad tea—but one knew what was tolerable, good, and certainly not good. And fostered inclusivity of spirit and bonhomie. Even if not enjoyed, the final billing from Kirk was always, '*woo-waar, woo-waar*'. A non-descript recall to 'We are, where we are'.

The Three Trees

The next day was the final weekend before lockdown again. At the City-Zen Café, Pancake Day and St Valentine's Day were being jointly celebrated. For the Belton folk, the day ushered in a renewed lack of independence. The virus had re-emerged, a deeply vengeful Venus rising from the sea, beautifully deadly.

Maybe Christmas and then Eid had been a call too soon for people to go back to the places of their birth. Even to go to Bethlehem for the Holy Family had been full of vexation with no room at the inn and the birthing place a barn with a manger. But they did not have SARS Cov-2 to contend with then.

The Three Trees, so-named Holly, Ash and Hazel were to perform their medley of melodies—in a slightly aggressive punky style—but were still very pleasant to behold visually and musically despite the odd vibrations thudding through your body, if you walked past the speakers at an inopportune time.

So many of the folk there now knew of the expedition that Guru Pi had embarked on that they almost lined up to talk to him and sat in pairs with him a few minutes and proffered choices and why. Anju and Kirk left him alone as they caught up with ex-lovers and made up with people, they had had infractions with and made up over mead and wine, and beer mainly.

Tactics were discussed and it was generally agreed again that books by the ilk of David Baldacci, Harlan Coben, Michael Connelly, and James Patterson had to be included. But these specific authors had already been added to the tower. Some queried the quality of the books though.

But surely, 100 million instances of people buying their books could not all be a subset of humanity that was critically speaking illiterate; they must definitely have experienced a cracking great read. Pi informed all that would listen that 100 million books at 45 millimetres would be over 500 times the height of *Chomolungma*—the Mother Goddess of the Earth.

She was otherwise known as *Sagarmatha*—the Head of the Earth that touches the heavens, aka Mount Everest to celebrate the adulation of Andrew Waugh, the Surveyor General of India for his erstwhile boss, Sir George Everest, a Welshman born on an American Independence Day.

Peak XV was an even less inspiring name than Mount Everest. To be perfectly fair to Sir George, he had objected and wanted to call the peak by the original native name Chomolungma. But the Royal Geographical Society had decreed that it would be called Mount Everest. An evidently impartial view.

But also, because the books were thick, often around 44 millimetres, as they were made up of at least 10% blank empty pages. One merely started the next chapter on a fresh page—often a few further white blank pages later. Especially if the place of action shifted to a different country.

For example, London to Moscow to Dubai to Delhi to Singapore to Shanghai to Sydney to Johannesburg to Buenos Aires to New York and back to London. Flight time. A *tabula rasa* that Pi would sometimes doodle abstract art on.

The more challenging had been the John Grisham and Lee Child but these were thrillers and must-reads anyway and were 36 millimetres thick to boot. Kirk reiterated the fact that one could never go wrong with a Lee Child book. The plot was summarised by Kirk.

Kirk: Jack Reacher walks into town. Finds a criminal problem. Finds potential partner. Crunches bones. Sleeps with partner, if ethics allow. Notices dirty underwear. Buys fresh clothes. Move on. Wait for next instalment.

But it was the must-read classics that led to the most animated discussion or arguments, to be honest. Pi was grateful for the cleansing of the mind and restoration and recreation of certain ideas it always seemed to offer. One would hope that this mix of the common and vulgar, classic, and important would please Sir X and Anton. One could not risk Sir X's minor wrath even at the end of the task, whether it was finished or not. Pi had not failed to enjoy any of the books he had read. He had even thoroughly enjoyed *The Killing Floor* by Lee Child. Incidentally, this author could be one of the literary triumvirate deities of Coventry and Warwickshire. Shakespeare—the creator Brahma, George Eliot— the preserver Vishnu, and Lee Child—the destroyer Shiva. *A thought best left unshared,* thought Pi.

Pub Talk

From a swift quenching of their thirst in the Temperance Bar, Kirk and Pi wandered off to the Frederick Merrick, previously the Elephant Man. The pub was named after a local celebrity, albeit an unwilling one. The full story was in the windows co-located with the menus. Here, less temperant beverages were enjoyed.

Mundane problems dissolved, it would be for the clientèle to solve all the problems of the world, two or three at a time. A heated discussion would always ensue on ptotic politics, real religions and agenda-ed versus avowed gender. All conversation was taken to a certain limit and then declared off limits as no one quite wanted to delve beyond the pale.

Politics riled up everyone. Pi was surprised that there were not as many political parties as there were Hindu deities. Although there was no rule as such, the conversation was tasered into a stunned silence as everyone observed Pi standing up, his facial expression poised to speak his first word.

Pi: Politics is just so easy! It is simply an algebra, within the confines of resources, of having the best ideas for advancing human rights of the individual in all the nooks and crannies of human communities, together with the agenda of Mother Earth to preserve itself from climatic and other forms of destruction and despoilment. Sorry, I do use the word algebra a lot.

After this remark was digested, no counter-response was offered and many drowned the dregs of their drinks and got another, acknowledging Pi on the way to the bar with a nod and a wink. The last drinks were being finished on the conversation that all could imbibe in and agree, mostly. The weather and football.

Pi stated the fact that most of the football supporters, the small coterie that it was, in Sundervagvela supported Manchester United. The supporters would often gather away from the town at a bar near Pulicat Lake—Manchester, after all, was only 8343 kilometres away.

Life-Back at the Becks

Ruth's biscuit club had met with their secretive agenda again. The rules were simple enough when Carmen and Ruth had set up the group. For each had agreed to a coffee in the park at the weir in the Soar. Both had brought along a packet of biscuits.

The cheesy ones were a great favourite at the initial meeting but had been banned after the revelation that the palm oil used in their making was grown in fields created by the mass removal of orangutans from their natural habitat.

Ruth had been extremely distressed in seeing the scenes of humans being forcibly removed from their slum homes in Slumdog Millionaire but at least humans would usually find another solution. For the orangutan, the Old Man of the Forest, there was only the prospect of impending extinction.

The club generally chose charities with running costs of 20% or less. *Médecins sans Frontières*—Doctors without Borders was discussed. Members wondered why only 13% was being spent on fundraising as every £1 spent raised

£8.14! At only 2% office management and 85% going direct to humanitarian relief—this was a commendably open charity. And who does not like to nosey into all the financial details?

All the charities were carefully filed by Ruth into a folder called Life. This had been a leftover from the Oxfam Campaign that she had led in Belton through the libraries, community centres and the gurudwara especially. Not to be left out, the mosque, synagogue, temple and some churches had also put-up posters.

The long and the short of it all was that a classroom had been built in Malawi that would be used as a schoolhouse during the term and day and as a community portal for health and other useful information outside of these times. A cup of coffee or tea and a peanut snack would be guaranteed with a nominal donation.

Western visitors were advised to pay 50% of what they would usually pay for a barista coffee at home. That would usually keep the running costs going for a day or two. The earning hour and life of the *homo sapiens sapiens var occidentalis* was worth a lot more than *homo sapiens sapiens var africanus*.

Pi had engaged a lot in these meetings. By attending and listening and just being there, he vowed to do the same back in Sundervagvela. He even had proposed a new name for the club. It would be called EK-ARTH. The way it would be written would lead one to read EK first and then the E would be re-used to be part of the word Earth. Ek—one—Earth is Earth and Arth also means meaning. This was accepted.

A pyrography plaque was commissioned from the local underworked pyrographer who also doubled up as the second-best tattooist. The idea of a tree logo with a few humans and animals and insects and birds around was proposed. But this might be too much.

Items of correspondence came first and many of these were beautifully crafted cards or newsletters providing a window to another country, to another people, another circumstance. The pictures told mostly of good news but ever so often the bad news remained as well. The correspondence was generally however upbeat, celebrating the success of their ventures together.

There was much to celebrate. The health camp had now been established now that the start-up cost of £24,000 had been met. It would run in Afghanistan for 12 months. The group felt good. They had contributed the most as a single donation of almost 10% of the costs. Hopefully, polio could be eradicated from that sector too, and they could give advice on other childhood vaccinations and general health.

Each new member had to agree to take on a charity for at least 1 year. Today, the charity under discussion was Practical Action. This one was new for Ruth and Carmen. Kite was the proposer. He was the local greengrocer who had been blessed with the gift of the gab and would sell you anything that you wanted in the edible vegetable and fruit world.

The legend was that Kite had even managed to procure 12 different types of aubergines for the Diwali stuffed vegetables stand at the Mela in 2019. Abandoned later for practical reasons, Covid-19, of course.

Kite presented the charity. He extolled the virtues of the small stove that Practical Action had designed to reduce indoor pollution in small dwellings and the wells that been dug and maintained, the low cost but effective latrines and of course the tree-planting.

The idea was quickly agreed on and there was broad enthusiasm that the initial commitment of £120 per year had been raised by the surplus created by the small donations that came in through the collection boxes in various businesses around Belton.

The boxes from several businesses rarely rattled; some because they were empty and others because the coins were muffled by the regalised polymer promissory notes of Churchill, Austen, Somerville with otter, Turner and the occasional rare but most welcomed Turing.

There had been a jovial interlude when Kite had showed the members of the group the card picturing two children in a verdant field that he had received from the inquiry pack.

Thank you so much for choosing to leave a gift in your will to Practical Action. Through this extraordinary act of kindness, you are helping to make a world that works better for everyone.

We simply couldn't do all the amazing transformative work we do without the generosity of people like you.

Kite did not recall to agreeing to all of the above. He was not prepared to die yet. He simply must have inadvertently ticked the wrong box. Though the moons, as for all of us, were slipping by. But Kite was in that state of *gemütlichkeit*. With each passing moon, he was seeing the yin and the yang in himself and the moon with greater clarity.

And also, in the carp jumping in the pond and the rabbit digging up the carrot. He also remembered that Pi had informed him that he was very likely only to ever see a thousand full moons in his lifetime.

Anton's Sit-Rep on Spikey

Instalment Twelve: February

Sir Tom Moore, now age 100, dies 12 days after contracting the virus and becomes just another national statistic. There will be a National Clap for him.

Vaccines would be provided to all by the end of the financial year, if adult enough. Then to the over 50s within a few months later. Progress does appear to begin to happen.

I have spent a lot of time explaining how the vaccine works to all that asked at work, at home, and in the local drinking holes, when and if open. That it worked by the fatty envelope containing a chit to the human recipient cells informing them of the recipe to make the spikey bits of Spikey.

Then to raise antibodies via the immune cells. These guided missiles would then kill off any invading COVID-19 virus. The other vaccine, similar but not quite the same. Was it vegan? I always refused to speak on this subject. Our event in the Covid Olympics has been chosen and for a big country, we are first off the blocks and are winning the vaccination event.

Both Elton John and Michael Caine urge us to get vaccinated. The Queen asks the same of us. The ethnics are compelled into vaccination by Meera Syal, Sanjeev Bhaskar, and Romesh Ranganathan. By the end of the month, we have vaccinated 19.6 million people. But many millions are still being shielded, alone at home.

Restaurateurs argue that the lockdown will cost lives because they are losing money and taxes will go down. There are many lockdown breaches on the beaches as the weather is surprisingly clement over the last weekend of the month.

The cost of COVID-19 has been £407 billion. But the debt will be easier to pay off if we save about a billion and a half, from disinvesting in our agreed budgeted plans on global poverty reduction. Honestly? But we imported 12,148 doctors recently. Thus, saving us over 3 billion pounds at £250,000 a pop. Many from the same countries we do not want to help.

Another great idea to raise money emerges. If you arrive from a country on the Red List, then you have to quarantine for 10 days at a government-designated hotel at a cost of £1,750.

Pi later calculated that Sir Tom Moore would have had to walk around the equator just the once to raise enough money for the COVID-19 excesses at his final rate of £12,000 per meter. Pi also found out that Sir Tom had been posted in Mumbai and Kolkata. Pi was oddly pleased with the link.

I had wanted Wacras to win our top award, the COVID-19 Leadership Award, and he did. Simply the best Clinical Director we have ever had.

Is the death rate slowing down? I think so. Re-opening of society is planned for March. The vaccinations are working, that I know. But the month ends with a recorded total of 147,951 deaths so far.

Chapter 14
Further Random Ideas of Pi

—It is easier to change a man's religion than to change his diet.

*—Never doubt that a small group of thoughtful, committed, citizens
    can change the world.*

—Children must be taught how to think, not what to think.

*—I was wise enough never to grow up,
    whilst fooling people into believing I had.*

Maxims of Margaret Mead (1901-1978). American Anthropologist.

Car-A Multi-Organ Failure

Anton had to take his beloved Triumph Spitfire to Speedy's again. He would
need to have a consultation with Yarran, and if need be, have the catalytic
converter mended. It had to be Ray, he had nothing against the other mechanics
but there were just those extra snippets of life that Anton was grateful for,
whenever he interacted with Ray.

The Polish, Zimbabwean, Afghani, and the others would do in an emergency,
of course. But Ray was Ray, the Sound of Music's *drop of golden sun*. Sir X had
once quipped that Ray had the tan to match that accolade. The flashing white
gnashers would greet you as a long-lost friend with the cheekiest of smiles and
the most astute business sense if selling you a car. There was always the
undercurrent of having just over half the fun being poked out of you.

In Ray's life, it was all the little things that had been neglected that had led
to his plight, although now he was holding his head above water. Unlike many
of his tribe that were still attempting the crossing of the Channel. Maybe he
should not have drunk 25% of his wages and smoked another 10% and he could
have and would have—alas all the failure in family, tribe and macro-politics had

led to despair but an eventual planting of roots in Belton and hopefully, forever. For he loved working at Speedy's.

Anton had to wait 20 minutes for the assessment. Pi was with him and 'calculated' the cost of the free coffee and how much it would have cost at the café down the road. It was incredible to be in a country where a tea bag with boiling hot water on it, plus or minus a bit of milk and/or sugar, costed at least 20 minutes of a minimum wage in some cafés. Or a good day wage in the for a quarter of humanity.

Pi suspected that the cost of the receptacle in which it was served had a higher asset cost. Especially if recyclable. Strange but that object could take 250 years to biodegrade, if at all, but it costed less than those made of paper ready to turn into compost rapidly. But there you are, the strange world of money makes the world go round, warmer and warmer.

Pi helped himself to a heap of the Haughty Elephant brand coffee from the 'overlapping' eco-landscapes of Vietnam, Laos and Cambodia. Pi would diligently collect the spent coffee and spread it, after permission was granted from the graduand of the Royal Horticultural Society, onto the herb and rose garden at the Beck Household.

Anton: Pi, make sure that that coffee has not gone through the arse end of a civet!

Pi was fortunate that he did not comprehend the meaning of this and enjoyed his coffee regardless. A lot of knocking, clanking, and grunting later, Ray came out.

Ray: The good news is that that the camshaft is perfect and would attract a whacking £350 when the car is eventually scrapped.

Anton so wanted to tell Ray that this was not a communication approach approved by the specialists in all things communication in his own work. Anton recalled training that he had had to endure early in his career before he chose to look at Petri dishes and life-forms that facilitated an easier mode of communication.

For him at least, less of the dreaded cycle of being sympathetic, then offering diagnosis and then poor prognosis and then thoughts about organ donation. He missed patients though, at times even their families.

Ray: The brakes are fine but only the two on the left side. The others have a hydraulic leak. The third piston is warped, and the Boxer engine is boxing less like Muhammad Ali at his best and more like a drunken has-been. The exhaust looks like a Wiffle ball and you could probably drive, thus exhausted, for a week or two. Then, the car will inevitably die. The alternator unit is good in parts, however, Dr Beck. The cat will attract a good scrappage fee. The minerals in it are really valuable. You know yours, being old, will have rhodium, platinum, and probably some palladium in it. They don't make that brown paint anymore either.

Anton: Thanks for that mate! Ray, is there really no prospect of recovery? What if all the parts were replaced?

Ray: To use Cockney rhyming slang, it is feathers plucked! There is no point in that at all.

Anton: That's not Cockney rhyming slang.

Ray: It is now! I am just trying to contribute to your culture.

Anton: But you are not Cockney.

Ray: Think of it as a gift. Your car would cost more to repair than the SUV on the forecourt, which is 6 years younger and cheaper and will give 25% more miles to the gallon. Your choice. The parts I can sell for more than the whole. In fact, my life is also worth more in parts than the whole.

Ray went off to field a query from Zim who was under a bus and needed help. Anton knew that the repair idea would be sheer folly to Anju and Kirk. But trading in a car for another seemed so disloyal. The sort of state of affairs he had envisaged in the book *Brave New World* where the people, especially if higher ranked alphas, could trade in their old, decomposing partners for the latest models. Actually, several of his acquaintances at work and the golf club were doing the same. On their own, not even needing Ray's advice.

Pi was playing with discarded car parts and was especially entertained by ball-bearing units that he span on his hand in the fashion of Vishnu, the creator. Then he went and picked some green flowered plants in the yard. He had hit upon the spurge, the milkweed.

He picked it and decided to taste the milky sap. It was acrid and many strange noises later, real milk and a biscuit were needed to assuage the acrid taste and tiny mouth blisters and ulcers that had erupted. *Clearly, plants were not to meddle with nor eat*, thought Pi. Pi was however pleased that he had discovered, *de novo*, that the sap was rubbery when drier. *Maybe they could make tyres out of it?*

With this interruption and Pi being ministered to by the tri-continental staff at Speedy's, Anton sat down to wait and thought about his problem of the skeleton in the garage again. For some reason, the selling of the catalytic converter resonated with the destitute man of Calcutta selling his skeleton whilst he was alive to pay for his daughter's wedding.

The book Lapierre's *City of Joy* had no answers on what to do with the skeleton, legally, that was now somewhat crumbling in his garage. Could it be cremated and dispersed into water as would be the wishes of the Hindu? Or just buried as other faiths required, ready to fertilise life again. Or what if Zoroastrian?

Then a tower of silence would be needed and the attendance of vultures. Anton also thought about some of the Covid-19 cases he had seen at work. Day one marked the diagnosis of the Covid-19 infection, usually affecting just the lungs. The illness had its entrances and exits—often direct to the mortuary and the non-attended funeral.

The sighing and hunger for air would lead to the need for more of the 21% of the stuff we were all so reliant on in the atmosphere. The ill were often put into the massage-position, prone, which strangely eased the breathing. The failures would start to kick in. Thinking of this soliloquy, a lot more ideas appeared in Anton's mind.

All the world was indeed a stage for the virus. The predicted case load was a few million per year. But this had been exceeded. The million deaths every 3 months had happened. It was the male *in fair round belly with good capon lined* that had most succumbed. And were the *pipes and whistles in his sound,* the throes of death? Certainly, the patient knocking at death's door was sans kidney, sans heart, sans lungs, sans everything into mere oblivion.

Ray finished the consultation. Pi was busy working on his smartphone, having established that Anton had had the Triumph Spitfire from new and that it had been driven 132,031 miles.

Ray: I am so sorry but there is not an easy repair that can be done. I suggest last rites and a dignified exit without much ado. Zim said that even in Tigray, he would not have revived this Frankenstein's monster.

Pi: Anton, a car that you have spent 4225 hours in. That is 176 days! Imagine that. You have spent half a year sitting in the car. I assume an average speed of 50 kilometres per hour. Please note we spin around with the Earth. At 460 metres, a second or over 1600 kilometres an hour. Less in UK at only 1000 kilometre per hour.

The slowest spinning are the Inuit people in the Qikiqtaaluk region of Nunavat in Canada. Then we spin around the sun at about 100 000 kilometres an hour! The sun then spins at 800 000 kilometres an hour around a huge orbit in our galaxy! Our Milky Way is moving at just over 2 million kilometres per hour! You appear to have driven the car equal to 5.3 times around the Earth, at the equator!

Yet we die because we drive our cars too fast, thought Anton.

Anton: Thank you, Pi. I am sure that is most likely very helpful.

Pi: The pleasure is mine. I am sure that you will get a fabulous replacement.

These were words Anton did not want to hear at all. He thought the last foray of words was surprisingly insensitive of Pi. Anton recalled all the music, news, travels, work, holiday, and just general daily living that had been facilitated by the car. He could not envisage using some new-fangled way of playing music in a future car.

He had loved his cassettes and CDs. He wanted the touch and feel of a CD at least, with the original designs and the art of it all. How could Sergeant Pepper's, Led Zeppelin, Bowie and even the classic Deutsche Gramophone CDs be replaced with anything non-tactile and non-visual and non-olfactory. The future was a little bleak because of this. It was tearing out a sense from the overall experience of the music. And driving.

The future was probably for some of these cars to be used as greenhouses to grow food. Alas, he had nowhere to keep the car. Duly, a photograph of Anton, Ray, Pi and the car was taken and put away to be treasured in his enormous collection of photos. The car was given up to be cannibalised after a quick call to Ruth, in case there was a deep sentimentality that would preclude the sale or paid donation as Ray put it. Ruth agreed with Ray.

Anton was still emotional about it all. He had spent a lot of his life in that car. He recommended to Pi that he read *Klara and the Sun*. He also said to Pi that he hoped his car had not been conscious.

Over a peg, Anton later informed Pi that Speedy's was so called after the original owner, Zim had immersed himself into the world of Mma Ramotswe and all, things Number One Ladies' Detective Agency. Thus unsatiated, with merely reading of the travails of Precious, JLB Matekoni (grateful husband) and the effervescent Grace Makutsi (assistant detective), he had gone on to visit Botswana and all the countries surrounding it with his Saxon wife.

The pride of place above the erstwhile owner's desk was a framed picture of the Queen, close to the first anniversary of her reign (unsigned), then the copper elephants, and then the picture of the owner with Alexander McCall Smith, the author of the world of Mma Precious Ramotswe.

And another factor that Zim was extremely proud of was that the author was born in his very own birth town of Bulawayo, Zimbabwe. The book itself was greatly enjoyed by Pi, though just another 16 millimetres was added. None of the other 21, to date, could be added.

Later at City-Zen Café, Pi narrated his trip to Speedy's and described the plant that had burnt his tongue. This was dismissed by the librarian as an obviously stupid thing to do as the plant was the euphorbia and it was the tree of the same *Euphorbiaceae*—that was rubber. Which was also acrid and not to be used as milk. She also informed him that the yield of rubber in UK spurges was too low to be economically viable. *She was distinctly more unsympathetic today,* thought Pi.

Book Choices

Pi had been appraised by Anton. He felt that the list of books proposed was perhaps a little insular. Very Indic at times.

Pi: Yes, but I am Indic, and one-sixth of humanity is too.

Anton: But in this experiment of yours there must be universality. I suggest you start marching around the globe and visit the lives of people in countries that you will probably never go to. Especially now that travel is banned or extremely difficult! The church library is awash with unread books.

I have no suggestions, but I think you should try this. There is a telephone box near us, which is a now a book swap shop. Only 50 pence a swap. The proceeds go to the perpetual Church Roof Fund.

Pi had got himself back into the *hygge* of reading his comfortable genres. He found that *Amish Tripathi's* mythic books were all that he wanted to read but could only add one to the tower that he was building. He chose to read the *Immortals of Meluha* for the tower.

To comply with Anton's edict, Pi went to the telephone box and picked up Legson Kayira's *I Will Try*. After duly depositing his 50 pence, he retired to the café. Pi enjoyed reading about the trials and tribulation of the long sojourn from a village in Malawi, then the walk of 4000 kilometres across Africa—barefoot with an axe, two books and some food.

Then the encountering of animals, humans and non-humans, each with challenges of hostility, but often friendly and helpful. Only to end up working and studying in the USA and UK. Having started at the age of 16, in former times, and especially in India, a new religion could have started with these escapades.

Although Pi had enjoyed all the detectives, especially Inspector Morse, Sherlock Holmes, and the erudite Monsieur Hercule Poirot, he did feel a re-read could not be justified. Sir X would not be impressed. There would be further opportunities in the remaining reading hours in his life. He was saving time in the future for a re-read of all the life and times Mma Ramotswe of the No 1 Ladies' Detective Agency.

Sausage

Pi then decided to set himself the challenge of further reducing meat consumption in the family. To be fair, it was not there daily, and usually of the highest quality. Or so newspapers and various food blogs had said. Vegan or even vegetarian the Beck household was not, and they could be askance in their thinking. But there would be always be an exploration of the diet of the celebrities.

Enjoying the incomes of these celebrities would undoubtedly be even more welcome. The towards veganism, just having more, rather than fundamentalist approach was worth a consideration but a denial of bacon would have been a deprivation of liberty and general human rights to both the Beck males.

But to follow in the alimentary gustatory habits of Ariana Grande, Zac Efron, Beyoncé Giselle Knowles-Carter, Venus Williams and in the other stages of life, so unimportant to Kirk, more important to Anton, were Gisele Bündchen, Madonna, Darryl Hannah and even the Clinton (Bill) and Queen Amidala herself.

Kirk thought an advert for the veggie stance with Natalie Portman stating in a galactic council of leaders as in that film would sell a tanker load of meatless but protein rich sausages, burgers, and faux bacon. An invocation often coming after the good morning. It would save the slaughter of a million animals.

In fact, more, as this could be a fair chunk of the eighty billion animals we eat every year, dear *Homo sapiens sapiens*. I ask again, why so sapien? Especially when the gaseous omission of the bovine were such toxic gases for warming our Spaceship Earth.

Kirk imitated Queen Amidala in Star Wars as he let rip.

Kirk: I was not elected to watch my animals suffer and die while you discuss this in committee and continue to eat loads more meat and pollute and cook the planet. It is clear to me that the governments of the world no longer function together. I pray you will bring sanity and compassion back to the galaxy.

For Anton, the not so useless calculation of the day by Pi, was that one less meat meal a day for the entire Chinese population would be the equivalent of the entire UK population becoming vegetarian or possibly vegan. Anton would be eternally grateful if that could happen, absolving him of much personal responsibility in this matter.

There was a return to the consumption of tofu in the family—high protein but not the best tasting unless expertly cooked. Nevertheless, Anton enjoyed the breakfast, vegan with the Beck tea. The vegan sausages he noted, although, 133% more expensive than Butcher's Best, were to his entire satisfaction.

The advertised knack of the sausage on biting in was to his quiet and considered gastronomic delight. An over-peppering, over-garlicing and fake gristle would be needed to conjure up the perfect open market European version though.

Regards Covid-19 though, there was optimism. Many had been vaccinated and the deaths may be reducing. Anton was always ready and willing to keep the Beck household thoroughly informed.

Why LCFC Are the Best Team in the World

A release from lockdown. Yippee. Just down the road, it was still lockdown. Magically not in Belton this time, where the gerrymandering had been perfect. Kirk and his mates had managed to get a table in a yurt at the Belton Rail Real Ale Festival.

It was just after his third pint of the real rail ale that Kirk decided that he was ready to launch into why Leicester City were the best team in the world and possibly the universe, if football was not played in any of the billion civilisations predicted by Carl Sagan. Or certainly Europe, at least.

Kirk: As you all know—Man City became top of the league halfway through the season and stayed there. They were the top of 20 teams. The European cup is only 32 clubs. But Chelsea beat Man City in the European Cup Final in Porto on 29th May. Therefore, they are better. *Comprendez?*

The small squad of close and stranger followers all nodded to this. Carmen's children, Patrick and Rikki had joined them. The Chelsea song span out across the outdoor bars, in a chant of—Chelsea, Chelsea, Chelsea in various tones which were shouted out and then repeated *ad libitum* until the next gulp of beer was due. A little too inebriated, as they were.

There was too much stimulation of the GABA brain receptors, and the euphoria was slipping into a little aggression and disinhibition. Some were nearing stupor. The latter group not having appreciated the strength of the beers brewed by the holy order of the English Trappists. Some beers were of the percentage strength of the legal age to marry with parental consent, that is.

Kirk: Therefore, Chelsea are superior! You agree? The FA Cup is the best of all—a record 763 teams have taken part before. Any registered footy team can enter. Please note that it is the oldest and most prestigious of them all—it held its first final in 1872! We then beat Chelsea in the FA Cup Final at the home of football—Wembley. So, we are the champions, we are the champions of the world. *Quod erat demonstrandum*—QED! Thank you!

The last was delivered with a reasonably accurate impression of Freddie Mercury. A karaoke medley of Queen songs followed. And as a final flourish as he was being escorted off the karaoke stage:

Kirk: If you want to win, Manchester United, Arsenal, Tottenham and Liverpool—change your kit to blue!

On sobering up a little, Kirk recalled meeting Julian Barnes at a book festival, where they had clandestinely shared the fact over the signing of *Chesil Beach* that both were ardent Leicester City fans. Julian had confided that this fact was not to be shared with his ardent intelligentsia fans who had elevated him above such mundane matters of supporting a football team. The book had been signed and dedicated to, at Kirk's request, Elsie and Effsy—Kirk's future potential children.

Chesil Beach had remained unread. Kirk thought it suitable for Pi as it was short and had sturdy thick covers. The lives of those in it would certainly be novel to Pi.

The Fête

The idea of bingo that Pi had for the fête was sceptically received by even Ruth. Ruth tried to convince Pi that a fête is more cake and ale, than quotes and education. This was especially never a school day. But Pi was very persuasive.

It was not actually bingo; Ruth called it that for want of a better word. Essentially, Pi created 35 index cards with quotes, four each from each of the following religions: Christianity, Islam, Hinduism, Judaism, Sikhism, Buddhism. And 11 for other traditions and secular points of view.

Each had a quote on it, and from the shuffled pack, one had to match the quote with the mainstream religion, other traditions or secular. It had proved impossible to win this particular version of the Elginesque puzzle and the highest score was a paltry 21 out of 35.

This was congratulations to the vicar aided and abetted by his catholic husband. The years at Divinity College sorting the chaff from the wheat had clearly not been wasted— too much. The most conservative of all (he had been the local MP) got precisely 0, which was a mathematical feat in itself. According to Pi. Pi also discussed the fact that the low score could be a testament to the retired MP's eclecticism or profound ignorance.

When Ruth took over the stall, Pi met up with Anju and perused the book stalls for suitable titles. In fact, one of the books that Anju saw—a steal at £1—was *A Suitable Boy*. Although a firm favourite of Anju's, she decided against it for Pi's labours. Why?

The lack of brevity at pages 1349 and the mere 591552 words. Though she did recommend for Pi to read it at a later date. But Pi had still read it, over 19 days, and simply loved it. And they all enjoyed the mini-series too. The perfectness of the characters played by the actors meant they should legitimately be banned from playing any other roles.

Tanya, Tabu, Ishaan, Rasika, Ram, Vivek, Sharvari, Shahana, and especially Namit would all need to be banished from the acting world. Much in the same way that the Mughal Emperor Shah Jahan is reputed to have blinded and cut off the hands of the architect of the Taj Mahal, so he could not create another such wonder of the world. Though many said this was untrue.

Anju felt as though some great decision had been made by her. Pi had agreed to Art Spiegelman's *Maus* and *Kindred* by Octavia Butler, both as graphic novels. The third was the already read *Swann's Way* by Proust. The final graphic novel was *The Handmaid's Tale* by Margarat Atwood. It was unlikely that Sir X would accept any others.

PS—the stall. It was deemed a great success and raised £137.77. This was a notable fillip to the funds, only to be outdone by the beer stall, cakes and samosas, and the plant sale.

The Recipe

And what did Pi and Kirk make for the feeding of the hungry? I promised you a recipe. You can have Pi's. In the Beck household, it had been established via Mejini, the TV dietitian, that the root of all evils, dietetic-wise, was not knowing and understanding the basics of satiety. Gastronomically speaking—not of the 4-fold life according to Pi of love, power, God, and sex.

Kirk: What shall we make? Let's put Mejini's idea in action! We should create a dish that is almost perfect.

Pi: We need protein at 1g per kilo of your weight. A bit of fat and some carbs. Fruits and vegetables and fluids. Done.

Kirk: Why?

Imitation in the sway and nod style of Mejini.

Kirk: Because we need to start with protein, which switches off our hunger the most—tick, tick, tick. Fat equally so—tick, tick, tick. Carbs less especially, if refined or disastrously sugary. Alcohol least of all.

The ticks in the conversation were supplied with cuts through the air using the right index finger in the manner of Zorro with a sword. Pi indicated that he wanted to talk with a half namaste.

Pi: That is why we must have nibbles with our beers.

After various attempts at googling the ingredients, it was formulated—*Prike*.

It was made of one-third rice, one-third quinoa and one-third red lentil. Added to a dash of oil. Spices to suit the Antons of this world but for Pi a bit more. Pi added these from his *hawejyu*, with a panache inadvertently imitating Jackson Pollack, a colourful dash of this and that.

The former and latter being jeeru, dhana, turmeric, garam masala, mustard seeds, ajmore and red-hot chilli powder. The latter was the best weapon in Pi's household to counteract burglars and nuisance calls in general. A hammer too, as the ultimate deterrent but one that could endanger a mutually assured destruction if wielded.

And from the lid compartment of the *hawejyu* its lid leaves of kuddhi, taj (very hot cinnamon, not the small supermarket pieces of tasteless bark or rawplugs), some mace flower, some grating of nutmeg, and a few cloves. Add water at double the volume of rice, dhal and quinoa. Stir.

Microwave for 8 minutes. Stir; and add vegetables of choice some onion, tomatoes (aka love apples!), okra. Microwave for 7 minutes. Done.

Kirk wanted it all costed. Anju helped here. The local spices from the delicatessen that is Alimentation Patel, the Francophile compatriot of Pi's would work out at just less than 9 pence per litre of *Prike*. The triad of the main ingredient would cost 93 pence per litre.

It certainly kept the munchies in retreat for a few satiated hours. All with this vegan blood streaming through the body and diluting the anguish of the eaten fauna. We all win.

The Sundervagvela Desi Stall

Pi often thought of his family and friends and missed all the aspects of home on a macro-level. It was in Belton that Pi felt that the smaller things in life had become even more important and integral to his way of living and thinking. He thought of Desi.

This chap on the fringes of the Sundervagvela Bazaar who sold peanuts, but with a business model that Pi though was unique. Kirk had agreed to discuss the idea with Pi. After his third pint at the Temperance Bar.

Kirk: What are you thinking about? Do you want to tell me about that peanut salesman?

Pi: My good *dost*—friend—Desi. He is a formidable businessman in Sundervagvela.

Kirk: Tell me more, tell me more, Pi. Did he get very far? In the world of business—will the company be launched on the stock exchange? Will the finances be secure? Has the business cash flow been hedged against the future rises in the cost of the raw materials—failed harvest, etcetera? What about the pension fund and what about inflation, depreciation of assets and the need to innovate and keep up with the competition?

Pi: I think you misunderstand. I meant no Tata, but a simple businessman.

Kirk: What is he; a small shop or a door-to-door merchant? How simple are we talking here?

Pi: He peddles. Both knowledge and nutrition. That is, it.

Kirk: How does he get away with the lack of a hawker's licence and rent for the space? Taxes?

Pi: Minor details. He invests only in land to rent out to others. He has enough for the day to day. He also has a small wife.

Kirk: I do not think the size of his wife is at all relevant surely?

Pi: But she is small.

Kirk: Ok, please do press on.

Pi: He believes that the only thing to ever invest in, is land. He will tell you that they are not making land anymore. I know what you are going to say, Kirk but land reclaimed or created is very expensive.

Kirk: The Middle East.

Pi: Yes, but that is almost a thousand dollars a square meter! People think that Desi has at least 1000 bighas of land. Did you know in Suryapet Mothy, a plot area of 4 square feet was advertised for 60 lakhs—that is 60 thousand pounds! Normally, land is about £1000 a bigha! But Desi has managed to find himself some land at a twentieth of that price.

Kirk: So, Desi is still a millionaire!

Pi: Much more so. In India, we call such people *crorepatis*. But nobody knows about Desi—he hides his wealth well.

Kirk: What does this guy actually do? Does he have an App for knowledge and nutrition? That is such a crowded market here, you know.

Pi: I am going to tell you. Firstly, he keeps the other businesspeople at bay by paying regular donations to the mosque, temple, gurudwara, church, synagogue and even the sacred grove area of the tribals dedicated to snakes. He goes to all the major festivals and leaves samples of his goods free for distribution as prasad.

Kirk: Marketing, Pi? Got it—the free samples are marketing! Yep, I have a clear idea of everything, except what he actually does!

Pi: It is just so simple that I wanted to give you the outcome first. You agree that it is a good business. For we do not have two bighas to rub together as assets.

Kirk just nodded, hoping that the conversation would finish soon. He was sure that the new ale on today—the Milk of Bacchus—would be running out imminently. It was the last cask. The hops had been particularly difficult to procure, all thing Covid-19 and the like.

Pi: What he does is that he sells just two items. The brutal hot days require adequate hydration and all that we need is provided by *nimbu pani*. There is minimum effort needed to make this. The recipe is iced water with a pinch of salt, masala and lemon, of course. A sprinkle of cumin is added too. And a leaf of mint.

Kirk: So, he makes curried lemonade! Is there anything that you do not curry?

Pi: As the sun is to the moon in providing light. *Nimbu pani* is just so much better. Masala *nimbu pani* is the best. There is no better thirst quencher. Desi normally uses lime instead of lemon. You drink this and wait for the monsoon!

Kirk: The bottle is recycled presumably, to be green, Pi?

Pi: Yes, in most cases, the *nimbu pani* was consumed there and then. A deposit would be taken out on the greenish bottle and reimbursed. Deposit only necessary if Desi did not know the customer.

Kirk: I will get a beer and wait with bated breath until you tell me about the rest of the business. What do you want to drink?

Pi: The same, please.

On returning, Kirk was very pleased that he had managed to secure his beverage from the dregs of the barrel. The unpasteurised curds evidenced this, floating gently to the bottom of the glass. This was a rare cask-conditioned alcohol-free beer. Kirk could taste the fermented afternotes and wondered whether it was an accidental kombucha.

Pi: So, where was I?

Kirk: The knowledge parts.

Pi: Yes, but the nutrition is not finished. He sells a mixture of nuts and dried fruits and seeds that is officially sanctioned by a paper in the All-American Journal of Nutrition. Apparently 30g—an old ounce or so—of the mixture has so many of the positive nutritional attributes that you people crave.

Kirk: What exactly is that? Though presumably most of the clientèle are locals.

Pi: Yes, but a lot are Silicon Valley wannabes of that sort. The mixture has good nutritional value as it will give you 580 milligrammes of the Omega-3 that you need of the 1000 milligrammes or more needed per day. Twenty percent of its calories come from protein. It is low in saturated fats too and has some other benefits that I cannot remember. That's it—manganese and selenium and iron and fibre.

Kirk: The latter to recharge the batteries! Ok, so people like it? It must be expensive.

Pi: It is not expensive. The main ingredient is dried peanut, with a few walnuts, flax and hemp and the rest is secret!

Kirk: I am intrigued about the knowledge part.

Pi: Well, the model of the knowledge distribution you assumed would be an App. But no—this was the application of pages torn out from books and then with origami transformed into a quadrangular tray. These are made by children but no more than 100 trays were bought from each registered child per month. So as not to exploit the child so much.

Kirk: Like a paper round without the paper round!

Pi: What?

Kirk: I was just thinking that my life would have been different if I had been allowed to deliver papers but the whole market was controlled by the Baxter twins.

Pi: So initially, the business ran into problems as the local thugs—and I am here with the thugs—were not pleased with pages being torn from their holy books to be origamified into envelopes for the Desi mixture—nutritionally beneficent though it was with a purported ability to contribute to a diet that reduces the risk of death full-stop and reduces cancer risk, diabetes and all things awful with the heart and brain. I think. There was a beautiful unity of the religious on this matter.

Kirk: I think I understood you, Pi. Having survived that issue with the thugs, what did he do?

Pi: I will spare you the details of his daily tortures. He kept up with the idea as the Silicon Valley sorts would enjoy reading a passage from the paperback editions of the Bible, Quran and the Gita and the other books. It was a daily snippet that resulted in sales. But sacrilegious it was.

Kirk: And?

Pi: He moved onto another idea for the paper, after his third fracture and the second burning of his stall. He would use pages from dictionaries, encyclopaedias, or magazines. The dictionaries were easy, and each child would be given one at registration after they had submitted 100 envelopes to the quality controller, Fatima Begum.

On selling the envelopes to Fatima, the child would have to elocute and explain the meaning and use of at least 20 words. Or have a chit from a parent or auntiji or uncleji stating that this had been achieved. The exploitation thus had an educational element.

Kirk: The encyclopaedia was the same, I guess? And the magazines?

Pi: The rules were complex but worked. The number of words and entries that had be to be said from each child was a function of the year they were in in school. The magazines were often like your fashion magazine that comes on Sunday.

These would be saved by Desi's airline hostess relatives. *The Week, Sunday Times Magazines, Cosmopolitan, Men's Health*, and *Women's Health* were the most popular. These envelopes were only made by adults though. Dictionaries and encyclopaedias were for the children.

Kirk: Yes, I can see why it works. On the commute in the bus, train, or the metro line. A bit of knowledge—a bit of nutrition. Tangible knowledge—an engagement with the wet brain rather than the dryness of siliconised electronic messages. And the paper would be recycled?

Pi: Yes. And the customer would bark out the order, "*Desi, one nimbu pani masala, one special mix—dictionary please.*" For the toothless, he would have an overnight pre-ground and pre-soaked mixture.

Kirk: I am not sure why we had this conversation but—

Pi: To pass time, Kirk, to pass time. One cannot live by beer alone.

Caste Out

The Beck family had wanted to know even more about the caste system. It was one recurring theme that always seemed to be mentioned in the charity magazines of Ruth. All incredibly useful charities that aided humans, animals and the ecology of Earth.

When it came to all things Indian, there was so often a prefix of some unfortunate Indic people being Shudra and therefore impoverished, and similar notes on the life of a person whose opportunities had been lost because of the accident of their birth.

The Beck family listened, questioned it all and felt a little more enlightened. They in turn were pleased that Pi was equally distressed by the casteism that was rife in his country.

Pi had been brought up on the caste system and it was as important to his society as National Insurance and NHS numbers were to navigate the new world that we had found ourselves in. Had you been vaccinated, or not? Did you need to show evidence; or not?

Being high caste certainly inoculated you with godliness, not just from an early age but from the inchoate embryo. He absolutely adored the lack of the caste system in the UK—at least in the areas that he visited.

The *Einwanderungsland* that was Belton worked well in its diversity. A recent sociologist had found 111 ethnicities and 61 languages. And that was without the creation of novel, unique often, mixed heritages and fresh new dialects of the children using a hybrid tongue from the mother, the father, and society out there. Caste and class at times appeared to be disappearing.

He had felt distinctly uncomfortable when visiting the golf club with Anton. The stares made him feel as if he was a Shudra walking into the religious inner sanctum of the Mahavishnu Ghats. A mistake that could be life-threatening depending on who was conducting and receiving the blessing of the Supreme at that specific time, and how much they had paid for the direct lines to the deities.

Interruptions were not allowed after the sacred contact had been established through fire, prayer and often some hard cash. A smartphone interruption would be most unwelcome. Even though it could be the sharing of a picture of a pizza overloaded Mondrian-style. There was also always the potential for instant forgiveness if there was further enhancement of the very voluntary donation.

Pi had seen the caste system in Aldous Huxley's *Brave New World*. The alphas and betas and deltas of humans thus divided. Unfortunately, in Sundervagvela, everyone knew the caste of a person as easy as if there had been a coloured square stuck on their forehead. You would be divided into the labouring Shudra, the trading or farming Vaisya, the administrative or security-focused Kshatriyas or the top dogs and learnèd, the Brahmins.

However, the intention of caste being cast forever in life had never been intentional. The *Mahabharata* although it may be difficult to locate within it as the longest work of mythology in the world at 15 times the length of the Bible and 8 times as long as the Iliad and Odyssey combined, declared that *only character and conduct can decide the caste.*

Pi felt that caste was more a job description than a restricted spiritual category or cut of the Supreme. Here was the problem; as this meant that castes were associated, by prejudice, with certain characteristics. The castes were aligned to the four goals in life.

These were *Kama*—the desires for fulfilling the body, and hence, the sutra. *Artha* is the gain and fulfilling of material prosperity and living well economically without debt, enjoying work that is mentally fulfilling. *Dharma* is self-discipline and ethical behaviour in endeavours in sport, work, studies or in martial encounters.

Pi always thought of Sunil Gavaskar, Sachin Tendulkar and Mary Kom as the best of all hard workers for their crafts. *Moksha* is the liberation; the end of a life fulfilled. The finality of being rich enough to live poorly and liberated from the ills of the world. These are aligned to the castes.

But it is so wrong to think of the crude alignment of these with each of the castes alone without any admixture. And then the third axis of the *gunas* or the properties of nature itself. The elementary attributes of all action or all that is. That is *Sattva, Rajas, Tamas*. *Tamas* being inertia, ignorance and lack of wanting to progress.

The *Rajas* the passionate, often angry, energetic way to do something and *Sattva* to be enlightened, progressing towards both a personal and communal fulfilment. And this, we have the *Tamas* as Shudra. The *Tamasic-Rajas* of the Vaisyas, the *Rajasic-sattva* of the Kshatriyas and of course, the *Sattva* of the Brahmin.

But life is far more complex than that. Bring on, Maslow! He could sort it for sure. In the end, Pi and the Becks agreed to steal, again, that phrase of Arundhati Roy's that life was an *algebra of things*—a bit of this and that and then a different amalgamation of attributes and feelings and doings.

Kirk made the point that the billionaire, almost trillionaire, almost inventor of the electric car was now living in a mobile home that was less than 425 square feet! Anton did not believe that, of course. But hopefully, always ethical and observing human rights. The world was fixed again. And only 2 bottles of the finest organic red (for less than £12 each), as per budget. The chateau-pyrographed corks were strewn at the base of the old honeysuckle. There were more important activities to undertake the following day.

How to Order a Zeer Beer

The Annual Litter pick around Belton had gone well and the 26 litter-pickers had collected 26 full bags of rubbish thrown out of cars or otherwise discarded by their fellow human beings living locally. The lakes, hedgerows, bridges, canal paths, and lanes had all been spring cleaned.

Gheewala Daughters and Sons and the local funeral director had sponsored the event by purchasing Hi-Viz gilet-jaunes for the litter-pickers and a lobster claw device that could pinch rubbish with a deft hand movement. The members of this Movement des Gilet-Jaunes were pleased to receive a Belton Voucher to spend in local pubs and cafés.

Pi, Kirk, and Anju decided to grace the untested new idea at the Temperance Bar—Zeer Beers. It had recently been refurbished and re-opened heralding a new era in all habits drinking. *Maybe intravenous infusions,* thought Anton.

Pi was perplexed, having decided to order a Zeer beer, having drunk the little free slurp on offer. There was no alcohol in it, hence the name, but it was certainly not lacking in gustatory and olfactory delight and often, if desired with the crunch of sharp bubbles dissolving into other universes. And always a mystique and novelty factor, inherent in the idea, for sure too.

The board was very much like the cryptic messages that were chalked up on the school room type blackboards that he had admired in the early morning on his travels through Sundervagvela Market. Those messages would be in relation to the different cloths, teas, fruits, and vegetables for sale.

The lower echelons of the boards were always reserved for spices and fish. Here, Pi had learnt the difference between dill, mustards, chillies, caraways, cassia, cinnamons, coriander, saffron, cumin, zedoary, cardamoms, clove, star anise, bay leaf, amchoor, nutmeg and mace, kalonji, khus khus, kabachini, aniseed, peppers, salts, anardana, sesame, ajwain, fenugreek and tirphals.

Priyali had been particularly impressed with this local knowledge of Pi's. And even of the 4 varieties of *patthar ki phool*—the lichens, the harmony of a fungus with an algae or bacteria, the stone flowers that in various combinations, juxtaposed with the family spice mix, would make up the secret blends of specific well-renowned biriyanis.

Pi doubted that now, post Covid-19, he could even discern his pepper from his cinnamon. He also had odd olfaction. At least, Anton had given them the charming diagnostic labels of dysgeusia and dysosmia. Or something similar.

Kirk: It's easy. Let me talk you through it. First the mash. Which?

Pi: OK that one is easy; there are only a few possibilities. This I assume is the body of the beer. A grain—steamed always and occasionally sprouted.

Kirk: There are three choices only. Which are?

Pi: Barley sprouted, wheat sprouted, buckwheat soaked.

Kirk: Anju, you explain the next stage, especially as you think that hops are drugs and cannabinoids!

Anju: Ok, sure. Hops are the female flowers or seed cones or strobilus of *Humulus lupulus*. Kirk; a member of the *Cannabaceae* family of wildflowers! That bit was easy. There are loads of varieties. The best are the Žatec or Saaz—the queen of them all as it used in Pilsner beers and Stella, of course. Impressed, Kirk?

Kirk: Almost and a little quicker, dear Sister, I am thirsty!

Anju: But Pi likes details. There are loads anyway: Amarillo, Apollo, Cascade, Centennial, Admiral, Hercules, Bo, Styrian Golding, Boadicea even. Goldings. Kirk, impressed even more?

Kirk: Yes, but doesn't help my thirst though.

Anju: There is a bitterness scale. The Bittering or IBU. The International Bitterness Scale. Its range is 5 to 120. But this could always go higher and off the normal scale. This is a bit like bitterness in humans, I guess!

Kirk: Anju!

Anju: Nearly there—we have 5 hops today—Crystal, Kent, Endeavour, First Gold Dwarf, Fuggles. Yakim Chief Simcoe has sold out already. Look, next month the Temperance is promised free hops courtesy of Big Tim- Savinjski Goldings, Celeia, English Cascade, Chinook, and Hallertau Blanc. An empire driven by the words of a teacher who had told Big Tim that he would fail.

Then onto the flavours. Today, we have 4 possibilities. 1 is no extra flavour, 2 is kriek—essentially a not too-sweet cherry, 3 is orange, 4 is lime, 5 is coriander.

Then, we go plus or minus a pinch of pink Himalayan salt from the nearest German supermarket. The little bit of lithium potentially gives a nice anti-depressant kick. Nearly there, next is the main liquid carrier of the Zeer beer. The water—flat tap filtered or sparkling—latter very sharp.

Pi: Wow! That is potentially 3 times 5 times 5 times 2 times 2 different types! 300 different types; that is amazing! Is the cost much? Who is Tim?

Anju: No, it's great value—£2 a pint or 3 pints for £5. Small crowds of friends are encouraged! Tim later!

As the pints were admixed, Pi remarked that 300 would be enough for each state in the world to adopt their own one. *This was potentially a useful addition to national identity*, Pi thought. Kirk had to search the internet.

Kirk: But there are only 193 countries as listed by the UN.

Pi: But India alone is 28 states. Also included can be Andaman and Nicobar as two states and then Jammu, Kashmir, Ladakh, Lakshadweep and possibly others. In fact, we recently created Telangana.

Kirk: OK, OK I surrender. We have Scotland, Wales, and a bit of Ireland, I guess. You will probably be a little short though and not quite get to 300!

The trio settled down to a Zeer Beer of buckwheat, Endeavour, orange, no salt and sparkling water. Anything to do with Inspector Morse would always find some sort of favour with Kirk, fond as this fictitious detective was of beer—though the Inspector's would always be with alcohol.

There was an animated discussion happening in the corner of the bar. Almost a fight at times. The gestures and words that could be ascertained were none too poetic. Often duelling with sharp incisive words of abuse. The topics were various; most often recurring was of course who to support football-wise. Why support Liverpool?

If you have never been there and were born in Hemel Hempstead? Or worse still, why would you not support Leicester City, it being the nearest major club? Politics and then war was covered. Then sport again as there was always plenty. Even darts and curling were given a good airing. Mother Earth and all her squabbling children. And so close to Mother's Day.

Pi Observations

Pi, went to get the next round of drinks and noticed that many of the citizens were heading towards Edgar. Edgar was poised to start another 10-minute lecture. He was so glad lockdown was over; for now, at least. The proprietors of the business were always personally and economically gratified with these lecture events, which Edgar's mind were not often enough.

For Edgar took weeks to prepare his lectures. The few champagne socialist types that Edgar brought along would buy, he would often remark, the ridiculous no alcohol gins and vodkas and rums and then have those in Martinis and Libre Rum and various other scandalously named cocktails. A dozen of these would bring in the same profit as looking after a score of other drinkers for 3 hours.

Pi noted that Edgar stood *à la Napoléon*. But why was it *la* that is feminine and not *le* as in the male? Edgar had his right hand on his spleen. Was it hurting?

This was perceptive from Pi, as in fact Edgar always had indigestion before giving a talk. Keke came in *à la Nehru*.

His right hand was holding his left upper arm from behind. *This*, Pi thought, *might be to relieve possible backache?* Almost late to the talk were three fashionable student who had come in right fist raised, *À la Mandela* proclaiming *Hiya comrades—a good day to us all*!

Edgar's talk today was on vegetarianism that he believed in, versus veganism. That he abhorred and thought most unnatural. All of the usual argument went to and fro as if they were playing competitive racket sports. Do adults really need to steal eggs? Steal milk? Kill for food? But we are carnivores; surely, look at our teeth.

But they don't look like the teeth of other carnivores; so clearly, we should be vegetarian. It was a football match, and you could not sit on the fence. You were either with them or against them in this fight. Pi put up this hand and this heralded a stunned silence as all looked in awe at the person who thought he could quell the fracas before closing time at the Temperance Bar.

Pi: Thanks to you for allowing me to voice a few words as a lacto-pisco-ova vegetarian. On holy days, I will be eating kebabs of course, and biryanis with my friends.

The punters looked to Kirk for a translation. Glances were exchanged between Pi and Kirk, and the latter interjected.

Kirk: Pi means that his diet is milk. With some fish and eggs, but he is mainly vegetarian. And on specials days such as Eid, Rosh Hashana and Christmas, he will join his friends in eating anything traditionally mandated. That would be a chicken biryani, a fish, whole with its head roasted, and turkey.

And 9 seconds later, Pi felt compelled to air his idea again. Why should his ideas be the private privilege of the Beck household?

Pi: Thank you, Kirk, as always. All that I am saying is that we have our 21 meals a week. Even if we all ate one less meat-based meal, the world would be a better place.

There was a lot of murmuring between those that were sitting on the fence and in between the trenches. Pi had succeeded in uniting the vegans with the vegetarians and the carnivores. He had united them all.

Pi: Look please. If we all ate one less meat meal a week, then that would be possible? Most of us would agree with the health and economic and climate benefits of this venture. No?

Kirk: That we can agree on—thanks to Edgar's snippets on the subject.

Pi: Thanks. If we all ate one less meat meal, then that would be equivalent to 3.5 million of us becoming vegetarian! We could start tomorrow!

There were murmurings as the numerically-challenged had this obscure fact explained to them. Often by a self-employed to a salaried person.

Pi: Some of you know already but if everyone in China ate one less meat meal a week that would be the same as all of UK becoming vegetarian. If the USA population ate one less meat meal a week that would be the same as the 17 million of the Netherlands, one of my favourite football teams, becoming vegetarian completely. Not the football team.

The accidental rehearsal at the Beck household had come in useful.

Usually, Anju and Pi never seemed to spend much time together. Pi told Anju that he had enjoyed the day particularly, as he spent so much time with her. They recalled their times together in India.

Anju and Pi

Anju fondly recalled her time in Sundervagvela. How her small project Fem and Aid had married the ideas of charitable aid, especially to the feminine base of society with also benefitting the world around them.

Pi had worked with her on so many projects for the simple fact of the matter was that Pi was desperately lonely and was still carrying a torch for his road traffic killed first love. The feminine workshops were advertised as teaching all things feminine in a gender-neutral environment, as far as possible.

It was actually very difficult to put this into practice. What had amazed Anju, however, was just how many boys and young men had signed up to the classes, which were relatively expensive at Rs 100 each. *A day's wage for many to keep out the unwanted*, thought Pi.

Usually, feminist workshops he had seen advertised were hosted by women's magazines and the more fashionable shops in the Grand Mall of Saviturbagh, where you would be guaranteed to pay more but would always have your goods carried home in a top-quality carrier bag advertising the shop that you had graced with your business.

The perfect business model of 'come here, we only have your sort of person here, pay more of course, take what you have bought home in a bag that advertises my shop and informs everyone you see of where you have risen to in society'. Hence, the customer was gainfully employed.

Even Pi could not recognise the women that turned up to these workshops in all the colours of the rainbow, especially the extra gaudy ones that they had added into the somewhat limited palette of the rainbow. What Pi discovered only after several of the events was that many of these beautiful people of all ages and occupations were the *dhobis* in the ghats smashing clothes against the well-worn rocks in the stream, the perfectly spined hod carriers of a dozen bricks, the beggars at the temple, the cooks at the government offices, road-sweepers, latrine cleaners, teachers, nurses and even the occasionally, the pandit's wife.

Pi shamefully admitted to himself that he had only seen people for what they directly appeared to be at work and not as humans to interact with. The workshops would often end with a song. The simple rules of *Antakshari* were that after a coin toss to decide, the chosen lead of one team would start singing a Hindi film song. All the main forces and concerns were represented—in fact, all of life itself.

The next contestant from the other team would have to start a song with the consonant or vowel that the previous contestant ended on. *Ad finitum* unless home calls. *Antakshari*, the game of the ending letter. Whatever you have just ended on, is the start of the next. A bit like life really.

The high poetry of many a Hindi, or even an Urdu song would be sung perfectly. If translated and published the output of any single game could be given a poetry prize. The joint understanding and communality of problems shared was a level unreached within his friends.

Although it was mainly women, men also added their baritones. There were also the occasional duets by the Kinnara Hijra twins of the transgendered community. Song and dance of the latter a mythological descent from the half-human deities.

Pi recalled having been told of the mythological origin of this community from the part human, part bird Kinnaras via Buddhism. Associated with music and love, they were also tasked to ensure the well-being of humans at times of distress and danger.

Pi felt that they were essential, especially recently with all troubles boiling over. In the home, workplace, society, the country, and the planet itself. Pi had spent many hours standing oft from the medley groups that would be playing *Antakshari* translating the words, usually Hindi, into English for Anju.

Mein pal do pal ka shayar hoon, pal do pal meri kahani hai —I am but a poet for a moment or so. My story will last but a moment or so.

Pal do pal meri hasti hai, pal do pal meri jawani hai—My existence will only be for a few moments, my youth will also last but a moment or so.

After a while, Anju felt that there was no need to read any new poems. In the late afternoon and evening, *Antakshari* was all that was needed. All of life was covered by those in the maelstrom of their daily lives.

The workshops had taught women how to make basic period pads, nappies, and clothes. There was bartering galore, with that most complex of bitcoins; the quantification of the value of your life per hours was compared. It was the stock market fractalised to the small veranda of the school after hours.

At the festive season, it was the flower sellers that did well, then the mango-sellers in the earlier part of the mango season and then when the glut occurred the prices would drop for the freshness of the mangoes to be frozen or tinned. Many were taught to read and write.

Though female illiteracy was not a great problem in Pi's part of the world. Simple basic cooking ideas were shared. Of course, everyone knew how to cook; but the ideas shared were ones of less indoor pollution and reduced energy usage.

Feminaid, the drink, had been jointly invented by Pi and Anju. Feminaid Ek, Feminaid Do, and Feminaid Teen. The Ek, Do, Teen referred to the amount of saltiness. Clearly, natural salt from Dandi only. Not crudely refined but virginal and hence higher in potassium, calcium, magnesium and sea-faring iodine.

On a hot sweaty day, it would only be Feminaid Teen that would satisfy the body's craving for salt. Otherwise, it was a concoction of lime, mango, banana, cumin, pepper and a sprig of coriander and turmeric pieces afloating to cleanse the palate at the end.

When the recipe had been sold to a smaller American Café franchise, a large amount of money had been generated and a large workshop area had been added to the school for the children during the day and the towns' people. There would also be a steady income to employ some health-advisors. Especially to advise on good mental health, diet, smoking, contraception, alcohol, physical activity, and the statin. The health-advisor would also navigate individual through to the treatment centres if needed.

Unfortunately, physical activity, was deemed unnecessary once a certain level of affluence had been achieved and indeed physical exertion, unless Lycra-ed or in shorts, was an activity of the poor only.

The most popular, by virtue of the waiting list was the Andro Workshop purporting to 'convert' males from a paternalistic view of life to one that affirm both and all gender-types. These were particularly popular among the boys and men hoping to make romantic intrusions on the feisty women of Sundervagvela.

They listened to all but aspired to the life of Pi's brother who appeared to have everything in life, a wife, who was also a conversational knife to cut through all things rubbish to practical fairness and a strifeless life. Albeit with the strange Pi as brother. And what was not to lose.

The statistical chance of dating increased with conversations suggested with a clear approach to individual continuous social and professional development. The latter often included advice from the advisors on trimming the artificial turf sprouting from ears, the nose, and escapees from the moustache.

Thus, stimulating local trade and an increase in the sale of beeswax. Another important topic was on adoption of more modern hairstyles, a general advice to move on from the early Amitabh Bachchan days and the Bradley Wiggins sideburns.

For the aspiring Romeos, when asking, 'Will you then go out with me? And be my soul-mate?'.

The reply, sadly for them, was often, 'I am happy—no thank you' or 'I am happy and gay'! Or the deeply saddeningly 'No-ways'! Or 'Why'?

Inspired by this recollection, Anju's recommendation had been We Should all be Feminists by Adichie of the fabulous prénoms Chimamanda Ngozi. Which Pi had re-read recently, short as it was and requiring to be even better understood and remembered by Pi.

Also recommended by Anju was Americanah by the same author, but it was deemed too dense for Pi to read and would be waitlisted until after the challenge. It could only be one or the other for the book challenge anyway.

Pi was a little despondent that the great little book was only 5millimetres thick but then again, it was only the area of a smartphone. Greta had greeted Pi, sternly and vested in yellow, from the back of the same-sized book. No one is too small to make a difference. And the less salubrious, but same-sized Ivan Turgenev's Kasyan from the Beautiful Lands. All three only 15millimetres, but a good result for an hour. And two freshly ground coffees.

The next week, Pi and Anju tried to enter into discussions at the City-Zen Café to resurrect Feminaid. This was needed just to generate some income to help the local women at the shelter. It was a sterling success but packaging for retail sale elsewhere was proving an insurmountable challenge.

The *'buy-in'* to the game of *'let's market a new product'* was just too low. It was too novel and not invented here. In the City-Zen Café, it did though live and breathe. It was also initially popular in the Temperance Bar of course, at half the price of beer.

A few early pioneers had discovered that adding a few drops of Devilishly Dastardly Deadly Hot Sauce Seven would result in a high at the level of a double vodka shot. Anton self-vouched to investigate this. And to produce a paper. After all that, these ideas failed to launch in the end. The drink was abandoned. Another idea would also fail to see the light of day.

Pi and the Car Ideas

It was a meeting of the underground club—the Homo saplings club to the current membership and their most stalwart supporters on the x, y, and z of the social media channels. The winds had been particularly strong, many trees had fallen over, uprooted, never to rise again, and the group were keen to replant urgently.

There had just been a harvest run whereby the sappers had searched the brambles and hedges for any small saplings that they could transplant to more congenial areas. They spent the time over the first drink just dividing up the trees. There would be great progress.

There were even three black poplars, the only British native representative of the poplar trees. They had 42 trees altogether. The random magic number of Douglas Adams. Apparently, it was nothing to do with 42 being 101010 in binary, or the fact that light refracts through water at 42 degrees to create a rainbow or even the 42 laws of cricket.

Pi could not read the book though. He simply did not get it. *The Man who Planted Trees* was easier to read. Although, it really was too thin for such a loud idea at only 5.2 millimetres.

Kirk: Ask Pi—he has an idea on everything honest. He will tell you how to lower CO_2 with his own ideas. Sometimes begged, borrowed, or stolen, of course!

Hela (with a glass half-full): Go for it, dude!

Pi: Well, if I can be as bold—can I give you three ideas that people are doing I am sure—for nothing is that original—apparently.

Hela : *Plus ça change, plus c'est la même chose.*

Pi: I am sure that what you have said is correct. I have three ideas for the 1.42 billion cars on Earth and I believe 38.6 million in UK. That was on the news. I did not count them personally!

Hela was a little but increasingly irritated by the 9 second pauses.

Hela: Please progress to the ideas.

Pi: Firstly, we do not need the spare wheel that is still in the back of at least half the cars in this country and more in the world? No one changes car tyres nowadays as it is too dangerous, I believe. So, not carrying a tyre would reduce petrol, diesel and electricity wasted. The latter via at best solar, wind, hydropower, and nuclear but mainly from oil, gas and coal. By a bit but even 1% would be 386000 cars worth in UK. Surely that is worth it. *Hanneh?*

Hela: Pray progress to the next idea—my glass is nearly empty.

Pi: The roof of a car could be a moulded solar panel. A car lies idle for at least 90% of daylight hours? This I did guess, dear audience. The car could be gainfully employed in capturing solar energy into the battery *hanneh*! I am not sure, but the non-reflection of the sunrays would be of benefit to not warming up the atmosphere?

Hela: My glass is empty.

As Chair, the glass was not allowed to be empty and a swiftly placed order meant that another pint of Alderman's appeared in the drinks lift and was handed to her by the Vice President, who would be in a similar position of ultimate power in a few moons.

Pi had attempted a lesser pause before speaking but this had simply not been possible.

Pi: And finally, the idea of the in and out battery—Bio-car.

Hela became a little happier, now fully stocked with her beverage.

Hela: Pray elaborate.

Pi: Well, I was in Haridwar where many of the tuk-tuk rickshaws are electric. Indeed, they had be to after the Swami Nathan edict of 2014—I believe. They are called Toto—the e-rickshaw. They have 4 batteries. They are Tata of course in the main. Like your Land Rover Jaguar. Some of your tea also, I believe. But the Toto only lasts for 34 kilos. The best trip that the Haridwar Toto driver can do is the trip to Rishikesh. The Firangi want to go here because they want to visit Chaurasi Kutia. Better known to you as the Beatles Ashram. This is where Maharishi Mahesh Yogi had his international origins, reinventing TM—Transcendental Meditation for the West. In a nice, not too difficult, technique that you could dip in and out of as you lived your usual life without interruption. The Beatles went there. Indeed, in the year and month that my oldest brother was born in. February 1968. And from Rishikesh, you could go to the market towns of Mussoorie and Dehradun which are near and well worth visiting. Because of the Tibetan goods from the permanent exiles, I have heard.

Hela: Do we need the details? —and you mean kilometres not kilograms, otherwise, not many of us here would fit into the Toto. And yeah—the Beatles worked on the best of all albums there—The White One. Ringo called it the spiritual Butlins! The naughty MMY could never be upset with Angels.

These remarks were given the accolade they deserved by the followers and especially the VP.

Pi: Yes, of course. The kilometre it is. But it is at least 21 kilos one way and the batteries are often low and the driver cannot return. What to do?

The VP was anxious lest another drink was needed for Hela.

Pi: So, the drivers, pop into the Rishikesh Battery Exchange and change their batteries—1, 2, 3 or all 4. And leave the old ones behind for charging. The charge cost is dependent on the age of the battery. Himat Singh would certainly not allow old batteries to be exchanged for new ones as in the offer of the evil magician in the Ali Baba story of Scheherazade.

Hela: 30 seconds left!

Pi: That is, it. In the future, the people in flats and terraces and council high-risers will have difficulty in charging their cars, so what we need is garages that take the uncharged battery and put in a new one. There is one more idea to share. I will have to leave that for another day.

The latter rendered of necessity in 27 seconds.

Hela: Good ideas. I think. But why have they not thought of them anyway?

On the way home, Pi discussed his Wisogrow idea. A really tortured acronym. Essentially, this was a wind turbine with several pluses. The deep digging in of a 60 to 120 metre wind turbine, to stabilise it, would necessitate that a depth of 15 metres or so is reached. There is access to warm earth from a depth of only two to five metres.

This would allow the ideal environment for ground source heating and possibly electricity generation. The wind turbine itself and any larger pieces of the ground source heat pump engineering would be coated in flexible solar panelling if exposed to sunlight. This would add the third source of energy to be accessed.

There would also be fast biomass growing around the base of the Wisogrow Superstructure. The biomass of rush grass, willow or even bamboo or whatever could be used for fuel pelleting, feed, toilet rolls, or whatever else possible to do so.

Kirk: Why Wisogrow?

Pi: I wanted to call this thing in honour of the Earthly contributions of Vayu—the Deity of the Wind. Surya—the Deity of the Sun, and Bhumi—Goddess of the Earth, and Aranyani—the Goddess of the forests and all the animals that dwell in them.

She's big in the *Rig-Veda*. Alas, this was not possible easily. So, I settled for Wisogrow. This is simply a combo of wind, solar, and ground. The 'grow' bit also suggests some growing? *Hanneh*?

Not every invention in life worked. Kirk told Pi that he would explore the ideas with his mates at the Number One Detective Agency-inspired Speedy Motors with Zim and Co.

Bookcase

Pi thought he would approach Peta with the other challenge. Not one that had been set by Sir X, but by himself. He declared this at the Temperance Bar. His idea was to design a bookcase that could store 1000 books. Pi thought that it could be done within a cubic metre. Most of his audience were circumspect to say the least.

Pi: That you would need if you read a book a week for 20 years, with the occasional break for the bank holidays and sick leave.

All had scoffed at the idea over a pint of Zeer beer. Pi started to work it out. It would need to be a cubic metre then. The average quarto book was coming in at 24 centimetres by 16 centimetres by 4.5 centimetres. A thousand of these would be far too for a cubic metre as each book would be 1728 cubic centimetres.

Maybe the task would have to be based on paperbacks, at 20centimetre by 12.5 by 2centimetre which be only 500 cubic centimetres.

So, a combination of the two would work. Pi took a scrap of paper and did the algebra. Respectful of and remembering the contribution of the Arabic Mathematician Muhammad ibn Musa al-Khwarizmi who had essentially invented algebra. Indeed, his Latinised name became algebra. He had also introduced the Hindu-Arabic numerical system to the wider world, the answer came to Pi. For a thousand books, 593 paperback and 407 quartos would do it. But to be sure and leave space for error, it would need to be 600 paperbacks and 400 quartos. He would check it later when he met Peta.

Back to reality. Pi was becoming acutely aware through his brother and others that Covid-19 would start to devastate and crash India soon.

Instalment Thirteen: March

Today, 4th March, the year that could have seen the virus renamed as COVID-21, maybe. It had disguised itself and mutated. It had taken on a multitude of costumes and avatars. All deadly to the right person. Or rather the wrong person. The most around was the Indian and then called B.1.617 then, now the Delta variant.

There is even a Brazilian variant. The original Alpha variant was now ancestor status and a mere B.1.1.7. There were just another 647 main variants. The vaccination drive continues to accelerate as millions of doses of the Oxford vaccine are shipped in from India's Serum Institute. Well over half the adult population of UK, that is 30,151,287 people are now vaccinated with at least the first dose. Thank you, India.

This is also the anniversary of the day that I had sent a confidential email to my MP and copied to the chiefs of the new health structures including the Chair of the new and fledgling Integrated Systems Health Initiative Team. I had called for a lockdown, to halt spread of the virus. But we had Cruft's and packed-out stadiums instead.

COVID-19 Globally? There were 2 million dead. The latter could be considered the main game in town. Is it though?

Let us record the Yemen famine. The Myanmar crisis and the deaths and the quietly slowing tears. Yet, the radio led on the protest of the sex-workers of the Netherlands. Of obvious interest, especially as they were semi-naked; this made for good radio.

I question not the authenticity or the need to address this; but maybe it could have been placed a little later on in the programme. Just my private thoughts. Despite the claps for healthcare workers, rather re-branded as heroes, the pay rise offered to the nurses is 1%. I have checked this—it is not a mistake.

Parents lobby for higher grades for their children in GCSEs and A Levels. Have the children really improved, despite lack of schooling? Are we implying that parents are better teachers than the actual school teachers? If so, a lot of money can be saved. Weddings are allowed for up to 6 people. Presumably, that means the couple and 4 guests. Or one of the couple and 5 guests. Or just 6 guests!

I think that Pi's task of reading his own height in books in a year is near completion. The height appears to be nearly there. In fact, it may even end up being a little higher than Pi. Kirk has done the forecast calculations and the height would be reached very soon. The tower does not need to be the height of a Sir Chris Whitty. But higher than a JVT. Possibly, and approximately, double the girth of a PM.

We continue to spend money that will now take the young decades to pay back. Unless we print it to ease the economy and render our savings worth a lot less. But really, I think the various triads on daily TV, had tried their very sincere best. We do need to learn for the future though and say sorry to those who died inadvertently.

Early in March, we had less than 100 daily deaths from COVID-19 for the first time since early October last year, but March end declares a total of 152,453 COVID-19 deaths.

This in the year of living dangerously in the times of COVID-19 in the best-prepared for a pandemic country on Earth. Even WHO thought so.

I need say, no more.

Chapter 15
To Infinity and Nearly Beyond
via the Temple

It is hard to be a diamond in a rhinestone world.

Dolly Parton. Actor, Singer-songwriter, Philanthropist.

The exercise of imagination is dangerous to those who profit from the way things are, because it has the power to show that the way things are is not permanent, not universal, not necessary.

Ursula Kroeber Le Guin (1929-2018). American Author.

Jatra

Anton dropped the trio of Kirk, Pi, and Anju off at Lambert Place. An erstwhile General Practitioner's surgery and family accommodation, substantial as it was. Although the Blue Plaque was there affirming its previous incumbent, Lambert Place was now the Samaj of Brahma Community Centre.

Today was the day of the pilgrimage to the various sacred sites in and around Belton in the three hours they had before Pi was due to give a speech at the Hanuman temple. After a quick *Aarti*, dutifully and beautifully, led by the Brahmachari Brigade at the Brahma Samaj, Pi stopped to admire the statue of Mahatma Gandhi outside.

The latter appeared to be striding in the general direction of Belton and away from the park dedicated to his disciple of *ahimsa*, Nelson Mandela. Meanwhile, Kirk and Anju had a discussion as to whether Lambert of Lambert Place could have had any connection with a man rather larger than Mahatma Gandhi.

Daniel Lambert had been a tad over a third of a metric tonne at over 52 stones and rather famous for his horse-riding and animal breeding. Surely, his horse would have been that most magnificent of English animals, a shire horse. They both agreed that a visit to the museum housing all his, Daniel Lambert's, paraphernalia was long overdue. Pi would surely be impressed. Such random thoughts over, they embarked on their *Jatra*—pilgrimage.

There was a quick explanation from Kirk that the Abbey College campus was Anton's infant and then junior school, many decades ago. There was a little diversion as the trio went through the park as Kirk wanted to point out some of the trees that the Homo saplings club had planted, unbeknown to the council. There was a sign, identically pyrographed to the one at the allotments that announced: "*Friluftsliv this way*'. Pi found a three-pronged samara, among the hundreds of the usual two-prolonged ones under the sycamore tree. He gifted it to Anju.

Then past the stunning stone architraves and lintels of St Mark's Church, they stopped for a quick breakfast, free as the weekly *Guru ka langar*, at the Guru Nanak Sikh Temple. All three admired the display on the histories of the Ten Sikh Gurus and how their collective wisdom had been left as the final scripture and authority on Sikhism, the *Guru Granth Sahib*, also known as the *Adi Granth*. And the little publicised fact that it had pertinent writing from mostly Sikh, but also Muslim and Hindu saints. The book was on display under a canopy within a palanquin, gently wafted by a yak tail-hair *chaur*. Kirk was so enamoured that he declared potential future conversion!

Next to the 900-year-old cathedral, via the infamous Jewry Wall, within which a Roman Temple was thought to reside to Janus of the past, the present, and future. Dedicated to St Martin the Merciful of Tours, the cathedral was just sheer splendour, especially now even more popular after the Plantagenet King had been found buried in the carpark, only to be interned in the cathedral itself. And as Anju was quick to point out, the dynasty had been founded by a certain Geoffrey of Anjou. Back to St Martin, why was he deemed to be so merciful? He had used his sword to cut his knightly cloak in half to share it with a rag-clad homeless seeker of alms during a freezing cold winter. His shrine was an also a watering-hole for pilgrims on the road to Santiago de Compostela in Spain. This had been the first *capella*, where St Martin's cloak or *cappa* was enshrined, later all small churches were often called chapels.

Pi found it thrilling that the monarchs had been so-called because of the yellow broom flower, *planta genista* that was their emblem. Anju also told Pi that the House of Plantagenet was also called the House of Anjou. Pi was then transfixed by the teasel heads blowing in the breeze with their elaborate arboreal architecture.

Pi also took a detour to say hello to the nurses and other staff at the Blood Transfusion Centre to thank them for the bronze medal he had received for his plasma transfusions. He also gave them a box of Indian sweets.

Then to the Jain temple via the outside paths along the museum for the Bengal Regiment. Twitter declared it a haven of all spirituality. And it was. Beyond the intricate lace and fretwork of the marble façade, there were esoteric painted panels and the 44 ornate columns of yellow Jaisalmer sandstone. The latter, Pi declared, were the most beautiful he had ever seen but he did go to state that he had only ever visited a single other Jain temple before.

But this Jain temple was the first in the western world. The basic tenet of it all was rendered in the marble deity Bahubali, standing naturistically, as digambara—sky-clad, in the *kayotsarga* pose, steady body, mind, and soul. Immune to the inclement weather and time long enough for ivy to establish on his legs. Kirk then noticed, for the very first time, that Pi's usual style of walking was much as if Bahubali would start striding. Hands close to the hip joints with very little arm-swing.

The temples to the God of football and rugby, the fox and the tiger respectively, could just be made out in the distance and were declared so and pointed out to Pi by Kirk. Beyond these stadiums was the abode of another skulk of foxes. That of cricket.

They then had an herbal concoction under the prayer flags in the Buddhist Meditation centre listening to the that most complex of mantras, the four-worded *Om Mani Padme Hum*, surrounded by serene, ochre-clad mixed gendered Bhikkhus spinning the mantra on their prayer wheels for universal peace and fraternity.

Then a longish trek to the station from where all of tourism had purportedly started, in all unlikelihood, commemorated by the statue of Thomas Cook outside, no doubt at the end or the beginning of his tour to the bell foundry. The central mosque was thereabouts.

The dome echoed the beginning of the universe to the trio, housing all of the faithful under a single umbrella. Here was by far the most diverse of worshippers there today. *Another religion to consider,* thought Kirk.

Alas, no synagogue was open, But Pi was equally enthralled by touching the door of the synagogue and feeling its carved Hebrew scripture. He was sure there was benevolence there. The synagogue will need to be visited at a later date by special arrangement. He had a tear in his eye wondering why the modern children of Abraham, Ishmael— the first son from Mother Hagar, and Isaac—the younger son by 13 years from Mother Sarah, fought so much. And why the life of one was considered 20 of the other in the calculus of contemporary politics and warfare. Never mind the contemporary political aftermath of the Sunni-Shia schism. He was speechless.

Then to the Shree Sanatan Mandir. Here, Pi was particularly animated. He pointed out the various deities, they all appeared to have assembled here. The larger murtis were of Vishnu and Lakshmi, Radha-Krishna, Sita-Rama, Lakshman, and Hanuman. And the rarer smaller ones of Brahma and Sitala-ma. The latter, the Goddess of smallpox that Pi had discussed with the Becks before. Baliadev, the deity to protect against measles and chickenpox was also present.

Pi stood for a distinct three minutes before the murti of Shirdi Sai Baba, the spiritual link between Islam and Hinduism. He was excited to notice the small murti that was Gita-Maa, the Goddess pertaining to his beloved *Bhagavad Gita*.

Pi was pleased that he had found most of the avatars of Vishnu, Matsya the fish, Varaha the boar, Narasinha the half each of human and lion, Vamana the dwarf, Rama with an axe, Rama with a bow, and Kalki still to come. The latter on a white horse.

Pi was perplexed as to why the tortoise, or was it a turtle incarnation? — was missing. Pi also smiled remembering the evolutionary theories in relation to the form of the avatars, but then again, he thought, *anything can be a story if there is interest or a lesson.*

Kirk disappeared to meet his old mathematics teacher and current president of the temple. He gifted him a copy of the wooden-boxed Vedic Foundation of Planet Earth's edition of the *Bhagavad Gita* that Pi had intended to promote until Covid-19 got in the way.

The final stop before the Hanuman Temple was the Swaminarayan temple. Kirk awarded this temple the most beautiful of architectures award. It created a sheer delight within the hearts of all the trio. All three participated in the family

Abhishek ceremony circumambulating the exquisite murti of a loin-cloth clad Neelkanth, the later founder of the movement.

The walls were clad with snippets from the speech that the revered inspirer of this, and the other 1100 temples and 3850 centres, had given at the United Nations Millenium World Peace Summit.

At this hour in human history, we religious leaders should not only dream of one religion in the world but dream of a world in which all religions are one. We must not progress at the cost of others but sacrifice a part of ourselves for the good of others.

Pi pointed out that the *Mir Vam* he had seen at Kyiv airports those several moons ago had the same meaning as the title to the quotes which was *Vishwa Shanti.*

And then there was even a quick trek, as they were tired, to that temple to nature—the allotments and small wood. Pi wondered whether all the places of worship in his *Jatra* would exist anywhere else on planet Earth in such proximity. All within a 12-kilometre walk.

The Hanuman Temple-Pi's *Toofan aur Diya* or Storm in a Teacup

So, now to the Hanuman temple. Pi created a storm. Albeit a little one. He clearly had not learnt a lesson from the time he expressed his views on the use of milk in Sundervagvela temples.

He had been invited to give a talk at this, the Old Vayuputra Hanuman, temple. The very cosmopolitan board of this temple had heard that Pi was from Sundervagvela, one of the few towns in the world that had a temple dedicated to Ardhnariishvari. *Vide supra,* or do you remember?

Krishnabaladevji—also known as Panditji, was the head Pandit. He had received Pi personally and given him (and Kirk, whilst Anju was escorted away by a small feminine throng) a second breakfast of chai—without milk—therefore if we're being picky, it was not real chai but black tea with chai tea spices.

This was accompanied by the yellow spongey 4 centimetre by 4 centimetre by 2 centimetre-high bricks that were *dhokras* (made from dal and rice), accompanied by chickpea paste fries called *fafras*. These were accompanied by chillies that were definitely classed as high on the Scoville Index.

All of this had been generously gifted from the Rasta Fasta Nasta Café. Prior to Pi's talk, there was a rendition of the *Hanuman Chalisa*. The latter, as Pi later informed Kirk and Anju, was by Tulsidas. Yet another famed individual from the lands around Pi's town.

The Hariharan version of it had over 2 billion media hits. Pi knew all the words off by heart. Hanuman, to the billions of India, was a benevolent super-soul that had all the positive attributes of Marvel and DC heroes to rival Iron Man, The Hulk and Thor. He would fit perfectly into the franchise, being from the dawn of history at least 3500 years ago. Or so said Pi.

Pi was impressed by how many of the audience appeared to know all the words of the *Hanuman Chalisa* off by heart—well over a thousand words in some English translations but about half of that in Sanskrit compound words. Today the rendition was led by the 93-year old most senior doyenne of the temple. Pi thought that maybe they could contribute to the undertaking of Avadhoota Datta Peethadhipati Jagadguru Parama Sri Sri Sri Ganapathy Sachchidananda Swamiji's vision of chanting the *Hanuman Chalisa* 130 billion times for universal peace and brotherhood. This thought was even more ironic in the light of what transpired.

The first half of the talk went well. Maybe breakfast was keeping the attendees docile, so that they did not become hungry and less charitable. But then Pi, unusually clad as a teacher in cloth cap but with the usual Nehru gilet, thought that there was enough fraternity and positivity in the audience to share with them an idea. An idea that had previously laid nascent but could now be extant in the safety of Belton, rather than among the more volatile populace back home.

Today, he was wearing the mustard yellow gilet. He thought of his great friend Limu, who had been influenced by Goethe and had gifted this attire to all his closest friends as they would normally gather every December to celebrate the life and demise of Johann Wolfgang von Goethe's Young Werther. The book, *The Sorrows of Young Werther*, that Pi thought that he would definitely re-read and add to the tower. Werther's sorrow for his loss of Charlottle was akin to the loss that Pi felt so so often thinking of Priyali.

Back to the idea that he wanted to share. Pi's idea, back home, had the following of precisely 4 families. And this too Pi suspected was for economic reasons rather than reasons that Greta would be proud of. At this temple in Belton, Pi sensed considerable and significant female energy here as their spouses had disappeared, in the main. The matriarchy index was on the up. In fact, this new temple had a majority non-male board.

Pi: If there are no more questions on the Ardhnariishvari Temple and the meanings behind it, I would like to discuss another spiritual matter in the last 10 minutes before the *Azan* to *Aarti* at noon.

Panditji: We do not have *Azan*. You must be thinking of another religion.

Pi: But a bell is rung that we can hear every day. Those that are near then know that the *Aarti* is in 10 minutes and run in—no? Same function—is it not so? For a Muslim or Hindu or the Atheist. The latter for general time-keeping *hanneh*?

The Pandit scratched his breastbone and then benevolently nodded to him to proceed.

Pi: The Hanuman *diya* is interesting. The wick is made of cotton, of course. The fuel is from vegetable oil. In India, it is sold as arachis oil. But it is a 100% peanut oil. Not as refined as the peanut oil we use for cooking, but actually a little more expensive. Which is odd.

Panditji: We call it *diva* not *diya*. What is this lecture on? We do not have much time. That you know?

Many a times, Panditji's temple meetings had been hijacked by all and sundry—the politician who wanted the vote bank of the attendee, the invites to the rainbow parade, the Communists, the Fascist-lite fundamentalist, the revisionist historian, and sometimes, completely honest people such as insurance and double-glazing sales representatives.

Pi: I have an issue with the *diva* being made of ghee and cotton. I see my friends Anju and Kirk are standing together at the back. I will need to explain first. English medium, I will be speaking in.

Radiantly smiling, Pi noticed that there was consternation at the back of the hall as Anju and Kirk were whispering, whatever, to each other.

Pi: Please do not worry that they have not quite split like chromosomes into the two strands of male on the right and female on the left. They are brother and sister only.

Panditji was trying his best to conduct Pi and increase the pace of this last bit of Pi's talk. Also, his bladder was making frantic signals to his brain for easement.

Pi: The *diva* is basically a small wad of cotton that has a twisted stalk. This is then dipped into oil or ghee. Ghee is butter that has been clarified, further made purer, by taking off even more of the water. Dr Patil informs me that ghee is very bad for arteries, but we offer it to the gods. Too much can certainly speed us to God.

The *diva* is therefore a small candle. There is nothing that beats the glory of an *Aarti* on the banks of the Ganges in the evening fading light of the sun but lit up by thousands of *diva* after sunset. That much even I agree and am most enthusiastic about.

Panditji: Pray continue a little faster.

Panditji was also concerned that Gheewala, Sons and Daughter had sponsored the marble images of the deities and that further funding was likely if the relationship was mutually beneficial. They also supplied the ghee at a contract price. Future funds may be in abeyance. That much was clear.

Pi attempted a less than 9 second pause but alas, it was not forthcoming.

Pi: Ghee is clarified butter and yet, we are needlessly burning it everywhere in our religion and even in some Christian churches and mosques. In the former with incense. But in the latter is only to provide light and not a focus of worship otherwise that is *shirk*.

Panditji: Really! Really! Really! The ancient scriptures all specify, the very specific specificity of the use of ghee and you are de-advocating it! What is it that you know that we should change after 5000 years or more? Are you in a WhatsApp group with Brahma—God incarnate? Maybe with Vishnu and Shiva too?

Pi: No. No. No. Certainly not. But we evolve, it is no longer a recommendation that a widow, chooses to or is forced to, perform immolation when her often agèd husband dies. You will remember the scene from *Around the World in Eighty Days*? Also that most beautiful of queens—Madri—in the *Mahabharata*. We usually treasure girls more now and not drown them in milk? *Hanneh*?

Panditji was annoyed and felt that Pi was a South Indian upstart who had no role in attempting to evolve his rites, especially as Pi only been invited to give a short talk. And time was marching on towards the noon *Aarti*. It was the North India that had given all the material of his religion, the scriptures, histories, myths and legends that created the body Invictus of his beliefs and rituals.

Why evolve when his life was but a step in the long march of his religion? But most worrying of all was the potential for the loss of revenue from Gheewala, Sons and Daughters. He was also confident that the pronouncements of the *Sama-Veda* were set in stone and solid basalt stone at that. Not limestone to be eroded by rain and remodelled by the likes of Pi.

Panditji: Guru Pi, please we do have to finish very soon.

But it was also obvious to Panditji that the hundred or so audience were transfixed and wanted Pi to finish. Enigmatic he was and commanded time and space to finish. He had started and the audience would be with him as he finished. Agreeing or not.

Pi: Look, there are a billion of us that light *divas* then. Let me use your words earlier to me. Perfectly happily. Let us say—one *diva* per person per week.

The audience and especially Panditji surmised that this was a major under-estimation. They would like a *diva* per person per day—possibly. But none wanted to interrupt. A lesson had been learnt. It was clear that once the juggernaut of thoughts had started, they would be impossible to halt.

Pi: I agree that it is an act of piety and charity and for speeding one's messages to the consciousness of the cosmos. But ghee is ghee. So, one billion divas, at one cubic centimetre each would be a lot of ghee. One million would just be one cubic metre but a billion would be a thousand cubic metres!

A large shipping container is 66 cubic metres so that is 15 large lorry loads of ghee. This is if everyone, all of us, uses one *diva*. Which I think, absolutely minimum would be once a week, but it could be a lot more? *Hanneh*? If not, a lot more. So, should we change? No. One only would be 1000 metric tonnes of ghee!

Panditji: At 4 minutes to the *Aarti* bell, my answer is no. It cannot be as much as that Pi; you are simply wrong. Clever though you think you are! We cannot undermine what has happened for years and is mandated in the *Vedas*.

Kirk and Anju knew better than to argue with Pi in any matter mathematics. It would just be a waste of time and life wasted. Kirk knew that ghee as almost 100% fat would weigh less than water, of course. But overall, the point was reasonable and another tick for the vegans.

Pi: But—last comment, I promise. I have checked the numbers several times in my head in the last 10 minutes. So, I am pretty confident. Although please do check on the smartphone that makes us all smarter. That amount of ghee is the output of 66,666 cows on a single day. I am assuming an output of 15 litres a day, although I do know that the average in UK, on some farms, is a lot more.

Panditji: It is wrong!

Pi: I know—sorry, I made a mistake, Panditji. I forgot that we need around 16-17 litres of milk for to make one litre of ghee. So that is now over a million cows. Actually 1,100,000 cows, per *diva* per person. Usually, I think weekly as I said before.

Panditji: There is no doubt you have a miscalculation there. But why does it matter?

Pi: Because the milk can be spared for feeding humans, especially, back home where there is 33% poor nutrition. But also, to balance this fact, 33% too much nutrition. The rest just right. Because intensive milk production has its own list of non-*ahimsa* practices such as taking the child-cow away from the mother very soon after birth. The beef has to be there also. So, milk should never be cruelly wasted *hanneh*? For pizzas, I understand, of course.

Panditji: I would rather have less cheese on my pizza!

Pi: But cannot we just all do more of the great idea of this Vayaputra Hanuman temple and have a vegetable oil *diva* rather than ghee? Or even an electronic one that you generate the power for— by exercise? Maybe ghee only on Diwali, for example or the big days like the birthdays of Lord Krishna and Lord Rama? Sorry, I forgot Lord Shiva and Goddess Saraswati.

By now, Panditji was scratching his breastbone with both hands. Almost as if he was going to tear open his chest to reveal the fact that Rama and Sita, those standard-bearers of virtue resided in his chest and would agree with the ghee *diva*. After all, this was why Hanuman had become known as Ramabhakta Hanuman. Or more accurately as Sita resided, metaphorically, within a metaphor, in Hanuman's chest as well, as *Sitasameta Shriramapada Sevadurandharaya*. Roughly one always engrossed in the service of Sita and Rama.

Panditji: I have to ring the bell now. We have to do cleansing of the body, so let's all say thanks and leave. Please return quickly for the *Aarti*!

The associates and stakeholders in Gheewala Sons and Daughter were in a quandary. Supplying oil would be much cheaper. But they would lose the sales of ghee in their stores. There were many murmurings in the audiences and ones that had followed Pi closely got their calculator out for a final check on the maths.

Food for thought indeed. The bell rang and people scattered to their lives of joy and sorrow.

An Act of Kindness

At home, Ruth was writing a letter on a card to her friend, Fiona. Fiona was Dean at Harts University. Ruth had been emotionally struck down that morning after seeing a newly-released video of her friend, last seen by Ruth 3 years ago, graduating a student at home. Because the student was too ill. And would die. Very soon. From a brain tumour, the finality of a *Glioblastoma multiforme* in the brainstem. Whatever that meant. Other than death, sixty-one years too early in this case. On average, a mere 14 to 16 months of survival after diagnosis.

Ruth felt crushed by the plight of the student. And also wept because of the simple act of kindness. Number one in this category but a lot lower overall, she suspected than universities with the benevolence of endowments for whom acts of kindness and benevolent research had to be funded in advance and measurable against objectives and visions and strategies and the various indices in the Sunday papers.

It was obvious to Pi, Kirk and Anju that Ruth did not want to be disturbed. They had googol to discuss anyway. But then decided not to until the following day.

Size of the Universe

Pi and Kirk had planned to meet at the City-Zen Café. Pi had told Kirk at breakfast that he had some issues with imagining googol despite a few ideas on paper. This did not surprise Kirk. The problem had been similarly difficult for his fellow students at university, despite many attempts over beers and pizzas.

There was something fundamentally contradictory about the amount of matter in the universe and the limited comprehension of humans. Libation in tow, both settled down for a chat. Kirk's iPA meter pinged and proudly informed him that he had done his required and mandated 20 minutes of activity and 10,000 steps. The individualised physical activity meter had changed his life in that regard. He was now a slave to the iPA meter.

Kirk: I thought you might have a problem; you will do really well on the other tasks, so worry not, old chum.

Pi: No, it is much more an issue of what is already known and on the internet that is irking me to no end.

Kirk: Pray inform me.

Pi: The internet and your buddies inform me of three facts. One, nothing travels faster than light. Ever. It is a universal constant. If you travel very fast, then time will slow but you cannot ever travel faster than light. Warp bubbles are unlikely. Two, the universe is apparently 13.7 billion years old. Three, the size of the universe is 94 billion light-years across. That's what they said at the National Space Museum. NASA say so too.

I am amazed that you have a Russian Soyuz spacecraft so close to Belton. Oddly orbiting just over the café!

Kirk: Please do not detract!

Pi: The size is there in all the veritable websites including nine planets dot org and others. NASA even! Also, presumably Sheldon fact-checked everything in the Big Bang Theory?

Kirk: I am sure he did. You know it's fiction, right? But ok.

Pi: If the universe is 13.7 billion years old, then surely the maximum size of the universe would be 13.7 billion light-years radius from the Big Bang? Therefore, only 27.4 billion light-years across?

Kirk: Sorry, I really cannot help with this. Another drink? You need to ask one of the deities of space. Maggie Ebunoluwa Aderin-Pocock. I saw her at the Dark Matter Garden at the Chelsea Flower Show with Mum. I think Hiranya Peiris did a piece on this on Radio 4? Or if you have more time, Professor Brian Cox. You will like his pauses too.

Pi: What to do?

Kirk: Just fail gracefully. Read those books though. You need to speed up a little!

Size of the Universe, Again

This was vexing Pi. He would agree with everyone that he was just crudely reasonable at mathematics. If the universe started 13.7 billion years ago and nothing travels faster than light at a speedy 299,792.458 kilometres per second (or 300,000 kilometres per second amongst friends, or at 186,000 miles per second for older friends)?

Apparently, the speed of light was fundamental to the way things work in the universe. They quote: *Nothing can ever go faster than the speed of light, for the simple reason that space and time do not exist beyond this point.*

Yet, all the big websites on this state that the spot that we see 13.7 billion miles away has continued to move away from us as the universe had expanded. The self-same spot is now 46 billion light-years away. And now, ironically, the Earth is right in the middle of the universe, so the universe is thought to be 94 billion light-years across. That's the length that light can travel, at 300,000 kilometres, a second for 94 billion years. Pi was vexed—*But if the universe is 13.7 billion years old and nothing travels faster than light, then how can the universe not just be 13.7 times two across?* Anton listened to the arguments too and just declared — *hoc non facit sensum*— it makes no sense. But no use to Pi.

Sorry to spell out Pi's concerns for you, but they really were troubling him. And remember he had had a good thought on how to imagine a googol. But the book-reading was falling off again.

The only person who would be able to help him with another idea on googol was Rameshswaren Lodha back in the Sundervagvela Observatory. He could teach you anything in his field with the lucidity of understanding the 6 times table for the first time, and learning would be guaranteed. But his friend was ill with Covid-19. And dying.

Pi had an idea that he thought about in the early hours of morning observing Venus, Jupiter, and Saturn.

Pi on Googol

Pi felt that he had to get serious on imagining googol otherwise this labour could fail too. One idea he started to explore in his notepads was the final calculation in relation to a story of the grains of rice on a chess board. There had been many different versions; each a kaleidoscope of ideas based on where you were born or your culture and history.

The version Pi had created was taught every year as part of his Mathematics in Stories tutorial to his 15-year-olds. It was this version that Pi elaborated to Kirk and Anju.

A king was dying. As he approached death, he knew that his son could not inherit his lands as he was too young. A regent would be needed to rule instead until he became of age. The king had a younger brother. There was an older sister; but unfortunately, the world was not so enlightened in those days.

In Pi's version, it was the daughter that could inherit under an affidavit that was agreed to and pledged by the King's brother. The brothers were playing *shatrung*—chess. The dying king nevertheless kills the Sheikh and proclaims *Shaikh-mat*. The Sheikh is dead. We now say checkmate, of course.

King: Dear brother, I would like you to rule our lands, fairly and in the way that I have. There must be peace within our kingdom. Whatever language, creed, or location our subjects are—all must be treated equal. There must be no poverty of *roti, kapada aur makan*. All must have their food, clothes, and housing. Always also access to high quality state education and healthcare. Animals too, must be well looked after. The same goes for all prisoners.

There must be no violence against anyone. Any violence must be mitigated against, especially if against women. You must foster peace with all those outside of the kingdom.

It was clearly evident that he had been a much-loved, benevolent king. The brother, to be fair, agreed with everything that had been stipulated and was looking forward to taking on the kingdom rather than seeing it being frittered away on his niece. King Sharesh sounded great! The king announced his affidavit to the court and people's representatives.

King: I know my daughter Kuni is too young at present, but I would like her to have a chance at reigning. I would like to set you a challenge. Kuni is only 7 years old. She must be allowed to reign and take over the kingdom—it will then be a queendom—if you cannot complete a challenge.

The brother, Sharesh, begged to know the details of the challenge on bended knee and, presumably, notepad ready.

King: We have our 6 seasons. We have *Vasant Ritu*—spring. We have *Grishma Ritu*—summer. There is *Varsha Ritu*—monsoon and *Sharad Ritu*—autumn. And then *Hemant Ritu*—the early winter and then *Shita Ritu*—winter proper. The *en plein hiver* of the Puducherry court.

The brother was not entirely sure where this was heading.

King: Please look at this empty chess board. Start with one grain of rice on the first square of the board and double the amount every subsequent square every season. When you cannot give my daughter that amount of rice, please let her take over my lands for her queendom. Feel free to use as many boards as you need.

Pi recalled that 11 squares were needed to get up to 1024 grains of rice. 24 grains could be donated to the rats and mice that we class as vermin. But not bats or badgers or deer or kingfishers or sparrows or some pigeons. Bats are losing in the popularity stakes due to an aspersion with Covid-19, alas. Our prejudices are everywhere it would seem. Pi had always asked himself why the *Rig-Veda*, the oldest of his scriptures, had 1028 hymns when 1024 would have been perfect. Maybe 4 hymns could be amalgamated?

The donation of the 24 grains will allow for easier maths. Then just another 11 squares on, you would get to a thousand. Donate to the mice and rats again and we are still on a million. That is 10 to the power of 6. Pi carried over a cup of chai and concluded that googol would be easily reached by the square number 367 or so. This number of squares would be easy to accommodate within a board that was only 20 by 20.

Back to Kuni.

Pi had calculated that at 50,000 grains of rice per kilogramme, only a single standard chessboard would be needed. And that a decade or so later, Kuni would have to be Queen.

Planet Earth only produces 787 billion kilos of rice a year. Mill it and it only makes 480 billion kilos. Kuni would be Queen a lot earlier than her uncle expected. All of India's rice production would be reached within the confines of a standard chess board on square 54, at 50,000 grains a kilo — the global production on square 56. Kuni would be Queen well within 10 years!

Not that many boards would be required to imagine a googol either. But maybe googol could be imagined another way. What about the number of grains of sand possible in the universe in the whole sphere of space created from the creation of this universe? That had probably been done though. Needing to be rechecked, was his recent finding that there would be 1,206,900,000 molecules of water, in every litre of water one drinks, that had passed through any other human on Earth. Ever. But assuming perfect mixing with all the water on planet Earth. That would include Mahavira, Zarathustra, Siddhartha Gautama, Abraham, Krishna, Jesus, Prophet Mohammed (Peace Be upon Him), Guru Nanak, and rest of us all.

Back to the grains of sand in a universe 94 billion light-year across. Grains of sand, possible, at 94 billion light-year years across would only be 368.29×10^{87}, a lot less than a googol.

However, working with Anton, he wondered about the number of possible fully packed Covid-19 viral particles possible in a universe that was 94 billion light-years across. At a ten-thousandth of a millimetre across, you could, if you wanted to, pack in 36.829 googol virus particles into your universe. Yes, dear readers, you have the school day promised.

Pi: All Is Possible

Back to his labours. He was at a bit of an impasse. Pi had spent too long reading *The Idiot* by Fyodor Dostoevsky and *The Trial* by Kafka was still being read. The Dostoevsky was a creditable 41 millimetres but had taken 21 days. This was versus the 98 millimetres he needed to be on par. He was on a double bogey.

Kirk had gleefully informed him, that bogey originated from the Scottish Goblin Bogle and that Pi had progressed at only 42% of the expected rate in the last 4 weeks. All this had been worked out by Pi and had kept him awake at night. He really wanted to complete his allotted task.

Also discarded for his labours was anything by Jane Austen. The yield in height was simply not enough. Although he felt very guilty whenever he saw a ten-pound note and read that she had stated, *I declare after all that there is no enjoyment like reading*. And then not reading any of her works. Her *magnum opus* would have to wait until an attempt later in life. He had, of course, thoroughly enjoyed all three major filmic versions. Especially the Hollywood Bollywood one.

Enter another batch of the charity shop specials via Anju, the bricks. In came the tomes *The President is Missing, The Wrong Side of Goodbye and Casino Royale*. Some others, he had read though. Lee Child had declared the first tome as the thriller of the decade.

These three were a monumental 91.1 millimetres, at least. Happy days. Soaring like an eagle or gliding in now as an albatross. Thank you, *Bill Clinton and James Patterson, Michael Connelly, and Ian Fleming.* Heroes to the rescue indeed. Reliable friends when in need. All were achieved in only 6 days.

Sorry for another knight's move; but there had been an animated chat at the City-Zen Café that later spilled over to the Temperance Bar and much further afield. Another discussion on money.

Money

The rip-proof new synthetic notes were petrochemical-based. One could understand the need in Australia as surfers wanted to carry waterproof money! They also had in them a key admixture substance that had led in part to the Indian War of Independence when the Indian Sepoys had learnt that the cartridge grease for the guns was the perfect unguent to unite the Muslims and Hindus soldiers and ignite civil war.

The amalgam was pork and beef tallow—which was usually licked in preparing ammunition. This led to atrocities on both sides, with thousands of dead. Even the British officially lost 2392 lives. And the start of official British Rule in India.

The new banknote polymer also used beef tallow made from suet. The visceral fat from around the kidneys (beloved of our Leopold Bloom), guts and other bits and bobs of the culled creature. This was also used in soaps and candles. The five pound and ten pound and twenty pound and presumably the Turing fifty-pound note would all now be as intended, uniquely anti-static and anti-slip?

This had raised the hackles of many; and the most vociferous were the real burger enthusiasts. The vegans, vegetarians, many Hindus, many Sikhs and all Jains had all been upset. Checkmate had been the moment when the Bank of England stated in a missive that the cost would be 1.65 million pounds per year to change tack and that palm oil might have to be used instead, which had the risk of devastating the homes of even more orangutans—our far-off cousins (on Mother's side as Anton would quip to Anju and Kirk). Democracy in inaction, the parliamentary petition had been a bit of a cop out and failed too.

Infinity

There was also another heated discussion that I should tell you about. It all started when Kirk thought he had been insulted at the Temperance Bar. The incident had added a certain *je ne sais quoi* to the place just as it had begun to lose its edginess and had begun the drift into the insipid realms of the nondescript virtuous business, lacking character. A fight.

Some initial veritable facts, giving the story credibility, and then a tale that would be rewelded with every iteration. The story had started, I guess, like all such narratives did, with a sharing of news. An incident that would bifurcate at every retelling until one could have written a novella about it. The essential genes of the story were that, Pi and Kirk had distributed around 50 portions of their now staple meal for all who needed it for essential sustenance (and £7.99 with a drink for the rest).

Kirk: Pi and I had a great idea together this morning, guys. We're gonna tell you about it; see what you think.

Pi: Is this the one about infinity?

Kirk: Yep! Hey guys—what is infinity?

Various answers splattered criss-crossed between 13 people here and 13 there; there were at least 13 points of view that changed after hearing of the views of others. An organic creation of definitions, sensical and nonsensical as it would appear.

"All that there is!"

"All that there is and not there!"

"All that we can perceive with our science and objectively know in terms of quantum particles, energy interaction and the space between it all."

"An unimaginable largeness that we cannot comprehend!"

"Infinity that which renders us meaningless as we are just a mote in the gazillions of bits that make up the universe."

"That itself is wrong guys—you talk about a universe when that means a oneness of it all when there may be many."

"Many can still be a universe if you lump it all together."

Kirk: Pi, tell them. It is your idea—I will just help you with translating it into clear articulate English, as I so excel at it!

A few non-English hairs on the backs of the non-natives bristled a little. Hackles were raised.

Geraint: You are a complete Tyd! You serve the homeless. Now you want to start a new religion!

Unfortunately, at this stage, the violence gene was activated in the alpha males of all the home nations. Whilst the ex-colony and other nations looked on, the football and the cricket and indeed every single other sport, especially if televised.

"You don't be calling me mate, Kirk a tit. You practitioner of the solitary art of manual sexual gratification!"

Quick translations were offered to each other.

Geraint: I said complete Tyd not tit!

"So, he more than just a tit then—no bits missing like!"

Geraint: Tyd means Saint as in Tyd Dewi—which is Saint David's in Welsh.

"It's not actually. The Welsh for Saint is Sant. So, it would Dewi Sant. The place in English is called Tyddewi, which means the House of David! So, you called him a house. Not so rude! As to your Welsh, as our Dylan would say, you know Llareggub!"

Geraint: Never been there!

Geraint got punched. By the Englander. The Celtic nations joined in to protect Geraint. England quickly negotiated a treaty with the Polish contingents—taking mainly a neutral peace-making role, it would appear. The non-whites looked on—it was not their battle. Whatever side they took, they were liable to come out as the villains. Or so they thought, with a healthy degree of paranoia.

In the collective mind-set of the usually pacific clientèle, various historical facts came to mind about how the Welsh led by Vortimer (the real Britons, as they called themselves) originally defeated the Hengest-led Anglo-Saxons in AD 452. But to no great modern avail.

The early victories of Owain Glyn Dwr led to his eventual defeat, despite French help. Though he was never captured. The final laugh went to the Welsh as their King Henry Tudor won the Battle of Bosworth; the rest is relatively Modern History. The Scots and the Irish were not so easily assuaged.

The Scottish Independent Wars were a close draw until the end of the first spider-man, in effect, Robert the Bruce. And the whittling out of Scottish independence, 1547, at the absurdly named Battle of Pinkie Cleugh. The Irish had little to detail beyond the famines and Cromwell to feel all the anguish of the nation. And in the perfidy of the division of Ireland itself in an act of Solomon beyond the parable.

In more recent times, battles had been entrenched and bitterly fought out over the rugby, football, cricket and indeed any other sport that could attract enough income from betting, aftershave and razor blades to make it worth the while of the TV channels. And one day, they would be fought over women's sport too, one would hope.

Eventually, the discussion did get back to infinity. Pi finished off the discussion after several more definitions were mooted. The 9-second pause that was compulsory for Pi held everyone's attention.

Pi: Infinity is everything?

"Yes."

Pi: So, we are a part of infinity?

"Yes, but only a very small bit."

Pi: What is half of infinity? I would say infinite? Do you agree?

"Yes."

Pi: And even a small of infinity is infinite. So, we are infinite indeed. Therefore.

Kirk: Yep! *Quod erat demonstrandum*! QED, QED—let's all just drink! Watch the football, rugby, cricket, darts, snooker, anything!

This was all that led to that story being part of the essential DNA, the *sine qua non* of the Temperance Bar along with the diversity of the hops and the ancient grains that were used in the brews, that half genuinely loved, the other half tolerated for their virtuousness and idea alone.

The idea quickly spread to the City-Zen Café. Their regulars thus also felt really fulfilled, even infinite as they wandered in to fulfil themselves further, and downed a beer or two. They went home happy to have been declared infinite and originally from stardust, but living only because of the benevolence of a particular local star.

Anton Snippet

Anton was in a bad place. He was in his study, festering in his thoughts. The death of his father had hit him very hard again. The resolution of these times would be sought through his beloved Greeks and Romans. They had the answer to everything, according to him.

It was grating that a democratic highly developed set of nations that comprised USA, UK, France, Spain, Italy even had a very high death rate from Covid-19. They had discovered, or rather rediscovered and purloined, the world and developed it to what end?

The liberal democracies had reported at least a ten-fold increase in the death rate due to the virus *vis-à-vis* the well organised totalitarian states and the liberal stratocracies of parts of Korea, Vietnam, Singapore and others. The excuse bandied about was that these countries had learnt from previous pandemics. But we invented the pandemic game? Even WHO had declared our utter fitness to tackle these riotous pandemics a mere few months before it all hit.

Anton had always completed that most heinous of tasks, the tax form, as soon as possible after the end of the tax year. This year, he searched the net and concluded that we, all, had paid as we enjoyed a liberal life. But were the dying thousands, especially, in the homes of the infirm, signed up to this *laissez-faire*?

Especially, as Anton's uncle had served in war. He had fought in the Normandy landings and had eventually died from injuries sustained. Surely, it was not to give us the freedom to die needlessly? We have always allowed strictures on freedoms. Real freedom was the free-rolling traffic that allowed traffic lights to be ignored?

Yet, we were resplendent at picking up all such violators and fining them or putting them in temporary further education. *We of the autonomy of the person, the beneficence society, the non-maleficence, and the justice of it all had utterly failed*, thought Anton.

We were dying of freedom. This was not that removed from the invaders of the Capitol that had espoused a wish to be stupid. And free. Something was wrong. Maybe next year, we could sort it all out. It was all confusing.

Anton explained his thoughts to Pi. Who nodded sagely.

Pi: What is, what is.

Anton: That is profound; do you want a peg?

Anton had given Pi his signed copy of *Yesterday's Train to Nowhere* by Krishna Rau, which had made his way to him via his father. No doubt from an old army chum that his grandfather would have known. The stories had enchanted Pi (and made him less homesick). He was looking forward to finishing it later that day. But most of the stories mentioned a drink, alcoholic, and it often involved a peg or two.

A small one, *a chhota peg*, was recommended on the back cover by the Lieutenant-General. The peg served. Anton felt that he had to share his rereading of the maxims of Publilius Syrus with the whiskied Pi.

Anton: So much of what is happening would have been handled better if only the maxims of Publilius had been mission statements. For politicians and life in general. Our scrambled thinking would have benefitted from these—I will read a few out for you, Pi.

Oratory voice on.

Anton: *To do two things at once is to do neither.*

Once approving nods had been given (after the usual 9 seconds), others followed.

Anton: *Whilst we stop to think we miss our opportunity.*

Pi nodded.

Anton: *There are some remedies worse than the disease*—or so thought our politics and economists. But death is pretty bad?

Pi nodded.

Anton: *It is a bad plan that admits no modification.*

Pi nodded.

Anton: *Every day should be passed as if it were to be our last.*
Pi: But heeding to this maxim would pose many problems in reality. It would break up many relationships and families.
Anton: *Everything is worth what its purchaser will pay for it.*

Pi nodded more gently.

Pi: But you can be cheated.
Anton: Not sure, you just pay what you think, rationally, is the value to you?
Pi: But is it true that $69.3 million was really the value of Everydays, a digital collage. It is by someone called Beeple? But if the buyer Vignesh Sundaresan is worth billions, it may not be all that much of what he owns?
Anton: Clearly not. Surely a school or several hundred in Africa would be better?
Pi: For him, this non-fungible token is a reflection of the fact that life is non-fungible. Although I am not entirely sure what that means. But his family lives very near mine. He is also called Metakovan because Kovan means king in one my Indian languages. But I agree about the schools.
Anton: Non-fungible means a digital asset. It is there but not to hold. You can even buy special edition NFT Trainers! To show off on bloggs and bliggs. Everyone appears to live near you in India!
Pi: But it is true of the people I mention and many that I do not. Even APJ Abdul Kalam, the nuclear physicist and erstwhile President of India. He is Tamil

also. Also, Metakovan has gifted Everydays free to all to download. That means almost a cent, American, for every person on Earth. If they want it.

Anton: Great, Pi!

Pi: And it is 21069 pixels square. Which is about 26 pixels for every minute of his life, so far. I wonder if anyone knows that.

Anton: Really! Why is that useful at all? Two more from Publilius—*a rolling stone gathers no moss.* Also, *it is only the ignorant who despise education.*

Pi agreed of course, although some statements could be contradicting each other. And who defines what education is? Why is Welsh, Urdu, Gujarati, and Polish taught in school now, but not previously?

Anton was keen to add another string to his clichéd bow of cynicism through his beloved Horace. But just thought it through instead. We are dying for our liberated way of life. Wilfred Owen's old lie came to his mind—*Dulce et decorum est pro patria mori* —sweet and glorious to die for the Fatherland. *And ideally in it too*, thought Anton.

Even in these most peaceful of times the world, through Pinker spectacles. Dying now not from, mustard gas but because of the lack of oxygen all because of a virus. But he would never, ever, want to live anywhere else on planet Earth.

The sky would be particularly naked tonight from the App prediction, and he wanted to take Anju. He asked for another book recommendation before leaving. Anton told Pi that he would think about it.

The relevance of several of his ideas he was not sure of but wanted to go out for a walk to ruminate. Pi recalled and regretted not having taken a photo of the *Fota* that was the frog on the apple. That may have made a great NFT by Anju and Pi. But neither Anju nor Pi had remembered to pack their phones for that particular visit to the plotters.

They had seen a frog on an apple, and both agreed that it reminded them of the need to jump off our planet soon, as the sun would start to die in 5 billion years and no longer allow life on Earth. But Greta had sounded the alarms and had informed all that listened, that the dying had already started due to the Anthropocene warming epoch. It had started to accelerate in her lifetime and she was distraught. We needed to be ready to move to a different planet outside of our solar system probably earlier than planned.

In relation to this problem, he will need to have a further chat with Vik, a man Pi had kept in touch with from the café and Hanuman temple. If there was an eternal philosophy, *Sanatana Dharma*, and the Earth was destroyed and eventually the universe imploded, would *Sanatana Dharma* emerge again, or was it just one of a number of philosophies?

Was it inchoate to the universe to emerge life-forms of consciousness, because that was the inevitable outcome of the play of quantum particles? Or could nothing happen as it all might have happened by chance alone? Or will it all start again with the hominids and their accidental viewpoints and inventions. It was all a bit too much to tackle. Especially, after the generous pegs that Anton had put his way.

Final thoughts on his walk were how he had seen the stars and the planets in a different way, much informed by Anju. And how they had both agreed that people hurried too much on Earth. Pi was obsessed about his movement in three dimensions within the universe, again. Was not the Earth spin speed of up to 460 metres a second or 1000 miles an hour? (Kenyans mainly, is that why they run so well?). And then we on Earth (all of us now) spin around the sun at 67,000 miles an hour. Then we slowly, over 230 million years, spin around our home base galaxy, the Milky Way at 230 kilometres a second, 514,000 miles per hour. And the Milky Way itself is spinning 210 kilometres per second, like a frisbee, at 468,000 miles an hour. No wonder we humans are so dizzy.

At home Pi noted that the Covid-19 rash on his toes and feet was now getting better. The itchy geographical shapes were receding. The single larger map of Czechoslovakia was now just Slovakia. Cuba had disappeared as had Sri Lanka. That was the right foot. The other foot had an archipelago that was rapidly being cured. *Maybe this presaged what would happen with rising sea levels,* thought Pi.

And please note that the Krishna Rau was thoroughly enjoyed by Pi. But it was a disappointing 14 millimetres only.

Chapter 16
Passage to Victory

There are only two families in the world.
My old grandmother used to say, the Have and Have-nots?

Don Quixote. Miguel de Cervantes Saavedra (1547–1616)

Yagnas

Pi had had to spend a whole year for his 'Masters' in Hindu Studies. A year that had been spent sleeping on straw mats and a roughly hewn *charpoy*, albeit from the best sustainable wood from the hermitage forest. Incidentally, Pi informed the Beck household that *charpoy* is derived from *char* meaning 4 and *poy* from feet.

Then there was the daily upkeep of the ashram with its 'wax on, wax off' cleaning of the decking and the latrines, if you were so unluckily rostered. Or blessed, if you were particularly Gandhian in your attitudes. There was no discussion on the topic of performing the ashram's chores and other duties, for one had already signed an agreement to do so at admission.

There were no fees, but the authenticity of the place and its weekly worships attracted many donations from afar. They were especially interested in seeing the diligent band of youthful women and men who ran the ashram. These were the salad days, if that phrase could be transmigrated to Sundervagvela.

The days of being and spiritually-guiding, partaking in the most delicious healthy food and the sharing in the joy of others at *Aarti* times. Donations were plenty and the saintly budgeting of the son of the Pir ensured a healthy bank balance and that all amenities were well catered for.

A novice once had the temerity and audacity to complain about the *charpoy* that he was required to sleep. Akbarlal had pointed out that the *charpoy* was unaffordable to many in the West, as it was Rs 42,500! He would duly show them the advert on the internet. In the West, you had to be rich to live a life that was luxuriously poor and simple.

Pi recalled this thought but was struck by the Beck household and how it appeared to be practising the three daily Yajnas or rituals of daily life that he was taught in the ashram. These he saw observed every hour in Sundervagvela. These rituals that had made his life grounded and contented.

Even though they had clearly not had any association with the ashram as it had started after the conclusion of Anton's visit. Looking out of his window, he saw Kirk inhale sharply on his vaping device as he started to collect the spent birdfeeders.

The peanut one was empty as usual; beloved as it was by the woodpecker, the blue tit, the great tit, the coal tit, the nuthatch, and the occasional yellow hammer. The latter the magnificently-named *Emberiza citronella*, a hybrid of the Old German for bunting and the Italian for a small yellow thing. The water trough was empty but would need a good clean out. Apparently, there could be hidden parasites lurking within its innocent looking stone walls.

The sunflower seeds remained not eaten. The fat-ball holder needed a top up and the bird-seed thingamajig needed topping up too. This was *Bhuta Yajna* at its best. Pi had forgotten the meaning exactly, but was sure it would include bird feeding.

A blue tit at 10g and needing 3g of food a day—30% or so of its body weight could be fed for a whole year on just a kg of food. With the daily top up being around 1kg or more, Pi calculated, to no one's real benefit, that the Becks were feeding the equivalent of a flock of 365 wild birds a year. *Bhuta Yajna,* as the offering and receipted acceptance of food to the animal kingdom, was thus fulfilled.

Pitri Yajna was less evident but there were had always been the regular calls and visits to the agèd parents of Ruth and Anton, usually weekly or more often if need arose. But now there were no more parents for them. Unfortunately, many such elders still felt locked up and went unvisited in care homes, or worse still in their own homes. Sometimes, due to Covid-19. Sometimes not. The ancestors, living and dead, were thus remembered and served.

Nri Yajna as the gift of charity or help to the poorer and destitute was rendered most magnificently in Ruth's biscuit club, which was functioning very well. It was performing well beyond her initial expectations. The scheme had only started 17 months ago with lending of micro-loans to a diverse array of pig farmers, maize farmers, small shopkeepers, beekeepers, cooks and even solar panel repairers, which had been an interesting venture for Ruth's group. Loans of £15 had been duly paid off at 63 pence a week in some cases. An algorithm had calculated that the loans had helped the lives of 823 people.

The triad of Yajnas thus daily adjoined at the Becks had created a sense of fulfilment that Pi oft observed and admired. The magic was often fissured by mundane daily chores, and especially the news items of rapes, murders, shootings, addiction, and wars, and drone attacks killing people at wedding parties and the plastic nooses around the heads of turtles and the famine in countries adjacent to countries that throw away 50% of their food uneaten, if served at all in the first place.

Yoga

The Becks caught Pi attempting his yoga exercises. Of which he had no inclination or skill in completing. But there was a general assumption that Pi would be masterful in yoga; particularly as he was known as Guru Pi, by some. Pi had then been obliged to join Ruth and Anju at the exercise fest that happened every Sunday morning at the neighbours.

Albeit with toned down music, so as not to notch up noise pollution too much. There was no doubt that the mysterious man in the duffle coat was out every day, virtually, with his decibel meter on his bright orange high viz hodometer. The benefit to the community was that he was creating a map of the woods and fields with all the landmarks. Together with an acoustic map of all the human noise levels.

He had been heavily influenced by his time teaching in the outback of Australia and New Zealand and had proclaimed to the parish council that he would create a living map of the woods, plots and environs. This would include all the noise-polluting, light-polluting, and general-polluting hot spots.

It was a laudable project, especially as it was very likely that locally-named areas such as Nikhil Path (and Point), Papa's Poplars, Mummy's Alders, Ba-Bapuji's Beeches, Sunray Oaks, Winter Wonderland, Gloria's Oak, Jolast's Coppice, Haiku Echo Point, Patient Oaks, Conker Threes, Tolstoy's Birches, Les Amis unter den Linden, Jack Frost, The Line of Religions, Narnia, Exact Centre of England (without Cornwall), Dead Fox, Duckweed Pond, and Stone Hex— would all make it onto this map.

Butterflies and moths were particularly abundant along Nikhil Path. These rare and beautiful *Lepidoptera* entities were often unknown but included the identified Red Admiral, Peacock, Green Hairstreak, Brimstone, Dingy skipper, Orange tip, Comma, Large white, and the exquisite Cinnabar moth.

Sound was not to be more than 50 decibels, ever. Even though bird calls were 40 decibels and light conversation, close up, could be 60. Otherwise, an email would be despatched to the council.

Sometimes, Pi attempted exercises with Ruth, usually reluctantly. After 3 bouts of exercises, close attention to which was lacking and of the calibre that would have earned a first-round elimination from Strictly Come Dancing, Pi was incredibly happy to be declared a Divine Goddess. This was by the exercise guru herself, Schellea, who had moved from her ancestral trade of being a fowler to promoting even healthier living and moving, hitherto, undiscovered muscles and joints, it would seem.

The second antipodean connection that day.

Shuggie

Pi in his conversations to the Beck household made it clear that he had cried several times during his book-reading. On reading *Shuggie Bain*, Pi wept. On reading *Night* by Ellie Weisel, Pi wept. On finishing the Indian-Canadian Rohinton Mistry's *A Fine Balance*, Pi wept. Shuggie Bain had been a Baedeker's guide to the Glaswegian dispossessed. A videocam could not have done a better job. Reading had allowed Pi unfettered time to join Shuggie in the awfulness of his life and that of his mother. The convenient gated communities were not electrified and guarded by dogs of war as in South Africa or the Utopic Communities in Asia; but they may as well have been.

The *fixité du milieu intérieur est la condition de la vie libre et indépéndente* of the well-to-do *vis-à-vis* the stormy daily travails of the not-so-lucky in life. The former with the thermostat that would control regular delivery of food, comfort, companionship and all things good mentally and physically and spiritually. And the others that could not.

Anton's Despair

Anton was drifting away from the sit back and leave society to evolve from the top down economically, mentally, morally, spiritually, and otherwise. There must be another way. On this score, he was askance with the ideas of his dear friend, Mark.

Anton was on his own with a peg or two of the *uisge beatha*. But even this 14-year-old water of life was not assuaging his despair. He had been particularly perturbed by the doom and gloom emanating from the various magazines cast all over the house by his untidy household.

He was heading for another one of his periodic *désespérer de l'humanité*— this was the official diagnosis given for his bout of low-grade depression. His despair with humanity was manifold and extensive. He felt that his was a euphemistic European life ignoring so much ill in the world.

Where was the baseline in human behaviour, why was it transcended so often? Humanity had repaired so much in the colander of evils that spewed out on a daily basis. Life was longer sure. There were less deaths in childhood. But why does rubbish continue to infest our environment. Discarded rubbish absolutely everywhere. But then the stories.

Really. PETA had had to rescue a horse that had been stapled shut. To prevent pregnancy. Except that she was already pregnant. Staples thankfully, mused Anton, of copper and therefore anti-bacterial. After the rescue Rudi was born. Happily, ever after. But the 3 score broken bones of a child. And then to die. Really? These people deserve respect and dignity. Do they?

The trafficking of drugs. To maim and kill and deprive families of a life less sorrowed. And the man shot on the wrong side of the spectrum of skin colours. He could not breathe. This criminality of skin tone. So difficult to atone for. And he was not unaware of the local evils. Never mind the national and the international.

Was this the world promised when we were good in the nursery, infant school, secondary school, work? And paid our taxes? Helped the old lady across the road? Bought the Big Issue? And always, almost, behaved well. A failed social-contract. At best. A conspiracy of minimal intervention and consequentialism, at worst.

Anton vaguely recalled a Dickensian novel where a man was killed by a horse after it had presumably declared independence and turned on its master. And also, the making of Boxer into glue in the dystopia that was Animal Farm, then, and awfulness of some of the Animal Farms now.

William Blake must still declare that all heaven is in a rage. The wanton boy that killed the fly has grown up. Behaviour unchanged. *Homo sapiens sapiens—* really?

Pi's Trial

Pi recalled that in Kafka's *The Trial*, at a respectable 26 millimetres, was one of the chosen few in the millennium library series of books. Most were too long for his endeavours anyhow. This set of books had been kindly funded by the weekly 40 or so million gamblers, on a one in 45,057,474 chance of winning the jackpot.

He had read it a few weeks ago but was now transfixed looking at the horizontal spine of the book within the tower of books.

The book reminded Pi of all the distress in the lawsuit over the ownership of the Sundervagvela Cricket Pitch (SCP) and Maidan. Remember the Maidan uprising protests in Ukraine? Probably, somehow related etymologically. Originally, this area was the private domain of one of the First Indian Generals in the British Army and as such the land had belonged to him. And then for reasons unknown, it had ended up in the hands of Pi's ancestors. Who had then bequeathed it to the pleasure of all. That was mainly male cricketers and their doting entourages. Although, a women's team had recently started to use the facilities.

The awesome Jeetendraprasad Pathanlal had incubated his skills at the pitch and a small, or was it life-size, statue of him adorned the veranda of the main Pavilion. The women had their set of rooms, albeit, with a larger kitchen as a bar was not needed. Jeetendraprasad had turned his handicap of a polio-affected upper limb into a hand that had won several scores of national caps at the under 19 level.

His whip hand spin bowling had terrorised all the other local and regional and national teams. Until he had leprosy. And then TB killed him. There was understandable pride in the history of the place and the SCP case had hardened the populace into the pros for the conversion of the area into a shopping mall and some pretend social housing as the sweetener for the higher authorities.

The cons for the project had wanted to die peacefully one day, knowing that the history of their memories of the place would be intact forever—the bazaars, the regional finals, the weddings, the birthdays and the melting pot of festivities of Islam, Hinduism, Christianity, Buddhism and even Judaism.

Although the latter had been depleted somewhat with the granting of the creation of specific areas for Cochin and Keralite Jews in Israel. This part of the public wanted to die with their memories intact in that unchanged world of old.

Essentially, it was the Proper Roti Flour Mills that had wanted the land for development and felt that it was theirs, as debts arising from loss of revenue from advertising panels was not forthcoming due to multiple cancellations of matches during the religious riots, and then the various political insurgencies. Now of course, Covid-19 cancellations no doubt were playing a part too.

Proper Roti Flour Mills had bought the largest chunk of advertising years in advance and hence their issue. They considered that the only recompense open to them would be to take over SCP and convert it into a commercial venture— the shopping mall. The court case was costly, but luckily for the cons, there were several *pro bono* lawyers.

It was bleak. At least not all the assets could be frittered away as land could not be carried away. *The Trial* by Kafka reminded Pi of the circumstances of the common human whose file, their livelihood, their respect, their dignity, their life was a folder in a dusty, spider-webbed room awaiting trial. The file locked up; a life locked up. The life becomes a number. 11-07-92M. The twelfth case lodged that day.

It had been long agreed that the suffixes I, O, U, Q would not be used as they would create possible confusion and it would be too difficult to handle any more than 22 cases between the registry staff of 4. Twenty-two could be lodged or inquired upon or to have evidence and affidavits and codicils added then that was that. Any in excess of 22 would need to return the next day.

There was a waiting list for the waiting. Several entrepreneurs made money queuing overnight outside the register. The hourly rate being the same as Pi as teacher. Pi knew that the situation in healthcare, in Sundervagvela, was bleak too. For operations, mind treatments and tablets and potions.

But here treatment, if given, gave quick results. The dichotomy of success and living a bit longer, or failure to be escorted into heaven or otherwise by the buffalo-riding Yama, God of Death.

The SCP case still remained to be resolved. For the other cases too, daily life frittered away. One day at a time, one moon at a time. Often to the thousandth moon. Insulted and humiliated, if at all aired and duly considered, by the late due process of law.

Pi Book Choices

Pi had decided not to read *Don Quixote* by the magnificent Miguel de Cervantes Saavedra, even though it had been strongly recommended by Anju. He felt that it was too thick, and the writing was too dense, and he had lost just too much time with his last book.

Don Quixote was also 345,390 words long. Pi did dip in and out of the book and admired its comedic genius, irony, and especially the lavish illustration in the form of woodcuts. Certainly, a book to read at leisure back in Sundervagvela.

Daniel Defoe's *Moll Flanders* was recommended by Kirk but also abandoned. He had shared this recommendation with his brother. The latter had vetoed it, based on it being too raunchy and over-sexualised to be included. Pi felt that the eroticism in *Ian* McEwan's *Atonement* would be difficult to beat anyway.

Hopefully, Pi's brother would never find that out. The book was hidden at a friend's house whose family were not interested in his reading list. Pi also felt a little ashamed that he had decided not to embark on a Balzac even though the Honoré had finished his mission of scientifically, through narrative, cataloguing the wiles and vicissitudes and loves and sorrow of all of humanity in *La Comédie Humaine*.

It was all about the private life, the provincial life, the Parisian life, the political life, the military life and the country life. A cumulation of all the different aspects of French life. There were 91 finished works in total, in 12 volumes at least.

Apparently, the sad times of Pere Goriot aka Old Man Goriot had to be read at least once in a lifetime, Ruth had told him. And also, that other ill-treated fathers included King Lear after which her home town of Leicester was renamed. Probably. And a play by Shakespeare. A bestseller. The Roman name *Ratae Corieltauvorum* is even more difficult to spell and pronounce.

It was ironic that immediately after his decision to not read *Don Quixote*, Pi had witnessed a taller horse with its head down. Its rider was equally downcast. The picture of desolation indeed. Just behind was a taller horse; both horse and rider were erect and aplomb, riding towards the wind turbines.

No one in the household knew what the book was, but Pi would go round with a thick book covered in brown paper. This obvious brick of a book was a knackered-looking book. Its spine was broken in 3 places, frayed cover through the brown paper, and obvious fungal black spots on the paper ends.

Pi was often observed cutting the pages open as well. It fascinated him that the need to cut pages meant that no one had read the book cover to cover. Or had bought their own copy.

If anyone asked him what book it was, then he would just change the subject. His excuse was that he was having difficulty reading it and was probably on the verge of giving up with it anyway. For a good 6 to 8 weeks, Pi was not seen with another book.

The tower of books had ceased to grow. Very much like those construction projects that would suddenly erupt to a fourth floor within weeks and then appear abandoned as the investors ran out of bricks, money, workers or all three.

The Tower of Books Topples

And then, there was progress. Presumably that brown paper-covered tome was finished. Pi's tower was coming along on track. The three little books that had been added in the last season had been deeper voyages to the psyches of the character. But these small reads were still progress; especially considering how much Pi had been setback by *The Idiot*.

For a period of time, Pi went around proclaiming to anyone that would listen that Dostoyevsky was the antidote to creativity. His brilliance in capturing the body, mind and soul of another and encapsulating it into words would be off-putting to all but the most inspired. Here was a writer that could not be bettered.

The tower of books then toppled. All the books on top of the Greta and Adichie were is a sorry pile at the base of the tower. It was as if Greta and Adichie had shrugged and pushed and thrown off a whole load of heavier tomes. To Pi, it was a metaphor of the new world of ideas that had to be recreated focussing on all things climate and environmental, and the feminine. Nothing else mattered that much at this present time. Kirk had remarked that the burgers had flipped. Pi, often, never really understood any of the comments Kirk made at the beginning of their conversations.

On tidying up the tower of books, Pi felt that his height in books had been read at last. He was happy. Moreover, the deadline for the task was approaching. A final reckoning and certification that the task was complete was needed by Sir X in the presence of Anton as referee, or would it be an umpire or adjudicator or even a judge?

It was arranged that Sir X would pop in to see Pi after his early morning jog around the lakes. And appear he did. Unfortunately, Anton had not arrived back from collecting the paper, on foot, that day.

The Reckoning

Pi: Morning Sir, I believe I have completed the labour set by you. The task is accomplished. I am pleased to say.

Sir X: Let me see, and by the way you created and set the task yourself—I just said, and probably know that it was a little too much. Let me be the judge. Let's go!

Pi regretted the fact that Ruth, Anju, and Kirk were not there. Or even Anton. Pi took Sir X to the tower of books and was confident that the tower's height was a little higher than his nature ordained stature.

Sir X: Very, very well done! But do let me check.

Sir X did accept defeat in his mind and was very curious as to what Pi had read and the calibre of the books. He was very pleased to note the eclectic nature of his reading—even a James Bond book was there and a Lee Child. He should read some of Pi's choices in the future too. He then frowned. And then a bit more.

Sir X: Oh dear! I must be blunt and honest! This is not cricket! The rules appear to have been conveniently re-interpreted! This is ball-tampering or bowling at the legs at best!

Pi looked aghast. Cheating is practically what Pi felt he had been accused of, especially with the references to cricket. Pi was thus broken in the midst of admiring the spines of *The Vegetarian*, *Beloved*, *Maus*, *The Space Between Us*, and many many others.

Pi: What pray is the problem?

Sir X: So many of these are Folio editions. I can see at least 9 here. They have thick cardboard slip-cases.

Pi: But the challenge was to read my own height in books. If some books have a slip-case box—then what to do *hanneh*?

Pi looked visibly upset. He was going to fail the challenge that his family had followed in Sundervagvela and his new friends—the plotters, the mechanics at Speedy's, the City-Zen Café lot, those he knew at the Temperance Bar and the

Gate. Pi was sure that Shuggie Bains and Prince Myshkin would be particularly upset too. He especially did not want to fail Ruth or Anju or Kirk, and especially Anton. The latter had backed him so many times, despite the negative vibes from Sir X.

Sir X: That is at least 5 centimetres in cardboard. The challenge was not to read cardboard! But books. Not wood either!

Pi: Yes but—

Sir X: But what? Look, here are 5 wooden—solid wooden boxes with books in them. Do you agree? Lovely volumes, I might even get some. What have we here? *Guru Gita, Principal Upanishads, Yoga-Sutras of Patanjali, Ramayana Sundarakanda*, and the other one. But you surely cannot expect me to count those 4 centimetres, at least, either? So sorry, you have failed your task. Shame really, I was taking to you, you know.

Pi's eyes welled up at this stage.

Over a quick cup of tea, Sir X agreed that the tasking of imaging googol had been achieved. Sir X gave Pi his final report that two out of three is fine, as Meat Loaf had thought too. A remark lost on Pi. Sir X also wished Pi all the best for the Carmen Show and that he would be there.

Team Beck

When the Becks assembled later that morning, Kirk and Anju were particularly incandescent with Sir X. Repeated mention was made of the fact that book coverings and housings had not been stipulated not to count and that was just unfair and typical of Sir X. Anton, tried to argue that maybe Sir X had a point and had really wanted Pi to complete his tasks. Ruth was visibly upset.

Ruth: Pi, I think you said that you were short of reading your own height in books by, what was it, 8 centimetres?

Pi: Yes, with the cardboard slip cases and the wooden covers. It is impossible to read that by midnight tonight. We also cannot confirm, Sir X said he was going away.

Ruth: A few things. You have several books on your bedside table? Why are they not on the column of books?

Pi: Well, with respect to the *Hanuman Chalisa*—is it reading when I know it off by heart?

Kirk: Absolutely! As long as you looked at the words too!

Pi: Well, I read it once a week, on Saturdays. So that is good, it is not so thick though!

Ruth: Is there anything else there?

Pi: I have the *Sri Ramacaritamanasa.*

It was definitely Anju's place to act as defence lawyer here. She had been itching to take part in the conversation.

Anju: Long title indeed! Why not include it?

Pi: It is just the one word for the Manasa Lake brimming over with the exploits of Sri Rama. That is all. I did not think it suitable as I read it every alternate year. One year that book, the next Valmiki's version. Which is double the length!

Anju: Let's leave the details out but there was no stipulation on previously read books! All books had to be by a different author. No more than 10% of the books being graphic, and some other crazy rules.

Pi: Well, it is by Tulsidas. So, I cannot put in the *Hanuman Chalisa*?

Kirk: Afraid not. I guess the *Ramayana* book is thicker—put that in.

Pi: Yes, it is at least 4 centimetres!

Ruth: What else?

Pi: The *Bhagavad Gita* is there too. Just a thin edition by Juan Mascaro, I think.

Ruth: What a centimetre?

Pi: Not quite?

Ruth: What about that book wrapped in brown paper?

Pi: I am struggling with that one. I still have 97 pages to read. I have only read 1201 or so pages.

Kirk: Read it then, you have loads of time. What is it?

Pi: Can I tell you later? I can read it at 10 pages an hour on that one only.

Ruth: Don't be nervous Pi. OK but reading that would give you another 4 centimetres at least, so you will then be well and truly completely finished!

Anton: If you finish the task, let's get Prof Marma to come and check. Then I will get Prof Marma to chat with Mark. If anyone can convince Mark, it would be her!

Pi settled down to read in the study. He was fed and watered by the Becks, mainly *Prike* and tea and masala lemonade and defrosted madeleines. Pi finished by late evening. Prof Marma was pleased to have been selected as the final arbiter, having followed Pi's progress with great interest over the past few months. She was delighted to see her recommendations within the tower. And pointed them out to the spectators that were the Beck household.

Photographs were taken and despatched to Sir X. A gracious and congratulatory return message was received. So, it could be 3 out 3. As long, as the Carmen Show happened according to plan. A piece on the reading of the tower of books would also now appear in the local paper—weekend edition. A local journalist had deemed it worthy, and was hoping that Pi's undertaking would spark a reading revolution amongst the adults and children of Belton, at least. Bookstores had bid highly for advertising space. Everyone won.

The Becks and Pi and Prof Marma were all quite contented. Hugs all round. All was well with the world. Pi did not sleep very much at all. He had still not finally created even a mental list of answers for the Carmen Show. And that he would need to forward his musical choices on waking.

Chapter 17
The Carmen Show

I carry my ideas a long time, rejecting and rewriting until I am satisfied. Since I am conscious of what I want, I never lose sight of the fundamental idea. It rises higher and higher until I see the image of it, rounded and complete, standing there before my mental vision

Ludwig van Beethoven (1770–1827). German Composer and Pianist.

Some parts of the show were becoming clear to Pi. He would be asked about all the nuts and bolts that made up a culture, giving its inhabitants something to grow up with, imbibe and then contribute to if so gifted, or not rejected. He wondered whether he could promote the idea of the square Beck Plate on the show for Anton, his domestic host.

That would be a kind and much needed gesture. Though there was always the possibility that it would not go down well with Carmen, who could be notoriously cantankerous on and off-screen. But on the flip side if Carmen said anything positive about the Beck Plate that would keep Anton in good humour for many dinners and drinks in the golf club.

The jigsaw pieces of his personal landscape were becoming clearer to him. There was an odd but close affinity in relation to music with all things Amy Winehouse. Her glorious guttural rasping was now a part of Pi's repertoire. Anju was pleased to note that Pi clearly did not understand all of Amy Winehouse's lyrics.

The high music was all the stuff we all love, the Canon in D by Johann Pachelbel. It had been a favourite of those who had walked down the aisle since 1680. Anton felt that it was an ideal choice for a wedding; later to be relegated and replaced with a Mahler requiem later in life.

But Pi chose the last movement of a symphony by Ravi Shankar—*Banjara*. The word, according to Pi, and unverified, means a member of the wandering musicians and general folk of northern India. The same folk as our Romany community, the previously called Gypsies who were thought to originate from Egypt. The final vocals were just spine-chilling, an appraisal and vindication of humanity. Poetically written, coloured, and sculpted in musical sound, delivered as if it was the finale to the Creation itself.

Art as painting was proving more problematic. As to some of Anton's favourite works of Art, Pi did like. But he was not sure if he had to exercise censorship over his choices. When was the show aired? Was it a 12, suitable only for persons of 12 years and over? Or would it be categorised as a 12A—accompanied by an adult (not defined). Or would it be 15 years old and over?

That didn't involve any specification on whether an adult was needed or not at all. And suddenly after completing your 17th year on Earth, you were suddenly permitted to see everything. If the censors had passed it in the first place. But I digress.

Pi had seen several episodes of the eponymous show and was struck by several points. The show was just so removed from the sugary or saccharin shows that he had seen in British TV, Hollywood, Bollywood, Tollywood, or even the occasional Nollywood show. Carmen was a veritable tour de force.

She carried herself magnificently, with a mega-Watt grin on her face as though she was the Queen of Sheba, no nonsense, but on your side. She could coax out a conversation from anyone; whether from the demure lecturer of African Studies at the local university or the inventor of the solar-panelled sunroof.

Someone did beat Pi to that one. This was a simple stick-on thick film that was largely transparent and allowed one to charge one's phone (or keep one's coffee hot). A solar panel for all; affording great value for the price of 12 takeaway coffees. Speedy's would fix it if it broke for the price of 4 more such coffees. The show was oddly interesting and diverse in what was aired.

A song that had lived permanently in Pi's brain since the last visit to Speedy's was the energetic Mory Kanté's *Yeke Yeke*. However, once the lyrics had been translated at the City-Zen Café by Keke, the rest of the day was spent in thoughts of Priyali, missing her deeply. He had learnt many aspects of African culture from Keke.

But not enough to confidently air on the show with Carmen. He was fascinated that in Dogon culture in Mali, the sacred star of the community is Sirius. This was the same for the Svana Tribe around Sundervagvela. And apparently the Seri, Native Americans. There was almost too much connectivity at times.

Pi enjoyed the dreamtime paintings of the Australasians, Albert Namatjira and Tarisse. The satellite maps of imaging from above the landscape via the mind. Painted and cast in time and space and story. Favourite films would be shared throughout the show. There was one about the Iranian girls who so wanted to see a football match. He had no idea what it was called though.

To Pi, it was as if Carmen was using the show to cascade down culture and meaning from the people she interviewed to her viewers in easily digestible morsels. He imagined Carmen as Shiva. Carmen would have made the perfect model for the descent of the Ganges as captured in the stone carvings at Mamallapuram. A UNESCO World Heritage site that was only a few hundred kilometres from Sundervagvela. Pi read up on some details. If possible, he would air the story on the show. Carmen would certainly appreciate it. The story was that the Ganges, one of the most abundant of all Earthen rivers, was needed for irrigation in order to sustain humanity and all other life in the arid plains below the Himalayas.

Indeed, there was a worldwide drought at the time. Himalaya, the Mountain God, had agreed for his daughter, the Goddess Ganga, to help humanity. The Goddess was cognisant of the fact that whilst the waters of the Himalayas would be life-saving, quenching thirst and irrigating fields, they could also wreak havoc due the power of the torrents and ensuing floods. These tsunamis could destroy entire lands and dwellings and cities and temples, rather than being of benefit.

The great King Bhagiratha petitioned the great Lord Shiva to help with this task, who agreed to help. Goddess Ganga riding Makara, a crocodile, poured these mighty waves of water through Shiva's hair, allowing controlled rivulets to stream down onto the lands below the Himalayas, all the way down south to sustain and feed millions upon millions for aeons to come. Thus the 2510 kilometres long River Ganges was created in myth and legend.

Pi was saddened to learn from Kirk that this romance with the river needed a reality check. It was also full of millions, even billions of items that added 100,000 tonnes of plastic and other waste to the sea every year. Or so the National Geographic had calculated.

Pi had watched the flow of all things cultural through Carmen's programmes to the thirsty folks that awaited the show every Friday with great impatience. Having heard on the news that the show might be scrapped because of lack of advertising revenue; they had flocked to Smorg's Supermarket and other local businesses and petitioned them to continue supporting the show.

Pi also really thought that the beauty of the head of Carmen would have resembled Lord Shiva's. Anton would often sit there mesmerised by Carmen and all that she did. This was an unreached Goddess to be admired. Though he was perfectly satisfied with the one he had been privileged with in Ruth.

Time rolls on and Pi was on the show. Pi is delighted that so many of his Belton friends were there. That itself moved Pi to a wet eye.

On TV and Radio

The introductory song to the show was *Resham Firiri*—a cheery Nepalese folksong that Pi had chosen and would be discussed if there was sufficient time. Pi felt as if he was a celebrity on that most watched programme in the planet—Amitabh Bachchan's *Kaun Banega Crorepati*?

Who wants to be a millionaire, adjusted into rupees? He was also not sure that the programme would work on radio but apparently, people listened to it and then saw the TV show on catch-up TV later on.

Carmen: I'll roll the dice and … you can have 7 pictures in your gallery, Pi. Please show and name your hangings.

Pi had had many a sleepless night to choose 12 and upon being asked to choose only 7 of the 12, he immediately began sweating profusely. He would have to leave out several including *Woman on the Stairs* by Gerhard Richter, a regret as it was searingly enigmatic and looked like a photograph.

He also left out Kandinsky's *Delicate Tension Number 85*, which had reminded him of the banked container ship in the Suez Canal with the destinies of people altered by the late arrival of the ship. This had been a favourite of Anju's.

He was only going to mention Jack Vettriano if the dice was to score very highly. Much as he really liked these paintings, he knew that Sir X thought them vulgar and not real art.

304

Pi: I give you Banksy, Rabindranath Tagore, Tarisse, Frida Kahlo, Frank Bowling, Sophie Arp, and Theodore Gericault's *Raft of the Medusa*. Sorry; I am aware that you had Arp recently. But what to do?

He was anxious to enunciate the title of the last painting in full as he had difficulty remembering it. He was a little worried about the little bits of nudity in it. Hopefully that would be glossed over.

Carmen: I really am enjoying your choices. I hope we did not stress you out too much asking you to leave out 5.

Pi had felt ashamed and particularly hoped he had not upset Anju.

Carmen: Let's get the film choices out the way. As you know Pi, we cannot show any snippets of the movies you choose but I am sure the whizz-kids in the back will conjure up a still or so and some credits. And let's roll.

Pi: I hope it is large number—I have many favourites.

Carmen: Just the three! So sorry! Ok, let's go to the ads. And thank you, dear sponsors!

Pi discussed that once again, this would be very difficult. He went for and explained the reasons for choosing *Slumdog Millionaire* (obvious), *Love Actually* (the Beck Household's favourite), and *The Lunchbox* (obvious to no one).

Carmen: Great choices—I think the bloke, in the *Lunchbox* was in the film *Jurassic World*?

Pi: Yes, yes, he was, that is Irfan Khan, of course.

Carmen: And now to the music choices! Let's roll the dice. Sorry, but in the interests of time, we can only do a maximum of … 6 choices today. Football is on at 2.45 pm today and we have had to shorten the programme, otherwise sales of beer would suffer. We certainly would not want that, would we?! Or any interference with the betting syndicates.

Pi: I picked 12 pieces of music rather optimistically. I would like to start with a prayer song to the eternal saints that we think about when we gather collectively and sing. It is *Duma Dum Mast Kalandar*. This is a most amazing Sufi Qawwali. No need to sing either. You can just sway, whether sitting or standing. Do close your eyes though.

Carmen: Whatever. Please do translate this for us—although we will be transliterating it as well. And probably badly as my audience knows well!

Pi, becoming almost oblivious of where he was, swung his head from side to side and launched into O *Laal meri pat rakiyo bhala jhoole laalan. Duma dum mast kalandar*—O red-robed being, may I always be under your care, my every breath is for you—jubilant saint that you are, Kalandar. Something like that.

There was a tear in Pi's eye at the end of the rendition. It was by the local Qawwali group in Sundervagvela, recorded shortly after the massacre of the 97 at the shrine of the aforementioned saint, Lal Shahbaz Qalandar in Sindh. Pi's chaiwalla's son Nidom had died in that incident.

Pi Reveals the Brown Paper-Covered Book

Pi had brought his brown paper-covered book with him to the Carmen Show. He recalled how he had successfully finished it last night out of the sheer necessity of needing those extra 97 millimetres to accomplish reading his own height in books in a year. It was, after careful measurement by Pi, found to be 56 millimetres thick. A great result indeed.

Pi: I can now reveal my favourite book. I note that you have already given me the *Bhagavad Gita*. Otherwise, I would have been in a real fix. So, thank you very much.

Carmen: Does no one really not know what the book is? Not even your friends at the Beck household? Remember, this is a book that you take to another civilisation if need be.

Pi: OK and then no to your first question. I wanted to hide it from them until just now. I wanted to reveal it to you first! You only, Carmen! I did not think I could finish this novel for my project of reading a veritable tower of books. It is 1298 pages long and 545,925 words, I believe. The pages on the sewage system were particularly challenging as the sewers themselves were for the hero in our book who had to wade through them. I think you know now?

Carmen: I actually do not! What a superb cliff-hanger! Please don't tell us yet. Let's come back after the break—how about to a track suggested by you, Pi?

The bidding had started and the advert rates went up 23% as the advertisers knew that their adverts would have even better traction. Even Gheewala, Sons and Daughter went for the increased rate.

Pi: For a music piece, I would like to suggest a song by Amy Winehouse—*Rehab*.

The audience gasped. This was quite a surprise coming from the traditional-looking Indian man sat on the stage.

Carmen: Why Amy Winehouse?

Pi: Well, why not, I ask you? Hers is the voice of all of humanity in distress.

Carmen felt that further conversation would not help, and the director cued to move on quickly. The track was played and the move to adverts took place in quick succession.

Carmen: The next track, please!

Pi: It will be, please, *Jangar* by Anda Union.

Carmen: I know it! Very strange! May be the absolutely strangest music I have ever played on this show. I am not sure Belton is ready for it yet! My good friend George absolutely loves that track— and the group. And is it Tibetan?

Pi: No—it is Mongolian. The capital of the country is—

Carmen: Sure—let's crack on.

The audience were absolutely not sure what to make of the track but there was a lot of dancing and jumping going on in the stalls. It was not just the children that were dancing, now that they had been allowed to join the show after the art pieces were declared safe.

Pi was a little put out by the fact that no discussion had taken place on his choice of the track. Pi had felt himself in a directorial mind-set as the climax of his book choice fast approached. The adverts finished.

Carmen: And the book please; do not yet tell us what it is but please give us a quick summary as to why you chose it from the 71 or so books that you have read as part of your odd crazy—*I will read my own height in books in a year*—challenge. For whatever reason. We all do rather strange things in life!

Pi: So, you still do not want me to reveal the book?

Carmen: No thank you, not just yet. You cannot tell what the book is by its cover in this case! You have entombed it in plain brown paper. But no vinegar.

Pi: Well, you see, I borrowed it from the library in Sundervagvela. I was to go back within 6 weeks. I have been here almost a year! No crime has been committed though; my brother has already replaced it. But still, I want to keep this copy reasonably pristine. I can also guarantee that there is no vinegar. Although cider vinegar has many health…

Carmen: We do not need such fine details. But thank you. Any general thoughts on the book?

Pi: I chose this as my book to take to another civilisation because it is about kindness. Kindness between people of different social circumstances; the rich, the poor, the young, male to female, female to male, the spiritual, the atheist, the older and very old even. There is kindness even to an ant. I think. It also explores the depths of human despair. The boundaries of the cruelty one human can inflict on another. Through personal actions but also through legitimised sanctions of society that allow awful social circumstances to prevail and then persist. It is a story that will long echo on Mother Earth and spread to every corner of the human world. It may even influence what we do to animals, flora, and the Earth itself. We could be kinder to Mother Earth, Carmen, if we wanted to.

Sitting together in the studio, the Beck household, Prof Marma, and Sir X were riveted at this stage in the proceedings for they had tried to guess the name of the book. A tome of an Indian novel had been suggested or a book from the BBC classics of all time.

All of them had slips of paper with their guessed choices—*Moby Dick, Midnight's Children, Frankenstein, One flew over the cuckoo's nest*. But surely not a Solzhenitsyn such as *Cancer Ward* or Tolstoy's *War and Peace*?

Carmen: Is it the Bible? Or the *Mahabharata*? You can tell us now; we're so close to the end of the show. We finish soon. The weather report waits for no one ever. We will also have three, seven second adverts, please. And please cue the adverts!

This was clever indeed, economically. After all, Pi would be pausing for part of that time anyway.

Pi: The books you mention are great choices of course, but difficult to access for everyone. Long though it is, I commend it to you. I do need to warn you that there is far too much about the Parisian sewer system in it. Even though it is on the sewerage system of a great European country.

Pi took off the cover, ripping it a bit in his excitement to reveal his choice. He held it directly aloft to the camera.

Carmen: *Les Misérables*! I really enjoyed the film and stage show. Must read it one day!

Pi: For 6 weeks, I have walked in the steps of Jean Valjean, Fantine, Cosette and the heroic Marius. I despaired at the behaviour of those rogues, Javert and the Thénardiers. And I cried like he was my own son when that little boy died. I forget his name.

Carmen: What a choice! The boy's name is Gavroche, by the way.

Maarsi and the Children

Carmen had a surprise for Pi. Virginia Spode and a few of her teachers, including Koki, entered the stage with two representatives from each of the classes at the Ellie Elementary.

Virginia: Pi, the pupils wanted to tell you that they read their own height in books too. Each and every class did that to the school nurse's stated average height for the year group! Some children even, individually, read their own height in books. There are 19 of these bookworms in the audience—stand up and announce yourselves! Some are now on the stage.

The aforementioned children stood up, started jumping and shouting excitedly—Guru Pi! Guru Pi! Guru Pi!

Maarsi was there and of course, Spode Junior. There was a veritable ziraleet in the studio. Pi felt his eyes well up. Busy lacrimal glands indeed. Pi saw his unborn child in these raucous children. Though not strictly sanctioned by the production staff and uninvited, these children then marched onto and across the stage, head-banded with the colours they had individually achieved.

Maarsi just walked up to Pi and stood there, holding his hand, utterly beaming, and waving to everyone in the studio audience. He was then surrounded by children in bandanas, belts, and tags. There were the blues, the reds, yellows and even several black ones. They all held onto a bit of Pi's clothing. He was reminded of the Bandi Chhor Divas Sikh celebration depiction of Sri Guru Hargobind being released from Gwalior Fort, with anyone that could hold onto his clothing also to be duly released as sanctioned by Emperor Jahangir. Thus, 52 Hindu Kings were also simultaneously released holding onto the Sri Guru's hastily re-tailored elongated robe.

Pi felt that he had actually exerted a positive influence with his idea. What more could he wish for as a teacher? As a human burden on Planet Earth. Maarsi tugged at his *bundi*, and beckoned him to bend down to listen to her. She whispered in his ear.

Maarsi: Guruji! I am now—the girl who read her own height in books! I love you!

Climax reached. The show ended quickly with thunderous applause. Sir X clapped the longest. But Pi felt uneasy. He knew that the Vedic Foundation of

Planet Earth's edition of the *Bhagavad Gita* had not been covered a lot during the show. This would be noted back home. However, things were not as bad as they could have been as the picture of Pi and the Vedic Foundation of Planet Earth's edition of the *Bhagavad Gita* went viral after he gifted a copy to Carmen.

The bejewelled *Bhagavad Gita* sold out anyway, within a few hours. The internet postie would faithfully deliver a copy within days to all who were lucky enough to order one before stocks ran dry. That specific edition of *Les Misérables* also sold out immediately. And a re-printing was ordered. The show was repeated many times on endless smaller and the occasional larger channels. And podcasted and radio-ed and social media-ed on many platforms.

The Tome Revisited

The Becks and Pi walked home in relative silence. They were exhausted emotionally. But it had all been worth it in the end. Pi elaborated on his book choices. The tower had been progressing slowing. And then he had decided to tackle what was a significant part of his baggage weight coming over from Sundervagvela. The tome that is *Les Misérables*.

Life had been on hold for about 6 weeks as he fell way behind on his trajectory. It was a new translation. Relatively so. But it was still no shorter. That was why he had abandoned it when he had felt sure that he had completed his task. Pi could smell the streets of Paris in his mind even though his sense of smell had been destroyed by Covid-19 at the barrier to the brain and all things osmic.

He felt the cold and humiliation of Fantine, the dharmic duties seared as a mission on Javert's brain—that he had to catch Valjean and imprison him. There was also Cosette's flowering of youth and Valjean's epic life through prison, Mayorship, industrialism and fatherhood.

And then the death of a beautiful life. A hefty addition to the height in the end. Kirk called it an own goal almost, a double bogey at least, as Pi had fallen so far off target at one stage in his reading.

There was also a heavy sadness. Pi would be leaving soon. Many of his family had been affected by Covid-19 and he felt duty-bound to return as soon as possible.

Chapter 18
The Leaving

When you arise in the morning,
think of what a precious privilege it is to be alive, to think, to enjoy, to love

Meditations. Marcus Aurelius (121–180 CE). Roman Emperor.

Pi had his black belt as did, he later learnt, as did both Virgina and Ruth. He had gone through the chakras faithfully. The *muladhara, svadhishthana, manipura, anahata, visuddha, ajna* and the s*ahasrara*. I am, I feel, I do, I love, I talk, I see, I understand that little bit more.

He really did feel this, having shared the lives of around 108 main characters in the books he had read. Pi had almost certainly had made that number up. It was the number of beads on his sacred *rudraks* mala or necklace. One for each of the main gods. *And why not?* Thought Pi. There were at least 108 people that he had met in the books he had read.

Tomorrow was the day of his flight to India. So opposite to the flights of so many to the lands of promise. Promise was certainly not immediately available in India. There had been so much devastation in the last year; at best an act of cruel nature or at worst co-created by election rallies, the Kumbh Mela and possibly, the early cricket season.

The Beck household nonchalantly ignored the fact that Pi was leaving. It was too painful to face head-on. It was going to feel like an amputation from the body of the family.

Anton and Kirk hid their sadness behind the football. There was going to be a special showing of the replay of the FA Cup final and then later on, the Charity Shield. The FA Cup final had always been a day resonating with his personal history. Anton recalled with utter despair how city had lost the FA Cup final well over half a century ago. The sadness especially as he had watched the match with his parents.

The prayers then, of his to the Christian God, those of his friends, Imran to Allah, Siddhartha to Buddha, Kayal to Vishnu and Jacob to the main God had all been in vain. God must have had a much more important agenda; possibly another, better, Garden of Eden to atone for the disaster Earth was transforming into.

Maybe there was consternation at the rate of the decline of species. Anton thought there could be many other reasons for the neglect of the Almighty on this occasion.

But today, was another chance to relive it all. There was no need to pray to his humanist God. *Tat twam asi*. But it, the pain of life, was often too painful to handle. And people needed their prayers. Complex calculations took place in his brain, less complex than incomprehensible in the human scheme of things. The banal took over.

The would-be escapees from the Premiership, the MuMcLi CAT half a dozen had not succeeded and were to remain playing with clubs worth less than 3 billion or so. Anton was simply delighted that his club worth a mere £420 million were to play a club worth just the 6.8 times more at £3 billion.

And the players were the workers on a mere £4 million a year. An amount easily earned by, a good nurse, in a mere 100 years. Something was nuts and Anton was beginning to understand Pi and his umbrage at the cost of water.

Anyway, Anton was duly rewarded with his city winning the Charity Shield! No further solace was needed for him or his family. They were in a place of joy. Except for the fact that Pi was leaving tomorrow. Their sorrow was shared over their last supper.

It had been a year like none ever. The plague had spread. It was just a virus. Not this time through *Rattus norvegius* via the oriental rat flea *Xenopsylla cheopis*. Cheops was forever remembered, even more so now, having previously only having commissioned the Great Pyramid of Giza.

From the flea to nice human to nice human to nice human. The spread was even more so when that specialist of all human fleas, *Pulex irritans,* took over as a vector of transmission. Coronavirus has also spread through the incredible complexity of human life.

The bats left the scene very early on in the first act. We humans have been the *Rattus* and *Xenopsylla* and *Pulex* all rolled into a giant super-spreader, carrying this virus all over the globe. Killing ourselves.

In UK, the numbers of lost souls had declined and UK lost its less enviable position of the gold medal for cases and slipped to the 14th position. India was indeed shining high, but the tsunami of cases was continuing in some areas.

And Pi lamented and wept. He was leaving.

The taxi—top Uber at that arrived silently, juiced by the aforementioned solar panels and the modern-day quixotic windmills across the lake. Guru Pi was allowed, today, to hug. It would be officially allowed again soon anyway.

Talk of keeping in touch and revisitations was enthusiastically endorsed between them all. There was real sorrow at the parting. There were hugs. No one was yet certain of what life would bring. Pi waved to the Becks, three fingers, with the thumb and little finger in a circle. As Pi waved good-bye, it all ended in an epizeuxis.

Pi: Life is beautiful.

Ruth: Life is beautiful.

Anton: Life is beautiful.

Kirk: Life is beautiful.

Anju: Life is beautiful.

Pi: Life is so beautiful.

Epilogue

This will jar. This is not a neat wrapping-up type of epilogue. I would leave reading this epilogue for a few days. I will warn you. But this is the whole reason why I wrote this quickly. These are my last words to you.

I wanted to give you a novel of deep characters and a plot that would excite and leave you guessing as to the end—a *bildungsroman* that would be a maze of complexities. I only had time to tell you about Pi in the main. He helped me so much that I cannot put it into words; but his story will surely help you understand what he did for me.

And I, yes, had some help. But in the end, I ran out of time in my life. Even though I had carried around the ideas of my own life, gone and its future, for earnest decades.

I am not sure quite how my wet brain managed to distil some memories and not others. Memory fails me at times. I made notes on a lot of the aftermaths of my conversations with Pi and his friends. The bits that I preserved are here, though clearly unbalanced. Yes, my biases are what you got.

In this story, you can read through Pi, about my life. My ups and downs, my loves, my family, my friends, my animals, mêmes, news, history, culture, religion, philosophy. The sum of all that would be the life cut short. A life that could have been so much longer.

I, born Elizabethan, will die Elizabethan. Proudly so. Although a few years Carolean of King Charles III, and then some of the Gulielean reign of King William V, would have been welcome. If that is not too greedy. But thank you, Queen Elizabeth II, my dear monarch. For all you do. For each of the 32 states you ruled. And now the 15. Although the errors of your 14 Prime Ministers, so-far, are still too clear and recent to forgive and forget. For people died, too early, or in misery. The life of Shuggie Bain still happens too much. And should not happen at all. Are we not rich culturally, ethically, and economically?

As I lay dying, Pi taught me to see Venus and all things Venusian in the morning mists and the most oddly coloured sky. I marvelled at its most unnatural and otherworldly beauty. He would ask me to see Venus and keep it in position among the leaden lines and curves in the windows, fixing the starting position of it for us in its trajectory in the universe.

He usually told me to close my eyes to hum or sing the *Gayatri Mantra* of his Covid-19 infected days, eleven times. And then to open my eyes and see if Venus had moved. And we would be moved by the fact that Venus was in a different place in the chart of the leaden lines and curves in the window.

Venus was a planet it had moved, it was not a star, as it had moved. I loved those moments, especially now looking back with the knowledge that 'my goose is cooked'; as Pi would so eloquently and nonchalantly express.

He also waxed lyrically about the stars in Orion's belt. And sometimes, we could see both Venus and Orion in the same windowpane. These things he taught me, I will always remember. They truly fascinated Pi and he was always one to share that.

The length of time for light to come to us from Orion's belt and the distance across the belt. There are many others; but I will spare you from wasting your time. You live busy lives.

Pi taught me to enjoy the colours even more. I have especially enjoyed the colour purple. The purples were all out on my last short walk, recently. Purple was there to behold and enjoy and show evidence of beauty. The early bluebells. The snake's head fritillary. The grape hyacinths.

The nettle-like plant, with the purple blooms. The harebell and the periwinkle and the very early, this year (for it is warm) the cornflower. And even the spotted pulmonaria. Reminders of the devastation that Covid-19 had wrought on the lungs of millions and the 5 million it had killed.

I will never be a great tree that falls. Nobody will ever need to read *When Great Trees Fall*—that great eulogy by Maya Angelou at my funeral. It is simply not fair. I am predicted to not get my modern ration of four-score years of life. Or even the biblical three scores and ten. And will get just over halfway. I will not get a chance to see Pi in India. I am to die early. The disease, *dis-ease*—what a lovely euphemism! It is a lot more than not a fulfilment of ease. The disease will take me.

Daily, it spreads within the three dimensions of my skull. And then there will be a fight for my body to thin my blood as it thickens my blood. One day, I will lose. Anton informed me that it could be a clot on the brain, in the lungs or anywhere else. Or a sudden end as the tumour bleeds in my cranium. My specialist had said the same, albeit less clearly and with undue optimism. My help will also be unplugged. Both of us never to rise from the ashes.

Sundervagvela will never be for me. I will never see the days of Pi living a world torn from RK Narayanan's *Malgudi Days* albeit with the internet and the fizzing bustle of the more modern India. I am sure that, no matter what for the next few decades, Sundervagvela will still be living in the three different centuries of the past, the present, and the future.

I would have happily taken my chances with the virus rather than my disease. The virus was a live or let die chance at least. My chances, with my relative youth, would have been good. Anton had told me that my ethnicity, weight, and lack of diabetes would also have helped ensure that I was a safe bet for survival.

Sitala-ma as Covid-ma, Pi and I could pray to, but not my awful condition. I had no specific deity to protect me. At least there was reincarnation if I switched religions. And I thought of how many arms Pi had said Sitala-ma had. Would each arm wave once or more for Covid-19? What would stop the waves once and for all?

Instead of helping me be lulled into a sense of final acceptance, Pi had continued to increase my zest for life. I was never sure what Pi thought after the death of a human. But for me, it was a cessation of the robot that was Klara. In the sun, we flourished and then we died.

Our life was the amazing blossoming of a wet computer that grew larger and became more adept at seeking new experiences and consolidating old ones. We had an incredible, but not infinite, capacity for memory recall and creating, from the complex algebras of different experiences and memories and calculations for current and future action That made us human.

And maybe to trick us into thinking that we were something unique and not fauna or flora or quantum life-form alone. But to what avail? I am to be disconnected from it all. Maybe from the Universal Consciousness, if there is one. Or, as Pi implied, possibly merge into it.

Pi had always repeated his favourite take on life; that we as individuals were never totally happy unless we were unique, rather than just a link in the chain of all that had happened since the Big Bang. He found it strange that the initial objectives of lucre, fame and even more fortune, when achieved, were never enough.

Other things were needed. A void often filled with addiction to the worst addictions. Why community happiness *against* the Growth Profit Theory? Why not, community happiness *and* the Growth Profit Theory?

Or was it more? I really do not know. And I cannot care anymore. I am not even sure of my thoughts. I blame the drugs. And incoherent algorithms. And my zeal for useful facts and the words we forget to use. And to what avail the drugs? The best intentions are there for sure, but the *phiximabs* and *kurinibs* simply did not work. Not even the new taxol from that yew that lives a thousand years.

I think there is a word for what Pi achieved. An *ataraxia* or even an *ikigai*. There was also the acceptance of a *wabi-sabi* in his life, with a *sprezzatura*, especially after Priyali died. Take your pick. I think I would have got there with an extra decade or so.

I told you that Pi taught me to look at the stars and planets. But also, the trees and plants and birds and bugs and lichen. Anew. The clouds even. The different types of rain and wind and heat and cold. Orion's belt is now my familiar sleeping constellation, as is Venus on waking. He taught me about the waning *Krishna Paksha* and waxing *Shukla Paksha* phases of the lunar cycle. So, few cycles are left for me.

Because I listened, he told me facts and figures about the galaxies and starts and planets that overawed me in the most. But the delight on his face was to behold and enjoy it all again. That Betelgeuse was Orion's right shoulder and Bellatrix was at the left. The former was a massive 764 times bigger than our sun, and the tenth brightest star. That our galaxy with its 100 billion stars has a dozen for each human; though we should share these with other life-forms all over the galaxy. That it would take light 10570 light-years to cross its quintillion kilometres. And that there may be 100 billion galaxies that we have observed somehow or other. And that in our 10,000 years of so-called civilisation, philosophy and thought and religion and science and industry and lack of peace we still had the capacity to destroy human life on Earth, forever. But I am to die, forever, soon anyway. So, I may be blamed less than you in the final calculus.

What Pi did do, was to buy me a star. I must name it soon. It will be a memory of me forever, whatever that really means. Apparently, it is not even in our galaxy. Maybe a bit too far away to visit then. The name of the star and my status as its owner will be registered in the British Library, of course.

It is all very well for Pooh Bear to say, *we didn't realise we were making memories, we were just having fun*. But these, not even 4 decades will be my life. Even Proust had more than a decade longer to write down his memories in an exquisite manner. Whilst mine are quixotic and influenced by the rage and subjugation of drugs. My search for lost time that will never be.

I offer sincere apologies for all the Latin padding. But Pi had loved it and it made up a lot of our cherished private conversations, though it was often challenging and oft required considerable research to advance the conversation on the next visit.

At least it made clear and logical sense, in the most part. Unlike the etymology of the Afghan Tragedy, the Yemen Tragedy, the Eritrean Tragedy, the Rohingya Tragedy. Let's not forget the seemingly unsolvable Tragedy of the insoluble peoples of the Sixth Commandment—*Thou shalt not kill*— in the Holy Lands. And the countless others that we had edited out of our news, as a rare teddy bear had been discovered and restored.

I return again to the fact, that our etymology itself is an oxymoron. *Homo sapiens sapiens* —Hominid wise wise. Really? Once we believed this accolade to ourselves, we became blinkered and proud. That did not bode well and does not bode well.

So, I girded my loins and my mind with choices that could assuage the feeling of death. I read *The Death of Ivan Ilyich*, and *Mortality* by the usually effervescent Hitchins. Then *When Breath Becomes Air* and mortality itself was programmed into my being.

It did not help. And surprisingly, neither did the spirituality of Pi and Kalushi. Nor Zim or Elle. Some things cannot be shared. Their smiles helped though.

And some of this was written in the euphoria of the drugs, legal, supplied by Koroni as my doctor and I struggled with the added burden of the long shadow of Covid-19. In this time, I re-read *Middlemarch*. Skim-reading this time, I must confess. The ending with Cyrus reminded me of Shiva and the hair of Carmen.

Have I told you that already? And in my seclusion, I completed Casaubon's Key to all Mythologies. It was quite easy in the end. In kindness lies the golden rule of all faiths, religions and for the irreligious, their creeds. It is simply the kindness of a Christ and the valour of Hanuman and a life through the Hadiths and the ethics of Buddha. I think.

But it angers me. The capital centre of my life will be this illness that takes me. And yes, quotes, clichés and programmes I have imbibed from books make up who I am. And contributions of the real and reel life characters that exist throughout our lives who serve to inspire and restrain us. All together. But most of all, you, my family, friends, and the nature that I stopped discovering and being awed by years ago. Until Pi happened.

The mundane wasted hours with the gogglebox. The tediousness of trawling malls. Versus the world newly discovered; by safari shopping in esoteric shops and hidden bazaars in towns and cities away from the homogeneity of modern arcades, and into the local watering holes. In the end, it produced the kaleidoscope of thoughts that was me.

Soon to be thrown back as the cup full of water that I am, back into that vast ocean of knowledge and consciousness. This life is my scrapbook. Of my less than four hundred thousand hours on Earth and my less than 500 moons. I hope you have your allotted 1000 bright new moons. I won't get even half. Please enjoy the 500 that I will lack in my life. Enjoy your extra ones.

I so wanted to live longer. Not for me alone, but for the others. The Earth would surely smile if you choose to protect the little ones and pass on knowledge. For joy, not tedium.

To be fair, all that Pi and his friends did was take the obvious picture of our lives and everyday living and give instructions such that we could paint a different picture, now knowing what other colours we could use. Previously having seen it but through me-tinted spectacles. That is my confession. Maybe not yours. I apologise.

Many a day, I would wake with the deep gravelly yearning of the throes of my early loves, with all the intensity of Leonard Cohen's *Hallelujah*. That was pain indeed, with no expressed joy at all. And the feeling that followed was about the loss of my allotted hours.

The hours that were sold to me as I behaved in school, work, and life generally. The teaching to live, less now and more later. What a waste! Now with all things Covid-19, I will never go to Mexico to see Frida Kahlo's house, or see the giant tortoises in the Galapagos. I guess David Attenborough's take on these things will have to suffice.

But I had wanted to ask a guide about what would happen if the blue-and red-footed boobies mated? Would the offspring have one blue foot and the other red; or would both be the colour purple? I recalled Pi's artist friend who had created *Man never having Flown*—which I felt applied to me. I felt as if I had been conned into a life of strictures, a life too short.

A job that I hated a lot at times. But sometimes, loved a lot. I should have lived, not just saved myself for a future I didn't realise that I simply do not have. I wish that I had been less of a *Fomo sapiens* too. I had a fear of missing out, but most of those things, I could have missed out on anyway with absolutely no personal consequence.

And always, always, thoroughly crushed by why the people of Gogol and Dostoevsky, Wiesel and Mahmoud Darwish, Tagore and Bano Qudsia, Rumi and Shakespeare, had to maim lives and often kill each other.

Am I leaving this world in the grip of the four horsemen of the apocalypse? Did this virus open the seven seals? Have we entered our downward trajectory; with global warming and the destruction of nature, the pestilence of the virus, famine soon to be followed with the death of humanity itself? Through a little war and then a big one. All having started with a single death. And yes, I must thank Anton for sharing his Sit-Reps.

But should we even be worrying, when for Earth, we are nothing but a tiny destructive parasite? Pi tells me that of, the difficult to weigh and confirm, 550 gigatonnes of carbon biomass we, animals, are just less than half of 0.1 gigatonnes! Plants are 450, bacteria 75, and fungus 10. Humans as a whole, are just the—one hundredth of a single percentage.

And we are less weighty than the total of the cnidarians, livestock, molluscs, annelid worms, fish, and arthropods. Maybe we matter to Gaia. Maybe a lot. Or maybe we do not at all. She has many children to look after with equanimity and fairness.

She has no Sophie's choice to make. Unless we have a role in maintaining the biodiversity and the health of the planet. In fact, today I shall declare to Pi, by text, that I have decided to become trans-species. At times, I do not any longer wish to identify as human, male or female, but identify as a tree. My humanness is obliterated. In my final hours, at times, I am Hova. *Homo obliterans var arbor*.

But these are my darkest days, and I will smile again. Of that there is no doubt.

In my final hours, I must research time on Earth. I hope that your future is bright, unflooded, cooler and peaceful. I needed to collate the scraps of my own life into a collection of thoughts, ideas and memories that I can peacefully die to. Pi, my family and friends, other animals, flora, Mother Nature; you will help me at the end, I know. Pi's story certainly helped.

May you live long and prosper. Climb up Maslow Mountain, have a peaceful lofty aim in life. If you want the esoteric and mystic, then you should behave in such a manner; believe that you are entering the fourth quarter of being and aim for the *moksha* that Pi so avouched. Have fun though. *Namaste*. Thank you.

And we will never forget. It all happened in the time of Covid-19.

Finis

Printed in Great Britain
by Amazon